# BORN *to* RUN

# *A note from the publisher*

Dear Reader,

If you enjoy riveting stories with engaging characters and strong writing as I do, you'll love *Born to Run*. It's an edge-of-your-seat political thriller, action packed with terrorism… treason… and murder. It follows a nation's desire for Isabel Diaz to be the first Hispanic and female president… but can she win? And should she? I couldn't put it down… *Born to Run* is a gripping read. *Born to Run* is John's second novel.

Did you know that big-name authors, John Grisham and J.K. Rowling, were rejected many times by publishers? John Green's own experience of this was one of the many factors that inspired *Pantera Press*, and our aim to become *a great new home for Australia's* next *generation of best-loved authors*. We think we're well on our way.

But there's even more to us… Simply by enjoying our books, you'll also be contributing to our unique approach: *good books doing good things*™. We have a strong 'profits for philanthropy' foundation, focussed on literacy, quality writing, the joys of reading and fostering debate.

So let me mention one program we're thrilled to support: *Let's Read*. It's already helping 100,000 pre-schoolers across Australia develop a love of books and the building blocks for learning how to read and write. We're excited that *Let's Read* now also operates in remote Indigenous communities in Far North Queensland, Cape York and Torres Strait. *Let's Read* was developed by the *Centre for Community Child Health* and it's being implemented in partnership with *The Smith Family*.

Simply buying this book will help us support these kids. Thank you.

Want to do more? If you visit www.PanteraPress.com/Donate you can personally donate to help *The Smith Family* expand *Let's Read*, find out more about this great program, and also more on the other programs *Pantera Press* supports.

Please enjoy *Born to Run*.

And for news about our other books, sample chapters, author interviews and much more, please visit out website: www.PanteraPress.com

Happy reading,

*Alison Green*

# BORN *to* RUN

★★★★★★★★★

## JOHN M. GREEN

PanteraPress
good books doing good things™

PanteraPress
good books doing good things™

First published in 2011 by Pantera Press Pty Limited
www.PanteraPress.com



A Cataloguing-in-Publication entry for this book is available from the National Library of Australia.

ISBN 978-0-9807418-8-9

Cover and Internal Design: Luke Causby, Blue Cork
Cover Image: © iStockphoto.com/Roger Zambrana
Author Photo: Courtesy, Phil Carrick, *The Australian Financial Review*
Typesetting by Kirby Jones
Printed and bound in Australia by Griffin Press
Pantera Press policy is to use papers that are natural, renewable and recyclable products made from wood grown in sustainable forests. The logging and manufacturing processes are expected to conform to the environmental regulations of the country of origin.

To my three amigos

"When I was a boy I was told that anybody could become president. I'm beginning to believe it."
*— Clarence Darrow, defence attorney and writer (1857–1938)*

"Can a woman be president of the United States? At present the answer is emphatically 'No'."
*— Eleanor Roosevelt, "Women in Politics" (Good Housekeeping, 1940)*

"Yes, absolutely. I think, you know, because why not?"
*— Arnold Schwarzenegger on allowing foreign-born Americans to run for president (60 Minutes, 2004)*

"The tree of liberty must be refreshed from time to time with the blood of patriots & tyrants."
*— Thomas Jefferson (1787)*

# THE FINISH LINE...

FOR ONCE, HILLARY Clinton and Sarah Palin are in synch, privately spitting their venom at the cloying barrage of TV images that show a beaming Isabel Diaz sprinkling her pixie dust. Even their own supporters, in a distressing groundswell these two political foes once craved for themselves, are leaping to their feet across the country, punching the air and chanting "Bel... Bel... Isa-bel."

As the race to win the White House hurtles into its final straight, candidate Isabel Diaz streaks lengths ahead. "She's not only smart, personable and visionary, she's got an impressive record of accomplishment," says *The New York Times*. "The nation, and the world, will be well-served if this woman occupies the Oval Office."

Diaz's well-chronicled slog to success is tunnelling her deep into the nation's psyche, making it very tough for her opponents. It's hardly wise politics to slam a minority woman who crawled out of a rank pit of poverty, alcohol and violence to emerge as the big-hearted owner of an admired family restaurant chain, and an active philanthropist to boot. What little mud her rivals have been able to dig up and toss at her isn't sticking.

It's true that some see her as too good to be true, but for

most, in a nation deflated after so many pumped up promises of change, Isabel Diaz offers a credible breath of fresh air.

On policy, not only has she won over the Democratic heartland for her stance on moral issues, offers of relief for the middle class, and her doable list of programs of leg-ups for the underdog, but the Tea Party also loves her for promising low taxes, small government and family values. Her running mate, the more traditionally conservative Hank Clemens who hails from North Carolina, helps her shore up the religious right.

The media are chorusing that Isabel Diaz is a shoo-in, and that her rival Robert (Bobby) J. Foster is outfoxed and outpaced.

Buoyed for weeks with a 70-percent approval rating—higher than the rapture for Barack Obama at his peak—the presidency is within Isabel's grasp.

And deep behind the scenes, a shadowy circle of zealots is conspiring to guarantee just that.

# 1

JAX MASON HAD heard of Isabel Diaz. Who *didn't* know about the famous Burger Queen? But the twenty-five-year-old Australian had no clue he was about to sacrifice his life for her.

Bent over tying his laces, his shoe on his skateboard and his fringe flopped over his glasses, he heard the elevator ping and, at 5 AM, he thought it had to be the night guard doing his final rounds. Jax looked up, expecting that at any second the doors would slide open on the old guy's barrel stomach and customary can of Pepsi Max.

Though Jax was currently visiting London from New York, where he rented an apartment, he really lived on the internet. He was a prolific contributor to WikiLeaks (though he'd never actually met Julian Assange), as well as Anonymous and various conspiracy theory sites. His thick Coke-bottle glasses exaggerated his nerdiness and helped him suit the label of the typical young math genius, though it was called maths where he was born, in Melbourne. His straggly brown hair was so greasy it looked black even in a good light, and his pasty skin was proof he was a night-owl, especially with his skateboarding. Neither travel nor late nights troubled him. Jax was not big on mixing with other people and even dismissed "social networking" as an ironic misnomer. His computer was his closest companion, closely followed by his skateboard. The only thing neat about him was his beard, a slightly ginger mouse-tail that made him look as though an amber exclamation mark was pointing under his lip.

If the Silicon Valley environmental software firm that had flown him to the UK had bothered with a face-to-face interview, they would have had second thoughts. Instead, they hired him on the strength of a single phone call after hearing of his reputation from his PhD work, even though it was unfinished. He'd dumped Princeton University and skipped to New York as a contractor, mainly so he could work on his pet project away from the prying eyes of deceitful supervisors. Like the creep Jax had overheard in the hallway mocking his stutter.

His current employers had installed their patented software for running the environmental features of a new five-star-rated building at Canary Wharf, London's modern financial district, but due to a serious systems glitch the local authorities were refusing to hand over their completion certificate so none of the tenants could move in. Jax was over here to fix it. "Don't leave the building till it's done," was his simple brief, but it was one he ignored daily, stealing a few hours here and there to take in the sights since he hadn't been to London before.

He flicked back his hair but, from out here on the terrace across the empty blacked-out floor, all he could make out was the elevator's flashing "14". He squinted, and when the doors shushed open, two occupants stepped out, not one. With the light behind them, he couldn't glimpse their faces but neither of their body shapes was anything like the nightwatchman's. Jax's smile dropped, sending a glint of reflected moonlight from his lenses to the visitors.

"Jax Mason, is that you over there?"

She was British, Jax decided, hardly surprised. He couldn't make out the badge she seemed to be waving in front of her, but her confident strides toward him and her stubby companion's menacing swagger instantly made Jax's skin crawl, and his head suddenly squirmed with the thought that 14th floors were usually 13ths.

A frosty wind blew up from the River Thames two hundred feet below, though he wondered if it was nerves.

"Jax Mason?" she insisted.

"Yeah, that's m-me. Y-you?" Jax tried to calm the anxiety trembling out of him. He stammered at the best of times, though this didn't seem like one of them. He took her hand, but her sneer suggested he should have gripped it harder, or maybe first wiped the sweat off his own hand on his jeans. She was an eyeful, for sure, but that only increased Jax's edginess. He wasn't good around women. Or men. But especially women.

"I'm Diana Hunter," she lied and, tilting her head toward her slightly hunch-backed colleague, continued, "And this is Lucky."

Even in this dim light, Jax noted that Lucky's face looked like he shaved with a chisel, possibly why he had the chipped front tooth.

"We're MI6," Diana explained, brushing back a strand of her blonde hair, but not so far back that Jax could have guessed it was a wig, even in good light.

# 2

MI6 WAS THE UK's secret intelligence service; Jax knew that. When he'd goofed off on a River Thames tourist cruise three days earlier, the loudspeaker commentary had specifically pointed out MI6's building. Some secret service, he'd smirked at the time.

As Diana kept a grip on Jax's hand, her piercing brown eyes bored into him so long he noticed that one of her contact lenses was askew. If the lights had been on, he might have detected that her real eye-colour was blue.

He coughed as an excuse to remove his hand from hers. "Like, wh-what do you guys want?" he stuttered, mainly out of habit and not entirely from fear. Where, Jax sweated, was actor Geoffrey Rush when he needed him, or better than Rush, a real speech therapist?

"Mr Mason. Recently you posted a blog about your subway shockwave simulation." Jax had posted several blogs on the web about his intricate computer model, boasting it was mathematical proof that terrorists could build up and hurtle a shockwave through a city's subway system that was so ferocious it could suck down and destroy the entire metropolis above it. All they needed to know was precisely on which platforms to set off a hair-trigger-timed series of relatively small explosions.

As Jax gripped the terrace railing, the cold metal drew the remaining heat out of him. Months ago, he had contacted the US government about his computer model, a radical step for an anarchist like him. But Homeland Security flicked him straight into crackpot corner. He tried to tell them: if Jax Mason working alone could create something like this, what could more malign parties do? But if the US government wouldn't listen, why was MI6 popping up out of the blue?

As if she could read his mind, Diana answered his question, "The Prime Minister is acutely sensitive after the bombings over here. He wants you to help us design baffles for London's Tube to prevent one of these shockwaves. For a considerable retainer, of course."

*They* were going to pay *him*? Working *for* the government? Normally that would be against his principles, but this wasn't *his* government, nor even his adopted government… and then there was the money.

He shifted his gaze from Diana to the other spook, but only for a second, chilled by the stare penetrating him from Lucky's pencil-points. Lucky usually didn't say much, words not being his preferred tools of persuasion. While Jax didn't know that, he somehow sensed that any hand big enough to crush his skull by itself would do Lucky's speaking for him.

"I'm s-sort of busy. I'm here on a j-job," Jax muttered, looking at his shoes and reminding himself he had been about to tie his lace.

"Six hours ago," said Diana, shaking her head slowly, "we intercepted an encrypted satellite communication and only finished unscrambling it an hour ago. The point, sir, is that you are in immediate danger—from a terrorist cell here in London. We are not the only ones seeking your simulation model. We know these other people, Mr Mason, and they are not the types to let anything, or anyone, stand in their way. We need to get you, and your model, to safety. Now."

That she whispered this only made Jax jumpier. "How l-long we g-got?" he said, not that he had a hectic day of meetings to reschedule.

Without answering, she pulled him inside, off the terrace. "Mr Mason. May I call you Jax?"

He nodded dumbly.

"Jax. Your software program? The simulation? Before we leave here, we must isolate and protect all copies in existence. We have people on standby."

"Over th-there," he said.

Her eyes followed his to where his laptop was on the floor, next to his backpack. "Show me," she said, guiding him over to it.

Jax sat cross-legged in front of the screen, and she gripped his shoulder. On-screen, he clicked an icon and a menu popped up offering three choices: London, New York City and Washington.

"Trash it."

He did.

"How many other copies are there?"

Jax hesitated, but her grip tightened.

"There's o-one in my b-backpack."

After ferreting inside the bag, Lucky handed a DVD box to Jax, who flicked through them and pulled out the relevant disk.

"Any others?"

Jax slowly shook his head and, as his situation sank in, so did the rest of his body.

"Jax! Surely, you've got a backup at home or on a server somewhere?"

He shook his head harder.

"Why don't I believe you?" She held the disk up under his nose, cutting its edge into his septum until Jax's tongue tasted the sharp copper tang of a drizzle of his own blood.

"Mr Mason. Very bad people want this, and they're on their way here. Right now. Unless you cooperate, immediately, millions could die. Our government can't permit that."

Diana watched Lucky loom up behind Jax. From the broken half-smile on his face she knew he'd enjoy this quivering wreck.

"Jax," she reasoned, "think about it. If *we* found you, so will they..." She shifted her feet and nodded to Lucky whose own paw started to clamp onto Jax's shoulder. He lent down and curled his left arm around Jax from behind, digging into his solar plexus until Jax bent forward, dry-retching.

Lucky released his grip and Jax, still twisted over, grunted, "I'll sh-show you." He quickly located the remote server and pulled up the program.

Diana knelt, her face close to his. She loved this work. Her cheeks were translucent, pearl-like, shimmering with a light tingly sheen, not that Jax noticed. What he did notice, lit up by his screen, were the soft pads covering each of Diana's fingertips and a wisp of red hair creeping out from under her wig.

"Trash it," she barked, giving him no time to freak over why someone claiming to be on his side needed to mask her fingerprints or her hair. He did as she demanded, careful not to press the wrong keys.

"Now, Jax. Last time I'll ask. The other copies? Where are they? All of them."

He looked at her blankly, but Lucky leant over again and burnt his breath into Jax's ear.

"There's j-just one," said Jax. "In my a-p-partment... in New Y-York." He explained it was taped inside the toilet cistern in his bathroom, in a waterproof Ziploc bag.

Lucky slipped a phone from his pocket and keyed in a number. Jax watched him walk toward the windows, the phone lighting up one side of his unyielding face.

All Jax could make out of Lucky's conversation were two words: "TriBeCa" and "john." Feeling like he was swirling in as much shit as a cesspool duck, he didn't focus on the fact that in London toilets weren't called "johns" or that he hadn't yet mentioned his New York address, which was indeed in TriBeCa.

# 3

FUND-RAISING IS always centre-stage for presidential election campaigns, but with Isabel Diaz it was different. Not because she was personally worth a fortune, but more due to her struggle to achieve it.

She cast her eyes around the glitzy crowd—four hundred black tuxedos and an equal number of sparkly cocktail dresses—and mentally ticked off the tally: nearly $2 million raised, just tonight.

Her eyes settled briefly at Table Four, where her campaign director was staring at her, quietly fuming. He'd obviously done the calculations too. "Every dollar you pull in for Triple-B is one less for the campaign," Gregory Samson had whined to her earlier in the evening. And he ran the same script at last week's fundraiser, and last month's.

But to Isabel this wasn't a zero-sum game. Running for president certainly gave her foundation a boost, but it was hardly to her campaign's detriment, as she'd insisted countless times to Gregory, reminding him that it wasn't just her policies that had shot her popularity to record levels, nor even his masterful campaign strategies. It was also her rags-to-riches success story and the philanthropy it had inspired: her charitable foundation for runaway kids.

A Triple-B graduate always delivered the after-dinner speech at these events, and as Mary Dimitri drove to her emotive conclusion up at the lectern, Isabel guessed tonight's might possibly squeeze out an extra half-million in donations.

"Without Triple-B," said Mary, her dark eyes scanning the crowd, "I wouldn't be here tonight. I wouldn't be a pediatrician either. Simply, I'd be dead… from drugs, from disease, from a bullet."

A hush smothered the crowd as they tried to absorb what she'd just said.

"But Triple-B is not just a get-out-of-jail card," she continued. "It's not just counselling or financial support through college and med school. As you've heard tonight, it's also Isabel Diaz. She is an extraordinary role model, a runaway herself who through hard work achieved so much yet is giving, and has already given, so much back. Ladies and gentlemen, your generosity tonight will help Triple-B continue this amazing woman's work and get even more kids off the streets and into productive lives. Like mine. And like hers."

As Isabel mouthed Mary a thankyou from her table just below the lectern, a yawn insisted itself on her and she quickly covered it with her table napkin. The months of relentless campaigning day and night were catching up.

Tonight, she'd spent the entire evening conjuring up her stock of old-style diner service tricks. Pasting on her best smile, she'd popped around to most of the taffeta pink tables, thanking as many of the guests as she could for coming, lightly touching an arm, pressing a bejewelled hand, squeezing a shoulder or just picking lint off it as a dear friend would. Flattery worked when raising money, especially if it came from someone who could be sitting in the Oval Office in a few short months.

No matter how beat she was, she knew she'd keep the formula going right up to the finale. She pushed back her chair to continue her rounds, and as she straightened out the wrinkles in her snug black sequined dress, the band struck up *Bésame Mucho*, stupidly dedicating the old favourite to her.

It was a bad omen.

A few minutes later, only two tables away, a waiter tripped on a diamante-studded handbag strap and crashed a tray of wine glasses to the floor. Isabel was mid-sentence with a stockbroker when she heard the glass shattering behind her. And with her being so tired… and with that damn song playing… the darkness started flooding back.

Gripping the back of a chair, she tried to stop herself swaying, and struggled to visualise her father's photo. His face… his calming eyes… his…

"You okay?" the broker asked, concerned and reaching for a glass of water to give her.

"I'm sorry," she said, blinking open her eyes. "It's a… a sudden migraine," she lied, and rushed for the ladies room to wait out her ghosts.

★ ★ ★ ★ ★

ISABEL was hunched over in the toilet stall pressing a wet napkin against her eyes. Her other hand was flicking nervously at the old scar that crossed her throat.

At her feet was an empty *Clip'n'Drip* pack. Thank God for her husband Ed's miracle drug delivery device, she thought yet again. The brilliant, under-skin implant always kicked in the relaxant much faster than any pill or liquid could, and it was less risky than a syringe, which would really get people talking if anyone saw it. Sure, *Clip'n'Drip* hadn't yet got government approval, so this was her and Ed's little secret. Or one of them.

So far, no one had seriously objected that she suffered occasional migraines. The research helped. It wasn't just the 25 percent of women who got them at least once, yet still lived a normal life. It was more Napoleon, Julius Caesar, Thomas

Jefferson, both Robert E. Lee *and* Ulysses S. Grant, and John F. Kennedy... all extraordinary leaders, despite their migraines. If they could, so could she.

Even if hers weren't really migraines at all.

Fortunately, glass didn't shatter around her too often in public places, though she always carried several *Clip'n'Drips* in her purse just in case. But tonight, with her being so dog-tired her normally strong resistance was low, and the sound of the smash had shot deep, like a shard of memory shrapnel.

Years ago she had seen a shrink, but the treatment didn't do much for her and she backed off when she started thinking about going into politics, worried that her depressive tendencies could kill her chances stone cold if they leaked out. Instead, she taught herself some quick-acting meditation tricks which usually worked but, when they didn't like tonight, a private jab from a *Clip'n'Drip* did the job.

The episodes were monotonously the same... if horror could ever be monotonous... *She is back in the grim trailer her mother rented...*

Isabel had long suspected her mother paid their rent by offering "favours", though it took two decades to admit that tasteless morsel of her family history to herself. And she'd never revealed it to anyone else; not even to her husband.

Ed Loane knew about the rape, though only the fact, not the details. Before they married, she had confided that it was why she could never have kids. He also knew about her dad's photo and how much comfort she got from it, since it sat on her bedside table no matter where she was. But he knew little about her mother; only that she'd been poor, a widow and Bolivian.

Isabel had never quite grasped why her mother soaked her once sweet soul with that sleazy swamp of "boyfriends" and bottles. Poverty was an easy yet unsatisfactory answer since most of Isabel's trailer-park friends' mothers, even the single ones, lived quite differently. None of them had Isabel's daily chore of tidying up and stacking their mother's empties outside, flanking their trailer like a glass wailing wall, a kaleidoscope stabbing green, bronze and yellow-white needles into her sad green eyes. It drove Isabel's determination that never, ever would she be her mother's daughter. For starters, she didn't touch alcohol.

# 4

ISABEL'S HEAD FINALLY hit her hotel pillow. It was close to midnight in Chicago, especially late since she always got up at 5 AM local time, no matter what. Waking early was ingrained, a habit from years of working the breakfast and every other shift. But it wasn't just that; the memories that washed over her every morning were a refreshing ritual she liked to take time over. Whether they were to remind her of who she really was, or because she couldn't forget, she could never fathom.

BY the time she had arrived at Half Moon Bay as a broken fifteen-year-old, the roadhouse diner's once bold, optimistic paisley swirls had been washed out by the torpor of year after harsh year of the Californian sun and the flagging energy of the couple who "ran" the place, Annette and George Hicks.

Originally called Big Bad Burgers, later rechristened by her as BBB, the restaurant was a tottering pillar of the second law of thermodynamics, the rule of inevitable decay that her physics teacher had once explained was why iron rusts and old eggs stink. But to Isabel, then so fragile, this tawdry diner was paradise.

The air had been languid that day, she recalled, so thick she could still lick it. The morning hung as lazily as the brown pelicans drifting on the bay's flat waters. A straggle of flies lurked around the plastic doorway ribbons, once a rainbow but now so drab and limp they couldn't even pretend to defend the entrance.

Isabel had prodded the door open with her walking cane. The sticky odour the flies had been soaking up glugged over her, sour though not quite rancid, like fat that had fried too many tomatoes. Yet strangely, even that had welcomed her.

The battered girl didn't know it then, nor did the Hickses, but their shabby 24-seat Cabrillo Highway ex-speakeasy would be the seed of the successful nationwide chain that the three of them, though mostly Isabel, would build up and sell almost thirty years later, reaping a fortune of over a quarter of a billion dollars.

A few days earlier, the old spinster sharing her hospital room had winkled out of Isabel her unspeakable story and, with the girl only just walking again, the long-retired librarian slapped a Greyhound bus ticket and fifty dollars into her shaky hand, urging her to flee as far away as she could, even with her limp and her cane.

Isabel had bussed west from New Mexico, not caring where she was headed so long as the Cactus Flower Trailer Park and her mami's sleazy boyfriends, especially that one with the wolf tattoo… and the broken bottle… shrank deep into distant memory.

THE white sheet pulled away from Isabel's olive skin as she leant over to the bedside table and wondered what the public or the media would say if they knew. "*Candidate Wacko – keeps shrine to dead dad on nightstand*," popped into her head before she could dismiss it.

Her husband Ed accepted it. War veterans had their own sacraments to the past and respected others for theirs, no matter how weird. George Hicks, effectively her adoptive father, he knew. His wife Annette also, but she was long gone.

Slotted behind scratched glass inside its battered tin frame, the glossy print was possibly the most travelled photo in the country. The zip pocket in her leather satchel protected it, keeping it in much the same condition as when she'd swiped it out of her mother's bedside table drawer. She could easily have replaced the frame or the glass as Ed had suggested many times, but that would have been a sacrilege. This was her greatest treasure, despite all her wealth. It was her only physical memento of the man who had kissed her only in her dreams: her long-dead father.

Without needing to look, though she did, she knew every striking contour of her father's face and cherished the differences from her own as much as the similarities. Was he tall, as she was? From this head-shot there was no way to know, but her mother had filled in the blanks, holding her hand way above her own short head, saying he towered above her "*like a Bolivian jacaranda.*" Perhaps that was where Isabel had got her own five-foot-ten. His charisma was "*as vivid as clusters of lilac blossoms*" of the same native tree. Maybe, Isabel wondered, she'd inherited her people skills from him; her mother's were certainly nothing to emulate. She briefly shuddered just thinking about her. Though the photo was black-and-white, it lent her father's skin a moody tone, which long ago she decided meant it was olive, surely, and velvety. Just like hers. And when she touched her own cheek, as she did now, she sometimes imagined it was his.

Hernandes Diaz. She loved the ring and the metre of his name, how the syllables and the Ds tapped out on her tongue. She could even smell the Brylcreem on the comb he would have brushed his shiny black hair back off his forehead with, hair blacker and thicker than her own very practical bob.

His bedroom eyes, black and soulful, locked right onto hers as though she were the only person in his gaze. Since her mother's eyes were brown, Isabel had always been curious about why her own were green.

Hernandes had died just before she was born so he never laid those eyes on her.

Of course, he never saw her scar, either. Thankfully. Her finger traced itself along the familiar track across her neck. She couldn't help it. Often, just visualising this photograph helped Isabel fend off her dark spells… and if it didn't, she always had what was in her purse.

# 5

ED LOANE'S EYES were bleak after three sleepless nights. It was lucky Isabel was away campaigning and fund-raising. On a good night, Ed could look out from his floor-to-ceiling office window and see his own reflection lit up in the brassy Trump Tower opposite him on Fifth Avenue, New York. But not now, with the midnight downpour outside.

He turned and stepped over the scatter of files he had earlier hurled across the rug, patterned with a subtle but patriotic motif of white five-pointed stars.

At ease, the former general commanded himself. His sixty-plus years had seen it way tougher than this. The last ten were here at the helm of a global Fortune 500 corporation, but the decades before were in active service… from 'Nam, Grenada, Nicaragua, to the Gulf. Heck, his epaulettes hadn't got their four stars from Special Operations Command just for spreading hummus on Saddam Hussein's samoon bread.

Yet Ed's most important work was today, helping to airlift his wife into the White House. Sometimes he campaigned with her and other times, like this week, his business kept him off the stage.

She'd be president, and he'd be right there behind her.

Some in the media, the liberals among them especially, were scaremongering how Ed would be the ventriloquist behind his dummy. "Elect her, but get him," they agitated, though because Isabel had such a strong persona, the polls said the public wasn't buying it.

He suppressed a smile.

Opening his beechwood closet, Ed shuddered at his weary image in the mirror. Thankfully, he sighed, his appearance on *Meet the Press* was last week, otherwise what would Fabio or Jason—whatever that fag TV make-up artist's name was—say now? Before the show, the little squirt had tut-tutted how Ed's dark gun-slits for eyes made him look cheerless, offering a dab of lightener to lift them. But Ed's aloof self-confidence was as much a part of him as his Medal of Honour, and no pillow-biter was going to fiddle with that. No sir, no way. Ed had said nothing, just clenched his square, jutting jaw. It was a subtle, practised move that made even the toughest adversary worry his face might get smashed in. Fabio got the message, dropping his cotton puff back onto his tray and backing out of the room, claiming he suddenly had an urgent make-up call elsewhere.

Ed's fingers prodded the bags slung under his eyes… As bad as his worst passport photo from his years in military intelligence. Not the American passport, nor the British. More the tattered old crimson Soviet one… Yuri Something-opov. What was that Ruski name? Instinctively, he scratched his scalp where the fur astrakhan had warmed it that long ago winter. To Ed, his long-standing buzz cut was a salute to his military career. He kept it so short that people could only guess his hair was grey, though his moustache gave a better hint of that. It was pencilled over a mouth pursed so tight they joked, if they dared, that Ed didn't eat his food, he sucked it. People trod warily round him. You didn't even need to talk to him to know: his jaw or, if he was simulating warmth, the crush of his hand, said it all.

He grabbed a tissue to wipe the annoying drip from his nose as he twisted his head, squinting out of the corner of his eye to remind himself where his left ear had been sewn back on, after Operation Urgent Fury in '83. His men had joked he'd had a lobe-otomy. In just twenty horrific seconds, three birds had gone down. Debris and rotor blades flew through the air, one fragment slicing off Ed's left ear and another his left pinkie as he raised his hand to stem the blood flow. He'd been lucky. If his hand…

It was mayhem. Others were wounded far worse. Three killed. For these men, the tropical island of Grenada was no paradise.

Ed tugged at his ear, marvelling yet again at the cosmetic surgeon's work. Hardly a blemish.

On three separate occasions, he had delicately tried to press Isabel into getting the same doctor's magic to fix the scar that carved across her throat, but she always put up a brick wall.

"It's my memory," she'd say simply, then change the subject.

# 6

THE WESTERLY WIND hurled fragments of London's distant Big Ben's chimes up to the 14th floor. Lucky snapped off his cell phone and looking outside said, "Hey, I can see MI6 from up here."

Jax was thrown, and not just by Lucky's American twang, tight, like a crab was pinching his lips. "No w-way can you see it," Jax spluttered, realising too late that contradicting this guy was not smart, even if he knew for a fact that MI6 was behind several bends as the river threaded west, so you couldn't possibly see it from up here, not at night, not even in daylight.

"Sure you can," said Diana abruptly, any pretence of her own fake English accent discarded. "I'll show you." She twisted Jax's arm with a grip Lucky would be proud of. "What a view," she said, manoeuvring Jax over the floor lip onto the windy terrace. "Best view in London," she added, but oddly she seemed to be looking down the Thames in the opposite direction.

"Who are you g-guys?" Jax flared, trying to twist out of Diana's grip.

She maintained her grasp and smiled.

"Wh-who are you, d-dammit?" If only he could get Diana to release her hold he could get the hell away from them.

Diana edged him closer to the railing. "We're y-your f-friends," she smirked.

To Jax, Diana suddenly appeared like a swooping hawk to a chicken the moment before the talons crush its neck. His heart was pumping faster than the supercomputers he'd done most of his simulation work on. With his free hand he took out of his pocket the remote control the nightwatchman had given him and pressed it so all the lights on the floor came blaring on full, including the bright spots above their heads on the deck, and he prayed someone in one of the other buildings would notice.

"Gimme that," screeched Diana who snatched the remote away from him. After checking her fingerpads were still fastened, she pointed it in various directions but it made no difference. She hadn't seen the switch on the back that Jax had flicked to the lock position. "Fix this, you Aussie fuck," she said, shoving it back at him. "We haven't got all night." To make her point, she kneed him in his groin.

Hunched over, Jax slid the switch to unlock and flicked all the lights off at once but, while Diana and Lucky's eyes were adjusting to the instant blackout, he tossed the remote over the railing and made a dash for the fire stairs.

It would have been easy for Jax to hop over the half-inch drainage lip at the terrace doors even in the dark, if only he had remembered it was there, but he tripped over his shoelace and sprawled out face-down onto the cold concrete floor inside. While he was scrabbling to his feet, Lucky picked him up by his belt and hoisted him back outside, with Jax kicking and punching the air. Then, in one long parabolic sweep, he hurled Jax over the railing.

"Let 'er rip," was all Jax could hear in the hot wind-rush.

Diana and Lucky peered over… two hundred feet straight down.

Jax's eyes did all the screaming for him.

With his torch, Lucky lit Diana's steps back to Jax's laptop. "Got his disk?" she asked Lucky, and checked her finger pads again. After his affirmative, she deleted the copy on Jax's hard-drive, careful to empty it out of the computer's trash can as well. Then out of her back pocket, she slid out a DVD and slotted it into Jax's drive, running the clean-up program off it so no cleverdick could recreate on the laptop what she'd just deleted.

As Jax plunged, the sweeping copper entrance awning loomed up at him at a sickening speed, and he slammed into it with a force that fortunately he could no longer feel. It bounced his body face-forward over the canopy's edge into the air, in a belly-flop dive that skewered him with a sickening *thook* onto the bronze spike of Robbie Burns' quill. The twenty-five-foot sculpture of Scotland's most famous poet had been installed on-site only the day before and, even though Jax should have been working, he had watched almost the whole show. Now he was part of it.

While the clean-up disk was running, Diana came back out onto the terrace to check on Jax. She couldn't tell, but felt sure his blood and other bodily fluids were inking their way down Burns' pen, writing their own ending.

DIANA had a couple more tasks before she was finished. She switched off Jax's wifi connection and located the clock on the laptop's system. Once she reset the computer's time backwards to 4 AM, she clicked open the second file on her DVD.

She scrolled through Jax's suicide note one last time: it was sad... pathetic. It was perfect even with the Australian English spelling, yet she hadn't met him when she'd composed it. After she block-copied the text onto the computer's clipboard and closed the original, she created a brand-new document, one that would forever record its time of creation as... she checked the screen's corner... 4:03 AM. She pasted the copied text into the new document, saved it on his computer, and ejected her DVD slipping it safely back into her pants. As her thumb withdrew from her pocket, the button scraped at the protective pad almost peeling it off, but she felt the glue unsticking and tamped it back down.

She checked the computer's automated properties for the suicide note to double-check her time trick had worked... It had. "Created at 4:03 AM."

Leaving the laptop on the floor with the suicide note open, she called to Lucky, "It's go time." From out on the terrace where he was relishing his handiwork, he came inside and, as they started across the room to the elevator, a crease of annoyance smeared across Diana's forehead. "Damn," she said, and sprang back to the laptop to set its clock back to the right time, and reconnect its wifi.

★ ★ ★ ★ ★

BURSTING out of the revolving entranceway, what hit her was how light the breeze was down here. And the silence. The wind had petered out; at least down here on the ground it had.

Lucky's legs were shorter than hers, so she easily strode ahead to the statue of Robbie Burns.

"I hope Jax liked poetry," Lucky said from behind her.

Diana's lips curled a little. "So the pen *is* mightier than the sword," she said, and began to hum *Auld Lang Syne*.

She unzipped her side pocket and took out her phone and a small grey box. She was about to jam them together when Lucky interrupted her.

"It's only midnight on the east coast," he said.

She didn't respond and kept walking, and humming. No matter what the time was, she knew that their leader, code-named Isis, expected a report on the mission.

Diana bent her head as she passed under the monumental sculpture, careful to avoid the drops of Jax's fluids still dripping, and without lifting her eyes. She stepped over Jax's jam-jar glasses, rammed the scrambler/voice masker onto her phone and keyed in the dialling shortcut.

While she called, Lucky stopped to check his work, enjoying the composition of Jax skewered through the stomach and flopped limp, like a frankfurt suspended on the tip of a knife. Lucky licked his lips. Wet work made him hungry.

A reflection sparked up from Jax's lenses on the ground and Lucky crushed them beneath his steel-capped boot.

Diana heard the crunch and, with the phone at her ear, turned toward him. "Idiot," she fumed.

"What did you say?" said a brusque female voice on the line, sounding a lot like actress and singer Bette Midler.

"Nothing, er, Isis," said Diana into the mouthpiece. "Hey, nice voice you got there. Maybe you should croon your way into the White House."

Isis was weary of Diana's jokes about the voice-masking software they used to change a speaker's voice randomly using a stock menu of celebrities. "Your report?"

"Mission accomplished," she said, words that would be as premature as they'd been for a former president. The line went dead. Even with scrambling, Isis didn't prolong calls longer than necessary.

The duo strode along Thames Path, heading east on the riverbank, steering clear of the battery of security cameras at the Canary Wharf River Dock. Though the sun was doing its best to rise, the waterway was still dull and leaden apart from the glow of the single white anchor light coming from the boat mid-river.

Diana keyed another number into her phone. "Now," was all she said before flipping it closed.

# 7

ELIA CACOZ CHECKED her watch and adjusted her hair elastic. The TV current affairs researcher pulled back her hair so tight that the smooth, shiny blackness emphasised the Asian hints she'd inherited from her grandmother as well as the smudges under her eyes.

"You're working late, Mr Mandrake," she said, seated at her desk as Mike Mandrake walked up behind her. She still couldn't believe he wore a suit when he wasn't on-air. No one in LA did that. She was in a simple black T and black skirt. But Mandrake was from Washington, the new front-of-camera talking head who'd just joined the line-up on *Close-up*, the network's national Sunday-night political program.

It was 9 PM, and Elia had only half-eaten the tuna sandwich that dribbled mayonnaise on her desk. With hours of work still on her plate for this fly-in show-pony, she took civility off her menu. She knew she should have bitten her lip but she steamrolled on. "No Hollywood starlets for dinner tonight?"

In her two years in this business, Elia had observed many strange things, the latest being this guy, Mandrake. Those who said they knew better, i.e. her bosses, claimed Mandrake's glittering newspaper credentials were perfect for *Close-up*.

The network president's all-staff email had almost shimmered out of her screen: how Mike Mandrake was a Pulitzer Prize-winner; how Mike had covered Washington in-depth for fifteen years; how Mike's both-sides-of-the-street stints at *The New York Times* and *The Wall Street Journal*, as well as *Newsweek* and *The Washington Post* gave him an unparalleled breadth of experience; and how, while this was his first TV gig, he was a natural for the medium.

"A natural?" she'd squealed at the water cooler. "With his pseudo beard and chintzy smile? With a head like his," she told anyone who'd listen, "the only electronic media he's a natural for is radio."

She seethed about Mandrake, and as soon as she could phone her boyfriend Simon without anyone eavesdropping in the open-plan, she gave him the picture. "When the arrogant shit got here," she whined, "he tilted his chair back, slapped his faux mountain boots onto the desk and lectured how his trip here to LA was real hush-hush. That he's doing some," she made air quotes with the fingers of her free hand, "deep, deep background on Isabel Diaz." Elia knew this would grab Simon's interest since like many former runaway kids he owed a great personal debt to the candidate.

Mandrake's segment would be on air in a couple of weeks, she told him, but it wasn't going to be the usual gloss, or dross. "He's chasing some new angle."

"Is it that Karim Ahmed terrorist thing?" Simon asked.

"Can't say," said Elia, pissed off that Mandrake hadn't admitted her inside the tiny circle of those in the know.

In the team meeting earlier, Mandrake had held up a print-out of the latest nationwide voter approval chart, clocking Isabel Diaz at an extraordinary 70 percent. "At that level, a Diaz White House looks a certainty, but you can never tell what might jump out of the woodwork," he winked.

Yet he wouldn't disclose even a glimmer of his focus to her, instead selecting individual team members, Elia being one, for seemingly unconnected tasks.

But now, with only the two of them left, and with him leering over her shoulder as though he was checking whether she was wasting time on net porn, Elia's fuse finally blew. "What's your damn angle?" she demanded, swivelling her chair around, her penetrating eyes only inches from his.

Mike's face flushed almost as red as his tie. She suspected it was because the loner was finding this teamwork thing tough going. But the truth was he had been running on bluster. He hadn't found his angle, not yet. All he had was an idea, and a lead. It was a great lead, but only that, so far. He stiffened his back and swung his head around, double-checking that they were alone. "It's the truth about Diaz... about her parents."

Elia's face screwed up as if she'd sucked on a lemon and, though it was too late, she grabbed her tuna and mayo sandwich as cover. This guy won't last, she told herself as she took a bite. And if he did, well, her backpack was already stuffed with written job offers from FOX and Sports TV, the latter job reporting on her real passion, baseball.

Here goes nothing, she decided, glancing at her bag for security and swallowing quickly, "Hello-o-o!" Elia knew she was risking her job but, as her dad used to say, if you don't make a splash, you don't get wet. "What more does the world need to know about that doped-out lard-factory George Hicks? Or his wife, what was her name... Annette? Yeah, Annette... Anyway, she died years ago."

What was Mike Mandrake thinking? For a Pulitzer winner, Elia thought he was acting like a pretty big schmuck.

"Not her diner parents," he said, his eyes flicking nervously around the floor. "Her *real* parents."

Elia paused, weighing the sandwich on her palm as if it were one of the baseball gloves she sensed she'd be seeing a lot more of. What could this guy have up his sleeve? She had to admit that no one had ever gone very far down the "real folks" track, mainly because it was so long ago, Bolivia was so far away, and frankly it wasn't likely to be interesting once told. But then, she paused, what about all that birthist crap about Obama? His Kenyan father, his Indonesian step-father, and whether he was a Muslim, or had *really* been born in Hawaii… All that had all blown up into a huge storm of a story. So why couldn't this?

In her head, Elia sped through what the whole world already knew: Isabel was born in Newark to a destitute Bolivian mother, spent her childhood being dragged from trailer park to trailer park until… yada, yada. What more could Mandrake have?

"Okay… so why LA? Why are you here?" she asked him, intent on taking it as far as she could. "Last anyone heard about Isabel's natural mother was in New Mexico almost three decades ago, right? And her dad? He died in Bolivia before she was born." She rubbed her chin. If any clues were out there waiting for Mandrake to find them, she thought, they'd be in East LA. Hispanic central. Not, she smirked to herself, where he was swanking it up in his four-room hotel suite, three heel-clicks off Rodeo Drive where pretty much the only Latinos were the housemaids.

Mandrake held her stare. She guessed he was debating with himself whether to bring her into his circle which, from all the hush-hush, she knew was a tight one.

"Look," he said eventually but softly. "I've tracked down the guy who ran that trailer park she ran away from. He lives here in LA, and I'm meeting him tomorrow." He'd have savoured the sight of Elia's mouth dropping more if she had swallowed all the tuna. "So," he added, getting to why he'd come to her desk, "have you dug out her birth certificate for me yet?"

As Elia kicked her chair back, rolling herself backwards to the printer, Mandrake ticked off the prep he'd done so far: "This guy is the best lead I've got. He's the only one I could find from her New Mexico days. You wouldn't believe who I've spoken to… folks from Half Moon Bay, early BBB workers, members of her campaign team, kids from her runaways charity, grown-ups who've graduated from it…"

Elia considered telling him her boyfriend was one of those graduates but, certain he'd ask her to fix him up with Simon for an interview, she kept silent.

Mandrake went on to explain he'd done all the hunting and all the interviews himself so far. It was the print media way, not the TV way, he said. "I know all of you are cheesed off with me. You think I don't trust you which, to be honest, is true. But frankly, I *should* have let you do the pre-interviews." If Elia could have read his mind, she would have known it wasn't because he'd just had a revelation about the value of the team, but because none of those interviews had gone anywhere.

Mandrake was mentally shaking his head that if he had to sit through one more jerk-off repeating the same sickeningly sweet accolades about Isabel, he would gag: decent, intuitive, insightful, loyal, empathetic, committed to the common good, having the drive and organisational skills to achieve goals, compassionate but decisive, a practical visionary, blah, blah, blah.

Bor-fucking-ring.

No way was his first TV piece going to be about some namby-pamby Little Goody Two-Shoes. The network hadn't lured him from the peak of the print world for that. *Close-up* only did controversy.

Typing was Mandrake's preferred way to think. "Who is the real Isabel Diaz?" his fingers had tapped out on his laptop days earlier. "Mary fucking Poppins?" He hadn't been able to find one bastard out there with a bad word to say about her. Even how she was dealing with the Karim Ahmed scandal showed her in a depressingly positive light, despite the Democrats trying to whip it up as her Trojan or rather, Arabian horse. Mandrake had been weighing up tossing in the whole story when he had stumbled over the whereabouts of the trailer park manager.

Elia pleaded to have first shot.

"Not this time," he said. Mandrake had a gut instinct about this one. He was going to change the course of history. It was why he won his Pulitzer. And he badly wanted another one to prove he hadn't lost his magic just because he had sold out to television.

# 8

"ANOTHER MARGARITA," MANDRAKE winked to the bartender for the third time, "and another Wild Turkey for my friend. How 'bout a double this time, eh?" The wink was a coded conspiracy against Mike's drinking pal, a signal he'd agreed earlier with the barman to hold back the tequila from Mike's own drinks so he'd stay clear-headed while the former trailer park manager spilled his increasingly well-lubricated guts.

Mike now knew he'd been right to do this prep himself, and alone. Willy Nesbit would be top TV talent. His baggy, crumpled surf shirt was styled—though that wasn't quite the right word—for someone thirty years younger and twenty pounds heavier. Nesbit had filched it from an unattended pile at the laundromat. Mike sniffed Nesbit out as his program teaser. Willy was one of those tall, scrawny sleazebags whose rust-bucket of a truck would sport a peeling bumper sticker like, *You think this pick-up is filthy? Just try a night with the driver.* Willy's head was a total razor job, the shave exposing a macabre tattoo: two rats with their thick pink tails slithering down his neck. Perfect for TV.

Good journalism was in the details, Mike knew that, and at last they were coming to him. Like the "Gappy Hooker".

Mike couldn't believe his luck when Willy blurted out the pet name he'd given thirty years ago to a woman he knew as Maria Rosa, Isabel's apparently toothless mother.

"It had its benefits," Willy smirked, digging an elbow into Mike's ribs.

When Mike was slow to follow, Willy worked his lips into a big O, bulged his eyes cartoon-style and, placing one hand at the back of his neck right on top of the tattooed rats, and a finger of his other hand near his mouth, he bobbed his head up and down so his mouth slid over his finger. But it was Mandrake who gagged: a performance like that, while the tape was running… could he slide it past the network censors? Willy Nesbit was a repulsive toenail-clipping of a man, but Mike Mandrake was pumped.

Luckily, Willy couldn't recollect Maria Rosa's surname or the name of her daughter and Mike didn't enlighten him, worried that if the creep did remember he would hotfoot it over to another network, get plastered again for free and spurt out everything to the competition.

Willy's story was gold. Maria Rosa had paid him in kind for her trailer's rent. It was handy not having to stray from his Cactus Flower Trailer Park to "get done", he said, even if it had to be during the day. "At least the kid was at school. The ma didn'a want her to know nuthin," he said, "but she had to know somethin'. She was fucken smart, that kid. Won some prize, I 'member… from the, ah, Rotarians. Made some speech to 'em. Maria Rosa got the spoils after the girl scooted. I 'member it cos there weren't no monkey business goin' after that an' she give me the winnings for the rent. After that, Maria Rosa just shut down shop. With her legs closed, she couldn'a pay rent no more, so's what could I do? A man's gotta eat, right? So's I kicked her out."

"Why did her daughter leave home?" asked Mike before taking a sip of the drink the bartender had just slid in front of him.

"Was bad, man," Willy said, doing likewise. "One of Maria Rosa's boyfriends... she liked callin' all us regulars her 'boyfriends'... he did her, you know what I mean?"

"Ah, not really."

"He fucken did the kid."

That Isabel had been the victim of a serious assault was well-known, but this...

"He'd been round a couple weeks, Mr Mandrake. I even sorta liked him. But not by the end. There was fucken blood everywhere, man. I had to hose out the fucken trailer after the cops left. He fucken slit her throat 'n all."

"Her throat!" Mike pictured Isabel with her fabled scar. So she didn't get it in a mugging. That was the story the public had swallowed, but Isabel had always refused to confirm or deny it, and the media had let up on it as private. Until now.

"The kid was lucky. But fucken ran away from the hospital after'n she got fixed up. Never even brought her sorry butt over to say adios to her lovin' mami," Willy said snarling, his lips pulled back over his teeth, revealing Maria Rosa wasn't the only one to have lost a few. "Broke Maria Rosa's heart, Mike. Broke her fucken heart."

"Where'd she go?" asked Mandrake, meaning the mother. His stomach clenched for the answer.

"Don' fucken know, don' fucken care. What she did to her bewdiful ma, man... first class fucken A-grade bitch, pardon the French. I loved her ma, Mike. Really loved her."

"I mean the mother. Where did *she* go?"

"How the fuck would I know? Had to turn her out, like I said. It was hard on me to do that, man. I loved her."

"You must have some idea."

Willie looked hard at the four fifty-dollar notes Mike had slipped out of his wallet and placed under Willie's Wild Turkey. "Went back to Bolivia," he said, taking another swig of his drink and pocketing the cash. "Prob'ly had a few boyfriends back there… Lucky fellers, if y'ask me," he said, breaking into a sneer and again poking the cracked grey skin of his elbow into Mike's blue cashmere sweater, this time catching a thread. But Mike didn't care.

# 9

THE REPEATED LATE nights were getting to Ed Loane. He jerked open his closet drawer and picked out one of the small foil-wrapped *Clip'n'Drip* cylinders, this one an antibiotic. He peeled back the foil and after marvelling at the sharp, cone-shaped pellet spiking out of the cylinder, he ripped open an antiseptic swab. With the four good fingers of his left hand, he yanked the front of his shirt out of his pants and swabbed a few inches from his navel. Bunching up the little skin he could—even at his age Ed didn't carry much flab—he placed the cone point over the sterile area, jabbed it in and pulled the spike back out clean, implanting the biodegradable dose-release pellet.

Debbie Branson took a breath as she turned the handle on the door to Ed's office. She'd been his personal assistant for years, yet it always felt like she was creaking open the gate on a lion's cage. She'd open it only a crack and he'd already be roaring his instructions at her, with her dodging to avoid the claws tearing at his many bugbears.

Despite knowing he'd pulled his third all-nighter in a row, today was one of the rare quiet times, though the churn in her stomach suggested it was just temporary. She saw Ed tucking his shirt back in, but discreetly kept her eyes cast down at the files he must have flung over the floor last night.

"I can't afford to get the flu," he volunteered.

Her raised eyebrow suggested he said it with a touch too much guilt. Of all people, she fretted, the chief executive shouldn't be breaking the law. But she said nothing. Ed could react like a switchblade: whichever way he flicked, someone got sliced.

He plucked another tissue from the box, wiped his eyes and blew his nose. A ruse, she assumed, though he really did have a sniffle the last couple of days and was looking pretty run down. The last few weeks had been exhausting, even for her, and she didn't keep anything like his hours.

Ignoring her—or perhaps because of her, Debbie couldn't be sure—Ed tipped his head back, sprayed some drops into each nostril and sniffed them in.

Debbie knew that Ed's personal trialling of their big new drug implant product was for the company's benefit, but she would never take that risk herself. One of those things would never get jabbed under her skin until it got the all-clear from the Department of Health's Food & Drug Administration. Not if her life depended on it... though, given her husband's history, maybe she would in a case like that.

Over the last twelve months she had sent hundreds of letters for Ed: to the FDA, the World Health Organisation, senators, congressmen, committee chairmen. She knew the corporate spin by rote: "Our *Clip'n'Drip* dose-release pellet is so minute and non-intrusive, so reliable that once implanted, patients can simply forget about it and enjoy a normal life again with confidence. The automatic releases of life-saving drugs in pre-programmed doses last up to one year per implant. Great for children scared of needles, a boon for forgetful seniors, and perfect for the unreliable, such as addicts. We also have radio-activated *Clip'n'Drips* for when there's worry about an epidemic, but authorities only want the drug administered if the peril actually eventuates. This homegrown American invention can save millions of lives. You sir (or madam), should be championing it…"

Ed was glaring at her. Suddenly recalling why she'd come in, she straightened her tartan flannel skirt. "President Clinton's office is on the line," she said, avoiding Ed's eye. "They're asking for a meeting… for later this afternoon." She assumed it was about Clinton's foundation. Debbie still had a soft spot for the former President and suspected he wanted to press Ed to donate some of the company's wonder drugs to Africa.

"Fuck that," Ed muttered, not meaning for Debbie to hear, though she had. "And why," he said, "does that sleazeball still get to call himself President?"

She said nothing, though her eyes couldn't help scanning the plaque on Ed's desk:

GENERAL EDWIN (Ed) D. LOANE
United States Army (Retired)
Chairman and CEO

"Why the hell should I want to see him?" he said as he picked up the framed photo of his son, Davey. "Tell them I've got a subsequent engagement. Ah… ring Davey's school. Yeah, I'm taking him to the zoo… this afternoon."

Even Ed's distaste for Clinton couldn't stop him returning his eight-year-old's smile beaming from the photo. He remembered exactly when Davey had taken the photo, only a few months ago, by pointing Ed's camera at himself into a mirror. "And see if Isabel can squeeze in to fly back to join us. It'll be hot for the evening news."

Debbie checked the notepad she always brought in with her. She and Isabel's campaign manager swapped their bosses' diaries every day so they could keep tabs just for times like this. "Ms Diaz is meeting with Congressman Prentice in DC and then has a..."

Ed set down the photo and banged his fist on his open closet door so it slammed back against the wall. "Spencer Fucking Prentice! What *is* this? Be-Nice-to-Democrats Day?"

To Ed, Spencer Prentice wasn't just a Democrat, he was far worse: not only had he once been one of those investment banker scum who'd almost ruined the global financial system, but also Isabel had an affection for him.

Ed knew that Spencer returned his scorn. The last time he'd been over for dinner—yes, she invited the liberal bastard into their fine Republican home—he'd overheard a snippet of their conversation when he returned to the dining room after taking a phone call.

"Isabel, Ed's… using you."

Ed saw her give Spencer a twisted smile, "What makes you think I'm not using him?"

It was a disquieting question. One neither Spencer, nor Ed, had ever entertained before.

DEBBIE knew this would be a bad day. An hour later, the FDA's latest rejection of the *Clip'n'Drip* technology came in. She had tiptoed the letter into Ed herself. And to make matters worse, the Karim Ahmed affair had reared its head in Isabel's campaign yet again. Debbie had never heard so many "fucks" in one day, not since she stayed at that Nantucket hotel with the paper-thin walls on her honeymoon thirty years ago.

Even with Ed's heavy office door closed, she could feel the expletives pound into it from the other side. So no way was she going to disturb him to take a call from some sweet-talking *Close-up* TV researcher.

Ed was a man people admired when it was opportune and loathed when it wasn't, but those people only knew the rigid, unyielding Ed, the *it's my way, or the highway* Ed. Yet, as Debbie knew, if anyone demonstrated commitment and loyalty to him, he returned it and multiplied it, whether they were the men and women from his service past or even the lowliest worker in his sprawling corporate empire.

Debbie had been with Ed only eight months when her husband Angus was diagnosed with pancreatic cancer. Debbie, a professional, imagined she'd left her troubles at home but by the second day Ed had sensed something was amiss and pressed her. He dropped everything, made calls, got Angus moved into a more comfortable room at the hospital till his battery of tests was completed, arranged for the best oncologists to be swung onto his case, including the now-eminent son of one of Ed's combat troops, and insisted on taking care of any expenses not covered by health insurance. Despite Ed's doggedness, they had to wait nine long days of Angus's life before they got the prognosis… he had six weeks left.

"What's that?" Debbie asked when Ed placed the thick envelope on her desk. She opened it slowly. Two tickets to Edinburgh, Angus's birthplace. Pre-paid hotel vouchers. Thirty thousand dollars in cash.

Ed could be as tough and gristly as a five-dollar steak, but if you looked after him, he looked after you.

THOUGH Debbie didn't know it, Ed's mood that morning had also been also cranked up by last night's *Nightline*, which he'd seen on his office TV and replayed twice. The interviewer had hit Isabel with a crack Ed had heard several times before, though until then it had never been dignified with the gravitas of a major TV current affairs program.

> It's Inauguration Day… America's first female president has her hand poised over the Bible ready to swear the oath, and her mother's down in the front row. 'Hey,' her mom says proudly, nudging the dignitary beside her. 'That woman up there… *Her* husband's a *general*!' A reaction, Ms Diaz?

Isabel was clearly her own woman—few others had ever turned such hardship into a fortune anywhere near as big—yet there she was locking horns with yet another pundit over who'd really be wearing the pants in her White House. Ed, and everyone watching, knew the journalist's biased intent: to pitch Isabel as a floppy female glove-puppet who'd dance to the finger-touch of an unelected military, outfitted in the regalia of him, her husband.

If it had been him being interviewed, he thought at the time, he would have stared the liberal bitch down, but Isabel declined the dignified silence route and shrugged it off. After a few theatrically demure blinks from her green eyes, she flicked her black bob behind her ear and said, "Molly, Ed Loane is my husband, not my ventriloquist. If the people elect *me*, they'll get *me*."

He doubted the answer would finally park the topic. With the frequency it had been coming up in one offensive form or another, Ed knew it was no trivial issue for many people.

Soon enough, when America would be forced to confront it seriously, it would be no joke either.

# 10

EVEN WITH WILLY Nesbit's interview in the can, Mandrake needed his crack LA researcher to burn a bit more midnight oil. He'd seen that Elia Cacoz got results. She had spine too, so maybe, he thought, he'd consider letting her screw him. Being on TV had to have some side-benefits.

A simple internet search of "Isabel Diaz's mother" got you *Maria Rosa Diaz* in a millisecond. But where was Maria Rosa now? That was Mandrake's question. Nesbit had speculated she had returned to Bolivia. Mandrake already knew from one slammed down phone that she wasn't the Argentinean senator of the same name. One down, a thousand or more Maria Rosas to go.

Locating Isabel's mother, even just discovering whether she was still alive… that was Mandrake's mission. Voters needed to know what really triggered the fifteen-year-old Isabel to run away. If Nesbit was to be believed, it was rape… and an especially horrific one. It gave more colour to the scar. Mandrake was already convincing himself that this was the dark secret that drove the candidate.

He'd already got Willy Nesbit on camera drooling the snippet that Maria Rosa had been loose with her morals, if not a whore, and was relishing how the Republican National Committee might choke over that morsel on prime-time. But that was only an appetiser, nowhere near enough for the splash he wanted to make... needed to make. Nesbit's memory of the rape was too vague to pin his story on. He needed more.

Another key, he was convinced, was Isabel's father, Hernandes Diaz, but so far he'd drawn a blank there too, despite it being a name that was as common in many South American phone books as a Kennedy was in Cape Cod.

Virtually every Isabel Diaz feature ever written painted Señor Diaz as a successful Bolivian industrialist whose life ended when he was kidnapped and killed in La Paz, sentencing his pregnant wife—who he'd had the foresight to send to the US shortly before—to penury. Mandrake might have read it a hundred times, but he wanted proof. Mandrake always wanted proof.

According to Elia, such murders were commonplace in Bolivia back then but official information from that era of Bolivia's past no longer existed. The Presidential Palace in La Paz, Elia told him, was called *Palacio Quemado,* the Burnt Palace, for good reason.

★ ★ ★ ★ ★

"NO find no *empresario* Hernandes Diaz, Señor Mike... no, er, businessman. But..."

"But, nothing...," Elia heard Mike yelling into the phone as if it would motivate the La Paz gumshoe she herself had spent hours tracking down and hiring. As well as being a part-time investigator, Carlos was also a *cocalero*, a coca trafficker, which she guessed might be a synergistic vocation.

"...but I find 'nother Diaz," Carlos continued, ignoring the interruption. He knew he'd have Mike's attention even if the gringo at the other end of the line seemed incapable of understanding him. He spoke slowly and loudly, the same way gringos often spoke down to him. "Name of other hombre has letter 'z', not 's'. So is H-e-r-n-a-n-d-e-Z. He is no businessman too."

Carlos's slow measured pace only riled Mike more, "Then you've got the wrong guy," Mike screamed. "Wrong spelling *and* wrong job."

This wasn't an attitude the two-hundred-pound Bolivian was used to. "You hear me, Señor Mike…"

"You hear *me*, Carlos. Find *my* Hernandes, not some other Hernandez." Mike was about to slam down the phone on him.

"Señor Mike! I am find him. You fucking hear?"

Mike was silent.

"I find you fucking Hernandez, okay? He *diplomático muy importante*, but he no businessman. And he from Chile not Bolivia, but he live in Bolivia. He vanish exact year you say. His wife… she from Bolivia; a *paceños* family… indigenous, you say. I got wedding announcement from friend in Santiago. Chile have good records. This *diplomático* Hernandez with 'z'… he has one wedding party in La Paz and 'nother *grande* one in Chile. Later, *un periódico*… a newspaper in Chile say there is trouble in Bolivia and he send his pregnant wife away, maybe to America. Then he vanish..."

Carlos had to be on the wrong track, Mike was sure of it. "Carlos, you say you got the wedding announcement… what's the name of the wife of this Hernandez-with-a-z."

"*Un momento*… her name… Maria… Maria Rosa."

★ ★ ★ ★ ★

OFTEN when she was alone, Isabel hugged her father's photograph while her mind played back that morning… *She is fifteen… it's the last kiss she will ever give her mother…*

The terror of that afternoon attacked her whenever it wanted to.

The shrink she'd seen briefly years ago told her that her preoccupation with that kiss, that morning, and with her father, was her brain desperately trying to supplant the horror of that afternoon.

Mostly it worked.

Isabel knew that it was this momentary heaven set against the hell that had driven her to succeed, so that she would never again get close to that life, and could help others to avoid similar fates.

She replayed the morning over and over, seeking both comfort and pain from each tiny detail. It wasn't pretty, but it had been her life.

*IT'S 7:15 AM and Isabel's mami is flaked out, flabby and naked. Isabel is standing over her. Mami is beautiful, apart from her bruises. Her boyfriend is sprawled out beside her and the yellowing sheet with pink flowers half covers the couple. He's been mami's boyfriend for two weeks. Isabel has chalked him up as staying twelve nights straight. Suddenly, his arm moves and the snarling tattoo on his bicep, a wolf, disturbs her. Scares her.*

*She runs to tidy up the mess from the adults' party from last night. She tosses out soggy trays of half-eaten nachos and curling pizza, and using her fingers as stoppers manages to take out six of the eight empty beer bottles in one trip and lays them like bricks on the wall she's been building outside. She's already folded the newspaper he'd brought home with him from the plant. That was the only good thing about this one: twice a week he brought home the newspaper. Her mami never bought one, preferring to zone out in front of the TV.*

*Last week Isabel gave a speech for the local Rotarians' school citizenship contest and her teacher said she might win a prize. Her mami could sure use the money.*

*After Isabel picks up and folds her mother's clothes, she silently slides open the bedside table drawer and takes out her father's photo, their only picture of him. Mami hides it in there to avoid trouble with the boyfriend. Isabel loves how handsome he was; she strokes the glass protecting his movie-star hair. She holds it to her heart and turns her head to the bed.*

*She reviles this man with the wolf tattoo. If her father were here, he'd fix him. Isabel's black eye shines back at her from the glass. She touches it gingerly but it throbs, and in her fright she drops the photo-frame.*

*Her mother flips up in bed, instantly terrified: "No wake him," she mouths. The boyfriend stirs and the two females are frozen but he rolls over, smothering his wolf under the pillow.*

*Maria Rosa slides very, very slowly out of bed. Ignoring the stains on yesterday's dress, she slips it over her head. She looks around the trailer, nodding approval at Isabel's housework, and whispers: "*Vaya, go to school,*" and adds, "*Rápidamente,*" as if she needed to. Isabel is happy to escape from Wolfman.*

*She is an odd fifteen-year-old: she loves school and hates weekends. Maria Rosa's boyfriends fancy their Friday and Saturday nights wild, so there's hell to pay on the mornings when there is no school to flee to.*

*Her mami walks her to the trailer park gate, one of the few tokens of motherhood left. It's as much routine as mami can muster. Very gently she stretches up to brush the bruise around Isabel's eye with her lips, smiles and says, "¡Chao pescado!" See you later alligator, or a close approximation of it. It was her father's expression, apparently.*

*Isabel embraces her mami, careful to avoid the welt on her back, and leans down to kiss her beautiful cheek, and caresses it, knowing to ignore the foul breath of morning and alcohol.*

*They part, and Maria Rosa turns around to saunter back.*

*Isabel stands at the gate watching her.*

*Her mami is singing the bolero hit she's sung ever since Isabel was in a stroller: "*Bésame, Bésame mucho…*" Isabel thinks it's for her, but her mami is singing, and swinging her hips, in the hope that Willy the trailer park manager will see her.*

# 11

IN 1968, LAND-LOCKED Bolivia was South America's most destitute country. Within its rigid, polarised society, the grinding poverty of the Andean Indian majority had more in common with sub-Saharan Africans than with the lifestyle led by their Spanish-descended elites.

The host in the presidential library tonight is *el presidente* Barrientos. He drops into the sad leather armchair. He and all his guests are smoking the prized new Cuban *Cohibas*.

Despite the President's summons to sit, Dr Hernandez Diaz remains standing. A slug of thick grey ash precariously dangles from the tip of Diaz's smoke.

Barrientos's teeth crunch down onto his cigar and his stomach tightens. He waits. The President's shameless eyes look down at his other freshly imported extravagance, a hand-knotted silk rug that almost floats under their feet, a one-thousand-knots-per-square-inch red and gold Persian tapis. His eyes flick back and forth between the carpet and the ash from the contemptuous Chilean dog.

Alfredo and the others watch silently, knowing from experience that the insult will not go unanswered. But there is time. Here, there is a time for everything.

At over 13,000 feet above sea level, La Paz boasts it is the world's highest capital city. Yet, economically Bolivia is rock-bottom though *el presidente* René Barrientos Ortuño, gallantly propped up by his CIA friends and his cronies at Gulf Oil, regrets he has little time to dwell personally on his people's poverty. But he is a fine orator, in indigenous Quechuan as well as Spanish, and his diamond-encrusted finger always points to where the blame really lies: the irksome Cuban-inspired insurgents or, when it suits him, Bolivia's land-thieving neighbour and Dr Diaz's homeland, Chile.

At least, Barrientos smiles to himself, the insurgents no longer pose such a problem. Sawing off both of Che Guevara's hands after his murder was a nice touch by his colleague and former junta co-president General Alfredo Ovando Candia. Earlier that evening, as they were slicing into their steaks, the subject of Che had come up, with Alfredo accepting the plaudits with all the grimness his high forehead and clipped paintbrush moustache could muster. To Barrientos, Alfredo's stern appearance seems a little comical: his thin, pursed lips make him look as though he is secreting one of Guevara's rings in his mouth.

The old chesterfields lend an enveloping cosiness to the animated after-dinner discussion that hardly reflects the roles of these six men, or the tension tingling in the room. "*¡Ruiro siki!* You round ass!" laughs Barrientos only just concealing his loathing for Dr Diaz, the only one still on his feet. Is Diaz standing to show he can or because his stature, such as it is, will be lost in the sofas?

Unresponsive to Barrientos' jibe and feigning indifference to the damage his cigar ash would do to the rug or his smoke inflicts on the prized volumes lining the walls, Diaz, whose doctorate is in Spanish literature, pulls a heavy early edition of *El Ingenioso Hidalgo Don Quijote de la Mancha* off a shelf. He weighs it in his hands and loudly contemplates the irrelevant coincidence that its author, Miguel de Cervantes Saavedra, and William Shakespeare died on the same day: April 23, 1616.

Diaz rests the book on the lid of his pot belly, round as his head is bald. He tugs the antique leather-bound cover open to find the contemporary hand-written inscription:

> *My dear René,*
> *Our two countries: great friends,*

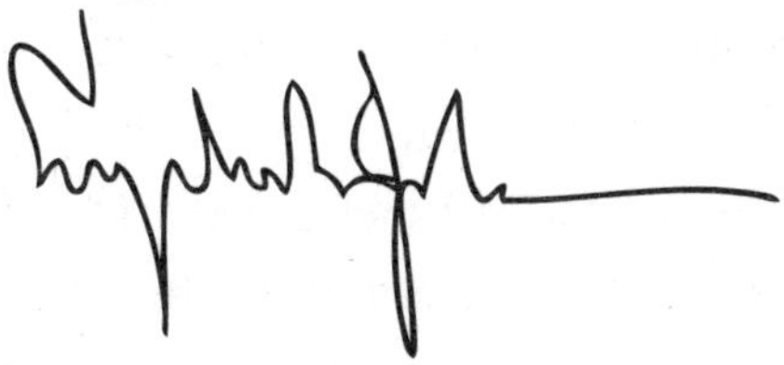

US President Lyndon B. Johnson's personal message is dated three weeks after the 1964 coup that installed Barrientos as Bolivia's president. Diaz masks his disgust with a long puff on his *Cohiba* and replaces the volume.

Chile and Bolivia broke off official relations in 1962, years before Diaz was sent by Chile to quietly negotiate their re-opening. "You Bolivianos have such light-headed views. Perhaps it is because La Paz indeed touches the sky."

"*Baja la música.* Turn down the music," Barrientos grunts to an aide who obeys immediately.

Diaz is disappointed; the turntable is spinning one of his favourites: Lucho Gatica singing the bolero hit *Bésame Mucho.* The orchestra played it five times at both of his wedding receptions—the first in La Paz and the other in Santiago. Oh, the tedious lengths an envoy must endure if he marries a local girl. Despite the cheerless outcome of that politically convenient tryst, he still loves the song.

*Bésame,* (Kiss me,)
*bésame mucho,* (Kiss me a lot,)
*como si fuera esta noche,* (As if tonight…)
*la última vez,* (…is the last time.)

"Hernandez," continues the President, one of only two present with no moustache but possessing the gravitas to interrupt Diaz using his first name, "The music is like the poetry, si? It can sometimes be prescient." Barrientos tips his widow's peak lightly as if signalling a farewell. Diaz doesn't quite follow, but sees the others understand.

He almost lets his suspicion screw up the folds in his pudgy face, but he restrains it and forces a smile, allowing Barrientos to continue uninterrupted.

"Why do you tell such stories, Dr Diaz? Maybe it is because you Chileans get to enjoy the sea air that Bolivians cannot. Is it so fanciful that Chile should restore to our beloved country her legitimate rights to her Pacific coast?"

Not even tonight, ostensibly a social occasion, can Barrientos restrain himself from rebuking his guest's nation for strangling the economy of his own.

Once more, Diaz sighs. It is tiresome, having to tolerate this monotonous gripe time and again. He knows the whining is just a crowd-pleaser, even tonight. It has been the same all along the conga line of Barrientos's predecessors, ever since Chile's glorious victory in *La Guerra del Pacífico* in 1883. Name just one Bolivian administration in the eighty-odd years since, he ponders, that has not sought to smokescreen its own economic bungling by agitating against Chile's seizure of the Atacama coastal corridor.

Diaz dares to yawn, secure that Barrientos's own jingoistic arrogance will not interpret it as the disrespect he so unquestionably intends; Bolivians have a saying that if La Paz itself won't take a foreigner's breath away, the altitude will. There is truth in this.

Diaz also blames the thin air for his brainless decision to marry Maria Rosa, but he will not share that regret with these Bolivianos.

"Señor Presidente," says Diaz eventually, without looking at Barrientos as would be the custom, "your hospitality is, as always, magnificent. But I have an early meeting with the *yanqui*, Señor Smith."

All present are well-acquainted with the sharp, green-eyed Smith, a CIA operative whose real name has been the subject of continued speculation. Barrientos owes Smith and his colleagues big-time for providing the intelligence that enabled his US-trained battalion of Bolivian Rangers to track down and kill Guevara, ending Castro's efforts to spread his leftist revolution to Bolivia. Between Chile and Cuba, Barrientos had previously had his hands full; now it is just Chile he needs to worry about.

Diaz also owes Smith. Kindly—too kindly?—Smith had procured a US visa for Diaz's wife Maria Rosa, no questions asked. Why Smith was so helpful still isn't clear to Diaz. Perhaps Smith has eyes for Maria Rosa. But with the escalating troubles, there was no way Diaz could let pregnant Maria Rosa stay here in La Paz. He couldn't pack her off to Chile; his diplomatic career would not survive long if he let a woman like her loose in his country. It was the best way. He would probably have had to find another, regrettably uncivilised, method if Smith had not been so cooperative.

"Please remember me to him," says one of the other guests, though he needn't have bothered. He is Mario Vargas Salinas, a member of the nocturnal detail that secretly buried Che's body in a grave outside the mountain town of Vallegrande. "We must thank Smith for ensuring the good doctor didn't stay under our skin for too long, eh?" Salinas laughs.

At first Dr Diaz takes this as a personal insult till he appreciates the joke: Salinas isn't referring to Diaz, but to Che Guevara's professional training as a dermatologist. Yet, in the carefully worded world of diplomacy, Diaz can't discount it as a double entendre.

"Maybe you should take Smith to the *Mercado de los Brujos*, the Witch Doctors' Market, and buy him some dried llama fetuses," suggests Salinas.

"A waste of time," says Alfredo. "Smith worships power, not *Pachamama*, the goddess Mother Earth."

"Unlike the six of us," Barrientos laughs, though it is a little hollow. Barrientos—always pragmatic—certainly worships *Pachamama*... why cut off options unnecessarily?

DIAZ wants to chew over the night's events with a clear head, so he instructs his chauffeur, Felipe, to drive him along the road towards Coroico. Felipe raises his eyebrow but Diaz waves him on. Hardly a road, more a one-lane track, it is cut into the side of a mountain and twists almost continuously with blind hairpins often with dripping wet rock overhangs that obliterate the stars. For good reason it is known locally as *El Camino del Muerte*, the Death Road, and is possibly the most dangerous road anywhere. Diaz detests having a driver, even more so on an exhilarating and challenging run like this, but both his position and the times dictate it. Felipe is also a crack shot.

Before they leave the grounds, Felipe jumps back out of the car into the freezing night air. Like Maria Rosa, he is a local. Diaz smiles. He has witnessed this ridiculous rite many times though it is true that it has so far protected his life on their many trips on Death Road. Felipe takes a bottle of pure alcohol from the trunk and splashes the liquid on each tyre, blessing the vehicle with a *cha'lla*. After taking off again, he stops at various points along the road to appease the *apus* mountain spirits, by making offerings of *mamacoca* coca leaf, and adding a rock or two to several of the many rock cairns by the roadside that mark where people have died. Fortunately tonight, perhaps because it is so late, none of the mangy rabid dogs come out to him angling for food. There are many deaths along this road, and not just from dog bites. Several vehicles per month tumble over the side, plummeting for 1,200 to 3,000 feet down precipitous sheer cliff drops.

Tonight Felipe meets no oncoming vehicles, or one of them would have had to back up along the track several hundred feet to squeeze past the other—terrifying at the best of times, unthinkable at night.

While Hernandez's adored silver-grey 1957 Mercedes 300SL Gull Wing is the best car in the world, according to him, with state-of-the-art fuel-injection being just one of its features, it is hardly the most appropriate car for this particular pastime. When Felipe has to lift the upward-opening door to climb out for one of his rituals, he has to avoid parking under the many rock overhangs or his boss would whine about the hand-tooled llama leather seats getting soaked from the drips.

Diaz affectionately calls his car Rosinante, after Don Quijote's scraggly horse. He loves this car and as a bonus, has found its whisper-quiet action useful.

Ten miles along the road, Diaz instructs Felipe to pull over at a wide bend, his favourite thinking spot, and to switch off the headlights. "The light will interfere with my thoughts," he says. He pushes up his half of the door and, with some difficulty, his rotund frame spills out of the automobile, leaving Felipe at the wheel. He buttons his coat, pulls on his hat and gloves and waddles over to the edge, carefully. He sucks in the chill air. Apart from the stars and a fingernail of moon, there is nothing to see. Everything is black, even his thick coat. He is cold and, even though he knows it will only make a psychological difference, he takes a cigar case and lighter from his inside pocket and extracts his own Cuban, biting off the end and lighting it up.

Felipe's sharp eyes catch a split-second glimmer in the rear vision mirror. It isn't Diaz; his Chilean boss is twenty feet ahead of the car and is humming that damn *Bésame Mucho* again.

Felipe turns silently, his intense eyes scanning, his hand imperceptibly reaching for his shoulder holster—in this country you can't be too prepared—but he sees who it is and his arm relaxes. Stupidly, he eases off the brake so Rosinante can canter quietly down the slope in the moonlight but her tyres crunch the stones and snap Diaz out of his contemplation of the evening's events.

Before Diaz can complete his head-turn, a shot rings out and the bullet punches through his neck, catapulting him over the edge.

Like many before, and after.

Diaz's favourite tune floats through his head as he falls: *como si fuera esta noche, la última vez*; as if tonight is the last time.

Music can be prescient. Barrientos was right.

# 12

ISABEL'S CAMPAIGN MANAGER crossed his legs, tugging the navy blue extra-fine merino wool cuff down over his red sock just so. Gregory Samson knew they were silk Zegnas; the socks, that is. The suit was Armani, made from Australian super-fine wool, but Gregory wasn't one to shout out his discernment for fear it would be yet another way to bring attention to his prematurely balding head.

The only obsession Gregory fussed over more than his appearance, apart from his fix of Diet Coke twenty-four hours a day, was managing Isabel: her program, the ads, the slogans, her speeches, whom she spoke to, where she went, how she got there, what she said, where she ate, what she drank—usually water, occasionally a Virgin Mary—what TV programs she appeared on, what TV she watched, what she wore, and more importantly, what she didn't wear. Once, he had tried to get her to wear high necks to hide her scar, but she refused, saying, "I am what I am." She did go along with greys and blues though, to distinguish her from the shouty reds and other bright colours so many other women politicians favoured and to avoid, as Gregory said, the inevitable cliché with Rosa being her middle name. Gregory worried about every detail.

He wasn't as snug with Isabel as family, he knew that, but he was as close as any outsider could get. At least he believed so. Maybe not as close as Democrat Spencer Prentice—a relationship Gregory considered weird—but close enough. Nothing but nothing went to Isabel without it coming to Gregory first—everyone in the campaign knew that—unless some pushy press reptile managed to slither past, in which cases the candidate annoyingly did as she pleased, which was usually fine he had to admit, and which infuriated him even more than the reptiles themselves. But really… it was his job to keep her clear of the mundane and, despite her instincts, there was no way she could see all the balls being tossed at her. She was only human, a weakness his campaign strategy had turned into a strength… a giant, hopefully sustainable and therefore unbeatable 70-percent strength.

Gregory spoke at a hundred miles an hour, and he thought twice as fast which meant he sometimes fell over himself, not often, mind you; just occasionally.

Isabel adored him, but he made Ed cringe. To him, Gregory was a bald, pain-in-the-butt motor-mouth who, when he was a kid playing hide-and-seek would probably have been the one the other kids wouldn't even bother looking for. Plus Ed couldn't stand the guy's voice. It wasn't that Ed didn't like Aussies. He'd fought beside many of them, and they were top troops, right up with the best. But Gregory's stream of consciousness wrapped inside his nasal whine exhausted Ed. "Julia Gillard on speed but with better hair" was how one news clip had described Gregory's voice. Despite Isabel backing Gregory as being brilliant, Ed just didn't see it.

"I told you we had to watch out for this," Gregory truthfully reminded Isabel. "And when we least need it, just when we've got Muslim America back in our tent eating olives out of our hands, that twisted…," he paused when he saw her scowl, "… *creep* spits the damn seeds right in our face."

"Enough!" Isabel said, charitably assuming the pressure had gotten to him. "Our campaign doesn't talk or think like that!"

*She* didn't talk like that, but Gregory knew from his polling that 30 percent of Americans did; he took a slurp of Diet Coke to stop himself from telling her that. This time, his mouth had really got ahead of his mind.

★ ★ ★ ★ ★

KARIM Ahmed was one of Isabel's many success stories or more accurately, he had been. His father, Hakim, an Iraqi chemical engineer, had fled with his family as refugees to America after the first Gulf War. Hakim started out mopping floors in a Newark outlet of Isabel's BBB restaurant chain; coincidentally the city where Isabel had been born. Despite being a practising Muslim, Karim's father always hand-painted Isabel a Christmas card incorporating both traditional geometric elements and Christian icons—he was a fine artist who believed his new life exemplified how different cultures could cohabit contentedly. Every year his card offered his and his wife Najeeba's thanks for the opportunities Isabel had provided for their family. By the time their son Karim was graduating high school, Hakim had risen to become manager of the LaGuardia airport BBB, one of the chain's busiest and most profitable. Karim was a straight-A student, blitzing his final examinations and topping his class. He'd done well in his SATs and was desperate to take the undergraduate course at NYU's Stern Business School but he'd narrowly missed a scholarship and the fees were a killer.

Isabel had gone to LaGuardia to take the shuttle to Boston and, as she often did, wandered over to visit the BBB restaurant, one of the hundreds she already owned at that time.

"Hakim, why doesn't Karim apply for a BBB family scholarship?" she asked.

"There is such a scheme?" he asked.

There was, from that moment on, and Karim got to go to NYU.

To the Ahmed family's surprise, Isabel turned up at Karim's graduation, a tradition she maintained for all employees and their kids until she was elected to Congress and had to step away from the business.

"What's that?" Karim asked, looking at the envelope Isabel had just popped into the black mortarboard cap he was holding upside-down, like a dish.

"Murray's finally bought that ranch, Karim, and he's aiming to retire in a few years. He needs a number two."

He didn't need to be the whiz that he was to know that she was offering him a job as assistant to BBB's Chief Financial Officer, Murray Byron. Karim nodded, unable to speak. He knew about the CFO's long-talked-about retirement plans—part of his scholarship had involved him interning with Murray during university vacations—but this!

"Eventually, Murray's gonna head back to Texas to raise cattle, so BBB needs to start developing someone to jump into his saddle. Any ideas, Karim?"

Hakim and Najeeba looked at each other in disbelief. "We love America," said Najeeba, her smile broader than the Tigris. "And we love you, Isabel."

Hakim hugged her, "You are like a sister to us."

KARIM became one of Isabel's hand-picked business intimates and slid easily and naturally into Murray's CFO role two years before BBB was sold into an Initial Public Offering on the New York Stock Exchange. By then, she'd left the board and distanced herself from the business as part of her campaign to get elected to Congress. Even so, Karim's betrayal had come as a shock to her.

Spencer Prentice, too, had been aghast. Though now a congressman himself, but on the opposite side of the aisle, he had long been Isabel's confidante and during the IPO process had been investment banker to the deal. Having observed Karim at very close quarters he was impressed. At due diligence meetings, Spencer cross-examined the young CFO on everything: the budget items and expenses that concerned him, teasing out how reliable the revenue forecasts were, understanding what could go wrong with the business's profit levers, querying the veracity of the internal systems. Everything. Even in the face of sustained probing, Karim hadn't missed a beat.

"The best CFO I've seen in years," Spencer had told investors and analysts.

So it was especially awkward when, only two months after BBB listed on the exchange, one of the audit juniors unearthed the fraud. He'd been up late ahead of the release of BBB's first quarterly financial report and from the moment he tripped over the first tiny irregularity to Karim taking flight, it was only a few hours. Karim had misappropriated over four million dollars.

Market confidence in BBB Inc. was punctured the moment the chairman simultaneously announced the fraud and Karim Ahmed's disappearance. The stock price haemorrhaged. BBB had been sold into the IPO at $30 per share. In those first two months of public trading, despite weak markets, the stock had still spiked up a solid 20 percent to $36, so the sudden plunge to $20 had seriously hurt.

Investors, the media, as well as Isabel's opponents wanted a scapegoat. Fingers pointed in every direction, many at her. The headlines and newsbars were already clattering: *Fraud smashes BBB but Burger Queen rolls in dough*, and worse.

As soon as she'd heard the news, Isabel got put through to BBB's chairman who was in the middle of a crisis board meeting. Spencer was with him, and they both left the boardroom to take her call.

"Isabel," said Spencer with more than a hint of anxiety, "This isn't your concern. You don't need to do this." She had offered an ex gratia payment, a gift to the company of the entire sum Ahmed had defrauded. Four million dollars.

"That's where you're wrong," she told the two of them. "The investors who bought in at the IPO saw BBB as my company..."

"But you haven't been involved for..."

"Whatever. They saw Karim as my man. They see this as my problem. Even if you don't, I do. You're telling me that Karim was doing this for years, so it started on my watch."

The chairman smiled into the speakerphone. "It's over-generous but you're probably right. And it'll certainly go a long way to relieving the board in the other room."

"Not the whole way?"

"The market will still be worrying whether there's more bad news to come."

"Same deal. If there's anything I should've known, I'm good for that too."

There was more bad news, but when it broke Isabel could do little about it. The Islamic charity in Chicago that Karim had been syphoning off the funds to was a front for a terrorist enclave.

Even though no one could seriously put that at Isabel's feet, it would continue to haunt her campaign.

# 13

IT TOOK OVER two years for authorities to capture Karim Ahmed and months after that for his trial to start, by this time smack in the middle of Isabel's tilt for the presidency. Each day of court proceedings aimed new shots at her campaign, but they were only flesh wounds so far, despite Bobby Foster's team blowing up every micro-development into a blunderbuss attack. Then one morning it stopped. The judge threw the case out on a technicality—evidence illegally obtained—and neither side of politics was happy.

> The Republican presidential campaign was rocked today by a shock decision by Judge William Thomas to terminate the trial of Karim Ahmed, candidate Isabel Diaz's former protégé… The disgraced chief financial officer of BBB Inc., the burger chain once owned by Ms Diaz, always protested his innocence and has now walked free.
>
> Ahmed had been charged with thirteen counts of financing terrorist groups on United States' soil, as well as eight counts of corporate fraud.
>
> While Ahmed's defence lawyer claims it is a victory for American justice, Democratic presidential hopeful

Robert Foster rejects that. From his campaign bus in Wisconsin today, Mr Foster said:

*Isabel Diaz's friend and confidant has walked, but not because he is innocent. That these grave charges were tossed out on a technicality leaves the American people troubled, with unanswered questions about Isabel Diaz's judgment and her fitness to hold office.*

Only five months ago federal agencies ended Ahmed's two years on the run. Authorities had been on the lookout for the Iraqi immigrant after Ms Diaz's restaurant chain revealed a multi-million-dollar fraud three years ago, only weeks after she sold the entire firm to investors for upwards of $250 million, some of which is funding her current presidential campaign as well as her nationwide Triple-B charitable foundation. The original discovery of the fraud sparked an investigation that extended into six states and has so far resulted in eight arrests.

We cross now to…

★ ★ ★ ★ ★

ED Loane walked into Isabel's mid-town Manhattan campaign headquarters, not far from his own office. Isabel and Gregory were hunched over a sheet of paper covered in scrawled boxes and arrows, the latest adjustments to the campaign strategy, Ed presumed.

"I just heard… Ahmed's off the hook. Damn lawyers!" he grunted, glowering at Gregory, knowing he had graduated summa cum laude from Harvard Law School after an undergraduate politics degree in Australia. "The bullcrap streaming out of Foster's mouth… And what about the freakin' judge! That conniving Democrat bastard chose his timing brilliantly, didn't he? To inflict maximum damage on you... Here's how it'll go: 'Ahmed's free to walk the streets, but he's not innocent… a threat to all Americans.' And he's *your* man, Isabel. End of story. Damn it."

"That's extreme," Isabel said. "Judge Thomas doesn't go for my politics but he's not going to endanger the country for that. Besides, while I accept Karim stole the money, I can't believe he knew the charity was a terrorist front."

"Don't ever defend that shit publicly," said Ed, walking to the window.

Gregory was about to give his opinion when Ed's head snapped round and the ice of his glare froze Gregory's tongue. Instead, he straightened his tie, a Versace, and let Ed continue.

"Ahmed has to go down for this *before* the election, or we're finished," said Ed. "I'm telling you this thing will fester, and it will screw your campaign. Trust me. None of those fancy arrows on that stupid sheet of paper will change that."

A silence jagged the air for almost a minute, a staggering time for someone like Gregory for whom speech and thought were almost indistinguishable.

# 14

SIMON KNEW THAT his girlfriend Elia despised Mike Mandrake. It wasn't merely that the journalist was a sharp-elbowed loudmouth from Washington DC, there was something else. Simon tried pressing the issue but Elia clammed up as she usually did about her work. "It's confidential"… "If I told you, I'd have to kill you, ha ha"… They were all excuses, not reasons. Whatever was behind it, Elia was continually pissed off about something and it was bugging their relationship.

"It's just *him*, okay?" she said, trying to push Simon off. "He's an egotistical bully and a repulsive shit, and… and he's got no background in TV, but then… you know, this is the thing… he's cracked something no one's managed to crack before. So I loathe the guy… seriously, but his work... it's…"

"This work. Is it worth the crap he's dumping over you?"

Elia's eyebrows rose like someone poised at the top of a cliff debating whether to jump.

Simon waited.

"It's about Isabel Diaz's past," she said.

"You already told me that." He stood and stretched his lanky frame. "Beer?"

She nodded.

He sidled over to the fridge. Take it slowly. That's what one of the fridge magnets said. He knew it was Elia's joke to remind him to fix the loose shelf inside, but right now he took it as a warning for this conversation. He noticed her fingers were fretting her bottom lip. "What is it, then?" He couldn't help himself. "Is he linking her to Ahmed's terrorists? Is that it? Jesus, Elia. How could you?"

Like many of the former runaways Isabel's charity had given a hand to, Simon was very protective of his benefactor. He didn't know her personally, not really; they'd only met a few times, but her Triple-B foundation had changed his life. At sixteen, he was doing drugs and living on the streets. It was his arrest for busting a convenience store that tripped him up. The duty lawyer hooked him up with a Triple-B guy in court that day for someone else, and who convinced the judge not to send him to juvy if he signed up for their vocational training program. It was hardly a choice, and he had begrudged it at the time. But it gave him the chance to pick up on plumbing and these days Simon's ample chest puffed proudly at being a solid citizen who made a difference to people's lives. He fixed their pipes. It was far better than living in them.

"It's a human interest thing." Elia was biting her lip now.

"So what's turning you inside-out?"

She glanced back over her shoulder, and shook her head as if realising the stupidity of the action. "We've tracked down who Isabel's father *really* was."

Simon handed Elia her beer and carried his over to the TV. "What? Was he a Bolivian drug lord or something? That it?" He kept looking at the screen, feigning the right level of disinterest to keep Elia going.

She cleared her throat. "Ah… here's the thing… he wasn't actually Bolivian."

"Huh?" He turned back so quickly he spilt his beer on the rug.

Isabel's father *was* Bolivian. A businessman. Everyone who'd been through Triple-B knew that. The story was famous.

"He was Chilean," said Elia, the sweat beading her upper lip. Normally, she'd never reveal a work secret.

"That's it? That's the big deal? That he's Chilean? Who the fuck cares…they're all Latinos, right?" he joked. Though he was sure the detail was important, he didn't understand why.

"Shit, Simon," she said. "Madeleine Albright … remember her? Bill Clinton's Secretary of State? I don't think she just toasted 'mazeltov' when she was leading the Middle East peace talks and she suddenly discovered her parents had been Czech Jews, not the Catholics she'd always believed."

"Albright, shmalbright."

"If you'd spent your whole life believing that your dad, who you'd never met, was a Bolivian businessman but, live on national TV, you get ambushed and get told for the first time that he was actually a high-ranking Chilean diplomat, don't you think it might matter to you?"

Simon ignored her glare and joined her on the sofa. 'He *is* dead, right? He's not gonna turn up on your show like it's *This Is Your Life* or something?"

"He's definitely dead," Elia said, pushing back a bang of her black hair that had escaped her elastic. "He died a month after Isabel was born."

"After?"

"Apparently."

"You think you should tell her this live?"

"My opinion isn't worth shit. It's Mandrake who wants to spring it on her, in front of millions. And the bastard's got something else… he won't tell me what it is… but he says it's huge, and he's dangling it out there like…"

"I hope the fucker chokes on himself."

# 15

LITTLE DAVEY LOANE was definitely his dead mother's son, and Ed was sick of people tactlessly reminding him of it. Davey's thick blond hair flopped just like Jane's used to and his open blue eyes lit up with her same buoyant optimism. But adore his son as he did, it meant occasionally... in a certain light... if Davey walked or ran in a particular way... his mere presence could reignite Ed's rage. Fury at the infidelity that led to Jane's death, and contempt for the man who caused it, often refuelled the suspicion that perhaps Davey was not his son at all. He'd thought about tests, but he didn't really want to know.

This Saturday morning, Isabel was at home for a rare lazy family breakfast. The house was way over the top for Isabel, but Ed loved it, more for its memories than anything else, so she had forced aside her discomfort over it. The six-bedroom, eight-bathroom mansion had been described in the realtor's ad Ed saw when Davey was born as "renowned and admired for over eighty years as one of the most important houses in the Hamptons, Long Island. It took the eminent Manhattan firm of Polhemus & Coffin seven years to build the home, which is listed at over 7,000 square feet and located on eight acres overlooking Shinnecock Bay and the Atlantic Ocean."

Why three people plus help needed so much space was not something Isabel could answer. Not even Ed liked entertaining or throwing big parties, but he did fish, so at least it had that going for it. And it was private.

George Hicks, Isabel's substitute father, had flown over from California to stay a few weeks to help with Davey while the campaign was in full swing. Ed wasn't thrilled about it, but tolerated him, which was not exactly hard in this house. Ed and George didn't see eye-to-eye on anything, apart from Isabel. And Davey.

Working his hands in American Sign Language, Davey had been begging George to cook up some of his famous ricotta hotcakes with honey. It was Davey's favourite BBB breakfast treat, which George falsely claimed he'd invented at the original Big Bad Burgers diner even before Isabel had walked in on the scene. Unlike Ed, who had mastered ASL, and Isabel who was adequate, George was totally inept so the boy turned his request into a kind of charades.

Davey loved it when George laughed—his teeth stuck out even further and his wiry grey ponytail flailed round so he looked to Davey like both ends of a horse. His bucktoothed grin was where George's nickname 'Buckets' came from; at least that was Isabel's child-friendly explanation. George had laughed when she told the boy that little lie. It had been the summer of '64 and George was on security for the Rolling Stones' first US tour. In those days George was always overflowing—with booze, drugs, whatever—and it was one of the Stones, Brian Jones, who bestowed the nickname on him. (Brian was the wild blue-eyed boy who ended up at the bottom of his swimming pool and, even then, people said he looked better dead than fellow Stone Keith Richards did alive.)

George, now in his seventies, hadn't done drugs or alcohol for decades, often joking he got the same effects these days just from standing up fast.

He was about to head off to make the flapjacks when Davey tugged at his shirt to stop. The boy turned to Ed and after asking him to act as interpreter for his new joke, he made the sign for "big" and thumped his chest.

"A big gorilla," said Ed, his grin widening.

Davey then put his finger to his mouth and his ear.

"Ah, a big deaf gorilla."

Davey nodded and continued.

"A big deaf gorilla… King Kong," Ed said, "is storming through a town… he reaches down to pick up this beautiful woman. She's deaf too. He has the deaf woman in the palm of one hand and says to her…"

Suddenly, Davey smashed his free hand down onto the palm that was holding the imaginary woman and started to jig on the spot. Ed cracked up himself and, until father and son composed themselves, all Isabel and George could do was look to each other, trying to guess at what was so funny.

"I'm sorry," said Ed, wiping a rare tear. "King Kong says to her in ASL," but he broke into laughter again. "Okay, this deaf King Kong says, 'Will you marry me?' But see, the ASL sign for 'marry' is to slap one hand down onto the other so King Kong, instead of asking her to marry him, crushes her to death."

Isabel leant over to give Davey a big hug as George laughed his way to the kitchen. Ed excused himself, too. "I'll be back in a few minutes, Davey," he said, and after stroking his son's head he walked off.

Isabel was so flushed with laughing that her scar stuck out against her neck.

"Why have you got that?" Davey signed when the two were alone. He reached for it and touched it gently, though to Isabel, his finger seemed to burn. Davey had asked before but she'd fended him off with her stock answer, "Someone hurt me once." Previously it had been enough for the boy, but he was getting older and more insistent.

"Who hurt you?" He pressed it this time.

The ASL sign for a man, Isabel knew, mimicked grasping the front brim of your hat, but gallantry was out of place. Her colour drained and she let Davey lip-read instead, "A man," she whispered. "A bad man."

"A boy hurt me at school yesterday," he signed almost immediately; Davey was, after all, only eight. "He whacked me over the head with his lunch box."

Isabel forced a smile. "I'm sure it was an accident."

"No," he continued signing. "He was angry because I hid his water bottle. How did the bad man hurt you?"

There was no way Isabel would reveal the shockingly sensitive details to an eight-year-old. She'd never publicly admitted it was a rape, just an assault gone very bad. Fortunately for her, the records from back then were patchy. "Davey," she said, "he cut me… with a piece of glass and…" Her voice broke off.

Ed walked back in. "Hey, big feller," he said, making sure Davey's eyes had followed Isabel's toward him, "Are you telling the next president how she should run this country, or are you still jabbering about gorillas?"

"A man hurt Isabel, daddy. With a piece of glass," the boy signed earnestly, then touched her scar.

Ed saw the silent wail on Isabel's face and the scatter of smile lines around his eyes fell away. "Isabel doesn't want to talk about that, Davey," he said. "Okay?"

Davey shook his head so his hair flew out at the sides, "Not okay."

Isabel rested her hand on Ed's arm, and breathed in, "It's fine," and turned back to Davey. "Davey, the man did bad things to me, so… so I can't have any children."

Davey absorbed the information for a moment, chewing his tongue and tapping Pip his stuffed toy penguin on its head. One of Isabel's campaign badges was pinned to Pip's chest—

the button with the red, white and blue rose. "But *I'm* your child. You said so!" he signed, a tear drizzling from his blue eyes. "Why can't you have me anymore?"

She shot a look of alarm at Ed. "Of course I can have you, Davey. I meant that I can't have a baby."

The boy nodded weakly, sniffed and wiped his eyes. "Did the man hurt you a lot?"

She nodded.

"Did he kill your mother too?"

Isabel's breath caught in her throat, hoping she'd misunderstood the signing but she saw Ed's jaw tighten and knew she hadn't. Ed had been right in trying to avoid this path. Often his relationship with Davey was excellent, like this morning, but it was sometimes marred, and not merely by a boy's typical disappointments over a busy father who wasn't always around. Wrongly, Davey blamed Ed for his mother's death and there would be days when he just wouldn't communicate with his father at all, freezing him out.

What was going on inside Davey's head became clear just after the wedding two years earlier. His doctors had suggested some new tests and it turned out that Davey wasn't mute at all. He was deaf, certainly, but there was no physiological impediment to him speaking.

Isabel had been witness to Ed's understandable tangle of emotions: delight his son had speech, but distress at why he refused to use it.

Off her own bat, Ed's assistant Debbie tracked down a psychologist who specialised in deaf kids. After three sessions with Davey, Professor Howard called Ed in. Isabel went with him and they sat silent, watching a video of the doctor interviewing the boy in ASL.

Isabel spent as much time watching Ed as the video. She could see Ed tearing himself apart at the boy's perverse theory. After his mother's car accident, Davey had read the lips of some adults gossiping that she had been "running off" with the man in the car. The little boy's twisted logic was that Ed must've done something bad to her to make her run away.

Isabel saw Ed shaking as Davey continued signing: "She went to heaven to run away from my daddy and I sent my voice up there to bring her back."

THE revelation turned Ed's already strong political partisanship into zealotry. Once he learned Davey was blaming him for his wife's death, his hostility to the Democrats and especially Isabel's opponent, Bobby Foster, became very personal.

Ed had explained the whole story to Isabel, starting with Jane's affair with former Democratic congressman Peter Jackson from New York. And if that wasn't bad enough, Foster had been the lawyer who helped the bastard escape any serious penalty for the charges, getting him just a paltry fine. A pittance for a life… lives.

"My wife dies, Davey loses his mom and that creep Jackson gets off scot-free, thanks to that slimy, sweet-talking Bobby Foster. Yet my son," Ed choked, "my beautiful boy… he blames me… and won't talk to me because he sent…"

Ever since, Ed had despised Robert Foster and everything about him: his role in Jackson's defence; his past career as a money-grubbing trial lawyer; even his glossy magazine good looks.

When Foster got the Democratic Party's nomination, Ed's investigations dredged up some of Foster's own passions; mostly of the tiresome variety that would plunge him into hot water with his wife if she ever found out, something Ed had toyed with facilitating many times.

But what haunted Foster's campaign—his own Karim Ahmed affair—was not his defence of Jackson, or even his infidelity… it was Joe Cook.

All these years after, few could stomach what Foster had done for his notorious rapist-murderer client. Harvard Law

School taught that Foster's strategy at Cook's trial was a model… of what not to do. He'd idealised Cook to the jury as an articulate and energetic white worker for black rights, a hapless victim of police who was standing in the wrong place at the wrong time. It wasn't even his gun! Mistaken identity. Foster tried it all, and enough of it worked. But within two months of the not-guilty verdict being handed down, cops from the next precinct shot Cook dead as he clambered over the tenement rooftop of a young black mother and her two daughters, aged twelve and ten. Foster's former star client had saved the mother… for last.

"The wealthy defence attorney with political aspirations," as the media liked to call him back then, took the opportunity to appear on TV that same night and, holding back tears, told the world he was ditching the law for a life of public service in politics. It worked, with most of the country applauding him for ditching money for public duty as penance for his mistake.

But Ed was not among them, vowing that one day Foster would pay. For all his mistakes.

# 16

SNAP! BOBBY FOSTER and his inner-circle were ensconced in the Democratic Party's campaign headquarters in Atlanta, behind floor-to-ceiling glass, partitioned from the bustle and clatter of the scores of volunteers working the phones. SNAP! Though neither Foster nor his running mate Mitchell Taylor hailed from Georgia, their strategists had picked Atlanta to boost their support in the South. Maine was Foster's home base and Mitch Taylor was an Iowa boy.

SNAP! The venetian privacy blind was yanked right up so—SNAP!—the "mamarazzi", celebrity photographer Niki Abbott, could take whatever candid shots she wanted yet still be out of earshot of campaign strategy. As always, her blue, signed Ted Williams Red Sox baseball cap was pressed down over her flaming red hair.

"Yes!" Mitch Taylor fisted the air with a spirited air-punch and shot a glance out of the corner of his eye to check if Niki had captured the moment for posterity. His victory cry would have made more sense if the Foster-Taylor team's polling had clicked over 50 percent rather than just 28 but, from the doldrums their campaign had previously been lolling in, any rise needed celebrating.

"Thank yo-ou, Judge Thomas," Taylor chuckled. The vice-presidential running mate winked at Don Thomas, the wily political strategy brain who headed up Foster's campaign machine. Don was a seasoned operator. He was also the judge's brother.

But Don, a lantern-jawed Kentucky boy, winced at the hint of complicity. Not in his family. No way. His brother had tossed out the Karim Ahmed case because that's how he cut the evidence. It had nothing to do with his political sympathies or even Don's job. Not with his brother's fierce love for the law above all else. It was why no one, not even Ahmed's defence team, had asked Judge Thomas to recuse himself from the case.

Yet Don was too excited to let the family slur intrude on the moment. He placed his hand on Mitch Taylor's shoulder, but—SNAP!—a flash from Niki's camera temporarily blinded him. "Mitch," he said to Taylor, blinking away the starburst, "at 28 we ain't even half of Diaz's 62, but one thing's for sure: our number's going up, and hers is coming down." Don Thomas's swaggering bravado seemed out of place for someone with such a pale face, bookish shoulders and a spine almost as bent as the question marks he always had on his mind.

"There's so much blue sky in here, we need sunglasses," Taylor smiled, posing for Niki Abbott's lens. Or was it for Niki herself? Don Thomas wondered, sucking in a deep breath of frustration.

# 17

AFTER ONLY SIX days of Don Thomas' revised election strategy playing out, Isabel was being pushed more and more onto the back foot. Karim Ahmed had suddenly vanished a second time. The entire nation's media mounted a massive search for him but was coming up empty-handed. The timing was perfet and Don Thomas had Bobby Foster asking all the right questions on every nightly news bulletin: "He won on a technicality, but does an innocent man run? Does he hide? This man, Isabel Diaz's star protégé, was claimed to have financed terrorists. Where is he now? Why won't he come forward and explain himself?"

That Ahmed was not a public figure was beside the point. That the judge had let him go, likewise. Isabel's support was nose-diving. *That* was the point. Down from its 70 percent to 55… already.

With seven weeks to Election Day, Isabel's chances of victory looked like they'd be pole-axed unless she could arrest the slide. Publicly, she remained calm and restrained. Stoic.

But deep in private, behind tightly closed doors, things were different. This was a crisis of the highest order for her campaign, for the Party… for the nation.

And it was time for a group of well-placed individuals to act. To take their next steps. Planning, precision, surprise and deniability were crucial. As usual.

They'd been readying for something like this even before Jax Mason's fall from the 14th floor of a London office building. It was time to use what they'd taken from him. The Diaz campaign was starting to reek with the stench of a slaughterhouse and they vowed, as such people do, to hose it clean. Isabel had to win; no matter what.

"It's not just that we'd miss out on the White House," Isis said, "though there is that. What stinks is that this pathetic duo, Foster and Taylor, might get to cup the future of this great nation in their mauling paws. If it wasn't for Ahmed, damn him, we'd still be wiping the floor with them… It's time to roll out Phase Two."

Diana was in Georgia and had dialled into the meeting on a secure line. She liked her code-name. Goddess of the hunt carried a certain class, she decided, and that Diana was an emblem of chastity added a pinch of somewhat ironic spice.

# 18

FOSTER AND TAYLOR had been dithering over whether to accept the Secret Service protective detail they'd been offered for the campaign, a privilege all major candidates were entitled to since Bobby Kennedy's assassination. After struggling with its privacy drawbacks, the pair had only just said yes, resigned that in twenty-four hours they'd no longer have some of the freedoms they liked to enjoy on the campaign trail.

Isabel had not a second's compunction about accepting the protection, though she hadn't expected her detail chief's bluntness. "Ma'am," he'd said when he first briefed her, "I don't want to create any false expectations. If someone's committed to killing you, well... they'll probably do it. My job is simply to make it as hard as possible."

★ ★ ★ ★ ★

FROM under her blue baseball cap, and with her camera tote bag over her shoulder, Niki Abbott phoned up to Mitch Taylor's room from the hotel lobby. "Ready for our breakfast shoot, Mr Vice-President?" she said provocatively. It was still weeks ahead of Election Tuesday, but she was confident he'd find it an alluring hook.

"Uhmmh?" He rolled over to squint at the clock. "It's only… ah… six. Weren't we scheduled at 7:30?"

"Oh, gosh, I'm sorry. You're right," she said, with a lilt calculated to intensify his memory of yesterday's seductive wink. She'd arranged to photograph him breakfasting alone in an elegant private dining room with the morning's papers spread out before him. It would pitch him, she said, as the contemplative man in the background, ready to step forward and serve as number one if needed. Though a Republican, Niki was fine with the scam. The shots would be huge for her, too; her agent had negotiated a five-figure pre-sale with Reuters for nationwide syndication. She loved elections.

Bobby Foster had already flown back to DC. He'd be breakfasting with congressional leaders and then had three back-to-back radio talkback interviews, all of which he'd planned for turning up the heat on Isabel over Ahmed's ominous disappearance.

"I guess," said Niki, her pout almost protruding out the other end of the phone, "I'll just have to wait by my lonesome down here in the lobby till 7:30…"

Taylor's bio described him as happily married with three children. His wasn't as long a marriage as Bobby Foster's but it was almost as tempestuous and, like Foster, that was mostly his own fault. Yet, Julia Taylor was always the good wife, putting up with his antics just as Foster's wife had so far tolerated his.

"Er, Niki, why don't we, er, do a pre-breakfast breakfast? You know, up here. Get to know each other a bit better. Then later, we can focus on the, er, shots and not the, er, small talk?"

She smiled as his voice struggled, trying not to crack like a teenager buying his first condom.

"I'll leave the door unlatched," he said, "while I'm, er, taking a shower. You can call up room service. I'll leave my order on the table and you can put it through with yours. Suite 2302."

A highly polished black brogue was holding the door to the suite open and, as she pushed inside, she heard the pelting of water in the shower—music to her ears. She picked up the shoe, looked back to check in the corridor and quietly double-locked the door.

She thought of snapping him in the nude—someone, though not Reuters, would really pay for that—but what she had planned would be better. Niki carefully put her treasured baseball cap on the hallstand and huffed her camera gear to the floor, lifted a pocket flap and pulled out two small objects and slipped them into place.

She decided not to call room service, not yet; she and Mitch didn't need interruptions or witnesses and, having turned up the radio in the room to muffle the noise for when the shower finished, she drew her one-piece suit's front zipper down from her collar to her crotch as she walked across to the bathroom. She smiled and paused when she caught herself in the mirror, and spread open her top to expose her breasts. She licked her thumbs and forefingers and tweaked and rubbed her dark brown nipples stimulating them into short thick shafts almost as hard as the shiny metal cylinder she'd slid over one of her teeth.

She didn't really need to be aroused ahead of what she was about to do but persuaded herself not to waste the opportunity. She flicked her red hair forward and curled her lips into her fail-safe fuck-me pout and stood for a moment, her hands on her hips, taking in the sight. Maybe she should get out a camera for a quick self-portrait? Niki worked as hard at her body as her moves. She was as taut and springy as a silk strap uplifting a porn star's bra, though with her mounds Niki never wore one, squeezing by with nipple-tight shirts and Ts.

She twisted round to see... yes, the flush had come to her cheeks and, yes, as always it made her tattoo down there glow. It was a red and blue rose, her smooth cream skin providing the necessary white. Frederico in Milan was truly an artist, she decided. He'd given her the tattoo years before she'd even heard of Isabel Rosa Diaz, but Niki tingled with a frisson of delight every time she spied one of the election posters or bumper stickers. Niki prized her body. She exercised daily, twice if she could. For her there was nothing better than working out on a simple bar, or sometimes two at a time.

Moments later, naked and very ready, she slid into the shower stall with Taylor and, before he could fake a protest or even turn his phony gape of shock into a hesitant grin, she dropped to her knees, her hands lightly stroking the insides of his thighs while her tongue flicked the water off the tip of his fast-rousing penis.

She knew what he was thinking: this was too good to be true… what if it were a set-up and someone came in… ummm… terrific… what if it wasn't a set-up but someone came in anyway… like room service… there could be a scandal… thnyumm… wonderful… This was the part, when he was pressing his shoulders back against the tiles and thrusting his hips forward, where she knew it'd be: *if only my Julia would do it like this… my god… ohmygod… oh, jeez-us.*

She'd soaped up her palms. This was the moment, she could feel it, and without missing a stroke, her mouth and one hand switched positions so Taylor wouldn't notice, not for a few seconds, anyway. At first she nipped him lightly, in play—she didn't want to hurt him. He moaned. And while one hand kept pumping faster and faster, she nipped hard and quick, his whole body convulsed with intense pleasure and he squealed. While still pumping him with one hand, the fingers of her other started caressing and massaging, delicately, the spot on his sac where she'd bitten into him. Finally, she wrapped her lips round him for his final spasm. She locked on to him, tight, and, at the perfect moment…

No, Julia never did that, did she?

Niki would have smiled… if she'd been able to.

"ONE thing I don't get, Niki," said Mitch Taylor, who was licking the twin peaks of whipped cream and wild berries that Niki had dolloped over herself in ways too daring and exotic even for the award-winning chefs in room service. "Here I am a Democrat, and you, not just a Republican but a raging hawk, and we're… you know… doing…"

Already slanted back on her elbows, Niki let her head dangle into the pillow elongating her neck into a silky arc that ached to be stroked, and she gurgled, "Mitch, sweetie… Fucking you Democrats… it's my life's work."

# 19

ISABEL WAS NO fool. She couldn't suppress her past forever; she knew that. How could she ask the people to elect her president if, whenever a glass smashed she'd risk losing it? It was time to confront it. For years, she'd been able to wave off probing journalists with "It's a migraine" or, if they pressed or it was someone close to her, a rehearsed and till now respected "Please, some things should stay private." But she knew that if she didn't tackle this herself, it wouldn't be long before someone's insistence would push her over, as Davey had almost managed the other morning.

"Ed," she said after the boy had gone off to play catch with George, "You've never pressed me, but the rape…"

"Don't need to know," he cut her off, but the furrow between his eyebrows told her differently this time.

"Maybe not," she said, taking a breath, "but I need to tell you…"

*SHE is fifteen. It's a last, fading June light. Biting her lip with anticipation, Isabel is hunched over the kitchen table in their grimy trailer, scratching at her homework under a single globe, anxious for her mother to wake.*

*Her English term paper (a ten-page essay prophetically entitled,* "If I were President…"*) is placed neatly at the corner of the table, the large handwritten red "A+" screaming to be complimented.*

*Maria Rosa's head is lolling on the arm of the sofa and a towel covers over the grey cottony tufts coiling out of the rips. The TV is on but the sound is down, and a half-bottle of cheap pink wine dangles from her fingertips, swaying precariously near the open bottle of gaudy red nail lacquer on the floor.*

*"Just brilliant." Her teacher actually said those words in front of the entire class. "Isabel, what you've written is beautiful. I would be proud if you became my president one day." Despite what happens that evening, Isabel will not forget those words.*

*Isabel's pride is aching to be shared. Repeatedly it drags her mind away from her homework and darts her eyes over to the couch. Unable to exercise restraint any longer, she slides noisily off the hard wooden bench and stands over her mother, breathing expectantly, making a couple of loud rasps. On the second, Maria Rosa stirs and absently grumbles a few low bars of* Bésame Mucho. *Isabel is pent up like a jack-in-a-box as she contemplates her mother's reaction: if the booze has worn off, she will be thrilled; if not… but Isabel doesn't want to think about that.*

*Outside, the steel mesh step creaks and Isabel's pride congeals into foreboding. The door swings open and Maria Rosa's latest boyfriend trips on the torn curl of carpet and lurches inside. The five bottles of beer he's hugging to his chest almost spring free but he manages to grip them even as he stumbles and swears—he never wastes good beer. Maria Rosa's eyelids attempt a flutter, like a flagging butterfly. A slit opens but reveals only the whites. A string of drool threads out the corner of her mouth and down her chin.*

*His presence compresses Isabel into a tight cold sweat. Her eyes focus on a cockroach, and she hunches her body into itself as if she too had wings. He says nothing to her, as if she's not there—which is how they'd both like it—and he sets his precious bottles on the table, directly on top of her essay. It is insensitive, ignorant, as if her sheets were merely drink coasters in a bar, but she knows he does it to make a point: she isn't wanted here. She bites her lip as the five circles of moisture spread themselves over the top page, and she pulls her eyes to the floor, unable to watch the evidence of her triumph dissolving into hollow pink blotted Olympic rings, blurry symbols of her former glory.*

*He snatches at Maria Rosa's bottle and in doing so knocks over her nail lacquer so it oozes like red mercury, poisoning the floorboards. "Drink without me, will you? Bolivian bitch!" The bottle flies out of his hand and smashes against the wall. The yellowing wallpaper soaks up just enough of the violent splash of pink liquor that it looks even more like someone had pissed on it than before.*

*Maria Rosa, startled, grabs her slippers and runs outside—she has good reason to fear this one.*

*Isabel cowers at the table, her eyes continuing to avoid his as if praying he'd go away. Now, it has the opposite effect, and he picks up the jagged green neck of the broken bottle, brandishing it at the girl as he approaches. "I'm not good enough for your fuckin' ma? That what you think?"*

*Still looking down, she shakes her head, but it is too robust to be convincing.*

*"Fuckin' liar!" He thumps at the table with the glass, and Isabel recoils fearing a shard will snap off and fly at her. It doesn't, and he stares at her as if undecided about what to do next.*

*She bites into her knuckle and looks at him. She has witnessed this one with her mother—the trailer is pitifully small. Already nursing a dismal black eye herself, she knows what he is capable of, and flinches from his gaze down to her books, and for a second, to her ruined class paper.*

*"Look at me when I'm talking'," he yells and swipes at the books, but misses. On the upswing, the edge of the glass slices across her neck, terminating just below her ear. Beads of blood form along the slash, then the red spills down her neck like a stage curtain.*

*But this is not the finale.*

*"Look at me!" His yellowing teeth push his lips back like a snarling dog's. "I'll show you how good I am." He slaps her face with his free hand, slamming her head back into the wall behind her.*

*Isabel is dazed and woozy. He must be swearing, she thinks, but isn't sure. ¿Dónde está mi mami?* Where's my...? *Isabel tries to scream her mother's name but no sound can escape the gurgling of the thick liquid mounting in her throat. Straining, she holds it back.*

*He shifts his precious bottles to the floor, almost delicately, but this time successfully flicks off her books with a rough sweep of his arm. He yanks her up onto the table and the back of her head smashes down onto her school paper. Her blood is soaking into it and finally obliterates what the five wet stains hadn't. The "A" is gone; no longer will she ever be able to boast of it. The "+" is still there, encircled by blood, like a shield against evil but it wards off nothing as she woozes in and out of reality.*

*He tears at the waist of her jeans and pulls them down to reveal her white panties. He rips them down.*

*The pain searing her neck and under her head blocks Isabel from fully grasping his intentions, at least until his filthy thumbnails are digging into the insides of her knees and he is forcing her legs open. She gasps with the shock as much as the rasping pain of his hard plunge into her. His forearms bulge with the power of desire and are pinning down her shoulders. His breath stinks of beer and tobacco and ham—honey-baked, she thinks, as though it might be important—and as she squirms, his spit slobbers into her eye. She can't wipe it, she can't do anything to help herself, and both terror and rage clash inside her.*

*Her vomit sprays over his neck and denim shirtfront. If only she'd had better aim... The rest oozes down the sides of her sad face, and the bilious chunks splatter and plop into the blood that has soaked and matted her once black hair.*

*¿Dónde está mi mami? She tries to wriggle free and vainly twists*

*her head searching. The startling pain again flares across her neck. His white-knuckled fist, an inch from her eyes, intimidates her even more than the macabre contortion of his scowl and the belligerent purple veins pulsing on his arm that make his wolf tattoo snarl. She can't think of… down there, but instinct, maybe disgust, sinks her teeth into his arm, just below his fucking wolf tattoo, and she clamps her eyes and her mouth till her tongue recoils from the repulsive taste of blood. His blood. She hopes it is his.*

*It is his turn to scream.*

*Good.*

*His spare hand grabs again for the broken bottle, "I'll fix you," he shrieks in her ear.*

*Bad.*

*She dares to open her eyes as he pulls himself out of her. He is towering over her, bristling, his penis still partially erect and flailing from side to side and his arm is soaring, brandishing the bottle neck, like a ghoul with a burning torch in a horror movie. His eyes are ablaze and his howl shrieks like a zombie's. One hand pushes her legs apart and his other arm winds back and round in an underarm so swift and sure that she faints in shock before he hits his target, a small mercy, so she never hears him yell, "You'll never forget your first fuck now."*

*He holds his penis fondly in his hand, the blood streaming from his wrist mingling with hers. He starts stroking. When he is finished and zipped up, he walks toward the door. "Tell your fuckin' whore mother," he spits out the corner of his mouth, "she'll have to get her booze from some other stupid cunt from now on."*

*A frayed grey bath towel is limp over the arm of the sofa where Maria Rosa's head had been resting just minutes earlier. He snatches it up and presses down on the blood on his arm. "Fuck you," he scowls at her and swipes the rag across his face and his shirt, but it just smears her blood and chuck into a fetid brown sludge. He tears the stinking shirt off and heaves it at Isabel. "Clean yourself up," he orders her, "You disgust me."*

*His foot has almost kicked the door open when he remembers his beers. He swivels back to the gory butcher's block and leans down to get them careful to avoid any of the red drips. Isabel's eyes stutter open and, almost instinctively, she pries the bloody shard out of her body, unleashing a venom that impels her to slam it down onto his bare shoulder, just above the wolf tattoo. But the arcing glass discharges a green glimmer of light that alerts the beast and he snatches her wrist just as it goes limp. Consciousness escapes her.*

*After the swearing and smashing is long stopped—Isabel has no idea how long—her mother steals back inside to discover her daughter almost catatonic, shivering and heaving without sound on the floor. A blood-drenched cushion is gripped between her legs and her once-white shirt is soaking red from the gash across her neck. Screwed up pages of sopping school paper are strewn all around her on the floor, the writing illegible.*

★ ★ ★ ★ ★

ED shouldered the burden of Isabel's story under a canopy of heavy silence. Like many, he'd heard the words "fifteen" and "assault" and "scar" before, a combination whose hideousness was tempered by its vagueness and so able to be touched on, though in hushed tones, in polite company and prime-time documentaries. He was one of the very few who'd also heard the word "rape" too, but apart from the original hospital and George's late wife, Annette, Isabel had never till now divulged to anyone how degenerate and degrading it had been.

In the deafening quiet, Ed stared at the wall opposite them, at the oil painting of golden haystacks, an original whose fanatical and intense swirls were now almost jumping at him. He touched his ear. How had she dealt with this… this horror? At fifteen, no less?

He pondered his own experiences; he'd averted his eyes from other fifteen-year-olds… some even younger… a lifetime of combat had taught him that nothing was unthinkable. He too had suppressed horrors and this was hardly the moment for them to arise again. Unlike Isabel's, his were in times of war. Raw as it still was, his first wife's adulterous and fatal car smash didn't remotely qualify, though the ache was with him daily. He tried to keep his own nightmarish images at bay, for a moment even closing his eyes as if to shut them out, Isabel probably thinking it was her story alone he was stressing over.

His arm hooked protectively around his wife. The two sat on the sofa and Ed glanced sideways to see Isabel staring blankly though the French doors, out to the patio where George and Ed's little boy were playing catch.

GREGORY was calling from campaign headquarters. "*Close-up* say they've got some new angle on your past," he told Isabel, the inflexion in his voice not able to hide his concern. "They're running it whether we cooperate or not." As Isabel gripped the handset, Gregory didn't even remotely understand her anxiety, but her tight mouth revealed to Ed that whatever Gregory was saying, it was not good.

She attempted to compose herself. Twisting back around to Ed, she said, "*Close-up's* got something." Her voice, already weakened, broke as she said it. "Gregory says it's about my past. Ed, they want me there, in the studio, but they won't say what it is."

"It's an ambush, that's what."

"God, if they found the rapist! Ed, I've only just told *you*. I couldn't face…"

Ed grabbed for the phone to speak to Gregory but pressed hands-free. "Samson," he said, "Isabel's in Detroit tomorrow with a zillion…"

"They know that," answered Gregory, "though they don't know about the debate preparation, which is secret… not listed on the published press calendar. The prep's only part way through when *Close-up* goes to air. The itinerary shows her with a night off, flying out to Des Moines, to be fresh for the next morning."

Gregory had a full production crew already at work dressing up an old church fellowship hall out in Detroit's suburbs to duplicate the actual set for the first presidential TV debate. Isabel's secret debate dress rehearsal was scheduled to be held there tomorrow night.

Ed wasn't in the mood for Gregory's blabbering. He stood, "Tell those fucks she'll do their show… from Detroit."

A surge of alarm shot up Isabel's spine, but Ed continued, his head nodding "it's okay" to her and his hand patting the air in calm. "Samson, but it's on one condition: they tell us what this thing is… Right now. Not later today. Not tomorrow. In the next five minutes, or no dice." He terminated the call before Isabel could intervene.

"It's not what you think," he reassured Isabel, praying he was right.

"But what then?"

Ed didn't answer her.

A contorted image suddenly loomed up in Isabel's imagination: she was seated on the studio set and from behind the curtains a muffled voice started humming *Bésame Mucho*.

"My mother?" Her heart hammered. "I won't see that… woman," she whispered. "Ever."

"You're as good as president. What's it matter?"

"How could you agree to me appearing without asking me?"

"Know your enemy," he said, only part-quoting the ancient Chinese warrior philosopher, Sun Tzu. He didn't think she needed to know the whole quote: "To know your enemy, you must become your enemy."

But Isabel knew it already.

# 20

"I JUST GOT off the phone from those slimeballs at *Close-up*," Bill Edwards wheezed down the phone. Isabel and Ed were listening on speaker and could almost hear Bill shift his trademark cigar from one side of his mouth to the other. "They had the hide to demand I get my butt over to their studios tomorrow night. Mine! On a Sunday!"

Bill Edwards and political muscle were Siamese twins; locked together, a freak of nature. Even at seventy-two, he was still a beefy six-foot-six and born to command. He'd been quietly pulling the Republican strings of power from on high for years, emphasis on quietly. Though a big man, he maintained a small public presence, speaking rarely and when he chose to, so softly that people had to strain to hear him, adding to the impression that whatever he said was worth listening to. In private, though, he never held back. And when Bill eventually let it be known he would, if asked, step out of the shadows to chair the peak Republican National Committee, all other contenders stepped back to make way for him.

"What did they tell you?" Isabel asked.

"It's about your past... big implications... national interest. Isabel, it's not like one of your long lost relatives died and bequeathed you a fortune; you're already richer than Croesus. Whatever this is, it ain't good."

She heard Bill take a long deep draw and imagined him tilting his head back, eyes closed, and contemplating the mess they seemed to be in. "Have they called Hank?" she ventured, knowing Bill would understand the implication.

"Damn, I should've thought of that," he said. "Lisa!" he screamed to his assistant, causing Isabel and Ed to flinch. "Find out if Clemens scored an invite to *Close-up*… Bel, if they did ask him, we're dead meat—who in their right mind would invite that turkey to his own Thanksgiving Dinner? Unless they had to."

She didn't remind Bill that he was the one who had foisted Hank Clemens on her as her running mate to help bolster her stocks with the conservative base. She'd agreed, for sure, but now realised how big a mistake she'd made. It was almost John McCain and Sarah Palin from 2008 all over again, except Isabel had insisted on Hank keeping his mouth closed, and so far he'd done that. She wasn't going to have her running mate shooting from his lip. Unlike Palin, who knew what she wanted to say but found it hard to put two words together, at least correctly, Hank's problem was that he wavered on policy, except on guns and moral issues. Unless he was closely scripted, he could take more positions than the Kama Sutra.

"The point is, Bill… if Hank's invited, it's me who's the dinner."

She heard Bill cover the mouthpiece, and waited.

"He's at his hoity-toity racquet club," Bill tittered in a falsetto whine. "One where the members can't use their cell phones. Bel, when you're elected, don't ever let Hank take you to his damn club if there's a war looming, okay?"

Isabel's other line was ringing. It was Gregory. She joined up the two calls.

"I told them," said Gregory, "you know, no info, no dice. Well, not those exact words, different w…"

Ed was shaking his head in disbelief that Isabel could have retained this verbal stumblebum as her key strategist. For Isabel, Gregory's rambling usually brightened up her day. He was an experienced campaign manager with the capacity to crack everyone up while making a deeply insightful point. She'd told him, many times, he was doing himself a disservice by it, since most people's first, and wrong impression was that he was a fool.

"Get to the point," said Bill, cutting Gregory short.

"It's about one of Isabel's parents."

She went as white as one of the Limoges porcelain figurines she'd bought for the Adam mantel. "Not my moth..."

"It's your father."

Thank heavens. She exhaled deeply, and her eyes rose to the high ceiling. All she knew about her father was the photograph... and the little her mother had told her. But had her mother lied about that, too? Had they found him alive somewhere? No... it wasn't possible, or he'd surely have revealed himself before now. In person. To her. Not on some TV show.

Ed's mind was also racing, and what started to emerge out of the bushes was the dread that Isabel's father's business activities might not have been very suitable for a US president's dad. JFK got clean away with a supposed bootlegger and stock market manipulator for a father, but Ed feared coca was in another ballpark altogether, especially these days with the war after war on drugs, none of which was ever won. Bolivia was infamous for its coca trade, and if her father had been a coca-runner it could be utterly disastrous, especially when added to the Karim Ahmed debacle that was still beating them up.

"So," snapped Ed, "what about him?"

"Ah... it's who he is," said Gregory.

Ed leant forward, close to the phone speaker on the white marble tabletop in front of them. "Who he *is*, or who he *was*?" He glanced at Isabel to see her fingers digging into her palms.

"Was. Sorry," said Gregory. "Yes, it's about who he *was*. My mistake. He's been dead for years… as we all thought… I mean, knew…"

"But," interrupted Isabel, "we know who he was. My mother told…"

"Apparently, we don't," said Gregory. "Your mother's story stacks up, according to… well, a source… except for two things, though I can't see why they're such a big deal…"

"What things?" asked Isabel, her stomach tightening even more, if that were possible.

"She told you he died before you were born. But it was after."

"No! How long…?" she jumped up, hating her mother even more, and starting to imagine all those years she might have known him and what they might have done together.

"It was only a month."

"But my birth certificate says…"

"If she could lie to you, why couldn't she lie to the hospital? Maybe it was to get higher welfare benefits as a widow? I don't know." Before Isabel could readjust, Gregory continued, "And she also told you he was a Bolivian businessman, right? Murdered for ransom?"

"Ri-ight," said Isabel, her hesitance apparent to all on the call. She'd been thinking the same things as Ed.

"Wrong," said Gregory. "He *lived* in Bolivia, sure, but he was Chilean. And not just any old Chilean. He was way up in Chile's elite... a diplomat, high-ranking."

Isabel started to speak, "A diplo…?"

Ed, a little relieved, interrupted and spoke from experience, "Chile and Bolivia haven't actually been the friendliest of neighbours…"

"Exactly," said Gregory. "Dr Diaz was an official envoy who Chile dispatched to Bolivia for secret negotiations aimed at resuming diplomatic relations. Isabel, he met your mother… a local… and one thing led to another, and they married."

"That's it?" said Bill.

"All I can get so far," Gregory responded, "but there's obviously an angle to this that we're missing. I've already put a team onto researching this guy… to see if there were any scandals."

"Greg, so what are your thoughts?" asked Ed, nervously scratching his pinkie stump against a knuckle on his other hand.

Gregory was taken aback yet felt foiled at the same time. When it seemed he'd finally earned Ed's respect, damn it, he didn't have the answers to keep it. "I mean, sure, call in Isabel and tell her on camera. Human interest… ra-ra… but why ask Bill? Unless it has… you know, implications." He said "implications" as if he'd put heavy quotation marks around it.

★ ★ ★ ★ ★

SATURDAY night marched up on them, yet nobody was any wiser. Isabel had packed for her flight to Detroit. Gregory was holed up in the campaign War Room to command the team effort. This would be his fifteenth call to her that day, according to the log he kept—for the eventual book—but this time it was to tell her to flick on her TV. Gregory already had Bill Edwards and Hank Clemens on the same line.

"Where were *you* when JFK was shot?" the crass voiceover teased with its text in white on a simple black screen. "Where were *you* on 9/11? And where will you be tomorrow night when *Close-up* reveals a story that will also shake the nation?"

The screen then cut to a clip of Isabel at one of her conquering rallies, and the announcer went on:

"Tomorrow night, *Close-up*'s new Pulitzer Prize-winning correspondent Mike Mandrake… in a searing, groundbreaking report… will reveal presidential candidate Isabel Diaz's *real* story. His report will fracture this election… it will change American history. Whatever you do, don't miss it. Tomorrow night…"

Unilaterally, Ed punched the remote and switched off the TV. "Why would your mother lie to you? Makes no sense. But who really cares if he was a Chilean diplomat? At least he wasn't a drug dealer!" Ed wasn't particularly directing his questions and comments to Isabel or Gregory or Bill Edwards or, for that matter, Hank Clemens, but all of them were mentally saying the same things.

"Mothers lie all the time," said Bill in an unusually flat, soft tone, as if he was trying not to remember something painful.

"Or maybe, Isabel, you remembered some things wrong?" suggested Hank.

"Gregory, I'm not doing the show," said Isabel, standing again to make her point though it was an unseen gesture to those on the other end of the phone.

"But Ed said… and I promised them," Gregory pleaded, brushing his hand over his bald head as if he had nowhere to hide.

"Tell them you misunderstood," she said.

Ed smiled, but Gregory didn't.

★ ★ ★ ★ ★

OVER in LA, Elia was pulling another piece off a *quattro stagioni* pizza. She and her boyfriend had just seen the *Close-up* promo. Simon muted the sound and finished chewing. "So?" he said, his eyes drilling into her.

Elia looked embarrassed and picked at a piece of olive. "Really, I don't know. Mandrake flew back to DC for the shoot and no one's talking. It's like there's a lockdown."

"You've got to find out, Elia."

"I can't."

Abruptly, Simon stood and stared down at her.

"Okay, I'll try," she said.

# 21

NIKI'S BUTTER-CREAM LEGS brushed against the green sheets, revealing her at her best...

Niki Abbott was no egotist. A hedonist, yes. A sybarite and a sensualist, absolutely. Tonight would be perfect. If you were going to do someone like Robert J. Foster, the presidential candidate himself, it needed to be momentous. Breathtaking. Tonight demanded far more than quickie sex in a vice-presidential hotel shower stall.

Tonight, Foster would receive more than he'd ever dreamed of, and given his track record that was saying something. In two hours, Candidate Foster would be on his own knees, praising the Lord.

She looked up at the ceiling mirror to ogle herself. Voluptuous. Niki loved how when you said that word out loud, your tongue did what it meant. Voluptuous. Loose lips sink ships, she smiled.

Niki's fingers feathered herself, and the high gloss of her nails winked sparks back at the sun that was streaming in between the slats of the venetians.

Bobby Foster would indeed have his breath taken away.

# 22

ELIA AND SIMON tore over to the studio in his plumber's truck. As though they were on a heist, he kept the motor running and she went in, heading upstairs for the office Mandrake had occupied but with no idea what she was looking for.

While the door to Mike's office was closed, she tried the knob and it unlocked. Betty was still working in the open-plan, so Elia mumbled she'd lost her pen somewhere, a Montblanc she'd been given for her birthday.

Thankfully, the cleaners hadn't made it to this floor yet. Three paper planes were lying in Mike's waste paper basket and, without unfolding them, Elia stuffed them into her bag. There was nothing on his desk or in any of the drawers. No, she was wrong: the third drawer down contained an unopened four-pack of Trojan condoms. Mandrake really was a sleazebag, she decided, but when she saw the box was still sealed she allowed herself a quick smirk.

Something else? There had to be something.

She punched 'redial' on his desk phone and wrote down the long grey number that scrolled across the small screen. She kept punching until she'd retrieved the numbers of his last five calls; the phones here stopped remembering at five.

She pasted a smile on her face as she left Mike's ex-office and almost skipped over to Betty. "Yay!" she shouted, holding up her pen and a finger to mock the V-for-victory sign. "Now I can sleep." She bounced over to her own desk, logged onto her computer, located the master contact list for the political campaign teams, and emailed it to herself at home.

ELIA approached Simon's truck with a bit of a shrug. It was running but he wasn't inside. She cast around and saw him loitering at the corner and signalled him back.

"Well?" he asked as he slammed the door shut beside him.

"A few scraps of paper and some phone numbers," she told him. "Can we get the hell out of here? I'm shaking like a leaf."

As he drove, she pulled the folded pages out of her bag and flattened them out on her knee. The first was a print-out of an email from Mike's assistant in Washington, confirming dinner for him with his wife when he got back. "Sleazebag," she repeated to herself as she recalled the condoms. The second sheet had *The Un-Making of a President* typed on it with *by Mike Mandrake* underneath, but no other text. She didn't need to remind herself about his ego. And the last sheet was the first page of the LA office's internal phone list which, no doubt, he tossed away knowing he wouldn't have to put up with the likes of Elia any more.

"And?" Simon twisted his head around to glance at the pages.

"Nothing here, but wait till we get home so I can check some phone numbers."

FOUR of the five numbers had East Coast area codes: Washington DC, New York City, Boston and Greenwich. The fifth was a number she already knew because she'd had to ring it herself a half-dozen times. It was the speed-dial for Mike's assistant.

10 PM in LA wasn't the best time to be making calls back east. "Here goes nothing," and Elia dialled the first number.

"*This is the Mandrakes,*" said the answering machine. Elia hung up. "Next," she said, punching in the second number. After one "Oops, wrong number" to a sleepy voice familiar to her as one of *Close-up*'s co-producers, followed by a ring-out, Elia felt this might be it:

"*This is the Harvard Law School office of Professor Robert Dupont. Please leave a message…*"

Elia didn't, but did an internet search on him instead, striking what she hoped was paydirt. "Simon," she yelled to him in the bedroom. "This could be something." He came over. "Mandrake phoned a professor of constitutional law at Harvard," she said. "This guy's credentials go way up to here," she added, her hand hovering above her head.

After speculating what this might mean, from absolutely nothing to damn near everything, Simon pressed Elia to contact Isabel's campaign office.

"At this time of night?"

"For this, absolutely." He could see Elia's anxiety growing. At best, she'd already breached her duty of fidelity to her employer; at worst, she was guilty of theft. "It's not as if we broke into the Watergate or anything," he said sincerely, but that only made Elia's mouth even dryer.

"Then *I'll* do it," he said, grabbing the phone.

Elia watched him, relieved. In truth, she wanted it done but she couldn't bring herself to do it.

"I got to speak to the guy in charge," Simon said. "My name's, er, Joshua and it's confidential."

"At 1 AM?" It was Julia Lee, a night owl who covered the phones in Isabel's campaign headquarters three nights a week, from midnight to dawn. She was a veteran Republican volunteer four campaigns in a row.

"Confidential *and* urgent, okay?" But Simon was getting nowhere. "Did you see the *Close-up* promo?" he asked.

She hadn't. She'd been staying at her sister's the last two days, and her TV had been busted.

"It's about that," Simon said. "Just find the head guy and tell him. I'll hold."

Gregory and about fifteen people had been locked up since well before Julia arrived. The receptionist she'd replaced at midnight had warned her there was some crisis going down about *Close-up*.

Julia grimaced as she went in: drink cans; half-eaten pizza cold and curling on sheets of yellow legal paper all over the central table; the close odour of people who'd been fretting sixteen hours straight. Disgusting… but she loved it. The acrid smells, the heat, the mess, the pressure. At first, no one noticed her. Several pairs of eyes were locked onto computer screens. Maybe eight people had their ears glued to cell phones in various parts of the room. For a second, she wondered if they were phoning each other—campaigns really could make people go nuts. Another two were tapping away on their BlackBerrys.

Gregory was speaking on a landline. Julia had already scratched out a note and put it under his nose. He gave her an irritated I'm-busy headshake but got the sort of stern response that only a sixty-year-old grandmother in a button-up pink woollen cardigan could give without uttering a single word. He read her note: "Joshua (?) holding. Re *Close-up*. Urgent AND confidential."

"Hold a second?" Gregory asked Isabel. She was on board her jet to Detroit. Whenever he thought about the plane, he smiled. Even now; he couldn't help it. *The Wall Street Journal* had christened the jet 'Big Red' after the rose icon they'd painted on the tail, but the campaign team had morphed that into the 'Big Red Bed' given how much time many of them spent strapped in it themselves. Originally, Isabel had been scheduled to arrive in Detroit at ten but, as things panned out, she hadn't even taken off till after midnight. Gregory read the note again and said to Julia, "This guy for real?"

She shrugged.

"Isabel, gotta call you back," he said. "Julia, I'll take it at your desk," and, after snatching a can of Diet Coke, he sprinted out ahead of her.

Simon introduced himself as Joshua again, no surname. "I don't know if this'll help..."

"We'll check it out. Thanks, Joshua. Hey, where'd you get this?"

"Sorry, can't say."

"Can I call you back if I need to?"

Simon had already hung up.

GREGORY got Julia to set up an urgent conference call. Apart from Isabel on the jet, the people he wanted would be at home: Bill Edwards who was probably snug in his Chippendale four-poster with a cigar and his latest girlfriend (not bad for a 72-year-old) and the campaign's chief legal-beagle, Oliver Pryor. Gregory chose to leave Hank out of this, justifying it to himself by assuming he'd be on a sleepover at one of his fancy clubs with no phones. At Gregory's end, he'd have a half-dozen of his key campaign people listening in on speaker with him.

Julia loved this job, even though there was no money. At least once in every campaign, there was a crisis on her shift and the sheer adrenaline was reward enough. It was years since anything else had quickened her heartbeat during that time slot. Her husband had died a decade ago.

Apart from his six senior people, Gregory kicked everyone else out of the War Room. The door closed behind them and the mystified outcasts floated en masse over to Julia; she had to be in on the gossip since she'd set all this in motion.

"IT'S Professor Robert Dupont." Gregory intoned into the speakerphone as if he were saying something meaningful. Gregory's people watched him slipping on his jacket and knew it wasn't out of deference to Bill and Isabel who couldn't see anyhow. It was obviously for 'The Book.' When it was all over, Gregory would want the world to know that at this crucial juncture he was not some tacky underdressed slob. No, tonight he was wearing Armani. "We've got word Dupont's involved."

"The *Harvard Law* Robert Dupont?" Oliver Pryor spluttered over the line.

Gregory wasn't sure if the campaign's chief counsel's reaction was awe or surprise.

"But he's on our side," the lawyer continued.

"Du-who?" asked Isabel, unsure of the name over the squeal of the engines. Her plane had just gone into descent.

This was legal territory, so Oliver Pryor responded, "Dupont, Isabel. Robert Fitzgerald Dupont. Emeritus professor of constitutional law at Harvard... former senior partner at White, Flom & Bay... chief counsel on constitutional issues to the National Security Council across two administrations, one Republican and one Democrat... the list goes on. He's one of the nation's most eminent constitutional lawyers. Refused Bush One's nomination in 1990 to the Supreme Court because it would be too boring. Oh, and he's, er, my wife's grandfather."

"Then patch him into this call," Bill instructed.

The lawyer knew this was not a good time to call the crotchety octogenarian but since nobody else was having much of a good time he'd do it. But first he needed the number. The house phone book wasn't in its usual spot on the hallstand by the phone, so he had to go hunt for it and, sure enough, it was on his wife's bedside table. As he slipped it away, she fluttered one eye open.

After he answered her, she strained at her bedside clock and said, "You're kidding, right? You want to ring Pa at this time of night… morning? He will *kill* you."

"He's against capital punishment, remember," Pryor joked weakly. He was visualising the old man creaking out of bed, perhaps wearing pyjamas overprinted with his trademark attire of red, white and blue striped tie, blue shirt and English tweed jacket.

As he tiptoed out, his wife said, "Once you've finished the call, place an order for your coffin. Good luck and," she rolled over on her side, "good night."

Gregory jotted down the number the lawyer read out and passed it outside to Julia. She phoned Dupont and, without a word, patched him into the conference call the moment he picked up; she wasn't getting caught explaining.

"Hello? Hello?" grunted the irritated professor. "Who the hell's there? Do you know what time…?"

"Robert, it's Bill Edwards. From the Party. I've got Isabel Diaz on line with me…"

"Hello, sir," said Isabel.

"…and her campaign manager, Gregory Samson, as well as your grandson-in-law Oliver Pryor." He chose not to mention the other six he knew Gregory had on the line.

"Hi, Pa."

"I won't speak to you," Dupont snapped.

If anyone could've seen Oliver Pryor, they'd have guessed he'd either just been hit with the first foul sniff of a dead elephant's rotting carcass or he'd discovered he'd been cut out of his inheritance.

Bill took the lead; Oliver's silence spoke to him louder than if he'd actually seen the lawyer's face. "Robert, on Oliver's behalf, on all our behalves, I sincerely apologise for calling you at this ridiculous hour but…"

"That's not why I won't talk, you fool," said Dupont. "And

Bill, cut the obsequious crap… Excuse the French, ma'am. I know why you're calling me and, frankly, I'd have called me too, but I simply *can't* talk, okay… lawyer-client confidentiality and all."

And may God bless you, Joshua! smiled Gregory though, on reflection, he hadn't counted on locating the magic box but not being able to pry the lid open.

"Then we're in a bit of a bind," Bill said.

"That you are," said Dupont, pausing for a moment as if he wished to say more. "We all are, actually. But, ah, the Constitution is the Constitution. Nothing we can do about that, not now. Ollie… you there?"

"Sir?"

"It's a shame you didn't call your old Pa before my, er, client did. Not that I could've changed the outcome… you just would've been more prepared. Ms Diaz…?"

"Professor?"

"The only thing I can say to you…," he paused, and everyone held their breath. The silence seemed to go on forever as the old man carefully collected his words. "…I just wish that old buzzard Orrin Hatch had got his stupid amendment through. Like I said, I can't talk. Good night to all you fine folks. You, too, Ollie."

"Well, that was useless," Bill snorted. "And he's supposed to be a friend?"

"He is that, Bill," said Isabel. "He was giving us a clue. People," said Isabel, taking control, "what constitutional amendments did Senator Hatch fail on?"

The call immediately descended into a rabble, with everyone trying to have a say, until Isabel spoke again. "Jack, are you on this call?"

"Yes, ma'am," said the campaign's research director, who was already typing and clicking.

"Can you get someone onto this?"

"Already have…"

Thirty seconds later, Jack came back on line. "Okay," he said. "I can only find two really significant ones… a constitutional amendment to… protect the rights of victims of violent crime…"

"No," said Isabel; in her case, that one was already three decades too late.

"Well, there's his Arnie amendment... Remember that? Here… I'm reading from the *Salt-Lake City Tribune*: '… Republican Senator Orrin Hatch wants to terminate the constitutional prohibition against foreign-born citizens such as Arnold Schwarzenegger and others from becoming president if they've been citizens for twenty years.' Hatch proposed it back in '03. Barney Frank—you know, the Dem. Congressman?—he drafted a similar bill before that but…"

"What's that got to do with us?" Bill interrupted. "Bel, you *were* born in Newark, right? Shades of Barack Obama's birthism, for chrisssakes! But really, if you were born in Newark, who cares where your parents came from… Bolivia… Chile… whatever?"

"The plane's about to land," said Isabel. "I can hardly hear now. Call me when you know something."

# 23

FURIOUS FUMES OF grey and white smoke—explosions?—billowed up from the sixteen bridges scattered around the edges of Manhattan. Diana, one of six around the country watching this on computer screens, spun her volume control to low, just loud enough to make out the blasts.

The silver-tubed Metro-North train was reversing fast, racing back over what was left of a blue bridge that a moment earlier had connected Manhattan to the Bronx.

Another ring of explosions rocked the island. These flashes were brighter, the smoke thicker, and darker, and the noise fiercer, even on her low volume setting.

In the briefing, Isis had explained that each detonation was precisely calibrated for the target it destroyed—for the subway stations, its depth underground, its exact position along the network, and the force of blast needed to intensify the shockwave it was intended to build. Who, or rather, what determined the calculations and the pinpoint timing of each explosion was a sophisticated computer program called Shockwave.

Every few instants a new and tighter ring of blasts rang out, smoking higher and fiercer until, perhaps twenty seconds later, a vast ball of flames erupted into an inferno at the centre of the island, around 42nd Street. Almost simultaneously, it heaved back out to the island's edge in a circular shockwave of such scale and intensity that it pounded everything in its path to the ground. Whole blocks fell into the vast fissures that cracked apart everywhere. Subways ripped open and fell in, crushing the rush hour commuters crowding the platforms.

Those above ground would be no luckier. If they weren't sucked into a chasm as the ground split beneath them, flying debris would pound them. Skyscrapers collapsed in on themselves pulping everything and everyone in their way.

What Diana and the others were watching was horrific. Beyond imagination.

But it was also virtual, not real. Not yet.

Isis explained it was an elaborate computer graphics simulation created by the young Jax Mason, whose brilliant career had been cut regrettably short, as Diana and Lucky knew first hand, "though not short enough," said Isis pointedly.

Silently, Diana squirmed.

Isis continued, explaining that in creating the program, Jax had conquered the complex theory of how shockwaves move through tunnels and up through the ground above them—the intricate technical interconnections between the mathematics, the fluid mechanics and the engineering.

Jax, Isis knew, had turned himself into a world expert on shockwave dynamics. On burst, airblast, yield scaling, overpressure prediction, dynamic pressure prediction, cratering, ejecta, airslap-induced ground shock, upstream-induced ground shock, shock spectrums, Brisance—shockwave energy—and Wef—effective energy. What Jax didn't know about displacement asymptotes and acceleration asymptotes wasn't worth knowing. One of Isis's team had found Jax's computer print-outs of calculations for "composite near-surface particle velocity wave forms" stowed under his bed, under his discarded dirty underwear and the research data on the Dresden fires in Nazi Germany he'd collected or, when he'd illegally tapped into the Smithsonian's World War II archives, stolen.

But Jax's work was not mere academic theory. This was his passion.

Jax had accessed and manipulated global geophysical data and research papers, and stress-tested his shockwave data on the actual geology of Manhattan. It was crucial to know, as Jax did, that from soft soil clay at the southern tip, the island's subsurface shifted to a ledge of hard rock by 14th Street which extended north, for five blocks, to the unstable schist ridge of Murray Hill. That, in turn, extended underground for twenty blocks north, from 22nd through to 42nd streets. Jax had reviewed material on Manhattan's geology all the way up to the 190s, near the Fort George portal where, according to the yellow Post-it-marked page of a book propping up a leg of his wobbly kitchen table, the rock was fragile, made porous by underground springs. The Fort George schist, like Murray Hill, could hide large pockets of decayed, shattered rock; important to know if you were going to send a shockwave through it.

With all that under his belt, Jax also researched the dynamics of explosives terrorists had used, or could easily get, and their specific blast characteristics.

He had turned himself into an expert on all relevant aspects of the forensic engineering of underground excavations in rock and soil, including the probabilistic modelling of bomb damage to tunnel linings, and the technical prediction and assessment of property damage caused by vibration.

People in the real world—engineers and insurance companies—did this for a living but for Jax it was a mission. If he had wanted to apply himself commercially, there would have been firms all over the world who would have snapped him up, despite his eccentricities. He knew who they were, since he'd hacked into them all.

To complete the picture, according to his blog, Jax had scoped out the entire subway network taking countless trips himself—his charged-up Metrocard had bought him trips up and down every line, at least twice, and he personally visited every station, taking as many photographs and videos as he could without arousing uneasy eyes. After Najibullah Zazi was arrested for trying to blow up the subway himself, Jax assumed as low a profile as he could while still needing to collect data, and took to using his mobile phone to take his shots, simultaneously pretending to be talking on it.

The kind ladies in the New York Transit Museum had even made him coffee while they helped locate old dusty drawings for him. Jax had been thorough.

Even on Jax's short-lived trip to London, all expenses paid, he'd completed the entire circuit of the Underground, but this time took no photos; Londoners were even more suspicious than New Yorkers—for good reason; terrorists had targeted their subway repeatedly. But they had been amateurs, Jax had heartlessly thought, so engrossed was he in his own plans to subvert them.

He'd spent hours in the London Transport Museum, located in the former Flower Market in Covent Garden, perusing relevant photographs and drawings and further updating his London computer model.

What a mine of information for terrorists Jax had found there, Isis marvelled: 80,000 historic engineering drawings including the original signed plans for several of the stations and tunnels. How crazy was the free world?

Jax hadn't yet done his step-through scouting of Washington DC's Metro. He'd temporarily put it on hold after public sensitivity and security were heightened in October 2010 when an FBI sting operation uncovered a ham-fisted terror plot to blow it up with wheelie bags, and he hadn't got around to finishing it.

According to Jax's logs, said Isis, the part Jax got the most thrill out of was sitting on a bench in Central Park and hacking into the municipal archives in London, Washington DC and New York to steal the actual detailed blueprints of their subway systems, including pinpoint precision data. That way he could overlay them onto his computer model. With New York, Jax couldn't believe his luck. The City's Office of Emergency had set up the Public Safety Geographic Information System (GIS) Data Development Centre to collect and organise geospatial data, and they'd already GIS-converted the architectural drawings for all 468 subway stations. The revised data sets displayed the precise locations and sizes of all tunnels, exits, including emergency exits for evacuations, and information on hidden spaces like storage and equipment rooms, corridors, and other sealed-off areas. Hacking into that had been a dream come true.

Incredibly, in just five months working alone—excluding his time at Princeton—Jax had developed workable, shockwave simulations for both New York and London, simulations that Isis described as chillingly accurate, and he had been partway with Washington DC when he was cut short.

The part Jax laboured over for the longest time was the most trivial, as it usually is: showing how clever he was by creating the glitzy, almost movie-quality computer graphics and animated video drama, which Isis was now playing to the team. "He made it to present his case as powerfully as possible," said Isis, "to convince sceptics not just with cold facts and threats but, according to one of his blogs, to 'scare them shitless'. But as we know, he had spent so much time on his simulation, he had only just started contacting those in authority and, fortunately for us, his letters, emails and videoclips had only got to minor officials who'd all dismissed him as a crackpot."

For the older members of this small group, the image that Jax Mason had edited in next evoked the haunting memory of a still photograph from a previous generation: one of a young Vietnamese girl screaming, tears streaming, arms flailing, running frantically for her life. For others it triggered flashes of ash-caked hair and the blank faces of bewildered souls straggling up from the World Trade Centre decades later, or blood-spattered commuters emerging out of the London Tube. Jax's own graphic was "shot" at the 42nd Street subway station. A young businesswoman, glued to her cell phone, was strutting up the subway exit steps when an invisible force hoisted her up off the ground and flung her violently forward through the air, her feet flapping unable to get purchase on anything, and slammed her with a nauseating thud through the side of a passing delivery truck.

Jax's simulation was sickeningly lifelike. One or two seconds later, while a number of Isis's accomplices were rubbing their suddenly parched lips or pinching the tops of their noses, the same truck was mashed by what moments before had been a 40-floor office building.

As the underground crater greedily gaped below, devouring whatever was fed to it from above, the tremor's assault drove upwards. The street above was an easy victim. They watched on-screen as Times Square split apart like a dry cracker and whole sections collapsed in single chunks into the widening cavern, dunking screaming street vendors, bumper-to-bumper cars and Yellow Cabs, and every other bit of human detritus unlucky enough to have been there.

Buildings shook, tall and small, glass blew out, shards speared bystanders frozen in shock. The famed flashing signs and illuminated billboards flickered, convulsed and randomly sputtered out. Almost one by one they tore loose of their moorings, segments swayed and ripped off, tumbling down to crash on the street or onto the few people still there, or into the ever-growing hole into which more of the roadway was still falling.

For the first time in its life, Broadway had become an understatement.

> "*Terrorists could do this*," warned the on-screen caption.
>
> "*If you don't want that…*," it offered a menu of the subway design modifications Jax was convinced were essential.
>
> "*This could happen almost anywhere: New York, Washington DC, London… any city with an interlinked subway.*"

"This is the key to turning the election around," said Isis, cool as ice. "If we need to do that, if things pan out so it is necessary, this is how we'll do it."

Even Diana swallowed.

# 24

ISABEL WOKE AT five, as usual, and leant over and picked up the photograph. "So I'm half-Chilean, half-Bolivian. Like an alpaca," she smiled at her father's picture, "though not so well-bred."

She swung out of bed, threw on a fluffy robe and opened the door into her hotel suite sitting room. A female Secret Service agent who'd flown in with her was on the lounge reading a book and jumped up to greet her, the paperback spilling to the floor. Isabel saw it had a pastel pink cover. The agent blushed and quickly pointed out the table laden with fresh coffee, bagels and a package of news wires and articles from the Sunday papers.

Isabel poured them both a coffee and took the news pack back with her into the bedroom.

Not surprisingly, almost all the newsclips were about *Close-up*. The free publicity they'd generated for tonight's show would be worth an entire month's campaign spending.

The speculation was rampant but not one paper had anything firm or believable. One ridiculous story had Isabel in an intriguing sex romp with a black woman, but that was in a British tabloid. Among the pages she was flicking through was a faxed single sheet with "*love Gregory*" scrawled across the bottom. It was headed "Scoop":

> Chilean to land-locked Bolivian: "*Definition of absurd: a Bolivian navy.*"
> Bolivian to Chilean: "*Definition of absurd: Chilean Ministry of Justice.*"

Isabel's spirits lifted. Gregory was her Mr Fixit, her cheerleader, her know-everything, do-everything. And yet, he could still take the time to lower the heat with a joke. After she'd worked her way through the pile, she switched on cable and flicked through the channels. The speculation about *Close-up* had hit rival networks like FOX, CNN, you name it. But there was no breaking news, not about her.

Not even "sources close to" the program were giving anything away. It looked to Isabel like the network had managed a complete lockdown on the story.

She switched on her cell phone for messages. Ed had sent her a text message at around 3 AM: "If UR reading this B4 I call U, go back 2 sleep. CU in Auto Alley."

She smiled and phoned him anyway.

Ed had heard nothing but told her he'd cancelled his London trip—he was supposed to fly out that morning—and was coming to Detroit to be with her. "I won't get there in time for Mass," he joked.

"Shame," Isabel retorted, "You're the one who really needs it."

"I'll get there for the debate prep, okay?" Isabel breathed a little deeper knowing he'd be there to support her during the *Close-up* timeslot.

AS Isabel went down in the elevator, she skimmed the background briefings on people she'd meet during the day. Her media arranger started giving her the rundown on what to expect with the press hounds waiting downstairs and on the radio program they were heading to: Bobby Foster's new tax policy, her promise for improved health insurance portability…

Isabel interrupted her: "There's only one issue today… *Close-up*. And," she said testily, "the only comment I've got to offer is 'no comment'."

Even good-humoured Father Lizewski at St Hyacinth's was stressed about the program. Leaning out from his pulpit, he blessed Isabel, joking in a preposterous mock-New-York-Jewish accent, "Like it couldn't hurt she's a Catholic?" When the chuckles settled, the priest looked out over the congregation and said solemnly, "What took God a lifetime of Isabel's hard work won't be undone in one 30-minute TV show."

Isabel was moved by the emotion that pulsed through the church. News broadcasts would replay the moment all day. When the service ended, swirls of well-meaning parishioners engulfed her.

"I am Democrat," said one woman who squeezed Isabel as if she were still wringing the washing water out of a bed sheet. "But November come and I vote for you. My whole family vote for you, good lady," and she presented Isabel with a foot-long knobbly pink kolbasa sausage. "I make this special for you."

Isabel smiled and took it, handing it to one of her minders. She had tried the fatty sausage once, as often as anyone would if they didn't have to.

The priest pressed a set of rosaries into her hand. "You might want these tonight," he said and softly kissed her cheek. Isabel wasn't much of a Catholic after she left the trailer park, but she thanked him graciously and slipped the beads into her jacket pocket. As the car shot off to the picnic, she pulled them out and held one of the rosary beads tight, recalling from when she was young the Glorious Mysteries, the first of which was the Resurrection. Well, here was hoping. And praying.

The high-security, deep blue Chrysler SUV that had been organised for the day was brightened up with magnetic stick-ons of her emblematic red roses, one on each door, standard fit-out for a campaign vehicle.

Her phone rang.

"I'm on my way to Detroit," Gregory said. "We've got nothing. No one's talking... no backgrounders... no off-the-records. No 'sounds like.' No 'hypothetically speaking.' No 'what ifs.' We've asked everyone, tried to pull in favours, pressed, cajoled, whatever. Nothing. These people don't seem to care that they're playing with the most important election in the world."

"Don't we just watch tonight, knit our eyebrows and say, hmm, that's interesting, we'll get back to you?"

"Not if they whack the ball right out of the field, we can't."

"Have you called Orrin Hatch's people?"

Gregory's silence told her she'd insulted him by even asking.

"What did they say?"

They hadn't been able to think of anything. "Here's the thing," said Gregory. "Scenario one is that this is all opportunist media hype and we've got nothing to worry about—about as unlikely as al-Qaeda cutting off their own heads—in which case we just go ahead with the debate prep; or... scenario two, whatever they've got is huge and we are... you know..."

"Fucked?"

Gregory had never heard Isabel use the f-word and after several empty seconds, he coughed. "Ah... yes, that. In which case, you and I and the team should ditch the debate and go out and get, well, ah, you know, pickled."

"I'm not a 'get pickled' sort of gal."

He didn't think she was a "fucked" sort of gal either, at least not until a moment ago, but there was a lot of pressure on her right now. "Yeah, getting drunk isn't classy." He thought of The Book. "If it's going to be the end, not that I'm resigned to that possibility, we will stand tall and with grace. Who knows, maybe there'll be a next time. Or maybe not. Whatever. So, if it does all turn to, er, shit, then we call in the media, including *Close-up*, of course…"

"To the church fellowship hall?"

"Exactly… out there in shabby real-town. We say, you know, no hard feelings… they were doing their jobs… we had no idea…"

"But we need one, dammit."

Isabel saw her team was fighting the last war, not this one. They'd discussed the need to create other options often enough but if a different approach was needed, it looked like Isabel would have to find it herself.

# 25

ISABEL'S VAN PULLED up for her debate prep a little late. "I had some last minute things at the hotel," she said as she walked into the secret location and joined her entourage around the large flat screen TV that Gregory had arranged to be set up. They were holed up in a vintage Detroit fellowship hall, last painted at least twenty years earlier, with quaint white gables and greyed, peeling clapboard walls. Any heritage value the building once had was lost on those present. They were here to practise the debate, but first they'd watch *Close-up*.

For the first ten minutes of the program, Gregory's theory proved correct: soppy human-interest stuff, but critically no surprises. No news, just background.

Ed had flown over as promised and a speakerphone line was open with Hank Clemens and Bill Edwards, as well as a few Republican officials in case they needed to coordinate reactions. The Party stayed rock solid. Not one representative with any clout agreed to appear on the program, a point Mike Mandrake tried shoving up them at the start of the show when he interviewed former Republican National Committee chairman, Michael Steele, who had nothing of value to say, much like when he was still in office.

IN the few hours' build up to *Close-up*'s timeslot, Isis wasn't the only one making moves. Despite Bill Edwards' advanced years, he moved fast too, shifting the entire inner core of the Republican Party organisation into crisis gear. What with the calls from CBS, the program teasers, and the intensifying media speculation, it was too much to leave solely in the hands of the candidate and her campaign team. What if this really was big?

Bill had personally called to put each member of the Executive of the Republican National Committee on red alert and, by the time *Close-up* was on air, Bill wasn't sitting on just any open line, contrary to what Isabel and the others in Detroit believed; he and the entire Executive Committee, or ExCom, were bunched around the massive oak table in his dining room. All their church-going and family Sundays had been cancelled and they'd jetted in from around the country to assemble at Bill's home. Fortunately, the secret gathering hadn't leaked to anyone, not even to the campaign. A news story like "GOP in panic" was the last thing Bill wanted, even if it were true. Actually, it was the second last thing he'd want.

Unhappily, he'd be getting both.

Bill had also dragged in Myron Kowalski, a wily old-faithful constitutional lawyer who, even more than that turncoat Robert Dupont, had provided the backbone of the party's legal advice for over thirty years, even if his own was clearly suffering acute curvature these days.

★ ★ ★ ★ ★

ISABEL was tetchy; who wouldn't be, waiting to hear about a past you didn't know you had until yesterday and having it broadcast live to millions of viewers?

But when the program ran an old scratchy newsreel, it gave her such a jolt that Ed put his hand on her shoulder to steady her.

The dateline on the screen was 1968. US President Lyndon B. Johnson was welcoming a line of Latin-looking officials to the White House, taking each of them one-by-one for individual photo-ops. As the fourth man, small, rotund, almost bald, was walking up to shake LBJ's hand, the voiceover announcer intoned, "*This man is Dr Hernandez Diaz, the father that, until now, Isabel Diaz didn't know she had.*"

"That's not him," she said to no one in particular. "They've got the wrong…" She removed Ed's hand from her shoulder. "This whole thing is cra… rubbish."

"You're kidding, right?" said Gregory, hoping she was not.

She held up her hand, and asked for someone to go out to the van for her satchel.

Bill Edwards spoke up on the open line, "Bel, what's that you say?"

"Bill," she said, "that man with LBJ might well have been a Chilean diplomat called Hernandez Diaz, but *he* was not my father."

"How do you know?" Bill asked.

At that moment, one of the Secret Service detail returned from outside with her bag. Isabel pulled the old photo-frame out of its zipper pocket at the side and held it up for all in the church hall to see. "Because *this* man was my father… Bill, I've got a photo of him here," she said in explanation. "It was my mother's."

A weird thing to carry around, thought Gregory—and most of the others—but even so, it was a lucky break. He dictated a silent "note to self": next campaign, check for rot in candidate's family tree, and always get mug shots.

The heavy mood in the church hall vaulted instantly to jokey bemusement about Mike Mandrake's very public, humiliating error, with enough bluster they could have been in a gym locker-room.

Isabel passed the photo-frame to Ed for safekeeping, and headed for the bar that had been set up in the corner for a spicy tomato juice. She needed a big hit of Tabasco.

The bravado and the barbs about Mandrake were getting somewhat offensive. Isabel hadn't minded the initial comments about his "radio head" and "newspaper voice" but the steam-letting was getting a little too warm.

"That jerk is so done with TV now."

"TV? After this effort, those whiskers won't even be welcome on a broom at any newspaper I know."

Ed stepped back to the buffet table and lifted a knife. Unnoticed by the others who were still enjoying their moment, he slunk to the darkened rear of the room.

"They're going to look like… like idiots when we get this out… So, Isabel? What do you say? Shall we call them right now?" Gregory suggested with just a touch too much glee.

She wiped her mouth and put down her glass. "Maybe we shouldn't. After all, what's it really matter, right?" she shrugged.

But it did matter.

★ ★ ★ ★ ★

MYRON Kowalski's legal research assistant phoned him on one of Bill Edwards' other lines to confirm he'd emailed through to Bill's house what the crotchety lawyer had hassled him for: a copy of a certain 1898 Supreme Court decision, as well as extracts from the seminal constitutional law texts, one of which the old codger had written himself.

Bill's live-in assistant had printed the email attachments and brought them in to Kowalski. The old lawyer skimmed them for a few minutes, nodding and smiling to himself, finally tossing his eyebrows over to Bill Edwards with such a theatrical gasp it was as if he'd just read that his revered baseball hero

Sandy Koufax was back on the mound and had pitched yet another no-hitter season.

Bill was familiar with Kowalski's tricks and punched the open line onto mute. What Kowalski had to say was not going to be shared with the campaign team. Not yet.

"Bill," Kowalski smiled, "our former ally Dupont is going to throw a fastball to our left over this 'father' issue. And were it not that this was a simple case of mistaken identity," he paused for effect, "it would be my sad duty to inform you that our star-hitter, Isabel Diaz, had suffered a hit to the temple, that she was down, and out, that the vice would have to go up to captain, we'd be bringing on a reserve and, after a decent moment for prayer, play would continue but we'd probably lose the game, and the season." The shameless egotist even quoted himself: "It says here in 'Kowalski on the Constitution'…" and he read from a review of a dusty old court decision that he was certain Professor Dupont would shortly be quoting back at them on TV.

Bill Edwards and Myron Kowalski went way back and to Bill, despite the annoying and often fumbled ballpark analogies the old lawyer inserted into almost every conversation, he deserved his own entry into the Hall of Fame. He'd saved Bill's skin, and even his marriage. Several of them.

With the assurance of Isabel's identification and Kowalski's opinion, Bill relaxed a little and called for whiskey and cigars all round, even for the women.

★ ★ ★ ★ ★

ISABEL quietly squirmed during the segment when Willy Nesbit, the sleazy trailer park manager, spewed to the world that not only had her mother been a drunk, which was not news, but that she'd also been a cheap whore, which was. They even put him to air leering about her expedient lack of teeth.

"*Gappy Hooker?* How can they run that on a Sunday night at prime time?" Bill Edwards boomed over the open line before slapping the phone back on mute.

Isabel knew she'd made the right decision to stay off the show. She peeked around the room; most of the smirks were hidden by nervous hands, but she could still see it in their eyes.

"What a dirtbag!" cried one.

"And that tattoo! Tell me it's not really rats doing… you know… to each other," another shuddered as the TV camera panned over Willy's neck. "A-a-w... Gross!"

"*…the kid ran away from Cactus Flower after'n she got outta [bleep] hospital. Little [bleep] never even brought her sorry ass back home to kiss her lovin' ma g'bye. Damn broke her ma's [bleep] heart.*"

When Mandrake revealed to Willy on screen that the girl was the same Isabel Diaz who was running for president, Willy splurted out, "*You shittin' me, right?*" but the network didn't bleep that.

For the mass of viewers it was top-rating entertainment and gave far more colour to what they knew about their next president than anyone else had ever attempted but, even so, they were still expecting more: the punch-line, the Kodak moment that the teaser ads had promised.

Now that Gregory was sure that whatever Mandrake was saving for last about Isabel's father would be a damp squib, he was finding it compelling viewing and the new insights into Isabel's past were fascinating. Frankly, they'd do no harm to the campaign, he decided; so what, her mother was a whore—it proved Isabel had politics running in her veins.

Gregory checked his Patek Philippe chronograph; to lesser people it was a watch. Mandrake dropped his long-awaited bombshell at 6:40 PM. Or 6:40:20 PM, to be precise for The Book. When the man draped with a red, white and blue striped tie, blue shirt and Harris tweed jacket appeared on-screen, no one present missed Isabel's chief counsel Oliver Pryor's stomach-churning groan.

WHEN Professor Robert Dupont's face appeared on TV in Bill Edwards' dining room, a wheeze of smoky air was inhaled as Kowalski twisted the knife, "Advising them in private, in confidence... that's one thing. But for Dupont to appear... to step onto the plate... *and* for the other team... What is the old fool thinking?"

On camera, Mandrake was seated opposite Dupont in a musty-looking office, whose walnut shelves were replete with hundreds of impressive-looking leather-bound volumes, most with slips of paper sticking unkempt out of the tops. After introducing Dupont to the viewers, Mandrake leant over the desk separating them and said, with a forced naïveté,

> "*Professor, until tonight Isabel Diaz believed her father was a Bolivian businessman, but we now know he was a senior Chilean diplomat. What's the impact of this on her crack at the White House?*"

"Absolutely nothing, you big fool. You got the wrong guy," shouted one of the team in the hall with Isabel and, when he caught the dark look she shot at him, he realised he'd guzzled one drink too many.

> "*Regretfully,*" said Dupont, "*it means everything. The wonderful lady's campaign is over, assuming your information about her father is correct...*"

"Which it damned-well is not," said Gregory. "Sorry," he apologised, to no one in particular.

> "*...and I stress, if. If that's the fact, then our Constitution dictates that I, and you, and all Americans will forever be denied the privilege of voting in Ms Diaz as our President.*"

At that moment, the station flashed to an ad for a nasal spray. "*All stuffed up...?*"

"If we didn't know this was built on a foundation of garbage," said a relieved but perplexed Gregory, "it'd be a disaster. But what's this Constitution thing? Oliver? You pointy heads didn't come up with anything, right?" He slurped on a silver and red can.

"Not yet, no," said Oliver. "We've got Professor Millie Wilkinson on retainer," he pointed to the phone he'd put temporarily on mute to answer the question, "but she's still looking." Oliver noticed the quizzical eyebrows, "She's a female version of Robert Dupont, but with better legs. And at Princeton."

No one laughed, though unknown to those in Detroit, Myron Kowalski was sniggering into his gnarled old fingers.

"Shh! They're back on," said Gregory.

Mandrake recapped before asking Dupont to continue.

"*Our Constitution, sir, insists that our president is a natural born citizen…*"

As Mandrake gravely nodded, the relevant text of the Constitution scrolled up the screen saying pretty much what Dupont had said, but with a lot more verbiage.

"*A rule that kept people like Henry Kissinger and Arnold Schwarzenegger out of the Oval Office can't be all bad,*" said Mandrake.

The octogenarian looked as if he was about to rebut Mandrake with a weighty list of twenty or more distinguished and naturalised Americans any of whom he would have been delighted to have seen as president, but pushed on:

"*The Fourteenth Amendment, Mr Mandrake, defines who is actually a citizen.*"

The precise legalese appeared on the screen.

"*But let me simplify it," said Dupont. "You're a natural born citizen if you satisfy two tests that most people wrongly read as one: you must be born here AND you must also be subject to our jurisdiction. Are you with me so far?*"

Mandrake looked perplexed:

"*But professor,*" he added, squeezing his bearded chin to emphasise the complexity, "*Isabel Diaz was born in Newark, New Jersey. Here's a certified copy of her birth certificate.*"

Mandrake waved a piece of paper, and Dupont responded:

"*Yes, Mr Mandrake. But, as I just said, we must consider more than mere birth… not only must a president be born here, he or she must also be 'subject to our jurisdiction' as I said a moment ago. The problem for Ms Diaz is that when she was born in Newark, as that paper you're brandishing certifies, her father was a loyal Chilean diplomat…*"

The camera flicked to Mandrake.

"*And…?*"

Dupont looked imperiously down his nose:

"*Please, sir! Any constitutional lawyer worth their salt will tell you that a diplomat owes their allegiance to the country they serve—you'd expect that, wouldn't you? It means, in the language of our Constitution, that they're not subject to our jurisdiction. You have heard of diplomatic immunity, yes?*"

Mandrake glared back at Dupont as if the old gentleman had severe body odour.

Dupont shook his head, and continued:

"*And it's the same with their children: the children of diplomats are also not subject to our jurisdiction. Mr Mandrake, birth and allegiance have been twinned together for centuries. That was so at the signing of our Constitution and it is still so now.*"

"*But why is that?*" asked Mandrake.

"*Why…?*" said Dupont, barely concealing a grimace. "*Because our founders feared foreign influence over our president. Just imagine if the father of today's president was a serving Iranian or North Korean diplomat or dignitary.*"

Mandrake nodded:

"*You're saying that the kids of foreign diplomats, even if they're born in Newark or Hoboken or Dallas or Washington, they're not US citizens?*"

Dupont smiled:

"*Precisely,*" he said.

The eyes of everyone in the hall flicked over to see Isabel biting her top lip.

Mandrake continued:

"*Including the children of diplomats who are long since dead, like Isabel Diaz?*"

"*Like she,*" said Dupont.

"*So that's your opinion, Professor?*"

He glared. "*It's the law.*" Humility wasn't Dupont's strong suit.

"*Who says so, Professor?*"

As Dupont paused to lean forward to answer, Isabel looked over to Oliver Pryor with some admiration, "Your grandfather is a surly old coot." Oliver's face flushed with embarrassment.

Dupont snatched up a large tome and levered it open.

"*I say so. And if that's inadequate for you, young man, the United States Supreme Court says so, too.*" He almost spat the words out, "*I refer you to the Court's decision in* US v. Wong Kim Ark. *It's older than I am. It's from 1898.*"

He slid his reading glasses out of his jacket pocket and perched them at the end of his nose. As he started to read the majority opinion, the relevant text flashed up on the screen together with the case reference: *US v. Wong Kim Ark*, 169 US 649 (1898). *Close-up* was leaving no doubt about where this was going.

Oliver was agog. Both his cell phone and Professor Millie Wilkinson who was on it dropped away from his ear. "So that's why he brought up Orrin Hatch… it *was* about the Arnie amendment. We just didn't figure out why."

Ordinarily, Gregory would've been furious at Oliver—the lawyer was paid to understand why—but here in Detroit where they possessed the vital detail of mistaken identity, Gregory was relieved. "Thank God not a jot of this legal crap matters," he exhaled.

Ed coughed, his craggy face suddenly as grey as a heavy cloud. "I'm afraid it does matter."

In a single sweep, all present turned toward him like sideshow clown heads.

Ed was walking back in from the rear, holding Isabel's photo-frame in one hand. Everyone could see he'd pried open the back. The old picture of Isabel's dad was in his other hand. It had been glued all these years onto a metal backing square placed under the glass—Isabel had seen it herself many times—but with the blade of the knife, Ed had painstakingly peeled the photo off the metal. He passed it to Isabel.

Handling her beloved photo like it was coated with poison, Isabel quickly saw that what she'd devotedly kept with her all these years wasn't a photograph at all… but a cutting from a glossy magazine cover. The name of the publication had been stripped off, but the caption beneath the face had been folded back behind the backing plate.

Yet another of her mother's lies.

Isabel's lip began to quiver as she read the text to herself:

"*Lucho Gatica: King of Bolero. His smoke-and-velvet* Bésame Mucho…"

That fucking *Bésame Mucho*, she thought, and slowly looked up at Ed. Her eyes, moist, went round the room, pausing for just a moment at each expectant face. Her shaky fingers wriggled into her pocket and locked onto the rosaries from St Hyacinth's.

Ed wound his arm around her pulling her close, and she tilted her head briefly to nuzzle against him.

The tips of one of Gregory's hands pressed against his lips and the fingers of the other hand were spread flat against his chest, as if he were palpitating and preparing to scream "oh-my-God-oh-my-God-oh-my-God" once Ed or Isabel explained what the heck was happening. One thing was for sure: the campaign was not looking good. Nor was The Book.

Isabel straightened up and inhaled. Her eyelids dropped for less than a second and, as she looked back up, her free hand crushed the once beloved picture into a ball and it dropped to the cold, wooden floor.

No longer looking anyone in the eye, but with a smile weakly hanging on to her mouth, she said, "No debate tonight, folks. Not ever, apparently."

And in the hushed gloom, the approaching noise from outside was all the louder… the long rolling crunch of gravel along the drive by CBS's outside broadcast van and three other vehicles as they drew up outside the hall doors.

For months, America had been clinging optimistically to Isabel's lustre like moths to the screen door of a lone shiny, bright room. Yet in fewer than thirty TV minutes, Mike Mandrake had doused those lights with a single flick of his microphone.

From that night, Isabel's election posters, still beaming her candour, high-mindedness and sense of justice, would curl up into relics for a disheartened nation robbed of a candidate they adored.

And Mike Mandrake, the man to blame, would become a pin-up of a different kind.

★ ★ ★ ★ ★

TERRIFIED eyes tried to meet through the cigar smoke, and Bill Edwards' colleagues startled when he stood his entire bulk, thumped the table, and bellowed, "Somebody… find me that damn Bolivian whore!" Myron Kowalski, of course, was snickering since, in their younger days, he'd delivered on many similar requests from Bill.

Bill had done all he could tonight, so he sat back down and puffed on his cigar, devastated, though the others in the room wouldn't be able to tell it from his rock-hard expression.

Bill was thinking fast. But as quick as he was, his mind kept taking him back to two years ago, when he had the vision to identify Isabel, from among the hundreds, as the best candidate. And how he went after her, chasing her, persuading her, cajoling her, using whatever influence he had to win her over. He'd watched her in action before that, and had liked what he'd seen. To him, she was the one way out in front, and it didn't matter a squib to this ancient conservative that she was female, Hispanic, Catholic, childless, rich, had a weird scar, or any of the other negative qualifications he could imagine being drummed up against her. It was Bill who, once he got her interested, used his clout and stature to dismiss all the party's teeth-sucking and hand-wringing—some of which, undoubtedly, was a smokescreen for racism and sexism. In fact, he boldly told his Republican National Committee, with Isabel—he had never been a Sarah Palin fan—the time had clearly come for a female president, let alone a Hispanic, and that he personally wanted the Republicans to have that first honour.

What were they to do now? The ExCom met around Bill's table till 3 AM, though Kowalski and other non-ExCom attendees had been dismissed at midnight. Bill, as chairman of the RNC, knew that the party rules bestowed enormous powers on ExCom, but filling a vacancy in the candidacy for president wasn't one of them. Under Rule 8, that had to go to the full RNC in five long days time, the shortest period of notice he could give.

For a brief moment, Bill contemplated substituting Ed as the candidate; the war hero was almost as well-known as his wife and, if Ed won, she'd still be in the White House. But even Bill knew that was an impossibility.

The debate about Isabel's running mate, Hank Clemens, raged. Only that day's *Washington Post* had them cringing over its accuracy: "Henry Samuel Langhorne Clemens III has as much grip on the major political issues as on a wet bar of soap." The feature on Hank was excruciating, detailing that while the Clemens family fortune was founded on hogs and river boats, he had spent his pre-public life making a hash of managing it. Hank was the classic butt of the old joke, "How can you make a small fortune…? First, you give Hank Clemens a big one."

Until Bill had pushed him forward as Isabel's running mate, Hank had enjoyed a richly deserved obscurity, apart from a stint as deputy director of Homeland Security, where the best that could be said was that nothing had happened on his watch. Even the Republican hard-core was underwhelmed, with the *Weekly Standard*, their bible, painting Clemens as "a shocker with no awe, a man whose very bright future lies behind him. His entire manner is a drawl, having lived his life like a shoe stretching out a wad of gum stuck to the sole."

But Bill had backed him, as a sop to appease the law-and-order crowd who saw Isabel as too soft. He didn't expect Hank would actually have to step forward, but so be it.

So, pressed hard by Bill, the ExCom decided four things that night: to convene an urgent meeting of the RNC in five days; to recommend that Hank take Isabel's spot; to recommend that Perry Patein, a Wisconsin congressman, become Hank's running mate; and to press Isabel Diaz to stay on the stumps and keep campaigning, despite her disqualification, using her charisma and the nation's sympathy to back up the new team.

Five turbulent days later, the RNC met, with little choice but to rubber-stamp the ExCom's recommendations—not least because, at Bill's insistence, Hank, Perry and Isabel, without missing a beat, had all three gone straight out onto the hustings to try to salvage as much momentum as possible; and because Bill had leaked the recommendations to the media.

This was a brand-new ball game. Bill... everyone... knew that. Like most vice-presidential candidates, Hank hadn't been taken seriously until now. The most flattering comment that could have been made about his public performances to date was that he hadn't said anything stupid, which was easy for him since he hadn't said anything at all; he'd just looked fine standing at-ease in the traditionally respectful spot back and to the side of Isabel at her rallies. And while he filled the minimum technical qualifications for president—over thirty-five and, yes, truly a natural born citizen—the public now needed to know exactly who this low-profile man really was, whereas the key task that Bill Edwards knew faced his Party was precisely the opposite: to prevent people finding out.

According to Gregory, when Hank was handed the nomination form where it said "Sign here," he wrote "Virgo".

It was why Bill knew he had to lean on Isabel to keep campaigning, though now for the team, not herself. In the current circumstances, if they didn't have her up front, the Party's chances approached zero. They all knew that when people focused on Hank he'd make even George W. Bush and Al Gore seem like they'd been jived-up marionettes dancing on crack. Hank Clemens might have a heart of gold but, as the saying went, so did a hard-boiled egg.

Perry Patein, the new running mate, had been Isabel's original preference before Bill Edwards had white-anted him in favour of Hank. Though also young, at forty-two, Perry was no dewy-eyed, Republican apple-polisher. He'd started life as a hard-hitting economist working on education policy, for the Democrats back then, as it happened. Isabel met him later when he was seeking funding for education programs that he was developing for Africa. That steered him toward gaining a wider experience in foreign affairs, including a short stint in Iraq, and it wasn't long after that when he won his seat in Congress.

That fateful night, Bill told his ExCom colleagues that even if Isabel's heart wasn't in continuing to trudge the campaign trail, the pressure on her would be enormous. And, when he called her in Detroit at 3:15 AM, it already was. She and Ed were still thrashing around the alternatives themselves. Gregory had just left their hotel suite for bed, Isabel only half-kidding that she'd ring housekeeping to remove the razor blades from his bathroom.

So Bill had an easier task than he expected. After what they'd achieved so far, there was no way Isabel and Ed could bear even the image of Bobby Foster's stockinged feet up on the desk in the Oval Office. They'd both known that much even without speaking.

Isabel and Ed didn't need Bill or even a poll to convince them that without the halo of Isabel's ongoing presence on the hustings and her strong advocacy, whoever they replaced her with was guaranteed to go down in a screaming heap. With her, they still might not win, but at least they'd have a fighting chance.

And besides, she was going to have plenty of free time—her Representative's seat in the House had just been pulled out from under her, too. Old Kowalski had contributed that fine piece of news to Bill Edwards straight after *Close-up*. He'd pointed out that for Isabel to keep her seat in Congress she still had to be a citizen, though unlike with the presidency, being naturalised was acceptable.

"No problem," Bill had said. "We'll get a naturalisation fast-tracked." Bill was already thinking about whose arm he'd be twisting for that.

"No," said Kowalski, "she's got to be a citizen for seven years first."

IN the lead up to the official RNC meeting, almost every lawyer in the country who'd been pumping for a Diaz win had pored over the Constitution and the case law. The Republican National Lawyers' Association had convened an urgent web conference of its constitutional law experts. The Heritage Foundation asked its legal scholars to opine. Major newspapers and magazines published opinion pieces galore on the subject. TV networks keen to prove Professor Dupont and *Close-up* wrong, especially FOX, scrabbled around for their own telegenic experts.

The Democratic Party was ecstatic. Bobby Foster was riding an all-time high, and it was with no assistance from unlawful substances.

Contrary legal arguments were dredged up, of course; even with just two lawyers you get three opinions.

But what was swaying the general public was the absurd notion that a fusty old legal judgment, based on the state of world politics more than a century ago was still the law today; surely it was merely a dreary relic of a quaint and distant past. *The Wall Street Journal* led that charge, reminding its readers that 1898 was the year the USS Maine was sunk in Havana Harbour triggering the Spanish-American War and the Cuban blockade; it was the same year a nest of white supremacist ideologues from the Democratic Party—yes, the Democratic Party—signed the scandalous "White Declaration of Independence" in Hank Clemens' home town of Wilmington, North Carolina: "*we will no longer be ruled, and will never again be ruled, by men of African origin.*"

But *The Journal* wasn't the deciding forum, and the antiquity of the decision cut no ice with the lawyers.

All the pro-Diaz legal lobby could do was say that the old case should be limited to its own facts; the most popular arguing that while Isabel was the daughter of a diplomat, despite his visit to see LBJ, he hadn't been an official envoy to the United States itself, so it didn't matter, or that since he was long dead, it rendered the Supreme Court decision irrelevant. There was merit in the counter-arguments, but the RNC's own experts didn't see them guaranteeing a positive outcome since it was inevitable the Democrats would challenge everything before the Supreme Court, the diversion throwing the election into total disarray.

Bill Edwards wasn't going to be deflected by legal maybes. He knew that with Isabel standing firm behind Hank and Perry, carrying the momentum on as best she could, they'd at least have a shot.

# 26

TWO WEEKS AFTER the *Close-up close-down*, as dispirited Diaz supporters had dubbed the depressing night, the temperature was dropping, not as fast as the Republicans' electoral prospects had plunged, though out in the skipping heart of the seniors' sunbelt, you wouldn't have known it. According to the placards, the crowd hailed from not only Phoenix, Arizona but from miles around: Scottsdale, Sun City, Mesa, Chandler, Peoria, and even the quaintly named Surprise.

To Isabel—up on the stage forcing a laugh and swaying arm-in-arm with Hank Clemens and Perry Patein—two things seemed remarkable. One was the vast difference from yesterday's rally in Long Beach, California: there, they'd been surging on a roiling sea of predominantly sun-bleached hair yet today they'd submerged into a languid grey lagoon, where the only buzz came from the faulty hearing aids and pacemakers down in the mush pit. The other was that Isabel was here at all.

As a tentative "Isa-bel" quivered over the somewhat ambiguous "Go Hank, Go" chants of the new campaign, she stepped forward to the microphone.

"Friends," she said, launching into the stock introduction she'd perfected over the last ten days, "Let's give a big, warm Arizona welcome to the two men with my vote for the next president and vice-president of the United States… my very good friends, Hank Clemens and… Perry Patein."

It wasn't as bad as Bobby Foster's rockstar version of "*Hel-l-o-o, Phoe-e-e-nix*," or Pi-i-tts-burgh, or wherever he happened to be, but she knew it wasn't a whole lot better.

★ ★ ★ ★ ★

TRAMPING city-to-city and breakfast-to-dinner, Isabel was doing her best to repair the damage she was responsible for, unwitting or not. Putting the Republican team back on top was what drove her, regardless of the painful fact she wasn't going to be the one enjoying the trappings of office. Despite her reservations about Hank, shared by many, she was convinced that the country would be better off with him in the White House than Bobby Foster. Especially with backup from Perry and with her in Hank's Cabinet, as his secretary of state.

Isabel had strong-armed her own campaign team to embrace Hank; especially Gregory, though he held Hank at a distance. They hired extra speechwriters. Hank's skills in the insight department followed the edict that genius is one percent inspiration, and ninety-nine percent perspiration. Merely giving Hank a pen made him sweat.

Isabel's stocks were still booming with the public, perhaps more so due to her demonstrable altruism. Almost instantly, "We was robbed" became a rally mantra.

The Karim Ahmed affair fizzled as an election truncheon since it was Isabel-specific and the Democrats couldn't beat Hank over the head with it; though Ahmed's disappearance did linger as mainstream news, peaking if someone reported a sighting. Between Elvis and Ahmed, shopping malls were getting crowded.

The Foster-Taylor campaign finally catapulted over the important 45-percent approval rating poll barrier, and was now tickling 50. With Hank cast against him, voting for Foster became enticing, like sliding into the driver's seat of a blood-red V-8 Mustang convertible with the top down. With Hank, it would be sitting astride a well-mannered thoroughbred, or rather a sculpture of one: graceful and born to lead, but going nowhere. Even if Isabel was in his Cabinet.

The Independents were thriving, too.

The only good news for the Republicans was that with Isabel their effort was resuscitating, and the Clemens-Patein team were pushing back up, to 35 percent and higher.

Inspired by Isabel's apparently selfless example, her supporters wiped away their tears and resumed campaigning for Hank. If Isabel could do it, they'd do it with her.

The Democrats fired off new sharpened barbs to keep their rising opponents down, especially on the theme that if Clemens-Patein won, they'd be Isabel's—or worse, Ed's—puppets in the White House. But they miscalculated the strength of the public's "she was wronged" sentiment, and the tactic backfired, boosting the Republicans up a few notches. Most Americans still hankered for Isabel in the Oval Office, so if Clemens-Patein was the only way to do it, well, that might be worth considering.

MIKE Mandrake's hate mail had started even before *Close-up* ran its credits that Sunday night. Within three days, he'd tallied six death threats and CBS was forced to give him a 24/7 bodyguard. Security in CBS studios around the country was bumped up: targeted protests were breaking out everywhere. It might have been synchronicity, but within four days, after several separate and nasty incidents of "mistaken beard", there was not a single hair left on any CBS chin apart from Mike's, and his was fast turning grey.

The network became a hackers' haven. For three days running, the nightly news bulletins were interrupted and each time it was with the same vision: Bugs Bunny, Elmer Fudd and the old Looney Tunes gang with the signature finale, *Th-th-that's all, f-folks* played on a loop for fifteen very long seconds, with Mike's face fading in and out before it burst into flames.

If Mike dared emerge in public, he was hissed and jeered. His car, a new Mercedes, was key-scratched along both sides and sprayed with ugly graffiti. Even his wife turned against him, courtesy of an anonymous phone call about his fidelity. What should've been Mike's finest hour was a fiasco.

The following week, CBS announced that Mike was on assignment outside the country. It was a lie. He'd gone into hiding.

# 27

"THREE WEEKS LEFT… this campaign needs something big... something to really stoke the votes… to start a stampede…" The six joined on this conference call were no bunch of hand-wringers or nail-biters; these were women and men who knew their duty.

"Obviously, I have to tread carefully about how far I go publicly," Isis added. This time the voice-masking software turned the words into those of a robotic Arnold Schwarzenegger, adding a creepy tone to the call, though any chance eavesdropper would have shuddered at the conversation even without that.

"Doing it in private is more fun," laughed Diana, her voice-mask mimicking the actress Meg Ryan.

Isis ran through the latest research. Even though the Clemens-Patein ticket was picking up steam, the experts predicted it would top out at 40 percent. The numbers were running marginally better in some of the all-important swing states, and even some traditional blue states, but whichever way the data was stretched, the magic 270 electoral college votes stayed just out of reach.

"We've upped the effort," said Isis. "I'm out there every day now, but we'll still have to activate…"

"The shockwave?" guessed Diana.

"Yes," said Isis.

Diana's face cracked into a smile; her work with Jax Mason wouldn't be wasted.

★ ★ ★ ★ ★

THE "One Hundred Club" dinner was at Harvard's Museum of Natural History. Hank's idea was to shift the campaign focus to his intellect, away from his wealth. Gregory sniped it would backfire: "So now they'll say Hank went to Harvard... for dinner." Isabel opposed the event for a different reason: the campaign couldn't afford to waste precious time preaching to the converted, especially this pile of withered old bones who shared more with the museum's skeletal exhibits than with the swing voters they needed to win over.

"Why'd they call it the One Hundred Club?" Isabel had asked Gregory before either of them knew it was the capacity seating.

Gregory scanned the crowd, "Minimum age of membership?"

The function ended at ten, late enough for most guests, so Hank decided to treat the travelling campaign team to drinks at the Railcar, a nightclub overlooking the tracks near the B&M Rail Yard. His family trust owned a one-third share of the club.

Once inside, Isabel turned to both Ed and Gregory—Ed was now also full-time on the campaign—"Not many voters... it's fake-ID-city in here." But over the pounding doof-doof of the music, if you could call it that, neither man could hear her.

Hank hustled them over to his showpiece. "My idea," he pointed to the Cocktail Wall.

"He's had an idea!" Gregory tisked.

Isabel didn't catch the comment, though his smirk told her it was a slam of some sort. She scanned the Wall, which was entirely black apart from the flashing fluoro discs, which were the glass faces of, she counted, thirty refrigerated cylinders slipped horizontally into the wall and filled with every vibrantly coloured liquor and cocktail imaginable. For a few seconds when the music faded down to the mere landing squeal of a passenger jet, Hank pointed out the six kinds of Daiquiris—from raincoat-yellow mango to fire-engine red strawberry—the hot-pink Cosmos and the Sex-on-the-Beach, even more candy-pink than the Cosmopolitans if that were possible. When he mentioned the Screaming Orgasm, Isabel lowered his arm, "Enough."

The sound built up and the spotlights behind the Wall started strobing randomly through the cylinders, making them jump like bouncing balls.

"Cost a fortune," Hank mouthed. He pointed to the nearby bank of speakers, now pumping harder than a steroid-sucking body-builder. "More power than the Pentagon." He laughed, but the strobes prevented him noticing that none of the others thought it was funny.

AFTER Isabel and Ed got to the sanctuary of their hotel—set back from Boston Common—the manager came up to their room to hand-deliver an envelope. It was marked "*Isabel Diaz: Important but not Urgent.*"

The term jolted her—until a few years ago she'd seen it typed on memos every day, until its devotee vanished, along with four million dollars.

"It arrived a few minutes ago," the manager told her.

How did Karim Ahmed know she'd be staying here? "Who delivered it?" she asked.

"Here's the thing," said the manager, "it just appeared on the bell desk… while the night boy was helping a guest to the elevator."

The letter weighed on her as she closed the door.

"What is it?" asked Ed, wiping his hands on a towel as he came out of the bathroom.

She waved it at him. "I think it's from Karim." She lifted it to the light and saw it contained only one sheet.

Ed took her wrist and brought it to his nose to smell the packet. He nodded and let go. Isabel sat at the desk and flicked on the lamp. She slit the envelope open. A single sheet… typed, but with Karim's signature. A scrawl that looked genuine.

Dear Isabel,

Like so many, I too prayed you would become President, so I desperately share your disappointment.

My only consolation is that ultimately your loss had nothing to do with me. But even so, I apologise for the pain I have caused you.

I was thrilled, as you would expect, when Judge Thomas threw out the trumped up charges against me.

Why then, you will ask, did I choose to 'vanish' after that? Not because of any guilt, I assure you, but simply to protect my family from again becoming a public freak show.

I had become very depressed when I saw how your opponents were using my disappearance against you. My heart went out to you. It still does.

For now, I will stay in hiding, though I will still do what I can to make amends. (You can be confident that I have some ideas.)

Please tell my parents I truly love them, no matter what everyone thinks of me. I am with good people.

Kindest regards,

*Karim*

Isabel sat quietly. Where was Karim? Who was he with?

Ed ruffled her hair.

Isabel knew what had to be done.

# 28

BY THE TIME Davey had scampered off to his bed, Isabel was dog-tired. They'd had a rare weekend at home, and just farewelled George who'd flown back to California. The stress of the last few months, especially the last couple of weeks, was catching up.

Even so, out of habit, Isabel flicked on the TV:

> "*…at least thirty people died in a nightclub fire close to Harvard University. Over fifty people are being treated for severe burns and many others for smoke inhalation. The Cambridge Police and Fire Departments have cordoned off the area. At this stage, it is unknown how the blaze began, but there is mounting speculation it was faulty wiring. The…*"

Isabel's eyes were drawn to the building on the screen. The shot was from across railway tracks. It was… she was sure… Hank's nightclub. Railcar.

Her hand flew to her lips.

★ ★ ★ ★ ★

NO matter what Hank could say to distance himself from the club—he only had a one-third share, he kept repeating, and even that was behind a trust so he had no involvement in management—the Republican ticket was again in diabolical trouble. The early reports of faulty wiring were accurate, and investigators had pinned it down to the Cocktail Wall, the wall which Isabel knew Hank took credit for.

The networks and cable channels were running newsclips of the blaze with tawdry newsbars like "*Republican campaign in flames*" and worse.

By the following Monday, the weekend polls were out and Bill Edwards' stomach was churning. Twenty… twenty percent! He phoned up Isabel and, with classic insensitivity, said, "We're dead."

★ ★ ★ ★ ★

THREE days later the CBS "eye" logo was overlooking a deserted Beverly Boulevard near West Hollywood in Los Angeles. This was the famous Television City.

The perpetrators had picked the hushed shadows of 2 AM to magnify the explosion's noise and minimise casualties. The stolen blue Mazda sedan lumbered slowly down Beverly and drew close. Telltale, it hung low on its wheels. It humped over the kerb and bounced up onto the sidewalk, pulling up sharp outside the newly remodelled front entrance. The car driver wore a red full-face helmet, curious only until he jumped out of the vehicle, sprinted to the rear and sprung himself onto the back saddle of the black BMW motorbike that had been trailing him. If anyone had later been able to view the security video shooting the street scene, they would have observed that the bike's plates were taped over with "Diaz for President" bumper stickers.

The bike rider, also helmeted, high-revved the throttle of the 1750cc engine for all it was worth, reared the machine up on its back wheel and squealed off leaving a black trail of rubber on the road behind them.

Ten seconds after the pair hurtled off, the pillion passenger pressed "redial" on his cell phone and swivelled around to rip the bumper sticker off the back plate. He tapped the driver's shoulder and she leant forward to do likewise to the front plate.

Five blocks back, the 300 pounds of explosives that were packing down the Mazda detonated with a fury. Even over the roar of the engine the rider heard it, shooting up her right hand in victory, and her passenger slapped the back of her glove for a plan well-executed.

The ground floor façade of the building sheared off. The blast ripped a wide gash, first across the pavement, then into the street, carving across five thankfully empty lanes. Four parked cars blew into the air. Car parts and leaflets showered over a two-block radius. Glass from the building's front doors flew inwards, spraying shards through the lobby, the force shattering even the bulletproof screen intended to shelter the new security desk. Fortunately, the night guard was up on the second floor and miraculously, no one was injured. Spouts of water from burst pipes gushed over the debris and, capped with heavy black smoke, the entrance flooded.

Thousands of charred pamphlets fluttered back down through the choking fumes… "*The Truth has Consequences.*"

Within thirty-five seconds, a coordinated hack attacked CBS stations across the country. "*We have* our *eye on* you, *CBS*," were the chilling words that unfurled out of the pupil of CBS's famous eye logo. "*And you, too, Mike Mandrake…The Truth has Consequences.*"

For Mandrake, it was after 5 AM. He had his back slumped against the pillows in a small room in Washington DC's infamous Watergate Hotel where he'd been holed up for days. His gut ached.

The truth has consequences… He didn't need these jerkoffs to tell him that. It was drummed into all journalists. But this morning, the words pressed in on him, the beads of sweat stinging his recently shaved upper lip.

Only an hour earlier the porter had slipped a copy of the paper he previously wrote for, *The Washington Post*, under his door. It was splayed open on his lap, at the editorial, "*Truth at all costs?*"

What did these people want from him? He'd done his job… and fucking brilliantly, he added for no one to hear but himself. Sanctimonious bastards! No one wrote this pious crap when Woodward and Bernstein busted Nixon over the Watergate scandal… here, in this same fucking building.

That Nixon was a crook and Isabel a saint didn't seem to gel with him in the state he was in.

He clamped his eyes, shutting out the TV and the room, but he couldn't shut out everything. His wife had kicked him out. CBS was publicly supporting him but privately wiping its hands of him, wishing he'd never existed. For security reasons, he'd shaved his beard and wore dark glasses and a cap when he ventured out.

What should have been the story of the decade had become a debacle.

Was no one interested in the truth any more if it had… fucking consequences? That was the truth's job, for chrissakes!

At that moment, his hotel room TV broadcast a newsflash about the blast in Los Angeles. His eyes blinked open but he could hardly watch. He recognised the building. It was meant for him.

Who were these fucking people?

He swiped his hand across the bed sheet in front of him sending the newspaper onto the floor and he jabbed at the "off" button on the remote.

His hand shook as he stretched across for the vial that was perched on the edge of his bedside table. It had been lingering there since ten o'clock last night when he had slipped it out of his toiletry bag.

Damn these childproof caps. Mike sat up straight and wiped his hands dry on the bed sheets and tried again. Third time, he succeeded. As he drank it, he remembered something his dad used to tell him as a kid when he was feeling down: if at first you don't succeed, forget the skydiving.

But this time it wasn't funny.

Hot sweat dripped down his back and the clear liquid streamed cold down his throat.

Truth.

Consequences.

★ ★ ★ ★ ★

IN London's St Bartholomew's Hospital, Registered Nurse Jeni Crompton was completing her morning rounds and came to Room 603. An insensitive creep had taped a hand-written sign below the room number: "Burns Unit". Jeni ripped it down. To her, the allusion to Jax Mason's shocking encounter with the famous Scots poet was not at all amusing. Inside Room 603 it was quiet… only the beep, beep, beep of Jax's heart monitor sounded. Here, no one answered back to her, unlike the man two rooms up.

She always spoke to Jax, babbled really, but had never got a single response in the month he'd been under her charge. Probably a good thing, given what she'd told him, otherwise he'd know everything about her sex life (lack of, really), her parents' divorce, the bank loan she was hoping for, and the fact she was sick of nursing and wanted to try out working in her sister's café (where she might meet someone "nice").

Jax's doctor had told her—probably the only time the old fart had deigned to speak to someone like her for more than three seconds—that he'd be surprised if Jax would ever come out of the coma; that the paramedics should have let the "poor young bugger" die.

Jeni rolled Jax over onto his stomach, untied his gown at the neck and laid it out on either side of him. She had brought in a basin of warm soapy water with her and bathed him top to toe, hesitating over the tattoo at the base of his spine, a disk with a "Y" stamped out of it. It was in fact a representation of an old New York subway token, but she guessed it was a peace symbol, though the words "Good for one fare" didn't really match with that. She dried him and rolled him over onto his back.

"You're a bit of a hunk," she said aloud for the umpteenth time as she sponged him down. He was her age, she'd noted from his chart the first time.

Just as she was about to shave him, her pager vibrated against her leg. Damn. Room 605. That bastard again. Why doesn't he just lie there like everyone else? Jeni towelled Jax down, dressed him in a fresh gown, tucked him in and left his room. She could shave him later. Or tomorrow. He wouldn't know.

As the door closed behind her, she didn't see the flicker in Jax's left eyelid nor hear the stutter in the heart monitor beeps.

# 29

ISABEL FIRST HEARD about Mike Mandrake's suicide from Gregory. A friend of his had been breakfasting at the Watergate. Habits are hard to break, and Isabel's former staffer called her even before he phoned Hank.

Hank's campaign was flailing. "I'm quitting," Gregory said, the real reason for phoning. They'd argued about this many times recently, but this was it. After the nightclub fire, he felt he couldn't keep working with Hank and retain any vestige of dignity. "I love a political joke as much as the next guy, but I can't work for one."

He was right about Hank, she knew it, but with backup Hank was still a better option than the alternative.

"Unless we pull a rabbit out of a hat, the campaign is D-E-A-D. It's..."

"You've got to hang in there, Gregory. He needs you... I need you." Her appeal to loyalty was a low blow, but she knew Gregory was nothing if not devoted to her.

★ ★ ★ ★ ★

"MANDRAKE?" Foster remarked. "What d'you expect from a beard guy? No beards in my administration... Note that down, Don." He glanced over to his deceptively bookish but hardnosed campaign strategist, Don Thomas, to check if he had.

What Don noted, though not in writing, was that his candidate was getting way too cocky. A bad sign. He knew voters easily detected smugness, and punished it.

SNAP!

"Damn that woman," Don swore behind the glass partition out of Niki Abbott's earshot. Why had he ever agreed to this intrusive photographic record? Each time he picked his nose Niki snapped him with her camera. Hell! He didn't want shots of Foster out there crowing like a rooster.

Spencer Prentice, visiting for an hour's meeting, also prickled at Foster's arrogance and shaded his eyes from the flash to cover his own crabby expression, the whole thing reminding him he'd rather be somewhere else; anywhere else.

"Diaz is out, and now Clemens is washed up…," Foster bragged, swinging his socked feet up onto the desk and puffing hard on his cigar. "So, what's next on my agenda? Solving world poverty? Get Bono on the phone," he laughed.

SNAP!

Don Thomas cringed.

Spencer's normally hard-to-read face recoiled at Foster's brazen conceit. Too late, he saw that Don Thomas, stooped on the airconditioning ledge over by the window, had observed him. "Robert," Spencer refused to call the presidential candidate Bobby, "that's how it looks today, but you know better than I do that three weeks are…"

"Yeah… a long time in politics. You came here for a reason, Prentice?"

Spencer was smouldering and cleared his throat to control himself. "Everything points to a win," he said slowly, "but that's not the point…"

"It's not about winning?" Foster said, unable to keep the smirk off his face.

Spencer bit on his scorn. "*How* you win is important, surely." How could it be otherwise? He glanced at Don for support but got the same sneer he'd seen on Foster. What was it with these two? "Robert, you're getting the numbers but unless things change you'll be seen as the usurper stealing someone else's throne."

"Hank Clemens?" said Foster, extracting his cigar and spitting some leaf to the floor.

SNAP!

"Oh, *fuck* her," Foster said, faking a smile through the glass to Niki's camera. "Hmm, maybe I will… fuck her. What do *you* think of Niki Abbott, Prentice?"

"Wha…?" Spencer couldn't believe this. Through the glass partition he saw Niki posed behind her camera in a body-hugging red silk suit and her ever-present baseball cap, its peak twisted to the right, just like her politics. "It's a signed Ted Williams cap, you know. Anyone who desecrates a Red Sox heirloom like that doesn't deserve attention. How do you work with her hovering around?"

"We manage," Foster said. "Prentice, what did you mean I'd be Clemens' usurper?"

"No, Isabel Diaz's," Spencer corrected. Was Foster really so thick?

"Her. You've always been, er, close to her, haven't you?" Foster winked, like a father discovering his son's stash of porn on his computer.

Spencer resented the implications—sexual innuendo, party disloyalty, ugh!—especially from this pretender, but he kept his face blank.

Don Thomas was now leaning so far forward on the window ledge Spencer worried he might fall into a duck dive to the floor. Unknown to Spencer, Don had given Foster a similar message two days earlier after he'd found a parody website called ImposterFoster.com. "Prentice," said Don,

"Seems you and me are sharing the same nuthouse. Come slobber over here with me."

"Buddy boy," Foster said to Spencer, the bounce in his voice barely masking a concern, "even if I agree with you, what can I do about it, exactly?"

Out of the corner of his eye, Spencer could see Don smiling. Then it dawned on him… this was why Don had invited him here. "You've got to show strong, uniting leadership… That you're for all Americans, not just those who vote for you." He braced himself, "In your victory speech, you should announce you're inviting Isabel Diaz into your Cabinet."

"Fuck! Fuck, no! Clemens has already promised *he'll* do that," said Foster, dismissively waving his cigar and casting a gruff eye to Don. "Newsflash! I'm way out in front," he continued. "I don't need to be Mr Me-Too."

"Clemens' offer was a desperate ploy in a struggling campaign. I'm talking about your *victory* speech, Robert. That way she can't refuse you, either. Bipartisanship... the right thing… bring the country together. All that."

Foster swung his feet to the floor and leant across the desk. "And if I don't want that bee-yatch in my Cabinet?"

Spencer was aghast, "Then you should offer her something else with stature… Speaker of the House?"

"Where have you been, Prentice? She can't even be a *member* of the House. You know… the Con-stit-u-tion? You Bostonians learn about that old piece of parchment?"

Disgust welled up inside Spencer but he controlled it. He'd heard worse and from "better" people. He eyed Don for support but the strategist had flipped his spiral-bound notepad open and was bent over it jotting, avoiding his eye.

Spencer shuddered just being with this pair, let alone with the notion that they would be in charge of his country for the next four years.

# 30

ELIA CACOZ WAS celebrating. She still had Simon and she'd cashed her first new paycheque. She clinked her beer glass against Simon's. "To my first story on FOX."

"Better than your last one at CBS, I hope" he said before taking a long draft. He belched and after wiping his mouth with the back of his hand said, "What's the scoop?"

Elia felt the drill of his eyes, chasing more. Spurred on by Simon, she had emailed her resignation into *Close-up* the night Mandrake's story went to air. When the credits scrolled past her name as assistant researcher, she couldn't help but squirm and found it hard to look him in the face. While she couldn't unmake that snippet of history, she wasn't proud of it and wouldn't remain part of it.

"It's a deeper trawl into Isabel's past… about what made her. But it'll only be ready to go to air *after* the election. So if Clemens wins, it'll be 'the woman thankfully behind the turkey' story."

"If Foster wins?"

She shrugged. "Why the slimy shit shouldn't have."

# 31

AFTER THREE WEEKS, Karim Ahmed was still holed up in the Philadelphia hideaway with his same four friends. The dilapidated row house was smack in the middle of Strawberry Mansion, near the east bank of the Schuylkill River. This place didn't look like the birthplace of the nation, not today. There were no mansions either, but plenty of decay. Row after rundown row, many houses had been abandoned and boarded up, and others with broken shutters were flapping to signal that someone was home, but wishing home was somewhere else.

Karim was making cheese sandwiches for lunch. "I'm tired of hiding," he said peeling the plastic wrap off the sunlight yellow slices he'd bought at the mini market down the block.

By the sink, Abdul was twisting the creaking faucet with a wrench to run some water for a cup of tea. "Soon, my friend," he said. "It is good there is enough money."

Mohammed walked in, carefully, over the cracked, lifting floor tiles. He snaffled a portion of cheese from the packet.

Their street was in a district with a Muslim flavour, though largely black Muslim. Around here, welfare was the biggest employer.

"We go tomorrow," Karim said.

# 32

"YEAH, IT'S A promo for some stoopid new TV show." The thick Bronx accent sashayed from a short, skin-headed man. "Some clever-dick guy upstairs dreamt it up so, by definition, it's brilliant. They gives me tree hours, yeah, tree. What, like I'm a magician? I ain't got that many people on call, which is how come I need you guys. So how many messengers you got you can send me?" he asked, drumming his fingers on top of the latest issue of *The Economist.*

He made a few notes on a pad and continued, "So to repeat, you'll send sixty—that's six-zero—guys here in plenty time to make all my drops, all over Manhattan at 17:25 on the button… Yeah, I said 17:25… You think I don't know that's rush hour? Listen, bro, I'm not the fat cat genius who thunk this up… Cool it, man. Don't shoot the messenger… Okay, you're the messenger—it's an expression. Now listen… If any of your guys ain't at the drops by 17:25, they don't get no money… Yeah, the packages are ready… The pick-up? Don't you listen? It's, like, where I told you… Yeah, that's it… Where? Christ, dude, where do you think...? Okay, it's just east over the Queensboro Bridge in Long Island City. Yeah, off 21st Street, a warehouse with a Big SatTV sign out front… your guys can't miss it… What…? No, our people'll be there to collect orright. The TV broadcasts go live at 17:35 so if our guys ain't at the drops at 17:25 to get the packs from your people, they'll be dead meat, so don't you worry... See ya." He terminated the call with a sinister grin.

"Dead meat. Great joke, Dwayne," his companion Gary laughed.

They were an odd couple. If Dwayne had any hair on his head, he would've resembled a furry bowling ball cover. He didn't look like a Dwayne but he kept the moniker his parents gave him because he enjoyed the cocked eyebrow that usually followed after he was introduced. Then he'd perform his party trick: he'd flex his pecs and then in theatrical waves, he'd send a series of tight ripples from his diaphragm at the base of his stumpy thick torso up to his shoulders—rounded by years of steroid-assisted weights; they'd turn and travel down the short but powerfully dangerous-looking limbs that sandwiched him, themselves covered with a protective shield of dark wiry hair, past his knuckles—graced with tattoos of "L" and "R"—to his fingers.

Gary, when he worked with Diana, had been Lucky, but since their London episode, Isis had shifted him over as Dwayne's sidekick for this part of the operation. Gary never needed to work out, yet he had a rapport with Dwayne. Maybe it was a height thing. Gary only went to gyms to ogle the women or steal their underwear. His nickname in high school had been heartless but on the mark: Ferret. He was short and spindly, like the snub-nosed screwdriver he used to keep in his back pocket for raiding the girls' gym lockers before he discovered the power of his bare fingers. It was his fingers he worked on; they had become Gary's ticket. With one hand, he could just about squeeze a piece of steel into a strand of wire that he could then wind around your neck to choke you.

"And your accent!" squawked Gary. "You shoulda been an actor."

"No time for flattery, Gary." Dwayne's now mellow timbre revealed his cultured roots, easily mocked in his profession, though never in his presence. "The messengers are on their way—our 230 unsuspecting shock troops from fifteen very ignorant delivery firms. They'll all be lining up here soon, and we can allocate the drop-offs. First in get the longest trips—that will make the fools happy. We'll send them on their merry ways and we'll tap-dance out of here by five."

★ ★ ★ ★ ★

"MAXINE" said the badge pinned to her uniform. With pink hair spikes gelled flat, she bounded up to the desk. It was just inside the doors of a warehouse huddled in an area she'd rather not be biking around. "Pickup for Crisis Couriers?" she said.

"Don't say," spat the walking neck. "An' I thought you was goin' to a costume party!"

"Okay, wise-ass," she chuckled, remembering the company logo stitched on her breast pocket. "You got my delivery?"

"42nd Street subway station, on the…," he looked at a control sheet, "A-train platform…"

"No one said anything about a platform." She'd assumed she'd be delivering to a store there.

Dwayne winced as though she'd dragged herself out of a dumpster. "Yeah, a platform… you know, what people stand around on waiting for trains. Here's a Metrocard," he said, handing her one of the pile of turnstile entry cards that would gain all the messengers entry to the subway platforms he was assigning them to. "Our TV broadcast team'll be waiting for the A-train heading north. You'll see 'em there with the cameras, can't miss 'em. Ask for…," he looked at his crib sheet, "… Vanessa. Like I told your boss, if you're there by 17:25, we pays. If you're not, we don't. Here," he said and pushed a small screen pad forward. "Sign for it."

"What're they filming?" she asked as she scratched her signature on the pad.

"Big promo," said the artiste-usually-known-as-Dwayne, his eyes lifted to the ceiling in mock derision. "It's called 'The First One'. Goes like this..." He lifted his beefy hands in front of his eyes into a camera view-square shape—his fat thumb tips were pressed together and his stubby fingers pointed up, his palms facing away from him so she could see his hardened weight-lifting calluses. "The train pulls into the station. The doors wheeze open. If you're first off the first carriage of the first train after 17:35, you gets a prize. This is the prize." He held up a black-taped white box that Gary had passed to him from one of the fast-reducing stacks.

She eyed it suspiciously but decided it would fit under the strap on her bike, only just, and as he handed it to her, she could feel its weight. "What's in it?" Maxine asked.

"Who gives a… The really big prize is they get to be on SatTV live tonight. They all love it. They get home and show everyone in the neighbourhood when it's replayed after seven. It's all marketing crap."

"Yeah, but the box?"

Dwayne glanced over at Gary and shrugged. "Don't know, don't care," he said, ending the conversation.

"But I'm the one carrying this," she said, a wrinkle of worry crossing her forehead.

This was taking too long. No more Mister Nice Guy. Dwayne furrowed his bushy eyebrow into the deepest vee he could muster, "Listen, I don't set this up; some guy with a big-buck paycheque tells me what he wants. And my job is to make it happen. If it's too hard for you, pink hair lady, we got plenty other messengers." He stabbed his thick stumpy index finger toward the line behind her.

Maxine took the hint, as well as the hefty box, and left the pair to deal with the couriers jostling behind her.

SHE circled the area around the 42nd Street subway looking for a railing she'd be happy chaining her bike to. It was near the corner of 44th and 8th, at the top of a subway ramp—the package was heavy and this would save time. It was 5:05 PM. She had twenty minutes to spare. She slid the box off her bike, supporting it on her hip, and headed into the subway, as fast as the weight of the box would let her.

She used the Metrocard, pushed through the turnstile and found the platform for the A-train heading north.

People crammed together waiting and reading. A few were chatting but most were avoiding eye contact.

Maxine was tetchy. She'd entered at the completely opposite end of the crowded platform and had to shoulder herself down its entire length to get to where the first carriage would open up.

After pushing hard and persistently, she reached where she guessed the train's first compartment would stop—only a few stragglers stood beyond that point. Her stomach tightened: no TV crew. It was 5:12 PM. Thirteen minutes to go.

The tunnel at the other end started to glow. If she didn't make the drop, she wouldn't get paid, plus she would've wasted ninety damn minutes. She resisted panic and waited, nervously on edge. They'll be here. She rocked up and down on the heels of her boots. Maybe the crew was coming in by train, this train.

It wasn't an A-train; it was a C sharing the same platform. It careered down the track and screeched to a halt in front of her—at least she'd positioned herself correctly. Swapping the package to her other hip, she wiped her forehead

The crowd surged around her toward the doors and she held back, shielding herself against one of the purple I-beam steel uprights as the doors shushed open to launch the contest between those pushing their way on and those forcing their way off.

When the closing doors signalled the battle was over, her eyes searched up and down the platform for the TV crew. They're running late, she decided, but the feigned confidence did nothing to ward off the mounting despair that she wasn't going to get paid.

5:18 PM, and still no sign. Maybe she hadn't heard the bald guy correctly and she was supposed to wait for the A-train going *downtown*? She gripped the box and raced through the nearby exit, tearing up the stairs and through the pedestrian tunnels. After what seemed like an age she flew onto the other platform, almost slamming into an elderly lady carrying a green Harrods shopping bag from London.

Her pulse pounded behind her eyes. No camera crew. But down the other end of this platform, she spotted one of her Crisis Courier colleagues with a similar box. Damn! It was someone else's platform.

She tried to calm down and pulled out her copy of the delivery slip to check the details. It was definitely the uptown train. Hell! She sprinted back, this time taking the correct stairway to deliver her direct to the head of the platform.

5:25 PM. On cue. Her head swivelled around and back like a police car beacon, but there was no TV crew in sight. She was in the right place; she was positive. She'd just have to be patient.

Proof. She needed proof she'd been here on time. She placed the box at her feet and her clammy hand yanked her cell phone out of her pocket and dialled her dispatcher, but there was no signal. Her hand punched down on her leg: who needs this shit? Maxine was tensed up. This had been a bad week for her. She wiped her face on her sleeve and picked up the box.

Next to her, a calm and Burberry-clad woman in her early thirties cradled a small baby. Oblivious to Maxine's plight, the mother's head was bent, cooing sweet nothings to her child.

She started the babble game and hummed a cute, vaguely familiar tune at the same time as repeatedly flicking her fleshy bottom lip with her index finger. The baby gurgled and cackled and those nearby grinned, apart from one ragged man who, undisturbed—or maybe not—continued rifling through an imaginary trashcan bolted to the wall.

"Excuse me, ma'am. I've got to deliver this box to a TV crew. They're supposed to be here. You haven't seen them?"

"We haven't seen any TV crew, have we Sweetpea?" the stylish woman lilted to her baby, not looking Maxine in the eye.

"See, if I can prove I was here from before 5:25, I'll get my money."

Maxine's box was too big not to notice and through the corner of her eye the mother also noted Maxine's pink hair and sweat-glistened face and the dark threatening circles spreading under her arms. She'd heard stories. New York went hand in hand with scams. Don't get involved.

★ ★ ★ ★ ★

ABOVE them in Times Square, the rush-hour traffic was nearing gridlock. Maxine was lucky not to have gotten caught in it and miss the time for her delivery altogether. On the sidewalks, motley street vendors hassled passers-by, indifferent to which were tourists, pre-theatre diners or office workers. Their sole concern was peddling assorted products of variable worthlessness: massive salt rocks pegged into hot pretzels; "gen-u-ine" luxury-brand watches for the price of a Texas Toast in a greasy diner; and pirated DVDs that were filmed with hand-held cameras in Chinese movie theatres.

Jaywalking pedestrians darted across the choked roads, dodging the honking Yellow Cabs, themselves ritually jerking from lane to lane.

The same chaotic picture screened all the way up past Central Park, and all the way back down Broadway to Wall Street where elevators worked overtime as neck-straining office buildings spewed out their human guts into the streets, into teeming rivers of floating workers bobbing home, thirsting for a cool can and a warm TV for tonight's big game.

★ ★ ★ ★ ★

THE train slithered in from Connecticut, against the tide of suburbanites on their rush-hour flow out of Manhattan. With busted airconditioning, thank you for nothing, Metro-North. Despite the outside temperature, it sweltered inside the railcar like a foil-wrapped string of frankfurts left out in the sun, with passengers' eyes drooping from the fixed windows as they wished the journey was over.

# 33

DESPITE THE BADGERING from the dwindling line of couriers, Dwayne and Gary completed their task on time, as Isis expected. In their circle, Dwayne's planning was revered, as was Gary's dogged execution. Usually. The episode with Jax Mason in London had been a rare exception.

With no more messengers or boxes, they ripped down the SatTV sign they'd hung outside the warehouse. After rolling it up and shoving it into Gary's backpack, they walked briskly into the loading bay, fired up the truck they'd stolen earlier that day and hammered it the six miles to LaGuardia airport's freight terminal, where twenty or so cargo planes were lined up. To anyone not blinded by the pink-washed glints of sunset, the odd-looking pair scurrying between the planes was like a silhouette of the nursery-rhyme dish running away with the spoon.

The pilot whose plane they were pacing toward was pumping his money into the vending machine in the waiting bay, a solemn pre-flight ritual that involved concentration and dexterity but, with years of practice, even this reformed drunk could manage it.

Three dollars for a cup of tepid coffee was a bit rich, he bellyached. Yet one more setback. He'd become a shit magnet he decided and, no longer caring, he dressed the part. His standard issue navy, tan and gold uniform was designed so even the most shapeless individual could impress; on most, it evoked the image of neat hospital corners, but on him it was an oversized blanket tossed over a sagging torn mattress. Self-esteem was not his strong suit. He hadn't seen a razor for at least three days yet no one would dream of complimenting him as fashionably unshaven.

He was in luck for a change. The click signalled the coffee was about to drizzle out. Gut-warming sludge it might be, but he loved the burnt aroma.

One of the planes taxiing off the apron shot a glint of the low sun into his bloodshot eyes and, as they swung over to check his own plane he puzzled, squinting at the two shapes he thought he saw clambering into his cockpit. "Hey," he yelled, abandoning his coffee. It was a reckless move. And they say that coffee kills.

He puffed and wheezed up to his Cessna just as its engines fired. Even if Gary and Dwayne hadn't been wearing headphones, the roar of the motors would have blocked out his screams. His fists slammed against the cabin door. Dwayne, focused on take-off, sneered at him and signalled to Gary to deal with the inconvenience. Smiling, Gary unlatched the door so it smacked the pilot in the head and yanked the dazed man up into the small two-seater cockpit.

Gary's serrated grin stayed fixed. With crazed eyes, Gary poked his scraggy nose into the man's terrified face and, without warning, roughly shoved the hysterical fumbler into the narrow space behind the seats that he and Dwayne had commandeered. "Shut the fuck up!" shouted Gary as his hand closed round the pilot's throat. Dwayne neither heard nor felt the pilot slump. He looked at his watch and remarked, "On time."

THE sweat dripped down the parcel courier's pink hair and trickled under her collar. The appointed 5:25 PM had passed and not even a hint of the expected TV crew had materialised. Maxine's eyes scoured the subway platform again. "Damn it," she blasted, out loud, but no amount of cursing would alter fate… that in three minutes' time nothing would matter to Maxine Powers.

When Maxine involuntarily stamped her foot in frustration, the already nervous young mother close by edged back and nuzzled even deeper into her baby's neck, as if their private bond would block out this crazy woman.

"Excuse me," Maxine persisted, shoving a crumpled dispatch voucher forward.

The mother flinched, keeping her eyes down.

"If you'd just initial this for me," she pressed, "to confirm I was standing here at this particular time." Her fingers tapped at her watch. "I'd be real grateful."

Out of the corner of the mother's eye, she could see that balancing against Maxine's hip was a strange white box strapped with black duct tape, but she still didn't look up; eye contact would only get her in deeper, embroil her, and she wrapped her arms even tighter around her boy. "Signing?" she said, shaking her head. "It's a bit diffic…"

As Maxine shook the ticket at her, the carton slipped and, despite her fumbling for it, it fell to the ground, breaking open.

The two women peered down at the contents and froze. They didn't need to know specifically that the exposed putty-like slab was a restricted-use, military-grade variant of the hyper-explosive C-4. But if they had known that impact couldn't trigger it, even if it smashed against the platform floor, their hearts might not have exploded into their mouths, gagging their screams.

Maxine's eyes were drawn to the blue blasting cap that was pressed into the white explosive. Bizarrely, she noted it was the same blue as the baby's bonnet and the candy petals on her cousin's wedding cake last month. Yet this would be no party. And only one of these two women would survive it.

With the presidential election in its final countdown, panic and terror were about to crack themselves across the nation like a bullwhip. It was calculated to spur a stampede, millions of skittish votes once again hurtling toward security.

The baby squealed as if he sensed the danger, and the two women's eyes paused only to blink at each other before they snaked along the two thin wires, one yellow, one green, that led from the blasting cap to the anodised aluminium cube on which a small screen was flashing a three-digit red number. It flashed again.

320...

Three-hundred-and-twenty what?

319...

Seconds.

★ ★ ★ ★ ★

AT Melrose Station in the Bronx, the train doors hissed shut against the few who'd run onto the platform a second too late to board. Phlegmatic, they shrugged and unravelled their newspapers as the train pulled out without them. There'd be another along soon.

Those who'd just made it and slid into their seats were hit by the acrid stench of body-heat that filled the car as well as the confronting racket that pumped out of the large black boombox in the seat between two scruffy teenagers.

# 34

ARMONDO CRUZ IN Pennsylvania's Office of Homeland Security had just placed his phone bets on the next day's card at Parx Racetrack when the call to the tip-off line came in at 5:15 PM. Cruz, a former cop had only transferred to POHS from Philadelphia's north-eastern 22nd District a week earlier so his first anonymous call, especially one so urgent, freaked him, though the caller with the middle-eastern accent didn't seem to notice.

Taking deep breaths, he meticulously followed procedures. Using the encrypted security codes he'd been given, Cruz's computer, as well as instantly alerting everyone up the chain of command and triggering certain pre-set actions, tagged directly into the hangar hidden in the city's outskirts—even he didn't know where—and set off an immediate dispatch of Captain Merrill Jefferson and his crack team of counter-terrorist specialists to the suspect address.

"Imminent threat. Alleged Muslim terrorists ready to launch," Cruz passed on. "Anonymous tip-off. Caller with middle-eastern accent. Immediate response required." Cruz was taking no chances.

Captain Jefferson's unit was primed and ready, as always. They clipped on their arsenal as they ran through the armoury toward their Huey, one of two unmarked UH-1 Iroquois choppers at their disposal. Their pilot, Terry Jarmin, was already firing up the rotors. Only minutes later, at 17:20, Jarmin dropped ten of Jefferson's men half a block north of the suspect address and they ran down the street spreading toward it. It was an especially chilly evening for October at only 5°C. A few rugged-up residents huddled on the street but when Jefferson's black-garbed men appeared, they all seemed to be summoned inside for various family crises—all except a waifish drunk in filthy coveralls who was slumped in the gutter between two vehicles, a burnt-out Ford Escort and an '83 Mustang. His—or was it her?—black dreads snaked out from under a grey baseball cap and his hands, with sky blue fingernails no one noticed because of the gloves, gripped a half-empty gin bottle, whose contents were merely water.

When the chopper pilot saw the men below were in position—two clustered at the steps of each row house either side of the suspect property, two crouched behind a '78 Chevy opposite, and four in the street at the rear—he hovered the Huey high and dropped the cables. Three men, including Captain Jefferson, slithered down to scale over the roof and launch themselves in through the upstairs windows. Over the city emergency radio networks, black and whites were ordered to seal off all streets leading to the area and to prepare to evacuate homes. Fire crews and paramedics were dispatched to wait silently one block back.

The pilot watched Jefferson and his men slide down the cables, smooth and fast until a sudden stop just short of the roof to avoid any tell-tale boot crunch. But the second their steel-capped toes touched, the front ground-floor windows blew outwards, the hollow-point bullets cutting clean through the Chevy and lodging into the walls of the houses opposite, missing the two men hiding behind the car by a hair's breadth. Someone had seen them.

The drunk, startled awake from his alcoholic daze in the gutter, lurched off in fright.

Two of Jefferson's men covering the sides of the house had already dropped to the ground with weapons positioned to retaliate, another two kicked in the doors of the houses next door and charged through to the back, scaring the hell out of the families already cowering in the corner after the blasts a few seconds earlier. The two men opposite watched. Those already in the rear jumped the back fence and stayed ready. Captain Jefferson, on the roof and still clipped to one of the Huey's cables, swung out and down, tossing a grenade in through a window. "Jarmin… all up," he commanded through his helmet microphone and, instantly, he and the other men on the roof were hoisted up about thirty feet until the blast cleared. The three then lowered themselves back to the roof, slipped down the slope to the guttering, flew over the sides and swung themselves inside the windows, guns ablaze.

★ ★ ★ ★ ★

318…

Don't panic, Maxine told herself. She and the woman clasping her baby stared at each other, too afraid to speak.

317…

Stay calm.

Even under this tension, Maxine could still calculate that 317 seconds was just over five minutes. Shaking, she was a good ten feet from the foot of the platform's exit stairway. Back further, she could see maybe a hundred commuters, and more were piling in. All these people…

316…

"BOMB!" she shouted, her lungs on fire.

For one, maybe five, of the next 315 seconds, those close by on the platform craned their necks to see what was going on, few trusting their ears. "It's a bomb," she screeched, "It's on a timer… Five minutes… Run!"

The woman with the baby was stuck solid in shock. Her adrenaline didn't seem to kick in. The baby laughed and gurgled, but this time no one thought it was cute. Maxine grabbed the mother's free arm, dragging her and the baby toward the stairs. Others were already running and pushing ahead of them, behind them, beside them. Maxine could feel the wave of raw panic surging up the platform. As they passed an alarm box she slammed her palm against the flat red button. The mob swelling behind her was shoving her forward, and wouldn't stop pushing to give her time to answer when the station attendant squawked "What's the problem?" through the speaker.

Maxine turned her head back but was propelled by the heaving crowd. She managed to cry out "Bomb" before her ankle twisted and she went over.

And under.

★ ★ ★ ★ ★

TWO minutes from Grand Central, the Metro-North train was already slowing.

At Grand Central, a courier stood waiting at the head of Track 110, unaware of the red timer ticking down inside the white box he'd lugged here. If he could've seen it, he'd know he had 280 seconds to get the hell out. It was the same for the courier at Track 45… and the one at Track 120. Grand Central was a big place.

279…

278…

# 35

SIX MORE SHOTS blasted out of the row house's ground floor windows, spraying what little glass was left after the first blast across the sidewalk. A quick radio count confirmed that none of Jefferson's men was hit. He ordered Adder, across the street, to wait five seconds and fire a flash-bang CS gas grenade in through one of the windows. Inside, and upstairs, Jefferson signalled to Smith and Fredericks to brace for the noise, slip on their gas masks and sweep the upper floor.

They found no one.

Jefferson heard the grenade whistle over the street. Even upstairs and muffled through his ear protectors, the force of the explosion stung. Downstairs the flash was solar bright, deafening, designed to stun its targets for forty indispensable seconds.

Jefferson two-stepped down the stairs first, the other two men covering him from above. Unusually, there was no coughing or moaning in response to the gas. Nothing.

A trap?

Jefferson took a turkey peek, hooking his head around the doorpost into the living room, and his left arm motioned for the other two to come down. His mask still in place, he took a long sweep before he withdrew his head back from the room. After one second, he swung back briefly as though to confirm something. "Five perps," he whispered into his helmet microphone when he was back in the corridor, his back hard against the wall. "Two immobilised, seated centre of room. Backs to me, facing toward front windows and computer laptop on coffee table. Two pistols on table… one's a Glock, the other's a Siggy P226." The Sig-Sauer was one of Jefferson's favourite hand-guns; he loved its Colt/Brown short recoil.

"Computer monitor shows a timer… numbers going down second-by-second. Last one I saw was 185. 185 seconds. Three other men… huddled below front windows… armaments at feet…. zero movement. Believe weapons to be MP5 and M16 fitted with M203s." Jefferson was impressed—these men carried some serious protection: the classic M16 was fitted with a 40mm grenade launcher mounted under the barrel, and a Heckler & Koch MP5 carbine that handled beautifully as a machine gun. Jefferson preferred it for its laser-sighted single shots. Giving cross-hair accuracy up to 600 feet, it fired the same 9mm Parabellum rounds as the Siggy, just a lot more of them and a hell of a lot faster, at 800 rpm.

"Jefferson, there's a bomb on a timer at 42nd Street subway on Manhattan. The caller suggested this might be connected. The two men at the computer? Are they functioning?"

Jefferson edged his mask back in again. The gas had pretty much cleared and the screen was already counting down to 178… no, 177.

Not even three minutes to go. They must be detonating the subway bomb from here. His bones told him it couldn't be a coincidence.

Jefferson stepped sideways and filled the doorway. "Hands away from the computer," he ordered. "Back off…! I said back off… now!"

Neither man moved a muscle.

"Back off or we shoot to kill."

One of the men shunted his arm toward the Siggy on the table. Jefferson fired, hitting him square in the back of the head and propelling him to the floor. The other man moved—maybe the first guy had nudged him as he fell, but no one was taking chances here and Fredericks, who'd followed Jefferson inside, fired a single shot into his back, smack into the curve of the "2" on his Michael Jordan basketball jersey, Chicago Bulls number 23.

One of the three men slumped under the window rolled his head, and his arm agitated toward the M16. Fredericks fired a three-burst shock round and took all three men out, though Jefferson wished he hadn't—they'd have no one to interrogate.

Surveying the dingy room for anyone else was quick work—there was scant furniture to hide behind. Fredericks headed back to search the rest of the ground floor. Smith did a dead-check on Fredericks' kills by the windows while Jefferson attended to the two computer jockies.

"Checking three perps below window… All in paradise fucking virgins," Smith reported into his microphone. He patted them all down. "No body weapons."

Jefferson removed a glove to pulse-check the necks of the other two. "Two at computer… same. Okay, men… all inside the house… NOW!" he ordered. "Full search. Fast."

As they entered from the rear and from the street, his men re-entered every room to search for anything or anyone missed by the first sortie, including booby traps. Cortes placed his detector near the phone and when it beeped an all-clear, he picked up the handset and dialled HQ so the line could be checked and all recent calls analysed, particularly any during the last twenty-four hours… who to… who from. After an automated phone drone identified these addresses in mere seconds, HQ would dispatch SWAT teams to "visit" them. If they were cell phone numbers, their locations could be triangulated from the network towers, provided they were switched on.

Jefferson's job was to work the computer. Time was not on his side. He dumped the body that was still on the sofa on top of the Chicago Bull on the floor, and was about to sit in his place to face the screen when he saw he needed a rag—the splatter of blood meant he had no accurate idea where the timer was at now, but he guessed it was down to around 85.

His eye caught the chicken-wire print of a Palestinian-type kefir hanging out of the back pocket of the topmost corpse, so he fished it out and dabbed the red off the screen as best he could.

His ear picked up something from the computer.

A hum? A voice?

Across the top of the screen, scrolling like a newsbar, were the words, "New York, New York." In the centre, the numbers were already down to 76…

If he wasn't tense enough already, what really did it for him were the inset frames that had popped up below the countdown: two side-by-side video frames, each one flashing up separate CCTV scans of subway stations, changing location every two seconds. The station names and platforms were superimposed over each picture, as well as the time, which was—he checked—current… these were live feeds direct from subway CCTV security cameras. In two sets of the paired shots so far Jefferson observed a striking coincidence: a loner in a courier uniform, agitated, glancing at his or her watch and hefting a large white box secured with black duct tape. Why the hell hadn't any of the turkeys watching monitors at MTA subway control picked up on this? What were they doing? Scratching their balls? Hell!

66…

With the rest of the team scattered elsewhere in the house, Fredericks and Smith searched the front room. Smith found a print-out of the first two pages of a typed document written by a certain Jax Mason. He scanned it quickly.

Jefferson noticed the pages were shaking as he took them from Smith. Like Smith, he only had to read the first two paragraphs.

"Penguin," he said, reporting to HQ. "You got to evacuate the entire subway…"

"But which…?"

Jefferson looked up to see Smith shaking his head and waving. He jabbed a paragraph below where his boss had stopped reading.

"Holy… this is impossible," said Jefferson taking a precious second to collect his thoughts.

He had to explain this carefully. And precisely. Millions of lives were depending on him.

"This laptop is programmed to detonate a pre-determined series of explosions only split-seconds apart, across over two hundred Manhattan subway locations. The explosions are timed to begin in, er, 52 seconds," he said, wiping his brow with the back of his hand. "They will start at stations… I'm reading here… around the island perimeter and work inwards, methodically, each ring of explosions timed to build on the passing shockwave and accelerate the force tearing through the tunnels so that when the shockwaves in the various tunnels meet at the centre of the island… here I'm guessing… maybe at 42nd Street… it will generate a massive explosion… nuclear scale, sir… which will radiate back out again with enough force to obliterate the entire island of Manhattan. Sir, if we can't stop this thing right here, in the next, ah, 50 seconds to be precise, we are totally…"

"I hear you. 50 seconds, you say?"

"49, sir."

"Can you do it…?" Penguin asked. "Pull the plug…?"

"I think there's something. Hold…" Jefferson clicked the mouse over the "New York" banner and dragged it lower down the screen. "There's a 'Stop' button. It was hidden. Could be a hoaxer… a booby-trap… could be real… no way to know unless…" Jefferson lifted his arm again to wipe his face with his sleeve.

"Do it," Penguin ordered unnecessarily.

43…

Jefferson's tongue licked dry at the corner of his mouth, and his entire body drained.

Smith closed his eyes.

Jefferson inhaled.

40…

He clicked on "Stop" and a shower of static hazed over the two inset video frames. They faded to black. The subway station camera links had been cut.

But the countdown ticked on … 37… 36...

# 36

IT WAS THE nightshift changeover at St Barts Hospital in London. The male nurse, a weasely man, locked the door of Room 603 behind him before slipping the patient's chart out of its slot at the foot of the bed. He checked the heart monitor: steady but weak. The chart graphed like this for weeks, apart from three valiant spikes that sustained themselves at close to normal levels for only a few hours each. The day-nurse, Jeni Crompton, had made a note next to the last one, "Encouraging."

"Touching," the night-nurse smirked, letting the chart drop to the floor.

There was nothing particularly remarkable about this man, or so the six other staff who'd seen him on duty would later testify to police, apart from some strange marks, tattoos maybe, on his knuckles.

"What were they?"

"No idea, sorry. Didn't want to look too close... It would've been bad manners."

"Had you seen him before?" Implicit in the question was "why'd you let him hang around if you hadn't."

"No, but with all the cutbacks, things have been a bit topsy turvy round 'ere."

THE "nurse" took the foil-covered cylinder from his pocket, ripped back the wrapping to reveal a cone-shaped dose release pellet at the end of a spike, and pressed it hard into Jax's heel, holding it there for a few seconds before pulling it away and slipping it back into his pocket.

The slightly hunched man stepped back and waited, an arched eyebrow impatient over the heart monitor. Finally, it flat-lined and he unlocked the door and strode out humming *Should auld acquaintance be forgot…*

# 37

"THE LINKS ARE down," Jefferson said, trying a workaround.

At thirty seconds to go, the "New York, New York" strip zoomed up to fill the screen completely. "I don't know what's happening here," said Jefferson, going even colder. He started to explain exactly what he was seeing when he said, "Hold it, the numbers are back… 26… 25… Shit. The 'Stop' button didn't work. Penguin, are you evacuating the stations?"

"We're linked direct into NYC's OEM," he said, referring to the City's Office of Emergency Management. "The Watch Command. They've turned all trains heading into Manhattan back, heading out in reverse. But they can't possibly evacuate the stations. Not in the time frame. The panic would be disastrous."

"So will this, sir. The flood mitigation barriers in the tunnels… can we close them, to stop the shockwaves building?" Jefferson was referring to sliding barriers that had been installed in some subway tunnels to contain flood by sealing off entire sections.

"Too late."

22…

At 17, the laptop's volume robotically spun up to maximum so the vague sound Jefferson had thought he'd been hearing for the last minute or so was blaring full blast, "… *It's up to you, New York, New York.*"

"Frank fucking Sinatra? Is this some kind of joke? Jesus…13… 12…"

He kept clicking on "Stop" but to no effect. Nothing… 10… 09…

He pulled the power cord out but, the battery was on full charge and, he checked, it was screwed in, and the heads had been mutilated to prevent quick extraction. There was no external cable going to an internet connection, so this had to be a wireless link.

Think.

Forget the battery. Disable the modem. Destroy the coordination and maybe stop the bombs. He located it on-screen under "Settings" but as he was about to do it, the song ended on its celebrated finale blast of brass. No.

07… 06…

He disabled the modem, and at 05 the countdown hung.

"It's frozen at 05… It's stopped."

"Maybe," said Penguin. "Hold your breath everyone… and pray."

# 38

THE NEWS BULLETINS worked hard to maintain a veneer of responsible calm, but the edge in the relief that night was razor sharp. Every so often the façade would crack. When the cell phone networks crashed repeatedly from overload, people suspected the worst, holding their breath, skipping their hearts, cocking their ears for... anything. Subways were closed. Roads were a mess.

The first panic surged through the city moments after 5:25 PM when word escaped from 42nd Street, but what really set off the storm was when the NYPD was ordered to evacuate every one of Manhattan's 468 subway and train stations. According to the two-page note in Jefferson's hand, there were 230 bombs, almost one every two stations, though pivotal stations such as 42nd Street and Grand Central had multiples. The countdown stopped without event, but no one in authority was taking chances. And even if there'd been a fine-balanced choice before, there was none once Captain Jefferson radioed in the name he'd found in one of the dead terrorist's wallets: Karim Ahmed, a man who'd notoriously been once charged with financing terrorists.

On current intelligence, there was no way of knowing if these 230 unknown couriers were suicide bombers programmed to explode their devices on-site if the timers failed. Jefferson heard the orders going out: evacuate subways; track down and secure all bombs; disable and arrest all couriers with white boxes on platforms. If necessary… take them out.

"PLEASE stay calm…"

Calm? Who were these people kidding?

All over the island, the undergrounds hosed out gushes of panicked commuters and subway employees. The couriers, shocked by station announcements that branded them, instructing them to put down their parcels and to lie on the ground with their hands behind their heads, couldn't move, and most were stuck to their spots cowering. Mistaking the reaction, emboldened commuters in several stations pinned a few couriers down, bumping the boxes to the ground and ripping them open, though wishing they hadn't. "Bomb!"

Hundreds of limbs cracked as the rush flung people beneath flailing feet or onto tracks—fortunately OEM had cut the power by then to the third rails.

The whole city was a giant whose stomach clenched in fear. Millions of breaths held in, but there were no blasts.

OEM had coordinated with Homeland Security to initiate emergency response procedures simultaneously with Jefferson's team lifting off for Strawberry Mansion. And when he radioed in the news about video feeds from scattered subway stations, those of New York's 35,000 police officers who were on duty, together with already alerted OEM and Federal Emergency Management Agency teams, were swiftly dispatched around the island. FEMA wasn't going to have any Hurricane Katrina criticisms about this operation, no way. It didn't take the authorities fifteen minutes to get each one of the couriers into temporary custody; this is what these guys were trained to do. Almost as quickly, 229 identical stories got radioed in, stories Emergency HQ backed up with the fifteen courier firms' own records.

CITIES around the nation shook with false alarms and rumours. The country teetered on hysteria.

Bobby Foster was at a campaign barbecue in Alabama when he was told the news on camera, and he dropped his mouth and his plate.

The plate was plastic admittedly, but his oh-fuck face would be memorialised in the press and on TV and no amount of wheedling explanations—"I was bumped," for example—could get the clip taken off the David Letterman Late Show's "Top Ten Stupidest Moments of the Year". Niki Abbott would have given anything to have been there. Almost.

HANK Clemens was in Charleston, giving an award for the best shag, the uniquely named state dance of the two Carolinas. He slowly put the ribbon down, wiped the corners of his mouth and, after taking a moment's breath, looked deep into the intruding TV camera's lens. "The men and women in our security and emergency response agencies know how to handle this threat." They were comforting though sombre words. "I know a little about these things myself," he said, "and I can assure you we are in good hands. Please… please, follow their directions until order is restored and then just go about your business. If we change… our routines… our activities… ourselves… 'they' will win… and we must not let that happen."

Gregory, who was there with him, was agog. Hank's quiet modesty. His confidence. His calm. Hank hadn't blown this. He wasn't masterful, he wasn't deep, but he was reassuring and showed a previously concealed hint of spine and resilience. It was lucky no one noticed, but a smile cracked open on Gregory's face. Hank had a chance at winning.

ISABEL Diaz was at a town hall meeting in Harlem when one of the TV reporters cleared by security barged onto the stage, stuck his microphone at her and demanded her reaction. The image that viewers would hang onto was her serene poise.

It was almost as if Isabel had prepared for this moment… that she knew it was coming.

At first it was unnerving—"how could anyone be so composed?"—but as the seconds dragged on, her unruffled tranquillity was soothing to those watching: how evenly she listened, how she asked the reporter a couple of sensible clarifying questions (which he had no answer to), and how she finished with, "My heart goes out to anyone who has been injured and their loved ones. My prayers…" She bowed her head for a moment and looked up again into the camera. "Please… those of you watching, please join me… and all of us here in Harlem… in a moment of silent prayer." The camera panned the town hall as everyone stood and bowed their heads with her and then, for fifteen long seconds, all that could be heard was an occasional shuffle of feet or a suppressed cough.

Finally, Isabel looked up and her eyes were grim, "Our world has hardened, but we must not. However, we must and we will defend our country, our way of life … and our families. I have confidence that our President, and our next president, will lead us in doing just that."

She paused for a moment, looked to the side and nodded, then faced the camera and said, "All of us who aren't in the front line dealing with the emergency, please stay calm. Do what police or other emergency officials advise you." She coughed into her fist and continued, "Perhaps the best thing for all of us here on Manhattan would be just to walk quietly on home and give our families and neighbours a hug. If you're sitting in a car in a traffic jam, check with the police, park your car and walk home… come back for it tomorrow. Tonight is a remarkable night. A catastrophe has been averted because we were prepared… Let us all sing songs of peace and thanks in our streets. If you can't get home, buy a candle and go to

Central Park, to any park, and sing for peace and thanks there. I have every confidence this will be under control quickly. May God bless America."

THE call for calm that the networks mostly kept replaying that night was Isabel's, not the official candidates' nor even President Joe Biden's, his own beamed from Air Force One, since he was mid-flight on his way back from a G20 meeting in Bonn when it happened.

Foster, who was until then poised as the clear winner would spend the next three weeks clambering back from his slapstick debacle.

Hank's performance would largely absolve his involvement in the safety code violations causing the Railcar nightclub fire and more, turn him into a mildly heroic figure.

And Isabel? Once again, she demonstrated her calibre; that she stood high above the others, with the mettle and the stature—though not the legal status—to lead the nation.

DESPITE Isabel's soothing message, by 10:30 PM Manhattan's 1.7 million residents, and the million commuters still stuck there were sagging. Not even the news that President Biden was diverting his flight to New York did much to lift spirits.

Around countless kitchen tables, hands were gratefully clasped. Bars and cafés were full, but hushed. Houses of worship across the nation, of all faiths, were open and overflowed. And parks and streets and neighbourhoods were alive with voices and restrained singing.

Midnight drew closer. A glittering sea of candles being waved aloft flickered across the city. Hundreds of thousands of citizens spilled out of their apartment buildings and out of Central Park and filled the grid, washing slowly down Broadway, Sixth Avenue, Park Avenue, as though sucked, toward the Twin Towers memorial. Police helicopters shone their spotlight beams over the crowds, not in search but respect. Arms locked in arms.

Manhattan's heart was beating back at the dark, refusing to die.

Behind all this, emergency services were tallying the damage and the casualties. Remarkably, despite the mass panic, and the hundreds of commuters who had been admitted to hospitals suffering bruises, cuts, shock and, in numerous cases, fractured ribs or limbs, there had still been only four fatalities directly attributable to the panic, apart from the five Muslim men in Strawberry Mansion and six seniors who suffered heart attacks after hearing the news.

One of the direct fatalities had been crushed to death at the 42nd Street subway station. The brave Maxine Powers.

★ ★ ★ ★ ★

HANK phoned Isabel, before the press got hold of it, to let her know that Karim Ahmed was one of the dead terrorists. He was surprised that she already knew, but he had bigger things to worry about, so he rang off.

"Ahmed got his just desserts," Ed continued, "for what he did to you alone." But what caught Ed a little short was that for the first time, Isabel agreed with him about Karim. No more defending him, nor dredging up spurious excuses for his behaviour.

Ed rubbed the stubble on his cheek, wondering what made her change her mind.

# 39

NAKED, DIANA TWISTED around and preened in front of her mirror. Her get-up as a dishevelled Philly drunk in the gutter had been good, but this was better. Squinting for one last careful inspection, she was satisfied every scrape of body paint was gone; it had been harder to remove than she'd expected. Her new sidekick, Daniel, had done too good a job applying it in the hard-to-get-to places, but then he seemed to be enjoying it.

"Perfectly executed," Isis had said. Like Jax had been, finally, though Diana didn't want to remind herself about that. She crooked her freshly shaved and moisturised leg over the lip of the bathtub and as she started to repaint her toenails, she mentally walked back through the operation:

*Tuesday night, 2100 hours*: Check equipment. Complete attire and make-up.
*Wednesday, 0100 hours*: Diana and Daniel drop in Philadelphia, two blocks north of suspect row house.
*0115*: Fix small (but loud) explosive canister under burnt-out abandoned car one block north, to be activated remotely later.

*0130*: Arrive at suspect house. (Even for the vagrant she had role-played, this was a filthy hovel; she shuddered just thinking about it and smudged a toenail.)
*0131*: Enter and check all rooms—Daniel upstairs, Diana downstairs. Find four men asleep in bedrooms and on sofas. Surprise one man hunched over on toilet, and pop him with a jab from a *Clip'n'Drip* pack. Pop the remaining men. Pocket all the used *Clip'n'Drip* packs. Forced sleep for all five men for eight hours straight. Dress all five of them. Another spasm of disgust… they were living like filthy pigs… and the guy squatting on the john… ugh! Carry them to the living room. (Daniel was useful.)
*0150*: Seat men according to plan: Karim Ahmed plus one at coffee table, three others under window. Plug laptop into wall socket and power up. Check wireless broadband link in full operation. Check and open links to subway video cameras. Check link to detonators. Remove weapons from carryalls and check ammunition magazines half-loaded. Place self-destructing bullet-launchers on inside of window casement facing street. Check loaded. Check remote sensor is operative.
*0230*: Sit tight. No lights. No TV. Sleep in turns.
*0930*: Bodies stir on schedule within five minutes of each other. Timing test: perfect. Top up tranquiliser doses. Use same dosage again, enough to dope up for eight more hours and be undetectable by the time the bodies are checked. Sleep in turns.
*1650*: Dwayne confirms all 230 packages dispatched.
*1705*: Prepare for exit. Set all weapons at allocated positions next to bodies. Plant "Shockwave" two-pager half under floor rug. Extract gin bottle and collapsed white stick out of microfibre bags. Roll up and shove empty bags down front of coveralls. Daniel to slip on

mirrored wraparounds and extend white stick. Diana to carry gin bottle. Synchronise computer and watches. Set computer's timer for 17:25. Check countdown sequence commences correctly. Check New York banner (with background music) to open up on laptop screen. (Nice touch.) Daniel to check street for passersby from upstairs window and get down fast.

*1707*: On signal, trigger remote to detonate explosive under abandoned car one block north. Check street again for witnesses—everyone is either running toward explosion or rushing into homes and slamming doors. Cover surgical gloves with woollen mittens.

*1708*: Exit building. Daniel taps stick as he walks away. Diana, the drunk, remains on street nearby. Work still to do. Slumps in gutter.

Perfect. She brushed a dab of blue on her toenail. Diana had a good life… And now, Isis was trusting her to set up the "what if the unthinkable really does happen?" scenario.

This secretive band was not the quitting kind and Diana savoured their next moves, in awe at Isis's fastidious precautions. The terrorist attack on the subway, specifically designed to fail in the last few seconds, was already working magnificently in stampeding the public to go back to voting "1" for security, and thus for Hank. But as Isis warned, stampedes can peter out as quickly as they start, and they can shift direction. She dwelt for a moment on the girl who died, as she brushed the final coat of lacquer over her toenails. Every war has collateral damage, she justified, and she slipped the nailbrush back into the bottle and screwed it tight.

Isis called. Diana had more crucial work to do and it was thousands of miles away.

# 40

THE NEXT DAY, President Biden's helicopter Marine One hovered over the Twin Towers memorial where people had stayed in vigil all night. It was a subdued crowd. After police cleared a space in the midst of the throng, the Sikorsky VH-3D Sea King dropped the President down to address them, and the nation.

Head bowed over heavy shoulders, President Biden waited till the clock struck noon before he stepped up to the microphone. He raised his head and cast his eyes in a wide curve across the crowd. "Despite what they do, we're still here," he said to heartfelt but restrained applause. "We will *always* be here, no matter how hard they try." The applause grew. "Once again, a President comes to this city at a tough time. But this is a tough city... and we are a tough nation. We will never cower before terror, nor be defeated by it." The applause was tumultuous. "And last night we were not..."

He praised the city's courage and preparedness, and thanked the emergency and security agencies in New York and Pennsylvania, and continued. "What we unearthed," he said, swallowing audibly, "was the unspeakable attempting the unthinkable," and, his hand unsteady, he sent a shiver through the crowd even though they were already aware of the horror that might have been.

What he didn't say was that despite all the last few years' efforts to upgrade security, including stationing federal and city employees at entrances to New York's bridges, tunnels, subways, airports, ports and major monuments, and equipping them with body scanners and radiation and explosive detection devices, these five dead terrorists were armed with none of the nuclear, biological or chemical weapons the pricey high-tech equipment was designed to detect. The C-4 they used was a new sniffer-proof variety that had only been available to the military.

"The evil plan of these men," continued the President, "was to wreak true mass destruction on this, the world's greatest city, by using conventional weapons but in a most unconventional way… And yet, what stopped them was conventional law enforcement."

Hardly.

★ ★ ★ ★ ★

TOPPING off Hank's brief but impressive performance that night, a susceptible public and media had finally started hailing him as a leader, and more amazingly, a hero. At last, Hank could crow about something important, and over the next few days it staggered even Isabel to hear him so coherent and passionate—her moments of toe-curling embarrassment were no more.

Hank's time had come.

The good guys were back on track.

Within a week, with only two more to Election Day, Hank's support was ratcheting up. Gregory had withdrawn his resignation on the night of the attack on the subway—"In the national interest," he claimed modestly—and was back in full flair directing the reinvigorated Hank & Perry Show. The tracking polls showed them bumping up to a more pleasing 48 percent. Bobby Foster had been dragged down, first as far as the 30s but he had started bouncing back and was now at 41. The "dish-drop drag" as Don Thomas had called it, was wearing off.

The election outcome was going to be close—very close—so Gregory's new campaign ads took on a vivid blush. He had his most aggressive fifteen-second spots playing six times a night in peak time, five nights running, on every network. One started with a quiet female voice over a blank screen with just a nudge of children squabbling in the background:

*Trial lawyers sure know how to side with a rapist or a murderer… but they never make the tough calls that could've protected the victims… us. America needs Hank Clemens, a man we can trust… with the experience to make those decisions…*

The clip ended abruptly with the crashing sound—but no image—of a breaking plate. The focus groups loved it. The lawyers hated it. The American Bar Association, no bunch of wimps, came out blubbering it was vilification, but apart from them few others cared.

The ad was working beautifully for Hank. And it was only one of four.

Don Thomas retaliated for Foster but made a titanic miscalculation. In truth, his ads were hardly more negative than Gregory's but the voting tide was rushing so fast ahead of him he couldn't seem to catch up. His most poisonous stole its venom from Hillary Clinton's "It's 3 AM and your children are asleep and the phone is ringing" anti-Obama ad during their 2007 primaries. Don's opened with a shaky nail-bitten index finger hovering over the nuclear button. A voice, genteel and plummy like Hank's, said "*Fire*" but what flashed up on screen was a newscast video of the Boston nightclub blaze. This time, the public rage was savage and Don had to pull the ad within hours.

"SO now I'm the desperate one," Foster fumed as he slammed down the newspaper. "Clemens attacks me and that's fine, yet I can't even whisper he's a fucking arsonist without it creating a stink. Go figure!"

SNAP!

"And Don, get that fucking Niki Abbott out of here. She gets no more, ah, access. None."

Niki had already enjoyed plenty of access to Foster. More than Don knew.

IT was getting down to the wire. Just as the polls had swung violently in Hank's favour a week ago, Gregory knew they could easily swing back, especially if the "old Hank" revealed himself. There was no way he, or Hank, or Bill were going to let up the pressure on their most valuable asset, Isabel. No way could they countenance anything short of stapling her to Hank's right hand during the final stretch.

"If I'm stuck here, courtesy of you," said Gregory in mock complaint, "you're going to stay here too. This could be..."

Isabel placed her finger over his mouth. She wouldn't be quitting, not after what she'd gone through to get to this point. This wasn't about her; it never had been. It was about doing what was right; about winning the best government for the nation.

And with the right backup, even Hank Clemens would do fine.

She smiled at Gregory like a cat that had just finished off a careless sparrow.

# 41

IT WAS FRIDAY before Election Tuesday. The weekend pundits were firming up their predictions for Saturday's editions. The near-miss subway attack had blown Don Thomas' strategy way off course and Hank had strong odds in his favour. Don had to manufacture an alternative scare campaign. It was a hackneyed classic, sure, but what else did he have? In it, Hank was portrayed as a lightweight, a stooge at the beck and call of sinister faceless men, all Republicans and thus evil, white, rich and old.

He didn't know how close he was.

Again, the public reaction was not what Don had expected. Was he losing his touch? What came back to campaign HQ from the focus groups was… Hank seems so, you know, nice, chirpy, and he does know about national security… and so what if he is a stooge, so long as he's Isabel's stooge, and she's rich, sure, but she's not evil, white or old. We like *her*, so…

With Isabel's in-your-face, day-in-day-out backing, Hank's mediocrity had strangely become an attribute and perversely Don's ad would only give it air.

Don's heaviest campaign burden had again become "that woman," a term he had winced at in an earlier frustrating era.

But *this* woman had clout with the electorate, not just sway in the corridors and closets of power.

Even though she wasn't officially running, Isabel Diaz was Foster's real opposition.

"This is a fucking phantom election," Don swore to Foster over the phone. "We're fighting Clemens, but everyone's convinced that a vote for him's a vote for Diaz. She's not even on the voting paper. How do we fight that?"

"You're asking me?" said Foster.

DON knew they couldn't attack Isabel—she was America's sweetheart, even more so after an absurd legal technicality had shouldered her to the sidelines. What the Foster campaign did now had to be directed squarely at Hank and yet, the cynical wine-soaked Washington media were already sloshing around and toasting the guy.

But Don had faith. He'd only lost one campaign in his long career and this wasn't going to be another. In his game, you could lose one presidential campaign and survive, but not two. He'd honed his instincts with experience and doggedness. His famous stoop developed over decades poring 24/7 over newspapers, newsletters, magazines, TV and web pages, never sleeping till every angle was covered, analysed and dealt with. A veteran of more campaigns at both federal and state level than almost anyone in the party, Don Thomas knew how to recognise a flake, and Hank was a flake.

He had to expose him… he just didn't know how, yet. And time was no friend.

Don cloistered himself in Democrat campaign headquarters' media room with a six-pack of Bud, two 25s of Marlboro Red and a small package from FedEx he'd just flown in—a DVD, according to the label his assistant saw before he snatched it from her hand and double-locked the door behind him. The tittle-tattle within the team was that Don had lost it; he'd given up on winning and had imported some porn, some beers and some smokes and was going to blow the campaign.

Don ignored the stares and elbow nudges as he flicked one switch to turn the glass partition opaque and another to cut the lights. He twisted his first Bud long-neck open and took a swig. The first Marlboro flew to his mouth, as if it were guiding his hand there, and he let it droop waiting for a thought to emerge.

It didn't. So he inserted the DVD and hit Play. He ran it for a second before skimming ahead on fast-forward. After a while, he paused it and lit his cigarette. He took several long drags as an idea staggered its way out, but he rejected it. He pressed play briefly then fast-forwarded again. He repeated this cycle ten or fifteen times. What was he looking for? He still had no clue. For the first twenty minutes it was an exercise in desperate hope, no more than a frustrating time-filler and an excuse to get through three cigarettes and two beers. By the third beer, his concentration was intense and he was leaning so close into the screen he was almost in it, almost tongue-close to the monitor. What gripped his attention was the brow that Hank Clemens kept digging into his face, filling it with soothing gravitas. At Don's insistence, this DVD had been loaded up with every TV interview Hank Clemens had given over the last rotten godforsaken week. The "brow" started with *Meet the Press* and, as the week's clips progressed from there, Hank's forehead developed more and more of these brows and the furrows notched in deeper and deeper. He was no Mr Country Club, not any more.

Hank was Mr Responsibility. Mr Trust Me.

Mr Fake.

Don banged down his Bud with such force that the geyser of beer it shot up spilled over the table. He drew back on his smoke. Don's revelation was about imagery, not Hank's actual words; especially since Don had intentionally kept the sound on mute the first and second times around. It was in the way Hank said whatever crap he'd been schooled to say. It was like the guy had just learned up the whole series of "How to Appear Presidential in Ten Easy Lessons," a course the GOP must have designed only after George W. Bush left office.

Why hadn't Don picked up on this before? It was so damned obvious.

Don lit up another cigarette unaware he still had one in his mouth. In campaigning, he reminded himself, there was nothing wrong or immoral about phony sincerity. Politics was built on it. What was wrong was getting caught.

No one had noticed it because they didn't want to or, like Don, they weren't looking hard enough. Don fumed at how the subway attack had played into Republican hands. The media, the public—everyone—had gone soft on Hank, respectful, toning down their previously harsh critiques… this wasn't the time to be petty… we need to elevate the debate… let's not sink into the gutter… or break a plate.

Don loathed that plate. If the election weren't being played on damn Queensberry Rules over the last two weeks, Hank Clemens would have been knocked onto the mat and counted out. It was time to rip off the gloves and go for the kill.

Fuelled by beer, cigarettes and rage, Don hunkered down alone for two hours lifting two- or three-second grabs from the DVD and, with the editing machine, he stuck together a quick-and-dirty ad with Hank himself doing Don's dirty work, all thirty beautiful seconds of it. Pure vote-catching magic.

"*So how will you deal with another terror attack, Mr Clemens?*"

The initial furrow of the brow, "*I was at Homeland Security as you know…*" The deeper crease, "*…and you saw what we… er, they… did this time.*" Crease unwinds into smarmy smile, "*I think the people can trust me on this one, Tim…*" Earnest puppy-dog brown eyes to camera, head tilting just a tad to flop his light brown fringe down to soften the image. Cut.

And so it was also with Julia, and Phil, and Barbara, and Larry, and... Whether these six, no seven, repeat episodes were conscious ham-acting by Hank or not, Don couldn't care. Jammed up one after the other—BAM! BAM! BAM!—they looked like it. The gestures, even the words, were pretty much identical, even down to the fireside golly-gosh ums and ers.

Don leant back with his hands clasped behind his head and took a deep, long drag of his sixteenth Marlboro—but who was counting? It was sweet. Very sweet. He had sniffed out the rancid whiff of the disingenuous Republican prick and he was going to dig right in, yank him out and pump the fucker dry for all he was worth.

Through the smoke cloud of three more cigarettes, the punchline for Don's makeshift ad materialised, "*So... WE'RE gonna trust HIM to do WHAT?*" It would be spoken over an old sepia snapshot of a young Hank bowing deep on a schoolboy stage, arms spread, soaking in his parents' uncritical applause. With a good ol' fratboy like Clemens, Don's media hounds would be able to scavenge a shot like that from somewhere, for sure.

And they did.

The ad got to air Saturday night and Don had it running all Sunday and all Monday. No voter registered in any of the swing states could have missed it unless they were on vacation and lodging their postal votes from New Zealand.

"HANK, this Foster ad is despicable," said Gregory, crushing his empty Diet Coke can for emphasis. It was still an hour before Don's new ad would first hit the airwaves—a "friend" at CBS, still trying to suck up after the *Close-up* debacle, had slipped Gregory a soft copy by email and he'd forwarded it to Hank.

"Why?" Hank asked, doe-eyed with naïveté. "It's what I believe... It's why we're winning."

"You are kidding, right?"

He wasn't.

To retaliate, Gregory upped the frequency of his negative Foster ads, turning the volume on the dish drops way up. He also revived an early one: a clip showing Isabel and Hank in serious discussion with the newly added caption, "*What Isabel Diaz likes about Hank Clemens is that he listens…*" If Don's ad got any grip, this one—Gregory was certain—would loosen it. If you couldn't trust Hank, don't worry; Isabel was behind him.

By Monday morning, Gregory felt sick. *The Times*' editorial stank and even the generally pro-Republican *Wall Street Journal* questioned his strategy. "Buy one Hank… get one free Isabel?" it asked, rejecting the notion.

The polls were no better either.

Foster was back. By a nose.

# 42

HANK'S ELECTION NIGHT concession speech was initially seen as respectable, mostly because it was short:

> *Just a moment ago, I spoke with Robert Foster and congratulated him on becoming the next president of the United States… What remains of partisan rancour must be put aside, and may God bless his stewardship of this country… I am grateful to all those who supported me and supported the cause for which we have fought… I know that many of my supporters are disappointed. I am too. But our disappointment must be overcome by our love of country…*

It was the usual billowy fluff that a loser would plump up to express his grace in defeat and to charm his followers into accepting that their months of unpaid toil weren't wasted. Yet, Hank's words failed both objectives and, worse, twisted themselves into the ultimate sword of humiliation, skewering any scraps of dignity his campaign workers and supporters had clung to. As headlined the following day, even in defeat Hank was a phony.

Bobby Foster had been ensconced in his hotel suite putting the final touches on his victory speech and his Big Entrance but, in case he needed to respond to something, he kept one eye and one ear on Hank's teary TV act. Hank wasn't long into it when Bobby's other eye was drawn to Don Thomas who he caught over in the corner mumbling. Mumbling was something Don, a stickler for the spoken word, never did. On closer inspection, Bobby thought he saw Don's lips flapping perfectly in sync with Hank's.

"How are you doing that?" Bobby asked.

Don knew Hank's words especially well since he'd written most of them. Word-for-word, Clemens was reciting Al Gore's concession speech from the 2000 election. Don would never forget those words… or the five seesaw weeks of legal wrangling that had hollowed him out and drooped his stoop by a whole other inch.

As Bobby and his swollen entourage swished out of the suite, Don stayed behind to phone Gregory on his cell; Don could see his peer's bald head on TV with Clemens—over to the side, of course—and he watched as he took the call. "What the hell was that?" snapped Don.

Gregory knew Don's voice instantly and, wisely, stepped off camera to speak. He too had recognised Gore's words. "So, Don," he said, wiping his brow, "WE trusted HIM to do WHAT? Your ad. That was the, ah, inconvenient truth, wasn't it?"

Don accepted this as the highest of praise from one professional to another; Gregory's own concession speech.

# 43

JUBILANT, FOSTER GRACED the lectern with eight flashes of gleaming teeth behind him: his wife and two children and his running mate, Mitch Taylor and his family. The Democrat crowd was in ecstasy: banners waving, chants of "Fos-ter… Fos-ter," torrents of confetti, balloons, pumping music, red roses tossed into the air…

From up on the stage, it looked great. It felt great. It was great.

Bobby embraced his wife, Marilyn.

Another cheer.

He managed one "Good evening, my fellow Americans" without interruption. For several heady minutes the cheering wouldn't let up. The flock of the faithful were in heaven, apart from the fifty people scattered among them who weren't. To slip past security all they'd had to do was smile, look neat—Democrat neat, not Republican neat—wear "Vote 1 Foster" buttons and carry their folded placards and their bouquets of red roses and plastic buckets full of petals through the airport-style metal detector at the entrance.

The group reached the centre of the vast venue and spread out. The network TV cameras panning the euphoria zoomed in on the red buds they were tossing into the air and the handfuls of rose petals they scattered over the floor. Simultaneously, the scene was beamed up onto the big screens hugging the walls.

At first Bobby lapped it up as yet another rapturous moment and he held the pause, goading the excitement even higher. The ex-trial lawyer knew how to play an audience. If you could do juries, he reminded himself, adoring crowds were a piece of cake.

But when the first unfolded placard shot into the air from the heart of the crowd, and then another, and another, Bobby's night of glory began its plunge: "*Bouquets for Isabel... Wreaths for Bobby.*"

"*Usurper.*"

And "*Wail to the Thief.*"

Eight different slogans, short and shrill. All with "ImposterFoster.com" slashed in red across the top corner. Ten stunned national TV seconds was how long the placards stayed up before the scuffles wrestled them to the floor amongst the torn roses. For the networks, ten seconds was ample.

Upstairs in the suite, Don was slumped forward more than usual. He was open-mouthed, gaping along with the thirty or forty million others also witnessing this abomination. He lifted his beer to his lips but as the infiltrators began their synchronised chants he set it down again without a sip.

"*Im-pos-ter Fos-ter.*"

"*Bel...Bel...Isa-bel.*"

The president-elect scanned the crowd. Where were the damn marshals? Who was behind this? Fuck. And fuck her. He read on, barely in control of himself, and his voice was shaky.

The uproar and scuffles continued.

Three pages into his speech, he paused and pasted a plastic smile on his face.

Don saw it coming. He felt it. His stooped frame shuddered from the base of his curved spine up.

No. Don't.

Don's hand moved to his heart and he felt the calm cool

of the pack of Marlboros in his shirt pocket. Almost without thinking, his fingers lifted the red and white box out.

The TV camera pulled in on Bobby for a close-up. Don saw the familiar lawyer's venom flare from his boss's eyes as he hesitated over the next page.

Don't.

Don didn't move. He caged in his breath and though he had no religious bone in his bent body, he prayed that Bobby wouldn't do it…

Bobby ripped the next page right out of his speech, crushed it in his hand and hurled it to the floor, staring at it as if it were vermin.

Don's fist slammed into the table, crushing his pack of smokes. "Fuck!"

Foster looked up and raised a hand in silence but this was no longer an audience the ex-lawyer knew how to play. It was out of control and his one chance of calming the mob was gone.

Don shrieked again, this time knocking his Bud over the coffee table, beer slopping all over his copy of the words Bobby's heel had trampled.

"Fuck!" he yelled again, not caring who'd hear. He struggled to find a Marlboro that was still vaguely smokable and hung it off his lip.

Don was seething. Despite the odds, he had personally dragged this ungrateful bastard over the line and instead of just grabbing the flag that Don had handed him and waving it aloft in their carefully thought-out victory move, Bobby fucking Foster had over-reacted and pissed into the wind and was going to get it back all over his face.

Don lit the cigarette and sucked as though this was his only way to get air. The smoke seared into his eyes, sending his tear ducts crazy. At least, he told himself, it was the smoke that caused it.

★ ★ ★ ★ ★

TWENTY-FOUR hours before Election Day, with Don Thomas' last-minute ad campaign turning the fetid tide, he again grabbed a longneck of beer and a package and, hunched over, ushered Foster back inside the candidate's hotel suite, closing the door behind them.

"What?" snapped Bobby.

"I've been digging around," said Don and he handed his boss the package.

The ex-lawyer noted the red ribbon. He pulled on the bow and, with his law background, was able to skim through the hefty folios of expert opinions very quickly. Bobby regarded himself as good a constitutional lawyer as anybody so, at first, the analysis Don handed him had stunned him. Three separate experts (from Yale, Harvard and Chicago) had opined, in writing, that the House of Representatives could virtually appoint anyone they liked as Speaker. The person didn't even have to be an elected representative nor even, more amazingly, a citizen.

"This says," Bobby noted with subdued deliberation, "that the House can elect anyone Speaker. Even a British monarch or an Afghani warlord. Or, for Christ's sake, Britney fucking Spears."

"Hell, no," said Don, a smirk spilling over his pudgy face, "it's got to be someone real."

Foster shot him an icy stare. "All the same, every single Speaker since Congress first sat in...," he looked down at the sheets for confirmation, "in 1789 has been a Member of the House." And as both men knew, a Member had to be a citizen of at least seven years' standing.

Don explained that though his proposal—okay, Spencer's, but he wasn't about to jog memories—had not one single precedent in American history, it was still 100 percent legal. "Sure, we've got over two centuries of precedent against us. But all that is merely what's *happened*; convention. It's not the law."

Slowly Foster nodded, and his eyes zigzagged down the

pages, carefully analysing the words of the Constitution and the commentary Don had put before him.

Don's nostrils flared as he inhaled the cool clean air. He needed a cigarette. The longer Foster took, the more he could feel the excitement brimming. He was going to say yes. This was going to be one of Don's finest moments; not only would his candidate triumph tomorrow night with the unofficial declaration of the polls, but he'd be forever marked as one of the few leaders truly able to unite a divided country.

He'd already crafted a spellbinding three paragraphs for Bobby to weave into his victory speech and he passed them to the candidate.

The writing was stirring—up there with his best—though, if truth be told, it was clichéd: that Bobby intended to be a president for all Americans especially in these troubled times; that sores needed healing; that Isabel had much to give the nation; that it was a tragedy she'd been barred from the opportunity of serving, but that Bobby had personally blazed a new track for her; and that, if she were willing, he would prevail on the House to propose her as its Speaker immediately.

BUT Don's plan went badly wrong… election night went badly wrong… Despite their preparations, no one in the Foster camp had predicted the turmoil that erupted on the celebration floor.

In the midst of his victory speech, before hundreds of supporters and millions watching TV, when Foster got to the page surging with Don's vibrant prose about Isabel and the Speaker's role, instead of galvanising the historic moment and pulling the rug from under the protesters, the combative trial lawyer still in Bobby had ripped out the sheet, screwed it up and hurled it onto the floor, crushing it under his foot.

No way was Bobby going to elevate that fucking witch now, he decided, not with those ImposterFoster fucks not more than fifty feet away wreaking havoc on his hard-won victory. This was orchestrated, he fumed as his eyes panned across the floor for clues.

Foster didn't know it, but Isis's plan had just reached its spectacular destabilising climax.

Yet those who had engineered the disruption had no idea their actions were self-defeating; that because of Foster's hot-headed reaction they had foiled Isabel's elevation as Speaker, something at that stage they didn't know was even a possibility.

More so than Foster's, their own victory that night was pyrrhic.

# 44

SEVEN LONG TRANSITION weeks later, Don hadn't stopped. "We can't keep doing nothing. It's Christmas. This could turn into an avalanche…"

"Fuck them," Bobby spluttered. "I'm President-Elect fair and square… no missing votes, no hanging chads, no Supreme Court… a good, solid, honest-to-goodness majority..."

"…by a mere 9 electoral college votes…"

"Excuse me?" said Bobby, his eyebrows arched. "Nine over's not good enough for you? Fucking *one* was good enough for Bush in 2000. Even JFK only got 34 over. Don, I'm sick of this 'ImposterFoster' bullshit… I'm sick of this Transition Office limbo. I've nominated my Cabinet… I've got 120 policy task forces running. I want to get on with the job I was elected to do."

Don turned his head to the window to hide his bitterness. Outside the Presidential Transition Office, two miles down Pennsylvania Avenue from the White House, a bunch of kids were making snowmen. They were probably midget Secret Service agents, he decided, though the thought did nothing to lighten his mood.

Inside the PTO, Don grit his teeth and turned back to see his boss stepping over to the bureau, again. For the fourth time in the last hour Bobby picked up the bottle of bourbon. He held it for a moment as if reading the label for inspiration, then topped up his chunky tumbler. He plopped in a couple of shrunken cubes from the melting bucket of ice and lifted the glass up to his tired, watery eyes. For thirty seconds, or so it seemed to Don, Foster's eyes searched into the gold liquid as though it were a crystal ball. He again drew the glass to his lips. Foster's drinking was out of control.

"That slimy Prentice's been slithering round here, hasn't he?" Foster slurred, his eyes struggling to keep focus and avoiding Don's pointed gaze. "He put you up to this?"

★ ★ ★ ★ ★

EVEN ignoring the protocols of Christmas goodwill, the antagonism toward Foster had not abated. According to Don, now White House Chief-of-Staff-to-be, the anti-Foster movement was accelerating.

The new Congress was due to commence its first short January session in a few days and, given the way the congressional elections had swung, it would be Democrat Majority House leader David Prescott who'd get Speaker. If Don could get Foster to agree, they'd summon Prescott back a few days early from skiing in Aspen and lay it on him. Prescott had been a congressman for sixteen years, and only last year was elevated to Democrat House leader. He'd want to be Speaker and there was no way he'd surrender that role, let alone to a Republican, but maybe a spot as, say, an ambassador would do it. They'd do whatever it took, as far as Don was concerned.

"Send *Prescott* to Turkey?" boiled Foster. "That's like sending sand to the Saudis."

"I don't care," said Don, hovering at the edge of disrespect before jumping over it. "Mr President, if you want to avoid trouble on Inauguration Day," only three weeks away, "if Prescott wants Ambassador to fucking Jupiter, you'll give him keys to the rocket."

"Maybe China, then."

# 45

FOR LITTLE DAVEY, Isabel's being scratched from the campaign and Hank's losing it were not big deals. Sure, with enough surly faces around to sour a month's worth of breakfast milk, he knew Isabel and Ed were sore but even so, this last week had been the boy's best lead up to Christmas ever. For the whole seven days, Isabel had completely pulled out of all her other obligations. George had come back from California. Ed was there for most of it, though Davey didn't much care if his dad had to be at work provided George or Isabel were around to play.

And play George did, though he suffered for it. Stepping back on the lawn to toss Davey a ball, he slipped on a patch of damp grass, threw out a hand to absorb the fall and strained his wrist.

AT Don Thomas' urging, it was Spencer Prentice who got to be Foster's emissary to sweet-talk Isabel. What Spencer didn't know was that the new Speaker's first task of gavelling open the year's first two-week sittings would come just two days before Davey's ninth birthday.

Isabel had promised the boy an extra treat, even crossing her heart over it, and Davey was still skipping around the house at the prospect of spending time with her and Ed for a few days' fun in the snow. She'd been pining for some refuge up in the mountains, far from the media, the pundits and the party. A few days there with her family would be perfect.

Until a week ago, her time hadn't been her own for almost two years. Once the campaign was officially lost, she'd been desperately looking forward to taking Davey and Ed away for a week of total sanctuary up in her hideaway shack in the Green Mountains in Vermont. But those plans had to be delayed by the drudge of mandatory party post-mortems, and the exhausting whirl of soirées and breakfasts all around the country. There was nothing to celebrate, but she knew her supporters had to be thanked, especially for sticking with Hank.

So Christmas was welcome, a time when she could legitimately say no to anything official. The shack was put on hold till early January. Christmas would be in Manhattan.

★ ★ ★ ★ ★

SPENCER spied Isabel before she saw him. He'd phoned earlier, asking to see her urgently, anywhere, just name the place and no, it couldn't wait.

It was 5:30 PM when she peered into the crowd as she and Davey skated the ice under Rockefeller Plaza's floodlights. Ah, there was Spencer's wave. He was leaning on the rail at the end, a golden aura glowing around him from the huge Grecian statue behind him. Where else would Spencer wait? The defiant Prometheus, the giant Titan who stole fire from the gods to give to humanity, would appeal to Spencer, she decided.

Spencer watched Isabel skate off the rink and leave Davey with a woman and her son. They were neighbours in the Dakota on West 72nd Street and Central Park West, where Isabel and Ed had their Manhattan pad, just one floor below

John Lennon's old place. Coincidentally, they were also at the Rockefeller Plaza's four o'clock tea with Santa Claus and they had hooked up with Isabel and Davey for skating afterwards. The mother was delighted to keep an eye on Davey, and almost as soon as the two boys got onto the ice they joined hands and were gliding round and round as if they were junior Torvills and Deans. It was better for Isabel than leaving him to George, her original plan: not only was his wrist strained, but these days his centre of gravity was a foot in front of him; not good on the ice. She left him sitting hunched in the café complaining about the coffee and the service.

It was while Isabel was crouched down lacing up Davey's skates that she told him Spencer was coming later to chat. With her head down, she missed the dark frown that clouded over the boy's face.

Davey had met Spencer a few times and knew Isabel liked him, but the boy also sensed his father had a different opinion; Ed made no pretence about things like that.

When Isabel skated off to the side to meet Spencer, she waved back at Davey, unaware it was how his Mommy used to wave, or so Davey's mind told him. Spencer waved too, just like The Man. And also like The Man, Spencer was an Afro-American. The "look at me, I'm skating" gleam on Davey's face dimmed as the memories filled his head and he dropped his skating partner's hand. Slipping backwards, he crashed onto the ice. He lay flat for several seconds, narrowly being avoided by several skaters till his friend's mother skated over, and since eight-year-olds don't have far to fall, she got him up fast. She mistook the tears and patted the back of his coat, "It's only a little fall," she soothed, careful to mouth the words slowly, but he wasn't crying about that.

He grasped her hand tight for the next ten circuits, whimpering each time he spied the couple near the golden statue, their heads close together.

ISABEL and Spencer finished their tête-à-tête just after Davey was off the ice and back with George in the café at the end of the ice rink. Davey's hot chocolate with two floating marshmallows was steaming on the table.

"What was so crucial Spencer had to interrupt your skating time?" George asked.

"A proposition," she said, and saw Davey's blue eyes clamp shut. "We'll discuss it later, George. Something's bugging Davey." She squeezed the boy's ear lobe and rested her hand on his cheek but his eyes stayed closed, damming back the tears.

The two adults were silent, contemplating, until George said, "The only proposal you should've accepted from Spencer was when he wanted to marry you."

Davey had cracked his eyes open and read George's lips. His body began to shudder, he couldn't stop it. "Don't leave us," Davey signed, his tears streaming.

"I'm not leaving you."

"He wants to marry you. George said so," the boy signed.

Isabel wanted to laugh, but was careful not to, "That was a long time ago. Now I love your daddy, and you."

Davey looked away. After a long pause, he turned his head back, "Why did he come?" he signed, his hand motions abrupt, angry.

Isabel inhaled deeply and spoke—quietly, of course—but paced to give just enough emphasis to her words, "The President wants me to do something important and he got Spencer to ask me to accept."

George was as captivated by this as Davey.

"But," signed Davey, his hands a blur, "we don't like the President."

"What does he want?" interrupted George.

Isabel could see Davey's lips pressed. "He wants me to become House Speaker."

"What?" George blurted, almost blowing his buckteeth out of his mouth. He sprayed with such force his puffy cheeks and turkey neck quivered.

"What's a house speaker?" Davey asked, imagining something like a talking building. Whatever it was, he knew it was bad, and it only got worse after she explained it might disrupt their planned special trip.

Davey signed, "I want to go to the shack. You promised!"

"We'll go, for sure, but it will have to be later."

Davey pulled his cap over his eyes and slumped in his chair.

"Say no," said George. "For a change, do something for yourself. And for Davey," he looked at the boy cringing into the back of his chair. "Take him up to the shack and damn them all. For once, Ed'll agree with me. You'll see."

Davey could see through the weave of his cap. George was Isabel's dad, sort of. She *had* to listen to what he said, didn't she? He pushed his cap up and sipped the last syrupy dregs of his hot chocolate. "Can I have another one?" Before Isabel could even swivel to signal, the waitress, who had recognised her celebrity customer even under the hat, came over. She explained she could sign ASL—her mother was deaf—and she winked at Davey and told them another hot chocolate was already on its way, with three marshmallows this time.

She also thought of phoning her friend at NBC to tell him the other snippet of their conversation she'd seen Isabel signing.

ED was late for dinner at the restaurant. Who was surprised? The mood around the table, already tense over whether Isabel would take the job, and whether Davey would get to go to the shack, stretched even tighter the longer they waited. The best George could suggest was another round of "I Spy" which, in ASL, was quite a challenge, especially for him.

Having delayed ordering as long as they could, they were just digging into their shrimp cocktails when Ed came up behind Davey and tousled his hair. Instead of getting a big hug from his son, all Ed got was a melancholic signing that dumped the speakership question at him, even before he had a chance to sit down.

Despite Ed's loathing for Foster—George picked that right—and the obvious jibe that Foster had to be desperate, Ed was as much for it as Isabel was.

"It *is* the country's third most important job," said Ed.

"Third?" asked George, wondering what Ed was getting at. Surely a Secretary of State or Defence, or the chairmanship of Coca-Cola rated over someone who banged a gavel every day.

Isabel explained it for him, "After the Vice-President, it's the Speaker who's next-in-line for the presidential succession." From Davey's blank expression, it was obvious he had no idea what she was talking about, so she tried afresh, "Davey, if something bad happens to both the President and the Vice-President, like they die or something, then the Speaker automatically steps up to become President."

"But not in your case," said George, "since you're not a natural born citizen, right?"

"You never know," she said curiously.

To George, the strange advent of both Ed's and Isabel's eager harmony set off his suspicions big time. He didn't let up, right through dinner. He kept pushing how she needed a break after the gruelling campaign but Isabel wasn't listening, he could see that. She maintained a look: an unfamiliar glaze. He imagined it was the wash of exhaustion, proof of his point, but the distance in her eyes and the flicker of a smile he thought he detected in the corners of her mouth made him wonder if it was something else? Ambition? Lust for power? If it had been Ed, for sure. But Isabel? No way.

She closed the debate when dessert arrived. She held up her spoon and said, "George, enough. I'm doing it," and then dug it into her pear soufflé.

Davey burst into tears.

THE four were back at the apartment in front of the fire, but there wasn't a lot of warmth in the room. Davey was pretending to fool around with his toy penguin Pip on the silk and gold-thread Savafid prayer rug, playing at being Eskimos while secretly reading the adults' lips. He didn't know, and wouldn't have cared that there are no penguins in the Arctic. Isabel wondered if Ed would ask the boy to be careful of his prized 400-year-old rug, but he seemed more focused on what her plans were.

She had been explaining that the House's first session would sit for ten days at the start of January before it recessed again until Inauguration Day on the twentieth. Then, there'd be a five-day session and a further break of around a week, resuming for the President's first State of the Union Address. He was delivering it early in February, she said.

"Pretty soft, this congressional life," said George.

"Oh, George!" Isabel sighed. She'd explained her new plan, a plan regrettably without Davey: that she'd still fly up to her shack, but it would have to be later and alone, for the few free days just ahead of the State of the Union.

She caught Davey lip-reading and looked directly at him. "Davey darling, like I said, you can't come because you'll be back at school and they need you for rehearsals for the school pantomime. But," she said, pointing between the two of them, "we'll still get up there one day, I really do promise… "

Davey's eyes dropped to Pip, and Isabel knew there was no point in continuing.

Suddenly, Davey jumped up and signed, "Goodnight," and without a kiss or a hug for anyone, not even George, he ran to his room.

George slumped back into the sofa as Isabel left to get Davey dressed for bed. He glowered at Ed, but the former general didn't notice or care; he had moved to the window and was gazing out at the snow flurries. After a minute, Ed gave George a curt nod, turned and walked off, leaving George to stew in front of the fire alone.

ISABEL sat cross-legged on the bed with Davey.

"A cross-your-heart promise means something," he signed at her. Deep in his own heart, he was sure she'd broken her promise because Ed had wanted her to. It was always Ed's fault. All Ed had needed to say was no. He was the man in the house. When Isabel ran for president, Ed was going to be First Man; the papers said so, and a First Man must be really important, or he wouldn't be first. So, if Ed had just said no, it would all be over and they would all go up to the shack. That's what George said, and George knew about stuff because he was old. But Ed didn't say no.

Davey pushed Isabel away as thoughts started pouring out to him; if only he knew how to sign them.

At least he didn't scream.

# 46

THE PRESIDENT-ELECT stood behind the lectern in the Transition Office pressroom, flanked by David Prescott and Isabel, and a wall of oak veneer behind him with a logo of "The Office of the President-Elect". His tone had been even, his demeanour calm but purposeful. With his announcement over, his eyes skimmed across the ragged carpet of raised hands and he gave the first nod to the *Chicago Tribune* reporter, who was guaranteed to ask a safe starter question since Don Thomas had set it up.

"Sir, can you give us some background to this appointment?"

"Sure, Anne. Representative… or should I say, Ambassador Prescott," said Foster, "has worked over many years developing close links with China…"

Don Thomas, standing at the side, twisted around to watch the press's reactions.

Bobby Foster continued, "and when I offered him the ambassadorship, not only did he accept but, conscious of his responsibility as the likely new House Speaker, he sought my counsel. Isabel Diaz was the obvious choice to us both… as Speaker, I mean. Unconventional, sure, but obvious when you think about it. I have spoken to the leadership of both Parties and, as I already mentioned, I am delighted to say that she has their unwavering support and we all expect the House to elect her at its first session on…"

"Doña Isabel, why are you doing this?" It was the correspondent from Miami*'s El Nuevo Herald*. He was fresh to the Washington press gaggle and blurted out his question without waiting for the President to finish, let alone being called.

Isabel tilted her head toward Foster.

"Go ahead," he said, forcing a smile through gritted teeth, and he stepped back from the lectern to make room for her.

"Thank you," she said, taking his spot. "For this phase of my life I deeply wanted to serve the American people but, in case you missed it, things didn't go as I planned…," though she did get the laughs she planned. "And you know," she shrugged, "when the President of the United States asks…"

"Ms Diaz…"

Another one! Foster was incensed.

"*Los Angeles Times*… Isn't there an irony here, ma'am? My read of the succession rules says you'll be next-in-line after Vice-President Taylor if anything, God forbid, should happen to the President. That's right, isn't it?"

The reporter's analysis was only half correct. As Don Thomas had explained it to Foster and as most legal commentators were now busy scribbling, there was simply no way Isabel could become president; at least not without a Supreme Court bench that would be bold enough to upend centuries of settled constitutional law, and that wasn't going to happen.

Isabel smiled at the reporter, "There's no irony. It's just plain irrelevant." No one seemed to mind she'd ducked the question.

# 47

THE REAL GOAL—panicking voters into Hank Clemens' arms to deliver the election—had failed. But after the guerrilla "ImposterFoster" campaign to destabilise Foster's new presidency had gone viral, it had paid off in an unexpected way. Levering Isabel into a post that was prize Democrat booty was a sign of Foster's desperation, which the conspirators had been able to relish for the few days prior to it becoming public knowledge.

"Outstanding press conference," said Dwayne. Despite being voice-masked, as they all were, his code-name flashed up on all the phone screens.

Isis snapped, "What was that?"

"The press conference. I said it was…"

"No, the background noise."

"Oh? I was riffling through the newspaper. Sorry," said Diana. "That line, *There's no irony. It's plain irrelevant.* How good was that?"

"Boot-licking isn't your forte," said Isis, though Diana wasn't quite so sure.

Dwayne spoke, "Some lawyer wrote it up in the *Post.*" No one said anything, so he continued, "He says if the President dies, the Vice-President *becomes* President—we all know that, right, but the crucial word is *becomes*, okay? That's the word the Twenty-Fifth Amendment uses… *becomes*—and to *become* President, the VP has still got to qualify with all the eligibility doodads, including the natural born citizen thing. But listen to this: if the Vice-President himself is dead or he won't stand… whatever… and succession slips to the next-in-line, which as we know is the… ta-da… Speaker, she actually doesn't *become* President under the law, she only gets to *act* as President, and… boom-boom… no eligibility criteria to interfere…"

"Tell me something I don't know," said Isis, cutting him short.

# 48

BACK IN THEIR home in the Hamptons, Isabel was stretched out with Davey on one of the soft lounges in the great room, struggling with the instruction manual, trying to decipher how to operate his birthday camera. George was watching from the red Regency récamier, and kept switching from one end to the other. No matter which way he lay, he couldn't get comfortable on the double-backed day bed, so eventually swung his legs off and moved to the chaise longue. Ed was stuck in a meeting in New York.

"It's totally intuitive," the camera salesman had told Isabel. Not for her it wasn't, though it was clearly different for Davey. He was way ahead of her, snatching for the camera, pressing this button, twisting that dial, tapping an icon on its screen, discovering shortcuts here and new tricks there. Naturally, she was worried he would press, pull, tap or twist something wrong and wreck it, but so far the slim-line digital camera with a thousand-image memory chip seemed Davey-proof. And apparently intuitive.

By noon, the boy fancied himself as a modern-day Ansel Adams, the photographer famous for his idealised landscapes of the American West. She'd recently taken Davey to an Adams retrospective at the Museum of Modern Art in New

York, where back in the 1940s Adams was instrumental in establishing the first museum department of photography. Contrary to Isabel's expectations, even after two hours traipsing around MOMA's tiring concrete floors, there hadn't been a single shuffle or yawn out of the boy. Davey was hooked and she knew what his birthday gift just had to be.

Davey dragged Isabel off the lounge and posed her on several of the antique chairs, first one way, then the other. And he had George prancing around like an arthritic old ballet dancer despite having an arm in a sling.

Davey scampered off to download his new snaps onto the computer in the family room. George fell back onto the sofa for a bit of shut-eye and Isabel kicked her feet up onto the glass coffee table to read a little more of the camera manual. Interesti…

SHE woke up to one of Davey's pinches. He was flapping computer prints in her face while jigging a little dance and, when he had her attention and pushed her feet off the coffee table, he spread the shots out, like a breathless artist revealing his portfolio for the first time.

"Very artistic," she said as she rubbed her eyes before even seeing the snaps. He had printed only six shots—his best, she guessed—and positioned them in two horizontal rows of three, temporarily masking the bottom row with blank sheets. The top three were grotesque blowups: Isabel's left nostril, her left eye and her shoe. "Excellent," she nodded. "At least you got my good side!" and she rocked her head back for a good laugh.

He peeled off the blank cover sheets on the three below. An eerie Dorian Gray intensity haunted the first, where Davey had snapped himself in a mirror. And the shot of George's bandaged wrist with his head lolling back, snoring on the sofa, bordered on the melancholic.

The third was a shot of Isabel's scar. Davey must have noticed her eyes avoiding it; he took her finger and pressed it to the photo, tracing along the line but he almost recoiled when he felt the shudder tremble from her finger up her arm.

Isabel looked over at George, hoping for a diversion, but he was still asleep. She hadn't felt this in weeks. She'd even been entertaining a tentative optimism that she'd got her dark cloud under control.

Why now? And with a photograph?

Her fingers found themselves combing through Davey's blond locks as tears streamed down her cheeks. He slid up on her lap and nestled his head into her shoulder. His stringy arms wrapped around her, holding her tight and then he did something he'd never done before: he lifted her hand from his hair and pressed it against his voiceless throat and, in turn, he stroked her scar.

Isabel caught her breath, and she felt it at the same time as she heard it.

A breath of a whisper.

"What?" she snapped her head back in shock. "Did you say someth…?"

Davey quivered a brave little smile. His tongue touched his top teeth and his breath blew a second time… slow and deliberate. The husky breathy sound was "love", she was sure of it.

She watched as his mouth formed an "O" and he exhaled again.

"Oo"? No, she decided, it was "you". It had to be.

"Love you."

Her bottom lip bled as she threw her arms around him.

"ED! Ed! Davey spoke to me…"

"Wha…? Tell me."

"He'll tell you himself," she said, crying with joy, and handed the phone to Davey.

Davey took it and held it, gazing into the handset. Finally, he put it to his head but made no motion to speak.

"Go on," Isabel encouraged him, wiping a tear from her eye.

"Davey," said Ed. "Isabel said you spoke... That's wonderf..."

Davey pulled the phone away from his face and stared into it again. He lifted his eyes to meet Isabel's and after a second, he passed it back to her and shook his head. He slid off her knee and, as she watched, he walked slowly to his room.

# 49

THE NEW FIRST Lady, Marilyn Foster, wriggled into the white silk pillows and surveyed the bedroom with a serenity she'd not felt for months. The Inauguration over, it was their first official night in the White House. She watched over her husband and toyed with his boyish front curl but stopped when she saw he was rousing. His blue eyes opened and fluttered a look around the hand-painted birds that dotted the walls.

"They match your eyes," she spoke softly. "Michelle was a clairvoyant." Michelle Obama had overseen the last major decoration of this room.

Bobby Foster stretched an arm over and caressed his wife's cheek. "Can you believe this, Marilyn? You and me… us… here?"

"We almost weren't," she whispered. "Hey, Mr President," she said with a lilt, "d'you think they video this room?"

"I checked. No way."

"Perfect." She slid down and billowed the sheet over the two of them.

# 50

ELIA CACOZ RUGGED up for her trip to La Paz but hadn't bargained for this. She'd skied when she was younger, so whistling mountain winds weren't new, but cheek-burn took on a new meaning at over 13,000 feet above sea level.

It was Elia's first visit to Bolivia and apart from the cold she'd prepared for it well. Her experience with *Close-up* had taught her to keep a lid on leaks and her new boss at FOX, Mr Devine, had approved of her precautions.

He was Mr Devine to everyone, though maybe not to Mr Murdoch himself. She was still pinching herself, though not from the cold. When she'd initially proposed her project—deep, deep research on Isabel's past—Mr Devine wasn't keen since Isabel was out of the race, old news. But Elia was positive she had a new angle and worked it up in her spare time. Six weeks later, on the day of the Inauguration, and with four other stories under her belt, good stories, she braved a knock on Mr Devine's door.

His head was bowed over some copy, his shiny liver spots flashing like idea bulbs as Elia swayed from side to side hoping her movement would attract his eye. The customary cigarette—in breach of office rules—drooped from the corner of his mouth. Still he didn't acknowledge her. She gripped the back of the lonely visitor's chair and held her breath as the smoke curled up and fingered through his salt-and-pepper comb-over.

Finally, she blurted it out.

Devine swung his head up at her, the sudden action seeming to drain the purple out of the alcohol veins on his nose. Heaving himself out of his seat, he waddled past her to shove the door closed. On his journey back to his chair, he plucked at the cigarette and stubbed it out in his famous water glass; it looked like water but there were rumours.

"Who else knows about this?" he wheezed, sprawling his vast bulk over the mottled green sweat towel draped over his chair.

"Just my researcher in La Paz," she said.

"Perfect. Better than perfect, missy," he said and, with the leaden point of a freshly sharpened pencil, scraped out a flake of tobacco, or maybe it was peanuts, from between his stained teeth.

Elia didn't like being called missy, or lovey, or sweetie, or any of the other endearments her old-school boss bestowed on every young woman who toiled for him, but she was new and they were only words, and since no one else who worked there had the guts or the boorishness to fuss about it, she wasn't about to rock the boat; especially not now; now she was better than perfect.

He gazed at her through his smudged spectacles, saying nothing, sizing her up. Eventually his hand, palm down, directed her to sit. "Let's get to work."

Within thirty-five magical minutes, he'd organised a crew, a plane, and a face: a TV reporter who'd front the camera and take as much credit for the story as the late Mike Mandrake would have wished he hadn't taken for his. She hadn't noticed it before but with the window behind Mr Devine, the wisps of his hair seemed to make him radiate. The harmless old coot could call her missy, or lovey, or sweetie, any time he liked.

"You're flying out at the crack of dawn tomorrow." He lit up his Zippo, a signal for her to leave. "You know," he added as he aimed the flame at his cigarette, "you get this in the can, *Close-up* will have more egg on their face than a year's worth of breakfasts." He took a long sip from his water glass, Elia watching in disgust. "Ah. That was good," he winked and licked his wrinkly yellowing lips. "Well, off you go, sweetie."

★ ★ ★ ★ ★

IN her excitement, Elia phoned Simon as soon as the Falcon tri-jet they'd chartered reached cruising altitude. She'd forgotten her boyfriend would still be asleep at home. "You won't believe this thing. It's got phones… well, obviously. And beds."

Simon wasn't impressed; he would have been if Elia had confided why she was going to an unnamed destination, or if he was the one sipping French champagne for breakfast, though Elia and the other FOX crew would have been wiser not to have indulged. By the time they were preparing to land in La Paz, even the burly cameraman—who'd guzzled more fizz than the others combined—had to pause taping the view from the air to press the sick bag up to his face.

Elia looked up in time to be sick again herself. In that instant before her head plunged into the brown bag, she noticed that the plane was on final approach into La Paz-El Alto airport, travelling at a crazy high-blower speed with the snow-capped mountains looming above them. Her eyes clamped shut as the wheels screamed along the icy runway.

The pilot ignored all the groans and, over the intercom, explained that, while fighting a thirty-knot cross-wind, she had needed to make the landing at twice the normal speed to avoid the engines stalling in the wispy thin air.

Elia reached for another sick bag.

# 51

YEARS AGO, LA Paz had attitude, but now, altitude was virtually all it had left to hang onto.

Spilling down the sides and across a rugged mountain bowl at around 13,000 feet, the Bolivian capital city had once held up its head, poised in a strategic sweet spot between the nation's bountiful silver mines and its critical Pacific Ocean ports. But things turned sour over a century ago when Chile and Peru ganged up on their small neighbour, with Chile nabbing the seaboard and Peru the rich lodes of ore.

Today, La Paz's remaining accolade—that it was the world's highest city with the highest airport—didn't feed the 30 percent of Bolivians living in poverty. They couldn't give a *miéchica* that their airport could headbutt Switzerland's Matterhorn on a clear day. Instead, with many scraping by on a measly five dollars a week, they hankered for the Swiss banks to reimburse the loot that some of their former kleptocrat leaders had secreted in their vaults.

In La Paz, the air was so thin that jogging would turn your legs to jelly. But few jogged here. There weren't too many places worth going.

ELIA had organised to do the shooting up in the slums of El Alto that evening, so her plan meanwhile was to wrap herself in the traditional *aguayo* shawl she was about to purchase and stroll around the old part of La Paz city. With snippets from *Lonely Planet* that she'd read aloud to the others on the plane, she'd captivated enough of the crew to join her; all except Shannon Reynolds, the face who Mr Devine had assigned to front the interview.

Reynolds decided to stay in. The flight had been nauseating enough but when the hotel bellhop slid the van door open, the precious star's stomach almost upended at the reek of the puddle of piss he'd stepped into. Spontaneously, he decided to leave exploring the marvels of this place to others. A market where you could buy llama fetuses, even dried ones, was suddenly of zero interest to him.

He commanded the bellman to wipe his boots. The withering look Elia gave him had nothing to do with the sharp smell. Disgusted with his *Don't you know who I am* arrogance—and no, the locals didn't have a clue—she and the others left their bags and a tip and made off, leaving him to drink alone.

Along the cobblestoned streets, the group kept bumping into women wearing shawls like the one Elia had bought, as well as voluminous layered petticoat *pollera* skirts and black bowler hats. According to the guidebooks, if a woman's hat was tilted to the side, she was single; square on top, she was married. Their skirts and striped shawls, brilliantly vibrant, were something else. Bizarrely, the shawls were often smeared with thick oily pig fat; at least they smelt like it to Elia. She'd bought one without the fat. It cost her less, though she would willingly have paid more.

Beggars wrapped as tight as mummies lay asleep, or dead—it was hard to tell the difference—under awnings or in doorways, and a loud gang of soldiers passed by, leering their gap-toothed smiles at Elia from under their riot helmets and waving their assault rifles. The grease they used on their weapons hung heavy in the still, dry air mixing with the thick fetor of pig fat. She decided that breathing through her mouth was a good option.

The wispy river Elia had spied as they had corkscrewed down the eight miles from the airport was nowhere to be seen, having oozed its squalid water under the city, the roads having been built over it decades ago.

★ ★ ★ ★ ★

CARLOS, Elia's local researcher, had arranged for them to meet the woman he claimed was Isabel Diaz's mother, Maria Rosa, up in El Alto over a *watia*, a dinner cooked in a traditional Andean earth oven. For colour, Elia had planned to stretch the interview across the meal.

Reynolds scowled as they drove into the worst slum he'd ever seen, or smelt. He knew of the Juhu slum in Mumbai, India—though the closest he'd come to it was watching the movie *Slumdog Millionaire*—and this was far worse. For starters, he was physically here. It was not a good place for someone with his finely honed nose for wine, or so he whinged.

"Let's skip the meal thing," he said, his throat gagging with the thick cloying stench of human sweat and shit, as well as other odours he couldn't avoid picking out: pigs, decomposing trash, rotting damp cardboard, wood smoke and the pungent ammonia tang of yet more urine.

"Is fixed, Señor," said Carlos. "We cannot cancel."

"Sure we can. We'll peg our noses, pick her up and take her back to the hotel. We can do the interview there."

"Not possible. Señora Diaz is spending many hours to dig meal for dinner."

The street—if you could so dignify a dusty dirt track strewn with scrabbling chickens, wandering pigs and, despite the chilly conditions, half-clothed urchins—was hemmed in by squalid shanties and lean-to huts.

An old woman shuffled out of a rickety metal and cardboard shack as their van approached. Maria Rosa's bowler hat sat flat on her head. Even if the bent old lady could stretch straight, she was nowhere near as tall or attractive as the woman she claimed was her daughter.

A few times, Carlos had to repeat things to her, and Reynolds got more and more irritable. "She's deaf, can you believe it?" he asided to Elia. "Of the five senses you'd be willing to lose up here, you'd go for smell, right?"

Carlos asked a question in Quechuan, slowly and loudly. Señora Diaz replied in broken English, "Paper is inside." She loosened her shawl and slipped through her doorway curtain, shortly re-emerging with a metal cash box, its red paint peeling. Pulling on a string around her neck, she drew up a key from between her ample breasts, then unlocked the box.

The page she withdrew from it and carefully handed to Carlos was yellowing and brittle and, handling it like a diamond nestling in his palm, he passed it to Elia.

"Bingo!" she said, her smile cracking through the cold. "A US entry visa… issued to Maria Rosa Diaz and dated… yes, just a few months *before* Isabel was born. Perfect."

Maria Rosa innocently looked up at Elia with an even more eager-to-please smile, though these days she had no teeth at all, distastefully prompting Elia to recall the trailer park manager's sleazy pet name for her.

"Can we just do this?" complained Reynolds, pushing forward. Three mangy dogs were nuzzling at his sharp-creased chinos and he wanted to get out of here before the mutts confused him with a lamppost. He surveyed the area and wrinkled his nose, indifferent as to whether he offended anyone, and his eyes settled on the hundreds of empty bottles piled up against a wall of Maria Rosa's shack. "She's a drunk," he boiled toward Elia. "I'm interviewing a soak? Puh-lease."

"She not have one drink today," Carlos interrupted. "I promise her ten bolivianos extra if she stay sober for you."

"That's what? About $1.40?" said Elia, peeling the money off her clip.

Carlos quickly wrapped his hand over Elia's, "No show money," he whispered. "No safe, here. Money you got in your hand is enough for food for many families for one month."

"Listen, Elia, do we really have to do the whole dinner shtick?"

Carlos cut in. "Is arranged, Señor Reynolds. Everyone make big preparations." For another five bolivianos, Carlos had got Maria Rosa's neighbours, whose hovel shared a rotting plywood wall with hers, to shift their chicken coops and pig swill to make enough space for the dinner, the cameras and the gas-bottle portable heaters he had hired, which were being fired up as they argued. He pointed Reynolds to a small hole dug in the ground with clods of earth piled next to it. "Is oven," he smiled, with more than a hint of local pride.

Reynolds noticed small, uneven dark lumps scattered around the hole, preferring not to think about the pigs he'd seen wandering around. He shrugged and headed back to the minivan to rehearse his intro. "Isabel Diaz," he said aloud, not caring who heard him, "couldn't be president because of a father she'd never met. But what of her mother, a woman she hasn't seen since she ran away from home at fifteen? I'm Shannon Reynolds for FOX. I'm in El Alto, Bolivia… a thousand feet *above* La Paz, the world's highest capital city. As you can see," and this is where the camera would sympathetically pan, "it's also one of the poorest. Tonight, I've been invited to a *watia*, a traditional Andean Indian dinner cooked in the ground, like a Hawaiian luau, and my hostess is… Maria Rosa Diaz, the long lost mother of Isabel Diaz, former US presidential candidate and soon, likely to be elected Speaker of the House. It's freezing here in El Alto, but what you'll discover tonight will make your blood boil. Stay tuned."

THE cameras rolled. Isabel's mother knelt in the dirt, the oven hole dug freshly in front of her. She selected the hardest clods and pressed them into the base to form the foundation, and then more for the sides. She huffed herself up onto her sandaled feet and walked purposely over to the nearby open fire where, knees bent, she lifted a smoking metal bucket filled with hot flat stones and brought it back to the hole, almost stumbling under its weight. Once again on her knees and this time with tongs, she placed the hot stones inside the makeshift oven, one by one. She piled yet more of the clods of dirt around the mouth of the hole, stacking them up until the structure resembled a dome. The small holes she left here and there were for ventilation, according to Carlos, and the stalks of *chaniua* she slipped in through them were for fuel.

When the oven was glowing red hot inside, Maria Rosa removed the stones with the tongs and replaced them with food: potatoes, raw leaf-wrapped alpaca, corn cakes and bananas. She covered it over with more leaves and sand and dirt, wiped her hands on her apron and heaved herself back onto her feet, all the while chattering away to Carlos in a language none of the others understood.

"One hour till ready," he said.

The cameras stopped filming.

"And we do what exactly during this hour?" asked Reynolds. "Sit on Mrs Gummy Bear's porch sipping mint juleps and watch the sun set over the horizon?" He swung around disgusted and almost tripped over the horde of open-mouthed children who'd come and sat silently behind them.

REYNOLDS and Maria Rosa ate seated on a brightly striped rug. It clashed with her shawl, but Elia let it go since everything clashed here.

So far as the cameras observed, all that warmed the diners was the heat radiating from the *watia* hole. "Alpaca. Mmm," Reynolds winked to the lens, "I never thought a sweater could taste so good." The flare in his nostrils was almost convincing, but Elia and the rest of the crew winced anyway, and she knew she'd cut it.

"Señora Diaz," he said after wiping his mouth. "You had a daughter when you were in America. Where was she born and what was her name?" He'd already learned from their off-camera rehearsal that if he spoke slowly, Maria Rosa would hear him.

"Her name… Isabel Rosa Diaz. Beautiful name, si?"

"And where was she born?"

"Ah, you ask me before… She born in New Jersey… in Newark. We live there first when we come to America—was cheap rent, but big troubles so we move."

"Tell me about Isabel."

Everything Maria Rosa recounted about Isabel and her early life had the ring of truth about it. Without giving Reynolds the details, she confirmed her daughter had run away from her at fifteen, when they were living at the Cactus Flower Trailer Park in New Mexico. After twenty minutes of what Reynolds would later describe as filler drivel, most of which would be edited out, he jumped in for the kill. "Your husband, what was his name?"

"Hernandez Luis Rodriguez Diaz."

"And what was his job?"

"He has big job. He work for Chile, for *gobierno*… the government, *sí*? He is *embajador*… ambassador… diplomat. I meet him here. No… there," she said, pointing down the mountain to La Paz, "and we marry there. *Celebración grande.* Very *grande.* And 'nother one in Chile too, for him family. I very pretty girl," she said, dropping her eyes as a petite smile curled her lips.

"When your husband sent you to America, did he know you were pregnant?"

"*Si*, is why he send me... because *bebé* is coming."

"Because you'd be safer?"

"No, was..." She paused, trying to find the right words. "...was *menos peligroso*—less dangerous, yes?—after we leave from here."

"But that's not what you told your daughter, is it?"

"*¿Qué?*"

He repeated the question slowly.

"I no want her to feel abandon by her father. So I tell her lie. I lie to her about many things; to protect her feelings. I pretend to her my husband is very pretty, but he short and fat... like Maria Rosa now," she cackled, the camera exposed briefly to the breathtaking spectacle of her toothless mouth.

"Is this a picture of your husband?" He passed Maria Rosa the grainy print Elia had given him. It was taken from the 1968 newsreel when the Chilean diplomat met LBJ.

"*Si, mi marido*," she sneered, spitting a large gob of yellow out of her mouth onto the paper.

Reynolds was ecstatic. Only a star interviewer could extract such passion, and the camera was getting it all.

"I don't understand, Señora Diaz. Why spit on him?" Come on. Do it again, he hoped. Tear it up. Burst into tears. He glanced up to see the second camera was framing her face but was pulling back the zoom enough to get her hands too. Marcus, the chief cameraman, was a professional.

"Because he throw me away," she said, her flabby arms suddenly gesturing so extravagantly she almost knocked the pitcher of water over. "I pregnant and he send me to America for get rid of me. Bye-bye me. And bye-bye *bebé*. He say, *Lloqsiy wasiymanta pantasqan qanwanqa karani*."

"Excuse me?"

"In Quechuan language means: *Get out of my house, I make mistake with you.*"

Elia could sense Reynolds' next question; it was as though a hangman's trapdoor was dropping open in the pit of her stomach. She saw Marcus preparing for it too, tightening his zoom in on Maria Rosa for a full-screen face shot.

"But why would he say such bad things to you?" asked Reynolds.

"Because his *amigos* tell him he is *cabrón*..."

"*¿Cabrón*?"

Her hands flew to either side of her head, her forefingers pointing upwards like horns. "*Cabrón* ... because *bebé* is not his."

"Hernandez Diaz... he was not Isabel's father?"

"He is husband, si. But no father. He go crazy with me. He tell me get out, but I say, *¿Y la guagua*?... and what of *bebé*? He say to me, he shout, I remember clear, *¡No estoy ni ahí*! *¡Vete al carajo*! *I no care! Go to hell!* Hernandez he say more very bad things to me."

Reynolds solemnly looked up to the lens, "As you've just heard, while Isabel Diaz's mother was indeed married to a Chilean diplomat, that man was not Isabel Diaz's biological father." He turned back to Maria Rosa. "Maria Rosa, tell me... who was Isabel's *real* father?"

"*Jardinero*. Can you believe..." she said, stretching her arms wide to take in their destitute surroundings, "I once has gardener work for me?"

"The embassy gardener?" asked Reynolds, feigning shock since he already knew the answer from their run-through.

"Si. He nice to me. But my husband go red. He say, *tú eres más falso que una pirata boliviano*—you are faker than a Boliviano pirate. He say that to me! Him... a Chile dog!" She spat into the dirt, just missing the rug. "He throw me papers and little bit money and he say ¡*Vaya*! Go! Get to America. ¡*Vete al carajo*!"

Elia's lips, dry from the cold, had split badly from grinning so much, but she couldn't care less. And nobody, not even Reynolds, was noticing the smells any more.

Eventually, Maria Rosa turned the questioning back on Reynolds, "Why you has interesting in Maria Rosa?" She'd asked this earlier, during the prep, but they had fended her off. Elia wanted her to hear the answer for the first time with the cameras shooting.

"It's your daughter, Maria Rosa. She was recently running for President of the United States."

"¿*Mi Isabel*?" Maria Rosa's eyes glazed over, then she smiled weakly, sadly, and for a moment she fell silent.

Elia imagined that all kinds of memories and what-could-have-beens were flooding Maria Rosa's head, details she'd long forgotten, or wanted to.

"Señor Reynolds," she said eventually, a tear running down her cheek, "Isabel want to be presidente since very little girl."

"America wanted it too, Maria Rosa."

REYNOLDS was already in the minivan, lounging smugly across a double seat, his legs spread as wide as his self-satisfied smile. The crew were packing their gear into the vehicle, but Elia stayed back with Carlos as he gave Maria Rosa the money he'd promised, in an envelope. Only then, did she hop in and tell the driver to head straight for the airport. She and Marcus already knew the satellite uplink in La Paz was hopeless, so editing the material would have to wait till they got back to LA. Reynolds seconded the motion, not because he cared about technical details, he just wanted out of this godforsaken hole. His work was over.

Within minutes of their departure, all the *paceños* who'd been squeezing into the cracks between the shanties so they could ogle the bizarre event had scattered back to their own squalid homes.

Two dark figures, their teeth glinting in the *watia* afterglow, sprung from the shadows. Maria Rosa saw them immediately. She'd been expecting them and greedily extended her hand for her second envelope of the night. She wasn't completely stupid, she thought, and now she knew the background for the first time she would ask these people for even more money than they'd promised. She'd met them twice now, the first time a few weeks ago, just before Elia had got her tip-off.

Maria Rosa ushered the woman inside the hovel. Diana's face was dark, her red cap peak pulled low over her eyes, and she was sombre as she handed the woman the fat wad. She placed her hand on Maria Rosa's shoulder and pressed her fingers in on the bone, "Maria Rosa, you must promise our secret will die with us both."

"*Si*," the bent old woman nodded, the pain in her shoulder and the mention of death hinting that now might not actually be the best time to renegotiate.

Diana smiled and slapped the old woman hard on the back. Maria Rosa felt a sharp pin-prick jab between her shoulder blades and was about to say something when Diana slipped out through the curtain and left. Maria Rosa watched the mysterious woman pass by the hot *watia* hole and drop something into it, rousing a brief flare to the dying fire. Even if she'd seen it closer up, Maria Rosa would've had no idea what a *Clip'n'Drip* was. She turned back inside and shrugged, a nerve pinching the same painful spot in her back, unaware that in two hours' time it would never trouble her again; and nor would anything else.

# 52

THE INTERVIEW ISABEL Diaz agreed to give to Shannon Reynolds had nothing to do with Reynolds and everything to do with Mr Devine, Elia's boss. Devine had been good to her over the years. It didn't hurt either that he too was a Catholic.

The set behind Isabel and Reynolds was a poignant blow-up of her mother in the doorway of her shanty, with three snotty-nosed, half-dressed urchins clinging to her skirt. "What can I say? It's history," Isabel said facing Reynolds on air, and brushing her hair behind an ear. Isabel was trying to emphasise closure, but all it did was show her vulnerability. "But of course I'm disappointed I didn't know about this before, or my nomination wouldn't have got scratched."

"And you'd be President now."

"Maybe I wouldn't," she shrugged. "In any case, Mr Foster was duly elected, he's been sworn in and, as a nation, we need to move on."

"And your mother, Madam Speaker? Seeing her again, on TV, in all that squalor… that filth? It must have shocked a wealthy woman like you."

Isabel snapped to ice so quickly that Elia, who was watching from off to the side, could almost hear her cracking. Elia had personally negotiated the ground rules with Isabel's staff. Anything about her feelings for her mother was strictly off-limits. She had agreed to the backdrop photo, but that was to be it.

"I have many regrets, Mr Reynolds, but I'm not disposed to sharing them with you. We agreed on that before this interview, as I recall." Delivering that last sentence through a sweet smile, she destroyed Reynolds' prospects of ever interviewing another serious political leader again.

After the interview, Devine wandered onto the set and signalled his nicotine-stained finger over at Reynolds. The "face" strutted over to his boss expecting dollops of praise for his last-minute attempt to throw Isabel off-balance but instead, Devine stretched his arm up around Reynolds' sculpted shoulders, slipped his cigarette out of his mouth, and edged the interviewer off to the side of the studio where they couldn't be so easily heard.

"Shannon, my boyo," he said, lowering his voice so even Reynolds had to lean down to hear him, "it's time you got yourself a brain to work your tongue. If you ever get one, call me; I might think of rehiring you. Security is clearing out your desk." Devine placed his fist in the small off Reynolds' back and shoved him forward and, for a change, the mouth was lost for words.

Devine wheeled around to find Elia. She had been watching the two men, wondering what was transpiring but Devine, without a word, pulled Elia's sleeve over toward Isabel. "Madam Speaker, before I apologise to you for Reynolds' appalling breach of our agreement, I'd like you to meet Elia Cacoz. She was the brains behind this story and you can be the first to congratulate her on her promotion."

"Mr Devine…," was all Elia could get out.

"Ms Cacoz. Well done," said Isabel, taking her hand. "If only I had you around last year."

"Actually you did," Elia said, slipping her hand out of Isabel's warm grip and hanging her head. "I was Mike Mandrake's researcher and, um, I sort of screwed up. I killed the research too early. I feel so, so responsible."

"Didn't you hear what Madam Speaker said during the interview, Elia?" asked Devine, smiling. "It's history."

Elia heard, but was not convinced.

Her instinct was right.

# 53

THE DOOR TO Ed's study at home was closed but Davey found it unlocked, and snuck it open to peek inside. His father had his back to him, and Davey could see from the green light flashing on the desk that he was talking on his speakerphone. To the boy, the grey phone-dome sitting on a 1930s bleached oak and steel Frank Lloyd Wright desk didn't look at all incongruous.

Nobody else was there except Ed and, with the drapes open, there was plenty of light for the bit of fun that Davey had planned. The boy slipped inside quietly and pressed the door closed behind him before sliding to the floor. Ed had chosen the same motif for the carpet here as in his office: five-pointed stars, though for the privacy of his home he'd gone for a less understated pattern.

Davey had already programmed the shutter-click on his camera to remain silent so his game would be as hushed to his father as it was to himself, and he started snapping. He began with four shots of the desk.

Eventually Ed swung around and as he did so, seeing Davey, his face compressed into a frown for a second, long enough for Davey to get him in the frame. "I'm on the phone," he signed, relaxing into a beaming smile and pointing to the console,

"Want to say something?" Ed's face was warm and open. He vainly hoped the boy would speak to him as he'd done for Isabel.

Davey shook his head, instead pointing to his camera, so Ed got the hint and shifted his pose so he looked mean, like a gunslinger sizing up his kill. Davey gave his dad the thumbs-up and clicked away.

"You still there?" asked Niki Abbott over the speaker.

"Davey's just come in… with his new camera."

"I should give him some lessons," she laughed.

"Not with what you'd teach him!"

"Funny man. I know he can't hear, but shouldn't…?"

Ed waved at Davey before turning away. "I've got my back to him now. Where were we?"

"You were saying it's two hours till she leaves. I'm getting wet just thinking about this," she said.

Ed shook his head. "No dirty talk."

"Ed, he's deaf!"

"I don't care," Ed said. Out of the corner of his eye, he noticed the light flashing red for an incoming call on the other line. "Our call's coming through…"

BY the time Isabel was ready to fly to the shack, Davey was back in happy-mode and she guessed it was the excitement of coming to the heliport.

His toilet break was taking time. The rotors had been spinning for five minutes and Davey hadn't made a reappearance.

"What *is* he doing in there?" repeated Isabel.

"Don't wear out your watch," Ed said, glancing at the chopper whirling outside the terminal not fifty feet away.

"It's not as if you have appointments at the other end," George added.

Davey burst out of the restroom door, his toy penguin Pip flying in one hand, his camera gripped in the other and his shirt flapping out from under his sweater.

"I hope you weren't taking photos in there!" George laughed.

Davey ran straight to Isabel and whooshed up into her arms, squeezing her with all his might. She tucked in his shirt as he hung there and hugged him back, and spun him around like the rotors, with so many swirls they were both giddy.

When she stopped, and was still swaying a bit, Davey slipped down and his blond head snuggled into the down-filled squishiness of her steel-grey parka. With cuddles over, he handed Pip to George and stretched his camera out in front and pointed it back at his face, snapping a big cheesy self-portrait. He held up his hand signalling to the others to wait for a moment—this was serious business. He had to check his work was of adequate quality, inspecting it on the camera's display screen. Finally, Davey, apparently satisfied, placed the camera firmly in Isabel's gloved hand.

He signed, "I *am* going with you." He pointed to the camera. "I'm inside there."

THE chopper was loaded up with more than enough provisions for her stay at the shack, long enough to recharge her batteries but short enough to make the President's State of the Union Address where she'd be officiating.

It really was a shack, not some millionaire's conceit. This was no mountain mansion with a staff of five and rooms for twenty. Isabel had bought the tumbledown log cabin from the estate of a recluse who'd lived there since before World War II and, apart from the roof and the walls, which she'd had freshly insulated, there wasn't much in it… All its magic was outside.

Over the years, so-called nature lovers wrecked great tracts of the Appalachians' fragile alpine vegetation, especially around the 2,000-mile hiking trail that spans from Mt. Katahdin up in Maine down to Springer Mountain in Georgia. If it wasn't trees lopped for firewood or soils compacted by walking or erosion, it was the food and trash left behind that weaned the wildlife off nature. You didn't have to be a tie-dye wearing eco-nut to want these remote reaches rededicated as wildernesses, though it helped.

In local Park Ranger Andy Goodman's case, his extra motivation was that humans hampered his grey wolf re-introduction program. Consequently, the deal he'd negotiated with Isabel was that she kept no foodstuffs stored at the shack unless she was staying. Nothing his wolves could sniff for.

Isabel's pilot and co-pilot were already inside the chopper. Apart from her food, she'd packed fresh batteries for the lanterns and a backpack bulging with her sketchpad and pencils, her laptop—she was working on a couple of speeches—eight spare fully charged computer batteries, an iPod, and some books. She'd thought of taking an iPad, but she was old-school about reading and loved the feel of books, even their smell. Besides, she didn't want to be reliant on batteries for everything. The shack had no power. That was not something the Fish and Wildlife Service rangers were prepared to budge on, not even if she paid for the line to be taken up there.

AS the helicopter skimmed across the tips of the mountain range, there was something ethereal about the white-dusted clusters of fir and eastern hemlock streaking below her. The word "privileged" did come to Isabel's mind; she knew there were precious few in the world who had their own mountain peak, let alone could access it in this style, especially if they'd come from where she had.

From the jumpseat, Isabel thought she caught the pilot's worried lips in the windshield reflection. She followed where she imagined his eyes were looking down and saw the landing pad at Roget's Peak, high ground that was normally flat bare rock clear of scrub about 200 feet east of her shack. She was guessing but, judging from the build-up against the walls of the shack, it looked like the landing pad was under three or four feet of snow. The crew were discussing alternative landing strategies since there were no snow ploughs or salt spreaders up here. Isabel switched on her helmet speaker to hear the two men debating whether it was dry enough to blow the snow away or whether they should drop everything in by cable, including Isabel. She didn't meddle but was relieved when they voted for the first choice.

The pilot shifted the chopper into a hard 30-degree tilt and she watched the snow shoot out in a wild sweep arcing back into the trees away from the shack. He held the slant steady for several minutes, but when the surface snow had blown off and they reached the denser packed mass, he added small vertical adjustments, tilting up and down a few degrees each way, manoeuvring the helicopter in a fan-wave rhythm. When her tongue-in-cheek welcome sign—*Shade'n'Froid*—poked out of the snow, he swung a 180-degree turn and, with a similar technique, cleared a path toward the shack taking care to keep clear of the trees.

Isabel jumped onto the cleared landing pad. "Cold isn't the word for it," she said, pulling her cap down over her ears and crossing her arms over and whumping her gloved hands to her shoulders several times.

"Good thing we got no wind."

The unloading was swift; it needed to be. The men refused Isabel's offer to help them carry the boxes up to the shack, insisting she climb back inside their machine and wait till they did their security check on the shack.

"I'm not entitled to Secret Service any more, you know," Isabel joked.

"Hop back inside and stay warm, ma'am. We'll take care of the rest," said the pilot, and he and his co-pilot hoicked up two of the boxes each, one on top of the other, and trudged through the few inches of heavy powder left lying on the path to the shack.

She smelled the fire they'd set even before she walked in but, once inside, the stubborn mustiness of ingrained mildew from the half-century the former owner had been cloistered here hit her. She had changed the furnishings last year but still the mouldy odour clung. It would lift in a few hours, she knew that, once she'd aired the place or got accustomed to it; though which it was, she was never sure. It seemed self-defeating having a fire and simultaneously holding the door open, but it always seemed to work.

Before the two men left, Isabel ticked through her checklist, opening up the lockbox in the cabin to make sure all her "outside" gear was still there and in order—thermals, cap, face mask, gloves, parkas, overalls, snow shoes, cross-country skis, poles, boots, rug, sleeping bag and blankets. The stack of firewood she'd collected last time she was here was untouched and still dry, and the three fire extinguishers were still rating well in the green safety zone. She inserted the new batteries she'd brought in the lanterns and checked the drawer for the spare globes.

"No radio, ma'am?" asked the pilot.

"That's the point… sanctuary. No radio, no TV. There's not even any phone signal up here."

BY mid-afternoon the next day, Isabel thought she had captured almost enough frames on Davey's camera to keep him happy. She kidded herself she was following in the footsteps of Claude Monet's famous painting series, *Cathedral at Reims*, by snapping her shack at various times of day from the same spot to reflect the varying shimmers, sparkles and moods. It wouldn't be long before dusk's fade to nightfall would drag her back outside to capture her stunning finale.

She'd sketched, too. Today, it was the unusually gnarled and twisted hemlock, the proudest in the stand not too far from the shack, and she had been pencilling it from three perspectives and in four lights, until around three when the wind blew up. At around 100 feet, to her, *it* was Roget's Peak. What fascinated her most was not its height or the knots that made it an unappealing construction timber, but its rough scaly bark, in the past valued by the leather industry for its tannins. What she had been drawing was the maze of cracked, carved furrows crossing and recrossing the trunk on their journey upwards through its arrogant upsweeping foliage, speedways and rest stops for ants and other bugs in spring. To her, it was like her political career so far: heading everywhere, yet arriving nowhere. Inhaling its Christmas tree perfume wasn't a good idea, rekindling her broken promise to Davey. As a sort of recompense, and she knew it was facile, she pulled out his camera from her pocket and took a few close-ups of the trunk. With the sun getting low, she packed up her sketching gear, and stripped some pine needles off a fallen branch.

When she was inside the shack, after rebuilding the fire, she connected the camera to her laptop, and as an afterthought tossed the hemlock leaves onto the flames. With her only companion the smoky tang and crackle, she opened up the trunk shot and continued to sketch it, until a distant wolf howled, startling her out of her solitude.

She put down her crayon.

Wolves. When she was buying the shack, she had been told there was a grey wolf reintroduction program up here, so she checked with the experts. According to them, there had never been a single documented attack on an adult by a healthy wild wolf in recent history. But that had never been a complete comfort to her. What if a wolf was unhealthy was the question she had asked to a blank stare.

She got up to latch the door.

# 54

THE NEXT EVENING, in his work cabin high above the small town of Manifold, Fish and Wildlife Service ranger Andy Goodman was fixing for a night out at Daisy's Bar & Grill. He was a regular, always cracking his jokes, and when he was sober, they were sometimes funny. When he was off duty, humour and booze were his crutches. Andy knew he wasn't the best-looking guy around; his wife had told him often enough, what with his big ears, his acne scars and the stubble he kept to hide them. She had complained so much, why she married him in the first place was a mystery to him, but at least, he thought, it would have a happy ending. She was about to be his ex.

Before leaving, he clipped the alert beeper onto his belt as he checked his wolf-scan. The GPS-based, radio-collar system showed all his seven wolves' heartbeats humming along, including that of Gretel, the alpha female. Sure, Gretel's heart rate was faster than the others, up at 125 beats per minute compared to Zane's at 84 bpm, but 125 wasn't out of the norm for an afternoon roam, and neither was 84. Zane, the wily old Casanova wolf, was probably letting the females do the hunting to save his energy for better things. A man after my own heart, Andy thought.

Andy set the alert to beep him if any of their heart rates hit 200 bpm or if any changed by more than 30 percent over a 15-minute period. Experience taught him that at even around 160 bpm it could be hackles up, snarls, teeth-bared, real back-off stuff, but not too big a deal. But at 250, it'd be a chase or an attack and Andy liked to monitor those, especially after learning Gretel was pregnant. The screen mapping her routes showed a significant shift in her habits; she was avoiding the edges of the pack's territory so he guessed she was looking to establish her den, even though it was a bit early in the season up here for mating. He had regaled everyone at Daisy's with the news that day, and the next, as proud as a husband who'd just learnt his own wife was pregnant… though if that lying, scheming bitch was, Andy thought, it wouldn't have been his.

He loved his *canis lupus* grey wolves for what they were, and for what they did. And for never accusing him of being ugly, or stupid. With their central role in maintaining a balance in nature, wolves were an "apex" predator. The remaining elk and deer herds around these parts got to profit from the wolves culling out their weakest, but being mostly killers of foraging herbivores, the wolves also boosted the survival of the region's delicate alpine flora, which in turn improved the perching and feeding prospects for birds and butterflies. Andy also saw his wolves as the mountain's providores. When they did kill an elk—mostly a sick calf or an old female—what they left of the bloody carcass would be a feast for a horde of scavengers: black bears, ravens, coyotes, golden eagles. Even the beetles and squirming maggots would be food for the regenerating flocks of magpies, warblers and nuthatches.

Andy loved his mountain, and he loved his wolves, and his bitch of a wife could simply go and fuck herself.

# 55

ISABEL GLANCED AT the grey puffballs flitting across the sky and saw they were turning just the slightest pink. With some regret, she thought, tonight's would be her last sunset this trip, with the chopper due the following lunchtime, a day-and-a-half before the State of the Union Address. It gave her plenty of time to get organised since it would be flying her straight to Washington DC, where Ed and Davey would be joining her.

Leaning down to place her sketchpad on the worn porch boards by her side, she rubbed her hands above the brazier at her feet, hoping the breeze would stay weak so she could stay outside and take more shots. Last night, even from inside through the window, the sunset had been spectacular drawing her back outside for its neon yellows and ochres slowly spraying across the sky, turning into oranges and reds, and eventually fading into deep, long pinks and satiny purples. The longer she'd looked at it, the more it sparked memories of George's favourite shirt back from when she first arrived at Half Moon Bay, the one he only wore on his and Janis Joplin's birthdays, claiming the singer had given it to him at Haight-Ashbury during the Summer of Love in 1967. She smiled, wondering if George still had the shirt somewhere and remembering how, whenever he told his Joplin story, Annette had always rolled her eyes and busied herself.

Checking the small screen on the back of Davey's camera, she noticed its disk was nearly full. She wondered why, since the guy in the store had guaranteed a capacity of a thousand shots and she had to be hundreds short of that.

She was right. The folder called PIX contained 202 shots, which from the thumbnails seemed mostly hers, and the other folder, labelled VID, only listed three. Videos, she guessed. Digital cameras could do that, she recalled, but thought they must be mammoth video clips. But she hadn't taken any herself, at least not intentionally, and started wondering if it was one of those annoying instances of accidentally tapping the 'on' button, with the video camera rolling and rolling and making a mind-numbing clip of the insides of her pocket, or something equally inane.

She sipped her Virgin Mary, its thick tang of tomato juice rolling over her tongue just giving it enough coating to take the big smack of spice and pepper she liked to lace it with. The breeze puffed an icy breath over her face before it moved on, tinkling the branches of fir overhanging just a few feet away from the porch.

She stayed curious about the videos. Maybe they were Davey's, and he'd shot a surprise for her, like his snaps of Ed posing in his office making cute faces. She clicked on the first one but no, it was her feet. Her snowshoes, actually. She decided it must have been yesterday when the camera was dangling from her wrist as she wandered around the hemlock grove. She deleted it, and clicked the second one open. It was indeed one Davey had taken, and showed Ed with his back to the camera.

To Isabel, it vaguely sounded like two people talking… Ed and… was it a woman? Yes, it was, but with the breeze picking up, she couldn't make out what they were saying. She moved onto the second clip, also Ed, but with more voices. Her eye caught a few flashes of green from the dome-shaped phone console on Ed's desk. He was talking on speaker, that was clear, yet the call couldn't be private or confidential since Ed was turning towards Davey to wave happily at the camera. He'd even signed: *Hey son, what's up?*

Isabel packed up her sketchpad, pencils and glass and brought them inside, then booted up her laptop to view her shots on the larger screen.

As she scrolled through them, first hers, and later Davey's, she leant back and smiled at Davey's snaps—of Isabel and George, her with Ed, the three of them together, and Ed in his office. It was such a shame that she couldn't bring him this trip but she would next time, she promised herself. Again.

With the video clips, she toyed with the sound as she enjoyed how Ed's shoulders never slouched, not even in private. But when his hand started rubbing across his buzz cut, a gesture he made when he was nervous or excited, she started wondering who was he talking to? Not that she cared. Or that's what she pretended. Maybe it was just Davey?

Eventually, after trying various sound settings, she succeeded.

"*You still there?*" It *was* a woman… a familiar voice, but not one Isabel placed immediately.

"*Davey's just come in… with his new camera,*" said Ed.

"*I should give him some lessons,*" laughed the woman. Niki Abbott? Was it Niki?

"*Not with what you'd teach him!*" Ed sniggered.

"*Funny man. I know he can't hear, but shouldn't't…*"

Isabel watched Ed wave his fingers at Davey and poke his pinkie up his nose playfully before turning, but unlike Davey, she wasn't amused, and her spine was stiffer than Ed's.

"*I've got my back to him,*" said Ed. And to me, too, Isabel noted. "*Where were we?*" he asked.

The woman continued, "*You were saying it's two hours till she leaves.*"

She? For Isabel, this was developing a very uncomfortable edge.

"*I'm getting wet just thinking about this.*"

Wisely, Isabel placed her glass on the coffee table.

"*No dirty talk.*"

"*Ed, he's deaf!*"

I'm getting wet?

Niki.

Niki Abbott and Ed?

"*I don't care,*" Ed said. "*Our other call's…*"

The clip cut Ed short, and Isabel slumped back into the sofa, taking one of the cushions and holding it to her chest.

Eventually she stood, a little shakily, and faltered over to the fire, placing her hand against the mantel to steady herself and let the heat sear her face dry, chalking her cheeks with two streaks of salt. She felt suffocated and wanted to rip open her throat to let in more air. She had to breathe… to do something.

The bastard… the fucking bastard. Wait till she got home. But that wouldn't be till tomorrow afternoon when the chopper came for her, and she had no means of calling it to come sooner. Damn this sanctuary shit, she screamed to herself.

She sat back in front of her laptop, staring at it like it was her enemy. The gossip… the snide innuendo. All through the campaign, she had dismissed the barbs, parking them beside malice or just plain jealousy. But here it was front and centre. True.

An image of Spencer Prentice wagging his manicured finger invaded her thoughts. He had been right, she knew that now. In his own genteel way, he'd always seen Ed as a scheming bastard who was using her. And what had she done? She'd laughed it off.

She wasn't chuckling now.

The acid of the betrayal was etching dark lines under her eyes and the scar on her neck bleached against the flush of red drowning her. Every one of her senses heightened. Her skin burned. The mustiness in the shack returned, but this time it stank so she couldn't stand it.

Had Ed loved her at all? Ever…? She slammed her fist on the arm of the sofa because plainly she had no idea.

Breathe deeply, she told herself.

*Bésame*… Fuck that song! Why did it have to enter her head right now?

Isabel played the video clip again. And again. With her hand trembling, she shook a few more drops of Tabasco into her drink and swirled it with her finger. She forced down a slug of the fiery liquid and then rested the glass, though well away from the table's edge. Both her hands rose to steeple just below her nose and she gritted her teeth. An observer might think she was praying, and in a way she was.

There had to be an innocent explanation… Maybe, she hoped, the second clip would give one.

She licked her finger and for several seconds it lingered, poised over the 'play' button but not quite ready. Pressing it could only lead to two outcomes, one good, the other unbearable.

She gulped another hit of her drink. *Bésame… Bésame mucho…* That damn song, and her drunken mother… she couldn't shake the tune out of her mind. Maybe if she walked around?

As she gazed out of the window, the deepening colours left her cold, reminding her she actually used to hate that old shirt of George's and how Annette got upset whenever he wore it. She shivered a little, and turned back to the fire to see the untended flames were dying. Like her marriage. She bent over to pick up the poker but her gut wrenched and her throat gagged and, suddenly, she threw up uncontrollably into the fireplace.

The fire sputtered... the embers dimmed to black-red... but as the steaming stinking liquid evaporated, they flared up more fiercely than before and the flames erupted afresh.

Isabel wiped her mouth against the back of her hand and turned back to the computer, and the remaining clip.

She pressed 'play'.

# 56

ISABEL NEEDED TO get down to Manifold, and it had to be tonight. Every hour mattered. Even tomorrow morning would be too late.

Why on earth had she come here with no phone... no fucking anything? She kicked herself. How ridiculous. How reckless.

With her head in her hands, she took deep breaths and calmed down a little, thinking it through. In daylight, even through snow, she knew that four hours at the most would get her to the town. That's how long it had taken her last year. But at night? Six hours? Eight? She had no way of knowing. It was 5 PM already and she no longer cared how awe-inspiring the sunset might be, just that it might eke itself out a bit longer so she could trek as far as she could before dark. After that...

She had no time to lose.

Quickly, she prepared her backpack. Even though the trip wouldn't last more than a few hours, doing most of it in pitch dark would have its challenges. She snapped open the lid of the emergency box and saw the yellow EPIRB on top, the Emergency Position Indicating Radio Beacon. She mulled over triggering an immediate distress signal for Search and Rescue. But with time so critical—with every second counting—she was certain she'd get herself to Manifold faster than hanging around up here wondering, but not knowing, if someone had picked up the signal while that… while Ed… and Niki…

The two Secret Service agents who had packed the emergency box for her were also keen mountaineers and had made the trek to the town themselves, plotting every mound and creek, almost every tree and burrow, and had printed and laminated the whole thing onto the mountain map sitting below the EPIRB. Even more thoughtfully, they'd uploaded a digital version of it onto her combination GPS satellite tracker/EPIRB. The device was working—she checked—and she stuffed it into her front parka pocket, together with a compass, just in case. Into various pockets and zips in her backpack, she slotted signal flares and matches, a whistle, a foil space blanket, a sleeping bag, a fluoro-orange plastic undersheet, chemical hand warmers, a collapsible hand shovel, a first aid kit, a miner's lamp to strap on her forehead over her pull-on cap, a waterproof flashlight, a coil of rope, a roll of duct tape, a penknife and spare batteries.

Isabel wasn't taking anything for granted, the way she'd done with Ed. She also shoved in an extra pair of mittens, hat, and even a second windbreaker—it didn't look remotely like it could rain, but if she slipped into a creek she could freeze to death without a change of top clothes. The pack was already bulging, and that was before cramming in food and water.

By the time she'd finished, she'd also scoffed down a full mug of the hearty pumpkin soup she'd been simmering to avoid having to carry too much, but even so she threw in a couple of ring-pull cans of tuna and spaghetti, and some Mars bars. Accidents easily happened in the wild, everyone knew that.

As she hoisted the pack on her back, it wrenched her backwards a step or two. She steadied herself, deciding she'd have to rethink the contents. She shucked the bag off onto the floor and wolfed down more soup while she pulled out what she thought she could risk leaving behind.

Winter, she knew, was prime time for dehydration. The colder it got, the harder the body needed to work to maintain its temperature and the extra energy demands called for water to fuel them, and plenty of it. So damn the added load, she decided, and stuffed two extra bottles inside even though they were in glass, not plastic.

# 57

DAISY WAS NO longer at Daisy's Bar & Grill but Brad kept everything else at Andy Goodman's after-work hangout the same: the Millers on tap, the long-necked Buds, and the kettle-cooked peanuts in the unsanitary bowls that customers slid along the bar to each other with a traditional mountain holler.

Andy was already three drinks down, and he asked Brad to pull him a fourth.

Through the bar mirror, Andy saw the mayor's daughter swing open the door, and he straightened his back and tucked in his grey work shirt. He knew she didn't like beer; she was a white wine drinker, a stuck-up toffee-nose if he was really honest with himself, but what the heck. While she wasn't as hot as a McDonald's apple pie, she still had legs… and after a few wines her personality might not be that unbearable. He hoped so.

"Did you hear?" she said across the bar, sloughing off her coat and slinging it at the rack near the door. "Taylor? Did you hear about Taylor?" Her gloves flopped onto the counter almost knocking over Andy's beer. "A glass of white…"

"… wine," nodded Brad. He'd snatched for the bottle the moment she pushed the door open and set the glass in front of her, giving Andy a wink. Lucky for him she didn't notice.

"Taylor who? Taylor what?" Andy asked, his eyes taking in her new jeans. Tight in all the right places.

"Like, hello-o! *Mitchell* Taylor… *Vice-President* Taylor. Brad, switch on the TV," she said, without a breath, "Taylor's dead. Can you believe it? Radio says he collapsed… died in the ambulance on the way to the hospital. Shh! There!" She pointed at the screen and took a gulp of her wine.

Andy sipped his beer. He was laconic when he wanted to be, and he didn't really give a shit about politicians. Continually dealing with the moans from Isabel Diaz's people about putting in access to the shack was enough for him. So what if some politician was dead, what did he care? There were only more of them lining up to suck the public trough dry.

According to the replay time clock on the TV screen, it happened twenty minutes ago. In an echo of President George W. Bush reading *My Pet Goat* at Emma E. Booker Elementary School on 9/11, Taylor was cross-legged on a rug at Columbus Elementary sweet-talking some kids at an after-school Book Week readathon. With a *Dr Seuss* book in his lap, he simply keeled over.

Secret Service agents appeared out of nowhere, guns unholstered and scaring the bejesus out of the screaming kids even more than having a weird old guy collapsing in front of them did. While other agents swept the area for an assassin, one knelt beside Taylor to perform the classic airways, breathing and pulse-checks. The agent's eyes were dark and his eyebrows heavy when he whispered into his cuff. He nodded a few times as he took instructions though his earpiece and, one second after he crooked his finger, three others crammed around the body with him and, cradling the Vice-President between them, whisked him out to the waiting car past the distraught children and stunned reporters.

"*We're crossing now to St Anthony's Hospital, and Dr Alison Martin…*

"... *Vice-President Taylor suffered a massive heart attack but died before reaching hospital. Despite all efforts, we were not able to resuscitate him.*"

"Well, cheers to Dr Seuss," said Andy chinking his beer heartlessly against his bar buddy's wineglass. "What's the difference between a politician and a trampoline?" he asked, and immediately answered, "You'd take your shoes off to jump on a trampoline."

She didn't return his laugh or cheesy smile, just eyed him as she would a smear of dog shit on her shoe.

"So," said Brad, not quite changing the awkward subject, "how is your dad, the Mayor?"

Without a word, she swivelled off her stool, grabbed her coat and left.

# 58

PRESIDENT ROBERT J. FOSTER wrapped his arm around Chancellor Kurt Schneider's shoulders. Thanks to the late nights and deep secrets they shared when they were Harvard Law roommates, America's relations with the Federal Republic of Germany were thawing. On their way to pre-dinner cocktails in the Blue Room, they were chatting and laughing like the old buddies they were, the only remaining chill being in the air as they bustled along the colonnade from outside the Oval Office alongside the Rose Garden.

This was Schneider's first visit during either man's term. He couldn't make the Inauguration, but came as soon as he could and the main topic of their talks was a free-trade agreement.

The Chancellor was as startled as the President when a posse of Secret Service agents appeared from nowhere, yanked Foster's arm off him and whisked the President through a side door, abandoning the Chancellor to ponder the cold outside alone.

Less than a minute later, the First Lady emerged from the same door and, wide-eyed as though nothing had happened, greeted Schneider. "May I escort you to the Blue Room, Chancellor?" She took his arm and added blankly, "The President apologises for the abrupt interruption."

Schneider noted Marilyn's strained formality, and couldn't help looking up to scan the skies.

"AT forty-fucking-two?" President Foster drummed his fingers against the rim of the Resolute desk, the one that most presidents since 1880 had leant on in times of stress. "A fatal heart attack…? You kidding me? Mitch worked out. Hey, Don," he nodded to his chief of staff. "Are we sure this wasn't…?"

Foster's teary, strained eyes fell to one of the quotes that President Barack Obama had asked to be woven into the Oval Office's centrepiece rug: "*The only thing we have to fear is fear itself.*"

"Mr President, nothing showed up in the bloodwork, and," Don said, checking his watch, "St Anthony's are doing a full body-scan."

Foster shook his head, "He goes through all the pressure of the campaign and… bam! We're in office a few measly days and his body packs up? Go figure. I've got to visit with Julia and their kids. The First Lady, too… I'll tell her to pack some things when I get to the Blue Room. There's no way I can dump the Chancellor tonight—Kurt just got here—so we'll fly out in the morning. He'll understand. Don," he added, "fix the rest, okay?"

"Yes, Mr President. There's something else…"

The President said nothing, but his heart was pounding.

"We'll need to announce your new vice…"

"Fuck that. This isn't the time…"

"It's precisely the time, Mr President. Section Two of the Twenty-Fifth Amendment requires you to nominate…"

"Not before I pay my respects to the family of the last one, it doesn't."

"Yes, sir, but…"

Exasperated, Bobby squeezed his chin and exhaled, "There

are no buts, Don. Even after I nominate whoever, it'll take months. Both Houses of Congress have to confirm it, and they're not gonna do that till after all the damn hearings, so a day here or there, even a week... it's all fucking irrelevant, orright?"

Don had gotten used to Bobby's temper. This time it was personal, sure, but the unseemly behaviour was nothing new and he would let it wash over him, as usual.

He scrolled his mind to the following morning when the President would run across the South Lawn to his helicopter Marine One, ducking to avoid the rotors. Don would be beside him, stooped no more than usual, but whether Foster wanted to read it or not, Don would be passing him a detailed brief on the succession procedures, including a list of twenty potential nominees.

It was a shock, for sure, but both men knew this was no unique moment in history, although the details would come in Don's brief, which three of his best staff were already preparing. It would tell Foster that no fewer than seven vice-presidents had died in office and two had resigned. In 1973 when Spiro Agnew resigned and Richard Nixon nominated Gerald Ford as his new Vice-President, it took nearly two months of Washington gum-chewing before Ford got to take his oath of office. When in 1974 Nixon himself resigned, Ford just one day later nominated Nelson Rockefeller as his Vice-President, but it took almost four months for Rockefeller to take the oath of office; four months with no vice-president to step up should President Ford really stumble. And neither of those precedents remotely compared to the days before the Twenty-Fifth Amendment got passed in 1967: Lyndon Johnson had no vice-president for 14 months after President Kennedy's assassination—some said there still wasn't one even after Hubert Humphrey was eventually sworn in.

"But sir, what if *you*, er, suffered a… um… a heart attack?" Don was getting to his real concern. "Under the succession rules, it's the Speaker—Diaz—who steps up. And after that FOX segment, there's not even a scintilla of an argument to stop her."

# 59

IN THE THIRTY minutes of snow and slush that Isabel had put between herself and the shack, she'd tramped not quite two miles, and had long discarded her snowshoes as virtually useless. The curtain of nightfall was closing in, and would slow her even more as the thickening cloud cover threatened to block the moon.

Her breath was streaking ahead faster than she was. Normally she loved it out here but tonight she felt totally isolated. Vulnerable. Petrified.

It wasn't the moose tracks that worried her; Isabel imagined she could deal with a moose. It was the ripped-open logs and digging marks, signs that screamed of a black bear. Normally, a bear would be no problem unless you got between a mother and her cub but, right now, Isabel could only imagine the worst. For comfort, she glanced at her handheld GPS map-tracker as though it could reveal the whereabouts of vicious animals.

The distant howl of a wolf stopped her, chilled her. But even that didn't pump her adrenaline as much as the dread of the impending dark and the many dangers it could hide.

BEFORE she had left the shack, she had plotted onto the laminated map with a marker pen what seemed like an easy path, and she was sticking to it as closely as possible, comparing it against the GPS tracker every ten or so minutes. "Easy" turned out to be a relative description, as her aching legs and back were discovering. It was heavy going over the thick snow and until now, despite the fading light, she'd resisted using her flashlight or miner's lamp. But it was no longer safe to advance without them. Her pack had been cutting into her shoulders, so she readjusted it, bounced it into the small of her back and retightened the waist straps for support. After ten paces, it was hugging a lot better so she strapped the halogen miner's lamp over her woollen cap and snapped on the light. In her left mitten, she had her tracker and map, and her other gripped a walking stick that doubled as a probe checking for crevasses hidden under the snow.

The miner's lamp was a mixed blessing. She could see whatever its fairly narrow beam illuminated, but out of the gloom at its edges a succession of sinister shadowy shapes kept looming, one appearing like an angry mother bear... another she lashed her hiking pole at, imagining that the branch was Ed.

Twenty minutes later, guided by the headlamp, she had already tripped four times—over semi-concealed rocks, tree roots, and twigs—so she dug out her flashlight and, despite some initial confusion with double shadows, the depth of vision was a welcome relief.

She trudged a mile down a slope packed with slightly thicker snow. Despite the deep holes sunk by each tiring step, her boot linings kept her feet dry.

A fallen branch, as grey in this light as the snow, caught her heel and she back-flipped and turtled, landing helplessly onto her pack with her legs and arms splayed out. She lay still for a while, winded, and scooped up some snow and sucked on it as she looked up, watching the tree canopy shiver as an eerie breeze whistled through. Suddenly realising it was foolish to lower her temperature, she spat out the remains of the snow, unstrapped her backpack and twisted herself out of it before getting back to her feet where, after wrapping her scarf around her face and yanking the hem of her parka down, she heaved her backpack on and continued walking.

This wind was going to be a friend, she saw. It was high, huffing away the clouds to let the moon through and a mellow light was already thankfully spreading around her. She paused to check her location—the base of Milligan's Hill—and she pushed on. Her steps still sank deep but twisted a little on the pebbly terrain below the snow. She guessed it was a deposit of scree that had collected during spring rains, so she went on even more gingerly, wary of her footfalls as well as the branches scraping her outerwear. She was rubbing her arm where a surprisingly rigid limb had ripped through her parka sleeve when her boot caught under a rock and she pitched headlong into a fallen trunk.

When her eyes opened again she guessed she'd been blacked-out for at least five minutes. Her head was spinning and her forehead was aching and when she went to rub her brow, she discovered that when her head had hit the log, her headlamp had smashed. As she drew her hand away, she saw blots of blood on her glove.

She wobbled herself up to sit on the trunk, and slipped off the lamp strap. Attempting to wipe her head with her forearm sleeve, the shot of pain through her right arm jolted her. She could see blood seeping out of another rip and, looking around, saw that the offending branch at the base of the log was waving a tiny flag of her parka sleeve. Below it, pink bloodstains had spread into the snow.

Her arm only hurt if she lifted it, which also made her woozy. She knew she had to stem the blood and stop the cold seeping in through the tear in the fabric. She had to go on. Turning back was not an option.

Her GPS tracker had perched itself on top of the log, safely she thought, and the strap of her flashlight was balanced on the tip of her walking pole as though she'd carefully hung it there herself. After she oofed off her pack, she took out the first aid kit and, puffing some antiseptic powder through the rip, plastered her arm and then, after removing a few shards of glass from her head wound, cleaned and taped that too. For good measure, she sealed the slash in her ski jacket with two strips of duct tape, making an X. Ready to move off, she reached out for the tracker but the pain from her arm scorched her again.

Bad had just gone to worse: the GPS screen was smashed. She guessed the EPIRB function was still okay, but had no way of knowing without setting it off. She slipped it into a pocket, glad she had also brought the old-fashioned laminated map and compass, and she slogged onward.

As she reached lower and lower down the mountain, the snow was thinning, in increasing spots fingering itself out to rock and hard, bare dirt. She sped up; not too fast, since it was still icy and she was fretful of her arm, steering away from stray branches, especially as waves of occasional dizziness washed over her.

The map showed that Major's Creek was coming up and she became tetchy about crossing it. Would it be frozen solid, or would the cover merely be a deceptive skin of easily cracked ice? She needn't have worried, not about that, since pretty soon it was clear she wasn't even close to Major's Creek.

Under her flashlight, she carefully checked and rechecked the map. Where had she gone wrong? She trudged on another few hundred feet; still no creek. She went back, at least she thought so, but the ground was starting to rise when it should have been falling.

Her arm was pounding and her head was no better, but she had enough sense to take another pause. She slung her pack to the ground, parked herself on it and, under the side flap, her fingers felt around for two Mars bars and one of her bottles of water. Steady methodical chewing. It was calming, but only until her mind was sucked back to Ed's betrayals.

She leant her head back to take a swig of water.

He must have been at this for months, she thought, the two-faced… Isabel replayed the sick, depraved banter in her mind.

She was lost, that was obvious to her. Three hours she'd been going and she didn't have a clue where she was. She knew she'd been crazy to try this at night. But should she have stayed up at the shack, set off the EPIRB and waited? More importantly, should she do that now? She slipped it out of her pocket and looked at the shattered screen as though it would reply for itself.

It was 8:15 PM. Yet even with the wrong turn she'd obviously made somewhere, she was sure she'd get herself back on track, just like she'd done with her life. If she triggered the EPIRB it would take Search and Rescue at least the three hours she guessed she still had to go—but there was a good chance they would wait till daylight—and she needed to keep moving, not to stay stuck in this frozen, godforsaken spot.

Isabel ate a second snack bar and stowed her trash, slipping the empty bottle into the mesh pocket on one side of her backpack.

Calmer, she studied the map and, after about five minutes of mental backtracking, she calculated there was a good chance she was near Potter's Mound, and if she simply headed west a little, she'd find a stand of black spruce.

SHE was right. Unfortunately.

She could smell the familiar earthy, sweet spruce perfume even before she saw them. Potter's Mound was smack in the centre of the wolves' urine-marked territory, and Andy Goodman's prize female had been out on the prowl for a couple of hours, always keeping close to the den she'd established for when her litter came. Gretel was big. Nose-to-tail, she was five feet long, last time weighing in at 120 pounds though she was undoubtedly heavier now.

Gretel whipped her tail out from behind an old hemlock and her glossy black nose sniffed out something tempting. Near to the ground, she stalked forward and a few shards of broken glass flashed the moon into her yellow-green eyes.

She drew up to the log and started to paw at the alien shiny parka material but drew back sharply… her paw had been cut. She spied the stains on the snow but knew instinctively they weren't hers, even before smelling them. Ignoring her paw—she'd had worse—Gretel's snow-white snout dropped back down and sniffed around the strange bloodstains. Her ear brushed against the torn piece of sleeve hanging from the branch and she twisted up to inhale its scent. Her long back arched and, with her good front paw, she jabbed at the spatters of blood in the snow. She seemed to make a decision and turned, low to the ground, making a slow, stealthy pace toward the stand of black spruce, a blood-spotted track trailing behind her.

Halfway along, she stopped dead. Her head lifted and she sniffed the air.

She pulled her lips back to bare her teeth and her menacing, guttural growl cracked the silence.

# 60

"SO FAR, SO good," Ed muttered to himself. Isabel was enjoying her last night up at her shack and Davey was at home in Bridgehampton with George and the housekeeper. Ed was overnighting at the Magiston Resort and had his head resting against the pillows before dinner, after a strenuous round of tennis on the indoor courts. He was here for his reunion of Loane's Rangers, his old unit, together with the usual hand-picked ring-ins. Every two years he hosted his buddies at the historic Magiston for a quiet dinner. No spouses or partners. Ed was devoted to his Rangers, many of them having earned a spot working in the sprawl of his corporate empire, or somewhere else on his team.

In pride of place in the centre of the grand table, always, would be the shot of Loane's Rangers taken twenty-five years before: Ed flanked by ten men in camouflage flight suits, one of whom was cradling his baby girl swaddled in a matching camy blanket. Mel Abbott had fought with Ed in 'Nam but died rappelling in the Rockies in the early 1990s. His daughter was Niki, and Ed and the Rangers had virtually adopted her when Mel died.

At college, her tuition paid for by Ed, Niki had signed up for the Air Force Reserve Officer Training Corps program.

Even as a kid she'd imagined herself as a pilot, unlike her dad; his passion had been fast cars and he'd even named her after Niki Lauda, the Formula One Grand Prix winner. What Niki loved most about flying was the exhilaration of calculated risk-taking, which didn't exactly make her a great fit for the disciplined life of the military.

However, it was her knack of capturing in her photographs that same sense of living on the edge that made them so sought-after. After ROTC, she'd trained as an Air Force pilot and, despite her notoriety for breaking the rules, she attained the rank of captain. It was ultimately because of that reputation that she was frog-marched out of the service and pushed herself into full-time camera work, well, mostly full-time, as her Loane's Rangers colleagues knew.

It was set to be a long night with much to celebrate, so Ed had taken an early nap. He bent sideways to check the hotel's bedside clock. It was around seven, half-an-hour before cocktails. He lay back on his pillow and imagined Isabel, extinguishing the shack's lanterns, her own head hitting the pillow just as his was getting up.

"Sleep well," he whispered.

Niki's soft blue eyes fluttered open and she brushed aside a strand of her red hair. "Wha…?"

# 61

IN AROMATHERAPY, BLACK spruce is used to suppress anxiety, but it couldn't help Isabel. She sensed a presence, and froze. Not a wisp of breath escaped her as her ears strained… At first, she heard nothing but the wind, until she detected the low rumble coming at her from beyond the trees.

She slid the tip of her hiking pole into the snow and, as quietly as possible, unbuckled her pack at the waist and let her shoulders and arms slip it slowly to the ground, her right arm causing her to wince, though only a little. Her fingers closed around the knife handle sticking up from her belt pouch and, like a reed in a breeze, she twisted around for the empty water bottle in the side mesh pocket of her backpack, gripped its neck and yanked it out.

She waited.

A flash of moonlight flared over near the stand of trees the growl was coming from. In the glow, an animal's snout began to make itself out. It was white. Abruptly, a pair of low luminous eyes blazed at her. Despite the tremble of panic, she calculated that they were too close to the ground… This was not a bear, it was something much smaller. And yet it was bigger than a snowshoe hare.

Instinct took over. She flicked on her flashlight and aimed it directly at the yellow-green eyes, praying the beam would startle whatever it was and make it scamper off.

Her torch lit up a wolf, and she almost dropped it in fright. Her heart was pounding as though she had already made a run for it, which her thrashing mind was telling her to do.

The beast defied the light, refusing to back off. It wouldn't avert its eyes. They were riveted on her, staring her down, sizing her up. She could feel them gazing up and down her body, like the sum-total of all those sleazy eyes she'd had to endure over those years waiting tables, but far worse.

Her blood ran cold, and she clamped her jaw till it ached as she tried to still even her slightest movement.

The wolf's sharp, bared teeth flashed the beam back at her as a thick string of saliva drew its way down from its muzzle to the ground.

Isabel was prey. She was sure of it. The assurance that *no adult had ever been killed in North America by a wild wolf* was looking scratchy.

She met its gaze halfway along her beam, and noticed a strange dark stain spreading out from under one of its front paws. In this poor, exaggerated light, the animal's paw seemed to be bulging. She moved her beam, just a little. It was blood. Her whole body shook, remembering that the advice had actually been that no *healthy* wild wolf had killed an adult.

★ ★ ★ ★ ★

ANDY Goodman's ears were assaulted by an unrelenting banging on the toilet door.

"You okay in there?" the barman shouted as he kept pounding. "Andy! You okay?"

"Hmm…? Yeah, I'm fine. Be out in a minute. Musta fallen asleep." It wasn't because of the booze; he'd only had four drinks the last couple of hours due to Brad knowing Andy liked to push it, but he'd started his ranger's rounds early that day, around six, and this was as good a spot for a bit of shut-eye as anywhere else.

Andy wiped his nose and sniffed. "Must be all that fresh mountain air in here."

As Brad swung out the door and walked back into Daisy's, he flicked on the extractor fan.

With a furry tongue and a dry mouth, Andy sat for a moment in the dim light—the bulb dangling above him was dead—and heard a buzzing sounds from within the confines of his cubicle. "Brad, hey… cut it out." His pants were still furled around his ankles but he now realised the noise was coming from down there, from his beeper hanging off his belt. It was flashing red.

Andy unclipped it and brought it up close to his eyes. Shit! Gretel was at 253 bpm. What the fuck was she doing? He scrolled back to read the log. She'd been up above 240 for fifteen minutes. Why hadn't he woken?

Was someone—or something—chasing her? Was she on a kill? Before he could answer with even more speculation, he watched as his wolf's heart rate slumped, in the space of a few seconds, to 83, a resting rate.

And then it plunged again, to 59, a beat of sleep. Or worse.

This was wrong. Way wrong. The beat drops were too rapid. She'd been attacked, or caught in a trap… bleeding to death. It had to be.

He was buckling his belt as he raced out through the bar, his head spinning around, searching for someone to help. Paul Dawkins was in one of the restaurant booths. Paul was a local garage mechanic and volunteer fire-fighter who had assisted Andy when Gretel was first introduced into the area; they had done the radio-collaring together. "Paul, Gretel's in trouble up there." He held up his beeper so Paul would understand. "We gotta go. Now!"

Paul was drinking margaritas with his wife and a couple Andy didn't recognise.

"Gretel?" his wife asked warily. Her finger wiped the salt off the rim of her glass. She didn't know any Gretels around these parts.

"One of Andy's wolves," Paul responded. "The pregnant one Andy was going on about…"

"Come on, man," Andy yelled. "I need help, like fuckin' urgent."

Paul's wife didn't hide her disgust at his language, but Andy was the only one who didn't notice; he was already out the door and Paul was following, leaving just a shrug and his party behind him.

★ ★ ★ ★ ★

GRETEL kept her head low to the ground. She began to slope toward Isabel, paw by paw, the dark splotches trailing behind her being whisked into the snow by her dragging tail.

Isabel didn't breathe. She didn't move. She kept the flashlight beam aimed directly at the wolf's eyes, hoping to blind it or push it back as though she were wielding a *Star Wars* lightsaber.

As the wolf drew closer into the long, narrow cone of light, the snow cover flared the underside of her muzzle and made the beast loom even larger.

Suddenly, Isabel spotted more blood splatters in the snow… in between her and the wolf. They were hers. The wolf had been tracking her. Sniffing her.

With her teeth, Isabel pulled a glove off her hand. Careful to avoid sudden movements she delicately pressed her arm. Her hammering heartbeats were spurting blood out of the wound—she could feel it—and saw it oozing out from under the X of the duct tape and dripping to the ground. She felt like a target.

The creature stopped... fifteen feet back from her prey. She arched her back and, snout down, nosed into one of Isabel's bloodstains. The animal stretched out long and taut and, as though she had made a tactical decision, lurched to one side and started to circle Isabel.

Isabel *was* prey.

Her knife blade was ludicrously short, fine for slicing an apple not for hacking at a leaping, snarling carnivore. She feared the bottle in her other hand was also next to useless. She needed a better weapon and dropped her eyes to her backpack… The shovel. She also spied a rock protruding partway out of the snow. Staring back at the circling wolf, as though that might warn her off, she forced her shaking knees to bend, taking herself down slowly. No sudden movements. With her eyes fixed on the animal, she deposited the flashlight on top of her pack, aiming it at where the wolf seemed to be heading.

Her hand felt for the shovel and unclipped it as silently as she could. With the handle tight in her hand, her other, good arm raised the bottle by the neck and smashed it down onto the rock, shattering the brittle silence.

Isabel hadn't expected it.

For weeks, she hadn't had one of her flashes … but now, years of trauma welled up inside her…

*She was fifteen… the gory wolf tattoo rippled on his tricep as that evil bastard lunged for her.*

Her body shook uncontrollably.

But who was holding the fucking broken bottle this time! She almost screamed it out loud, but let it gag in her throat, not out of fear… out of defiance.

This time it would end differently. This time, she would be no victim. Too much depended on it.

★ ★ ★ ★ ★

"THE networks say he's flying out to St Louis first thing tomorrow to visit Taylor's widow," said Niki, her voice raised so Ed could hear her in the bathroom.

He came out, looping his bow tie. "Perfect timing," he said, nudging her elbow. "To dinner?"

"Last supper?"

# 62

THE SNOW SUCKED the heat out of both bodies, gorging on the blood from their gaping wounds, turning itself into a stinking red slush. The two combatants were waning.

Gretel's blunder had been shooting for Isabel's neck. As the growling animal hurled herself up and her wild eyes met Isabel's square on, she sensed this mad woman was no easy victim.

Isabel's blood surged, roping her thick neck vein so it seemed to slash across her scar to make the sign of the cross that the ancients would wield to ward off evil. Gretel didn't know about such things, but she should have paid more attention to the shovel that Isabel had hoisted high, before she heaved it down, crunching it into the wolf's snarling maw. Gretel had pitched onto her back and immediately rolled, coming back for more, howling, almost losing her footing in her slippery charge. Isabel swept the spade wide and almost knocked her aside but Gretel managed to duck it, and gripped her fangs into Isabel's already weak arm. Jerking her head from side to side, she forced the weapon out of Isabel's hand before ripping into her limb.

With Gretel hanging off her arm and dragging her to the ground, Isabel clenched her fingers round the jagged bottle neck. She screamed a long gurgling shriek and heaved it down, straight into Gretel's eye socket, and twisted with all her fading might. She twisted again, but this time her own head exploded in pain, from her wounds and the memories she would rather have forgotten.

Both fell backwards, away from each other. The wolf thudded into the snow and her head thrashed around as she convulsed, trying to cast the glass out of her eye. Isabel tripped on a rock and her right leg twisted under her.

★ ★ ★ ★ ★

ANDY backed his flat-top out of his garage so he and Paul had more room to heft the snowmobile and the ATV up onto the tray. After lashing them down securely, Andy threw in the first-aid kit and a stretcher sled and they spun off. It was ten minutes of rumbling and bumping over rocks and roots and it was only after they'd passed three *No Vehicular Access* signs that Paul spoke, lifting his voice above the racket, "Bein' a ranger's got some privileges, huh?"

"Gotta save my wolf, man," Andy yelled. "Those're my signs, anyhow. Don't apply to me."

Half a mile higher up, their lights flashed on a *No Vehicles. No Camping. No Fires* sign. Paul said nothing. He was monitoring the GPS and Andy thrashed the pedals, concentrating hard in the dark, it being no mean feat trying to steer clear of ditching the truck or smashing it into the sudden succession of trees or rocks that kept materialising out of the blackness.

It took them forty minutes to reach Lambert's Crossing which, by necessity, was the end of the line for the flat-top. By GPS calculations, they had to cover two more miles to reach Gretel, but the pair could see the cover here was too patchy for the snowmobile. Andy hauled on the handbrake and the two men jumped out and bounced the fat-tyred ATV down onto the dirt. Andy strapped the stretcher sled and first-aid kit to the back; they hopped on and he revved off. Paul had charge of the tracker and the battery-powered spotlight but he couldn't grip onto Andy and operate the two devices at the same time.

"Stop," Paul shouted into Andy's ear.

He screeched to a halt. "What?"

Paul needed to rearrange himself. He slipped the GPS strap around the front of Andy's throat and over so it rested down his back and he could see it from behind. With one hand free to hold the spotlight and one to grip Andy, Paul was set. "Go!"

THE two miles were tough. Andy's tracker map was basic, lacking the detail of Isabel's but at least it was working. Fifteen minutes for two miles. Bluffs and cliffs and fallen trees blocked them. Repeatedly, they had to stop for frozen-over creeks to check for weight carry. By the time they got close to the clearing, Gretel's heart rate was almost flat-lining.

"Over there," screamed Paul.

Andy wrenched the throttle forward and they flew up and into the clearing, bouncing down about ten feet from the fallen wolf, but when he slammed on the brakes, Paul almost flew over Andy's shoulder. He managed to grip and stay on, though the spotlight flew into a tree and sputtered out.

Unexpectedly, another flashlight beam sliced across their route to Gretel.

"What the f...," Andy wheezed, surveying the gruesome scene. Dark—he assumed red—rivers were flowing out of both bodies. The broken neck of a bottle stuck out of one of Gretel's eye sockets twisting her into some rabid, R-rated cartoon character. A sickening concoction of shock and revulsion welled inside him, but loathing for the perpetrator kept it down. He stood still, to grip himself. Out the corner of his eye he saw Paul running to check the other body, whoever the fuck the murdering bastard was, probably a poacher. To Andy, he deserved whatever he got.

Andy lurched over to Gretel. Dribbles of her bile slobbered into the puddle under her pitiful head. Her good eye was almost opaque, the once luminous yellow-green had doused itself.

Gretel was gone. There wasn't even a squiggle showing on his monitor; not even a misty puff of air from her lips.

Paul shouted, but Andy didn't hear what he was saying.

"Andy, it's some woman."

Andy glimpsed over to see him rolling her onto her back, unzipping the top of her parka and feeling her neck for a pulse.

The loathing smouldered within Andy as he dropped, helpless, to his knees beside Gretel. Instinctively, he knew who the wolf-killer had to be.

What had that bitch fucking done? He removed his glove and stroked his wolf. The only trace of warmth left on her frosty fur was from his touch. His anger welled and he gripped his hand into a fist and pounded it at the melt beside Gretel, but smashed it against a thinly disguised rock. Absently and without a sound, Andy lifted his hand and stared as his own blood dripped out of his glove and mingled with Gretel's.

"Andy, get over here," screamed Paul. "Now!"

# 63

RUMBLING DOWN TO Manifold on the back of the flat-top, Paul moulded himself around Isabel like a hotdog bun, his arms and legs wrapped to radiate his body heat into the frozen woman. He and Andy, mostly he, had cleaned and patched her wounds and removed her wet clothes, replacing them with the dry gear they'd found in her backpack. Her space blanket as well as Andy's, and his crusty back shelf rug and sleeping bag were now swaddling the two of them, keeping the chill out from the air and the metal truck tray they were lying on. They'd left both the snowmobile and the ATV at Lambert's Crossing. Andy, a trained paramedic as well as a ranger, should have been the one to hop up on the back and care for Isabel but when Paul saw the rage steaming out of his friend's nostrils, he didn't even suggest it.

Andy drove with the two very premature wolf cubs coddled inside a blanket on the seat next to him. With his tears streaming, he'd sliced Gretel open to save her litter. There'd been five, but three were already gone.

When they got into phone signal range, Andy radioed ahead to alert the doctors at the county ER to scrub up for an emergency.

"Injuries…? Age…? Sex…? Name…?" grilled Emily, the triage nurse who took the call. Andy had dated her a few times.

"It's the Speaker of the House, orright? Go fuckin' Google her!"

Paul hugged Isabel close to him. Initially, he confused her shivering with the rough terrain Andy was bouncing the truck over and he called out to get Andy to slow down. But, once he realised, he worked harder at stroking warmth into her. Before they took off, Andy had explained she was probably in hypothermic shock, so Paul needed to get her warm and keep talking to her, pushing her to respond, to stay conscious. Paul spoke to her about everything and nothing, at least he tried, but his voice came out in fits and starts: whenever the truck would dip into a ditch or bounce off a rock, it would throw the huddled pair, and his words, off-balance.

"… so T-Taylor had a heart attack and po-popped it. It was while he w-a-as reading *Dr Seu-Seuss* to some s-school kids. C-can you believe th-that?" Paul asked, not expecting an answer.

Isabel coughed for the first time and, against his cheek, he felt an eyelash struggle to open. She whispered something Paul couldn't make out over the bumps and rolls. "Wha-a-at?" he asked.

She tried again. "Too l-late." Her hand, limp, did its best to imitate a fist against his shoulder blade.

Paul misunderstood. "Don't worry. You'll be fine. You'll see." Shit, he thought; she could've been President of the United States and here she was, thinking she was dying in his arms… Maybe she was, he shivered, but it wasn't just from the cold.

"T-too late," she repeated as her eye closed.

★ ★ ★ ★ ★

BY 9:30 PM, protocol formally reassigned the Vice-President's Secret Service detail to Isabel now she was officially next in line, albeit temporarily until Foster nominated his own choice as replacement for Taylor. They worked fast and would've acted even quicker if they'd known where she was and in what condition, but intelligence is hardly a perfect art, as the startling, unpredicted eruption against despots in the Middle East and North Africa proved yet again.

"She's up at her mountain shack," said George calmly when he took their call. "She'll be back in Washington tomorrow afternoon." He had also taken quite a few calls from media, but had told them nothing, not even that.

"No coms up there, right?" asked the Special Agent.

"Coms?" asked George, worried the goon was a Cold War throwback.

"Communications, sir. Our records say there's no phone line, no phone network or anything else up there."

"Correct. Taylor's death'll be some big shock when she finds out. After all she went through last year, to find herself now—what's the saying?—a heartbeat away from being president…"

"Yes, sir."

"You should phone her husband." George wasn't about to do it himself.

But the agent had already tried Ed's number, and had got a voicemail message.

# 64

THE COUNTY HOSPITAL pulsed as the staff prepped for Isabel's arrival. Normally not much happened around here at night, apart from occasional heart attacks that mostly turned out to be indigestion.

Dr Tom Cisco had been at his monthly Rotarians dinner when his pager buzzed, licking his lips and inhaling the window-sill aroma of the freshly baked green apple pie being brought around by the waiters. Even in Manifold, a deep Democrat town, the sudden death of a vice-president couldn't get in the way of the town's famous pie. But his pager could. Tom Cisco was on call tonight.

"We'll call you again when they're closer, so you don't need to come over till then," the triage duty nurse offered. She knew how much the hospital's head surgeon looked forward to his pie.

As his slice of pie was placed in front of him, Cisco held the phone and pondered what he'd just been told. The aroma of steaming apple, cinnamon and sugar was normally heaven for him, eliminating all other sensations, but now, all he could think about was how the more apt phrase would be the *hypocritic* oath, what with him being a committed liberal and now apparently charged with saving the life of the new, and Republican, second in line.

But then he recalled his med school buddy Joe Giordano's story. When President Ronald Reagan was shot, he was lying on Joe's operating table, and he looked up at him and quipped, "*I hope you're a Republican...*" Joe, a Democrat like Cisco, famously answered, "*Today, Mr President, we're all Republicans.*"

The nurse crackled into the phone. "Dr Cisco, hell-o-o-o?"

"I'm coming in now," Cisco said and hung up. For a patient like this, when the nation's eyes would be on him, even pie would have to wait, but he took a long deep sniff of it before he left. Then a forkful.

Two, in fact.

DR Cisco was already scrubbing up when Andy's tyres squealed into the emergency bay. The night crew knew that their initial task, in addition to staunching the blood loss, would be to get Isabel's temperature up. The first check had her well below normal but a touch above the danger marker for severe hypothermia.

"Paul... Andy," smiled the nurse, "you guys may have saved her life."

Andy shrugged as if he didn't care, which was not far from the truth. All he wanted to do was get Gretel's two pups to the vet. Paul was already on the phone to his wife, telling her the astonishing story.

As Isabel's gurney was wheeled inside, she drowsed in and out of consciousness. "Wha...s that?" she asked weakly, pointing to the warmed tube a nurse was inserting into a vein in her hand as they rolled down the corridor. She couldn't make out a name on the badge. Everything was too blurry.

"It's a heated drip, ma'am," the nurse responded, "to get your temperature up."

Isabel's attention focused momentarily on the second nurse, shooting the air and a stream of liquid out of a syringe, and her brow furrowed.

"And this is a pain killer," the nurse said.

Isabel tensed. "I need… phone… now. Must phone…"

"You've lost a lot of blood, ma'am," said the nurse, still wielding the syringe, "and you're hypothermic. We've got to get you warmed up before we take you into theatre. The doctors are already scrubbed and waiting." She peeled back a ripped piece of Isabel's parka and tried to swab her shoulder but Isabel struggled, and pushed herself back in the gurney as far as she could, her face twisting with the excruciating pain. She yanked the drip out of her vein and knocked the syringe to the floor, the needle scraping across her hand. The orderly wheeling the cart pulled to a sudden halt.

"Phone… Now!" Isabel screamed.

The two nurses looked at each other and then at the orderly. The patient was delusional. Hypothermia could do that. "I'll get the doctor."

"A phon…" Isabel tried to repeat, but she was fading, again.

# 65

DESPITE AN UNFINISHED agenda in their official talks, the German Chancellor had graciously proposed a raincheck on the dinner he knew had been elaborately set up in the State Dining Room. President Foster, though grateful for his old friend's consideration, declined to postpone, concerned that Kurt's voters might read it as yet another American snub, even though this time there was a perfectly understandable reason.

But as soon as was decent, Bobby pushed his chair back to stand. For an awkward moment his guests shuffled, unsure of whether to rise as well, but he motioned for them to be still. He put on one of his famous smiles and walked over to the stone mantel, to George Healy's famous portrait of President Lincoln. Below the great man's contemplative chin-on-hand, eyes-to-the-distance pose, Foster stood tall, and his own eyes glimmered with grace. He was in his element and nodded to the First Lady, reminding her what a thrill it still was for them both to be here.

He fingered the inscription carved into the mantelpiece. "John Adams," he said, "wrote this on his second night in the White House... '*I pray Heaven to Bestow the Best of Blessings on This House and on All that shall hereafter Inhabit it. May none but honest and Wise Men ever rule under this roof.*' And tonight, a most difficult one for us, we are blessed to have as our guest an honest and wise man who rules under a different roof but who is always welcome under this one."

Before the Chancellor could push his chair back to respond, one of the President's aides entered the room and whispered into Foster's ear.

★ ★ ★ ★ ★

ISABEL was hooked up to every relevant medical device the hospital possessed and no one dared ask her about health insurance.

Tubes snaked into and out of her in more places than polite company would like to know. The nurse glanced up from the chart to the cardiac monitor. She'd previously given Isabel a short bolus of five cc. per pound of 5-percent dextrose in normal saline and was now administering two-and-a-half cc. per hour as a continuous infusion. She was pleased, still, to see no arrhythmias.

A sweet wintergreen bouquet of birch oil overpowered the antiseptic hospital odour. Coldly known in the trade as methyl salicylate, the nurse had swabbed it over Isabel's skin as a vasodilator to enlarge her surface blood vessels. It was a strong fragrance even for this ER nurse, but for Isabel it didn't exist. All she could smell was humidified and warmed oxygen, which the ventilator clamped over her nose and mouth was pumping steadily into her at 40.5°C.

The nurse clicked an oximeter onto the tip of one of Isabel's fingers. This was a tiny but miraculous device: by shining onto the fingertip a small light beam of a very specific wavelength, it measured the absorption spectrum and estimated the oxygen saturation in her skin's surface blood vessels.

Dr Cisco was withholding surgery until he was completely satisfied that she wasn't hypothermic. Sticking to standard practice, the nurse was pumping Isabel intravenously with steady quantities of heated fluid. She checked a few more of the lines on the chart. She also checked the CVP line stuck into the large central vein in Isabel's neck, connected to a fluid status monitor by a dark pulsing red tube. Given the liquids Isabel was taking, she also needed a urinary bladder catheter and, to monitor her outputs and thus her internal temperature, Isabel's was connected to a thermistor, a heat sensor.

The nurse slipped the thermometer from under Isabel's arm. She checked her watch and, happy the patient had been stable for thirty minutes, she poked her head out into the corridor and saw the orderly crouched against the wall reading a copy of the *Manifold Tribune*. "It's time," she called and, together, they sheeted up the gurney to wheel their VIP to surgery.

★ ★ ★ ★ ★

OUTSIDE the White House, the silence of the night whooped to a roar as the long rotor blades of the President's helicopter levitated its payload to join up with the decoy choppers already hovering above. Tonight Marine One was the VH-60, a modified Blackhawk with medical evacuation facilities on board.

The President's immediate destination was Andrews Air Force Base where, with no time to lose, Air Force One was being primed for take-off.

The media that usually got herded in on the President's trips were nowhere to be seen. When they woke up and discovered what they'd missed, especially if it leaked that he'd flown off in the VH-60, they'd be grizzling about more than a skipped flight.

# 66

DAN CARTER'S CHEEKS almost matched the red of the scarf wrapped around them. For twenty sub-freezing minutes that began at 5.30 AM, the *Manifold Tribune* reporter—also its editor and publisher—was one of the fifty or more souls who, thirsty for the story, had been bunched up outside in the dark, cross-slapping their shoulders and stomping their feet near the cold stone hospital steps. In that throng of reporters who'd rushed here, Carter was alone in one respect: when the newswire came through, he was the only one who'd ever heard of Manifold, let alone lived there. He'd actually come here last night—the news had flown around the town—but Tom Cisco had insisted on the hospital enforcing a no-go zone, even for his friend Dan.

The jostling forward started as soon as the wash of yellowish light that had filtered through the glass front doors began flickering, telling the media that someone was once again headed up the corridor to come out to speak to them. This time it wasn't the nurse. Instead, the swing doors were pushed aside by the head surgeon, a distinguished, balding man with serious deep-set eyes and an arrow-point nose that Dan Carter knew was, for Tom Cisco, too uncomfortably close to a certain former president's. Instantly hit by the dazzling onslaught of the TV floodlights and camera flashes, the doctor stood at the top of the steps blinking and shielding his eyes.

Dan and Tom were fishing buddies and just last night, the pair were about to hoe into the apple pie when the doctor was called in.

Dan decided to assert his local *droit du seigneur* and got in first, "Dr Cisco, is Ms Diaz stable?" he asked.

Before Cisco could give his answer, another reporter stretched her microphone forward, past several sets of frost-pink ears and asked, without a hint of intended humour, "Has the Speaker said anything?"

The doctor peered down from the steps, trying not to squint. This was one of those moments, he thought, when it would be perfect to wear those pince-nez glasses, the ones that characters in novels or movies always got to stare down over the top of. But his perfect eyesight meant Cisco had to do without props, other than his forearm to shield him from the floodlights that had just been snapped on.

"Dan... Dan Carter," said the doctor bumping up his friend's status by using his name, "Ms Diaz is no longer critical. I'm relieved to say she is stable, and sleeping. But...," he held up his hand to halt the surge of interruptions, "you should know that Madam Speaker came to us in a most serious state, suffering acute hypothermia, massive lacerations and severe blood loss after an attack by a wolf up at Potter's Mound..." The crowd jostled in closer. "Two locals, ranger Andy Goodman and Paul Dawkins, found her up there. They immediately stemmed her blood loss and their quick thinking saved her from frostbite and, ah, much worse. Relatively, she's doing fine. But no, she isn't speaking. She's under sedation."

"Her family?" asked another hack, pushing up the steps and thrusting her mike into Cisco's face.

The doctor stepped back, his face twisting at the poor manners, but he collected himself and wrenched his features into a smile, "They're due here shortly. Perhaps you should go and greet them at our little airport." He prayed they would, especially this jackal!

A small pack did break off to go, but hesitated when they heard the next question, "When *will* Ms Diaz be able to speak to us?"

"That'll be up to her, but not before this afternoon." Cisco was being safe. He knew Isabel would be fine enough physically; she'd recovered quickly from the hypothermia thanks to Paul Dawkins' and the nursing staff's efforts. His surgery, though intricate, was pretty much a patch job. While her parts of her arm and leg had been ripped to shreds, her main problems were likely to be residual shock, lingering stings and severe throbbing, but with pain-killers he could get her hobbling about within the day, though he would not be recommending it.

For a county doctor, Tom Cisco was hardly garrulous, Dan Carter already knew that, but the visiting journalists' frustration was mounting. Cisco wasn't giving much away, so they pressed him further and further into the inconsequential, and Cisco reacted defensively, trying desperately to close it down and get back inside. But to the journalists, any personal tidbit about Isabel was better than nothing. Cisco detested even a flicker of publicity—it was why he'd moved here fifteen years ago. Each question answered on camera was another fingernail scraping away at his veneer of civility and as soon as decency permitted, he got himself back inside the sanctuary of his hospital, where he rushed into the men's room to wash the sweat dripping off his face.

CISCO drew back the curtain around Isabel's bed to check everything ahead of the expected invasion of visitors. As well as those who'd already arrived—her husband, a general no less, and her son and foster father—the hospital had been alerted to expect an influx of Secret Service and Administration personnel around lunchtime.

Dotted over the pale pink curtain around Isabel's bed were representations of Vermont's state bird, the grey-brown hermit thrush. For Tom Cisco, the chubby warbler's haunting, flute-like song was one of the reasons he and his wife used to relish their mountain camping summers when they were younger.

Isabel hadn't roused from the drugs yet, but observing the monitors, Cisco thankfully saw that she seemed to be progressing well. He reached over to her side-table for a tissue to wipe the stress off his brow but he accidentally nudged the chromium drip stand, causing it to rattle. He lunged to silence it.

Isabel's eye creaked open. A low voice grated over her sandpaper throat, "Foster… dead…"

Cisco automatically broke into one of those patronising smiles doctors spend years perfecting along with their terrible handwriting. Confusion or even slight hallucinatory episodes were common in cases like hers so, for added reassurance, he placed his hand softly on her good arm. "No, Madam Speaker. President Foster's fine. It was the *Vice*-President who died."

She was struggling to speak, but her throat gagged and her eye glazed over.

# 67

ED'S LEFT HAND brushed over his head. Tom Cisco couldn't avoid a spasm of repulsion at seeing Ed's stump for a pinkie. It was an odd reaction for a surgeon, he knew that, and he checked himself. He watched Ed's eyes fall on Isabel. "I know she doesn't look great," said the doctor, "but don't worry, she'll be fine."

★ ★ ★ ★ ★

ED had planned an exceptional celebration for his dinner companions the previous evening. As always his organisation was impeccable, down to the last detail. Apart from Isabel's accident.

After he listened to the message on his voicemail and left the table to speak to the agent who'd left it, and then to the hospital, Ed returned to his seat. He snuffed out his cigar in the dregs of his cognac, and explained why he had to cut the evening short. Everyone around the table started talking at once, until Ed raised his hand bringing immediate silence. "As I said, the surgeon's optimistic." After a contemplative silence, he stood and they all rose and manoeuvred into two lines, one down each side of the table, and stepped to At-ten-tion! before saluting him. After returning the gesture, he told them he had a surprise waiting for them at the airport and, without a further word, he turned and led them outside to the line of stretch limos which had already been packed with their bags. The drivers, not expecting their passengers quite so early, stubbed out their cigarettes and rushed back to their vehicles from under the mushroom heater on the other side of the driveway.

Niki held back to share Ed's car and slid in beside him. "How is she really?"

"Like I said, it'll mostly be trauma. When you cut through it all, the doc says the injuries were bad but largely cosmetic… hypothermic shock, too, but he's confident they've got it beat…"

"So what's your surprise?" Niki asked coldly, pulling the tight hem of her black dress down a little under her coat and letting the tips of her fingers rest against his leg where not even the driver could see.

"You're all getting a vacation on me."

"*On* you? Appealing…"

Ed ignored her comment but chose not to move her wandering hand away. "It's a week on Butaka, starting now. All their wives and girlfriends are in on it, and they're already there. I'll get a jet to take me and Davey, and that fat freak George, over to see Isabel first thing in the morning. But Niki," he said, arching his eyebrow, "don't worry. You'll find something to do on Butaka."

"Or someone," she winked.

★ ★ ★ ★ ★

THE next morning, Dr Cisco's *she'll be fine* still echoed in Ed's ears. He glanced up at the TV, which had been on mute since he'd arrived at the hospital. According to the text scrolling along the bottom of the screen, the man being interviewed was Andy Goodman, the local park ranger who'd saved Isabel. "Can we turn that up, Doctor?"

"I'd rather we didn't, General. The noise…" Cisco indicated the quiet hum of the sensitive apparatus around them but his resistance had nothing to do with the equipment. Thirty minutes earlier, when he'd seen this interview clip the first time, Goodman's brainless performance had discomfited him, and he was only Isabel's doctor not her husband, let alone a military hero who, judging by his bearing and the tight pursed lips under his pencil moustache, could probably suffocate an enemy just by sucking in the air from around him.

Ed reached for the remote control and pumped up the volume. Cisco blinked, held his breath and began an intense scrutiny of the ceiling tiles.

*… arrogant, when you come down to it, simple as that. And it's exactly because of her big-city rich-folks' attitude why we don't want people hikin' on their own up here. Especially…*

Cisco had counted thirteen squares when a newsflash thankfully cut off Goodman's even more offensive comments.

*We apologise for this interruption. We're holding for an announcement from the White House. Our Washington newsroom expects it will be President Foster nominating a new vice-president. Stay tuned.*

Cisco's eyes edged warily back over to Ed, expecting anger over Andy's distasteful remarks, but Ed's mask of cold fury sent a shiver up his spine.

# 68

BUTAKA ISLAND'S FRONT-LINE staff had just finished hand-brushing the last grains of sand off the blue welcome carpet on the tarmac when the jet engines whirred to a hush and its steps lowered. Though it was only sunrise, the temperature was already a comfortable 23°C, lucky for the waiting line-up of the resort island's valets, with their perfect bodies and crimson loincloths.

The fifteen valets stepped forward for the traditional welcoming ceremony, sprinkling petals of a rare crimson tulip along the carpet from the steps to each one of the sparkling yellow beach buggies. That this exclusive Caribbean island didn't grow tulips was, to those who knew the proprietor, the whole point. And these guests knew him well. They'd all been here before, mostly with Ed Loane. The proprietor had fought alongside many of them in Grenada in '83. After discharge, he came here, buying the island soon after and eventually making it off-limits to all but the super-rich, and his friends.

Mario, who'd been allocated as Niki's personal valet for her stay, whisked her away to her private grass hut, one of fifteen luxury bungalows scattered in remote seclusion around the island. Butaka was one of those elite resorts never covered in the weekend travel section. In all these decades, Butaka had never advertised, not once. No journalist had ever been invited, and none could afford to pay. It had no website, and even managed to appear as a vague unnamed dot on most Caribbean tourist maps. Butaka actively shunned publicity, which played to its privileged clientele. Any place that could charge so much had to be perfect… and it was. But for Loane's Rangers there were no charges. Never.

Mario showed Niki through her thatched cottage. She threw her tote bag and black stilettos onto the bed and dismissed him, noting his quiet grace as well as the bulge beneath his loincloth, but this wasn't the time. There'd be plenty of that later. With her Red Sox cap planted firmly on her head, twisted to the right as she preferred it, she strolled out onto the fine cream sand and padded down to her personal strip of surf.

Mario occupied himself by polishing his buggy outside her hut. He wolf-whistled, silently, as he watched her sidle toward the water, the sunrise with enough swing to it so that the black cocktail dress she'd been wearing since last night clung to her most intimate places. He loved his job.

He leant on the buggy and reassembled himself under his loincloth as he watched Niki wriggle her toes in the 24°C shallows. In the year he'd been here, the waters had rarely fallen below that. Mario tossed back his wavy black hair and tied an elastic around it at the back. Twisting into the buggy, he grabbed a tube of sun cream from the seat, squeezed a dollop onto his palm and slowly rubbed it into his hairless chest, waiting. He didn't have to wait long.

Niki crossed her arms over in front of herself, curled her fingers under the hem of her dress and in one sweep, drew it over her head, careful not to knock her cap off, and flung it behind her onto the sand. Hmm, Mario nodded. No underwear; he'd won that bet with himself. Niki stood for a moment with her hands on her hips, and her head cocked to the side, insolent to the waking sun, as though daring it to admit it had met its match.

By the time she slipped into the sea, leaving her cap on her dress on the sand, Mario had unfurled two towels from her bathroom rail and was walking them down to the water's edge for her… and hopefully for him.

Service with a smile was Mario's motto.

# 69

DR CISCO STARED at the hospital room TV, stunned over what he'd just heard. This couldn't be… Not after… His mind wound back to the reports of when Andy and Paul had rushed Isabel in. Her panicked intensity. Her demands for a phone. Even the confused ramblings he heard himself before she went under anaesthesia. What was going on? Cisco was tentative about Ed, but increasingly certain he should mention this. He heaved in a chestful of air but, when he saw the thin smile cracking Ed's lips apart, he hesitated.

The door burst open and Davey rushed in. He'd run from the cafeteria where, rather obviously, he'd been shovelling a breakfast of scrambled eggs and crispy bacon into his mouth.

George followed him in, panting, his liver spots blotched over the craze of veins on his cheeks, and his grey ponytail swinging. "Did you hear?" he said, before seeing the TV to realise they had. "Foster… The White House won't say where he is," he puffed. "What if *he's* dead, too?"

"That's what they've just been asking," said Cisco, pointing to the TV.

"Do you r-realise…?" stuttered George, shaking his head at the enormity of what he was about to say, "if Foster's dead, it means Isabel's…"

"President."

"It's incred…"

"It's justice," said Ed, tossing a serene shrug and turning to the window, observing the police barrier now encircling the hospital, and the milling security agents and local cops holding back the growing crowd of onlookers.

Both the doctor and George eyed Ed strangely, but George was less controlled and was about to say something he would have regretted when Davey tugged his sleeve and pointed to the TV. The nine-year-old had been doing his best to read the announcer's lips simultaneously with the newsbar scrolling across the bottom of the screen…

*ISABEL DIAZ… NEXT IN LINE AS PRESIDENT OF THE UNITED STATES… CURRENTLY UNDER SEDATION AFTER WOLF…*

Meanwhile, the TV commentator—a local—was mid-sentence:

*…last heard of on board Air Force One late last night. According to sources, the President and First Lady were flying to St Louis after Mr Taylor's fatal heart attack yesterday to sit with the former Vice-President's widow, Julia Taylor and their three small children. But Air Force One never landed at Lambert-St Louis Airport. The White House won't say where it went and has completely clammed up over the President's whereabouts, though senior officials insist off-the-record there is nothing unusual. Excuse me! Our Vice-President is dead, our President is unaccounted for even though he's due to deliver his State of the Union Address tomorrow night, and finally the next in line is discovered up in the mountains, by chance I might add, herself only hours from death. No wonder the conspiracy theorists…*

His eyes flashed off camera for a split second.

*Just a moment… we're crossing to Washington. Secretary of State Bert Robinson has just called a media conference…*

The Secretary stood on the steps of the Capitol, flanked by the leadership of both major political parties:

*...inform you that President Foster suffered an acute... a very serious... and sudden asthma attack while on board Air Force One on his way to St Louis late last night, but I am glad to say he survived it and is doing well. The White House Physician, Rear Admiral Dr Morris Blakeney was, as always, on board and, working with the aircraft's excellent medical facilities and crew, he arrested the attack. Despite the timing, we see no suspicious link to yesterday's tragic death of Vice-President Taylor. I'll take questions.*

The first rang out like a shot:

*"Mr Secretary. Where is President Foster right now?"*

*"He is safe, recuperating in a secure location."*

*"But if there is nothing suspicious, Mr Secretary, why won't you tell the American people where he is?"*

The Secretary's eyes moved in a manner that Ed's interrogation training told him that a lie or an evasion was coming:

*"I understand your concern, but please... the President is due to deliver his State of the Union message tomorrow night,"* the Secretary said, *"and he will."*

Another question immediately hammered at him. It was from an old hand in Washington, who had been around long enough to know personally that a president didn't actually have to attend Congress to deliver the State of the Union Address. Carter and Nixon had merely sent their last State of the Union messages in writing, as had Truman, though that was before his time, and he'd heard that Eisenhower had recorded one of his in a film made when he was recuperating from a heart attack.

*"You said message, not address. President Foster is going to deliver his State of the Union in person isn't he?"*

The journalist also knew that a president's address in their first year in office was not formally a State of the Union, but this wasn't the moment to quibble about trivia.

*"You can assume he will be there,"* said the Secretary.

*"Assume? You're choosing your words extremely carefully,*

*sir. My simple question to you is this: is President Foster alive and conscious? A straight yes or no, please.*"

Even to the untrained eye, the Secretary was looking uncomfortable as he shifted on his feet:

"*I am informed...*," he started.

"*Informed?*" the veteran reporter interrupted, stabbing the air with his pencil. "*You haven't spoken to President Foster yourself? You haven't seen him? How do you have any idea what shape he's in?*"

The questioner kept badgering him, almost hysterically now:

"*Mr Secretary... surely the people are entitled to hear from someone with first-hand knowledge?*"

The Secretary pulled himself up to his full six-foot-one:

"*President Foster is fully...* "

But the reporter wouldn't give in:

"*Mr Secretary, coming so close after the terrorist attack on New York, thankfully thwarted, can you assure the American people these catastrophes one after another are not part of some attempted coup, some conspiracy, some triple assassination attempt to overthrow...*"

"*America is not Tunisia or Egypt or Lib...*"

Ed grabbed for the remote and switched off the TV. "Triple assassination!" he exclaimed. "What crap!"

The screen-flash from the TV burnt Ed's strange reaction into Dr Cisco's mind. He reminded himself that he was drained from working under high stress all night without a break, and that it had been years since he'd felt pressure anything close to this, so he dismissed his jumpiness about Isabel's husband as being due to that and tried to calm himself by scratching useless notes onto her chart.

Davey tugged again. He signed, "Is Isabel going to die?"

"Ask Dr Cisco yourself," George said, letting Davey read his lips and swinging his own eyes back onto Ed. He had the same reaction as the doctor to Ed's comment.

Cisco had vaguely overheard George, but had no idea what question he would be answering for Davey so he slipped the chart back into its slot and raised his head, "Ask me what?" He licked his lower lip.

Without shifting his eyes away from Ed, George repeated Davey's question.

Cisco nodded and sighed, "Ms Diaz has quite a few problems," he began, and when Davey's hands flew to his mouth in terror, Cisco continued, "but she will be okay," saying it slowly so the boy understood. "We gave her some medicine to make her sleep. She'll be awake in…," he glanced at the clock on the wall, "two hours, maybe three." An assuring smile broke out over the doctor's tired, furrowed face and he tousled Davey's hair. "Can you wait till then, little man?"

Davey bobbed his head and gave a little gleeful hop, and took George's hand.

George's eyes kept drilling into Ed.

★ ★ ★ ★ ★

NIKI Abbott splashed naked out of the tropical waters to find her valet standing guard where she'd tossed her clothes. Mario had unfurled a towel like a white flag of submission and, as though they'd already been lovers, she ran up to him and let him wrap it around her from behind, snuggling her back into him.

The pair stood silently, both facing the sea. Niki nudged his arms aside and let the towel slide between them to the sand. Purposefully, she grabbed behind through Mario's loincloth and gave a strong tug, smiled and ran off from him high-stepping into the low lapping surf. Mario pulled the side-knot open and, inspired, hung the crimson cloth off himself and sped after her, laughing as the fabric flapped from side to side.

# 70

"CHIEF AGENT FRANKLIN, General Loane, special agent in charge of the President's personal protective division. I gotta discuss your wife's condition with the doctor, sir."

Franklin's tone and bearing were flinty and matter-of-fact, which even to Ed smacked as being frosty, as though the President's shock asthma attack before Franklin's own eyes had only been as bothersome as a fishbone in the throat. The arch in Franklin's eyebrow was pushing Ed out of the room, but the former general stood his ground.

But the special agent wasn't accustomed to resistance. "In private, sir," he pressed.

Ed drew back his cuff and glimpsed his watch. "I've got to make a call," he grunted and edged past Franklin out of the room, no mean feat since the man was almost as broad as the door itself.

Together with two members of the President's Cabinet and a crack team of security specialists, Franklin had just flown in on one of the President's two specially configured Boeing 747-200Bs. In this contingent, Franklin was the only one who had been with President Foster on his fateful flight the night before, though he wasn't offering any details, certainly not to Ed. Like Ed, the agent had not slept, so Ed decided that Franklin's personal presence here meant all was not well with the President, and that his instincts only a few hours ago when listening to the Secretary of State's press conference were correct.

Security in and around the hospital had blown out from locals leaning on the wall when Ed first arrived, to armed guards posted at every corner. The Secret Service had also set up outside the building a 100-feet, no-cross cordon, which was being enforced by police rushed in from all over the county and a few dozen more who'd come in from neighbouring counties even though they hadn't actually been asked to. The journalists, cold, tired and cranky were pushed well back, with all the gawkers, hardly the kind of equal opportunity that they believed America stood for.

Manifold was crawling with police and emergency personnel and security checks, and police roadblocks covered all incoming land routes. Continually circling in the air were two 767 AWACS—airborne warning and control system aircraft—with their distinctive thirty-foot rotating radar domes mounted above their fuselage. F-15s and F-16s flashed and boomed across the sky. Apart from these authorised aircraft, the town's airspace had been reclassified as a no-fly zone with a shoot-on-sight protocol, and the TV networks who'd pointlessly sent their news choppers were furious.

President Foster was alive and well? Yeah right, Ed sniggered as he glanced out of the hospital window at the frenzy. The media were thinking the same thing: if Foster was alive, why was Isabel Diaz getting all this, frankly, presidential treatment?

But those who knew the facts weren't talking.

# 71

TEMPORARILY ALONE TO make the call on the secure phone she'd requested from the special agent, Isabel pondered the answer she'd just been given and edged her head toward the hubbub of security outside her window. She winced as she turned back for a sip of water, resting the phone on her chest so she could reach the glass with her good hand. Refreshed, she picked up the phone again and said abruptly, "Noted. That's all from Isis."

THE hospital staff and security personnel couldn't help but notice Ed's exclusion from Isabel's room; and likewise George who, with Davey, was at the far end of the same corridor on their way back from an afternoon snack at the cafeteria.

"Why isn't she being sworn in right here and right now?" Ed demanded. Finally given the chance to confront the Secretary of State directly, Ed was going to push it, his pug nose a mere three inches away from Bert Robinson's as the two men faced off right outside Isabel's hospital room. Invading personal space was precisely Ed's objective. Isabel had been fully awake for two hours now and, for some unexplained reason, was conspiring with the recently arrived officials to exclude Ed from the discussions. Getting aggressive, he calculated, was the best way to insinuate himself back in, and he didn't give a damn who might be tut-tutting about it behind his back.

Ed was convinced that President Foster was dead but also that, for whatever reason, the Administration—or what was left of it—was concealing that fact from the American public, and thwarting Isabel's rightful elevation. What the hell were they up to? Ed pondered. Lyndon Johnson had been sworn in only an hour-and-a-half after JFK was pronounced dead in Dallas. The brief ceremony, Ed recalled from the famous photographs, had been held on board the presidential plane while it was still on the ground at Love Field.

Beneath his nose, Ed could see the Secretary's hand clamped over a thick dossier. What Ed didn't know was that it included those photos from 1963 as well as other, mostly classified, precedent material.

Ed noticed that the agent posted on duty at Isabel's door had turned his head away from the skirmish with the Secretary. Perhaps he was onside and signalling to Ed that it was safe for him to come forward. Ed stepped around Robinson and managed to open the door just a crack.

"Isabel...," Ed called through the small opening, pushing it wider but the agent blocked him from taking a step inside.

"Not now," she snapped from her bed, declining to even look at him and lowering her eyes back to the files spread out on her lap. Her commanding abruptness threw all of them, Ed included.

She buried her head in the papers and, when the silence in the room forced her to look back up a minute later and she saw him still standing with his hand on the doorknob, she insisted that the agent close the door.

Ed put her gruffness down to her trauma, or maybe the drugs. What else it could be?

George knew. At least, he knew the part about Ed's affair. He'd foamed when Isabel had told him. "Show me the damn video," he said, strangely satisfied that all his contempt for Ed was now proved justified.

But Isabel had refused. "Personal drama belongs in the background right now, okay?" she said. "But promise me you'll say nothing… especially to Ed. And Davey, too."

AFTER the Secretary of State's impromptu media conference in DC, he and Marcus Bentley, Foster's Attorney General, had buckled up next to each other on the flight from Andrews Air Force Base to talk to Isabel. They'd shared many trips over the years; both started in politics as assistant secretaries in the Clinton Administration and, during the politically lean years before Obama, managed to hew illustrious and remunerative careers for themselves outside politics, one in law and the other in electronics, crossing paths frequently and making life easier for each other when they could. They were great friends, and so was Mitch Taylor before his death. The three went back a long way, and with Foster too. But Marcus Bentley and Bert Robinson were also hard-nosed professionals and weren't going to let sudden personal grief blur their focus on the gravest matter of state either had ever been charged with.

Neither had been with the President when the attack happened, but they'd heard it all from Chief Franklin who had phoned the two of them at 3 AM, joining them into the one call and saying he was under strict instructions from the President to speak to the two of them, and only them.

Franklin had explained how the President wanted them to be ready on a moment's notice if, heaven forbid, his condition deteriorated and Isabel in fact needed to be sworn in. That was President Foster's Plan B, he said, though he declined to reveal Plan A even when Robinson pressed him. And despite both men screaming down the phone line, Franklin also refused to say where the President actually was.

Robinson and Bentley saw they were in the vortex of a potentially paralysing constitutional crisis.

They knew that under the Presidential Succession Law, if Foster died—or was *already* dead—Isabel would automatically step into his role. Permanently! After her mother's revelation on FOX there was no longer any impediment, since any doubt that Isabel was not a natural-born citizen had been quashed.

On their flight over to Manifold, even the engine noise couldn't drown out the concentrated hush that bore down on the pair as they read and swapped files, and exchanged whispers.

Neither man could believe the coincidences… first Mitch Taylor, then the President… thank God, Bobby was okay… well, at least Franklin kept telling them he was. But if he was fine, then why the urgency surrounding the contingency plan?

BACK in the corridor, Ed once again challenged Secretary Robinson, "The President *is* dead, isn't he? Yet you're delaying, putting up every block you can to stop…"

"You say that, General," Robinson replied, emphasising Ed's title to remind him that the chain of command was civilian over military. He stepped forward even closer. "But in case you hadn't noticed, we're still running this show," which Robinson hoped was true, though by now his need to speak personally to the President was reaching a point of quiet desperation.

"Robinson," said Ed, the snarl on his face betraying his contempt for the Secretary. "You call this running…"

"I'll take my chances with history," Robinson interrupted and, as he turned to the door to Isabel's room, the agent posted there started opening it for him.

Ed grabbed Robinson's shoulder and stopped him. "If the shit hits the fan, Robinson, what then? Who the hell's in charge of this country?"

"The President. Who else?" Robinson snapped, praying he was correct, though uncomfortably unsure. He hoped that would change after he spoke to Foster in an hour's time, a call Chief Franklin had arranged.

Ed swung himself in front of the Secretary. Threateningly, Ed let the tip of his nose actually touch Robinson's this time, then suddenly, as though he'd achieved his objective, Ed pulled back, knocking Robinson into the door before heading to the washroom.

Bert Robinson might have been as tall as Ed but he was wiry and slight. It was why he'd got the wading bird nickname Crane in college. He stood there shaking. To calm himself, he leant back against the insipid green wall and, to make his nervousness less obvious, he removed his glasses, held the lenses up toward the fluorescent light, and hurred two sharp breaths onto them before wiping them with his tie. But his heart wouldn't stop pounding. Winding the wire back over his ears and doing his best to mimic a cheery wink to the agent on guard, he took a deep breath and pushed himself inside Isabel's room to get back to finalising the arrangements.

To be truthful, Bert completely understood Ed's anger and confusion—what rational person wouldn't?—but according to Isabel, there were things Ed didn't know and shouldn't know. Neither Bert nor Attorney General Marcus Bentley knew them either and she certainly wasn't telling either of them, so Robinson was forced to accept that pragmatism was the only sensible course of action for now, no matter how awkward.

But the fact that Isabel was hiding the truth, whatever it was, from her husband as well impressed Robinson, certainly dismissing for him all those bitchy snipes during the campaign about Ed being the one pulling *her* strings. The woman had *cojones*, that was for sure, and after everything she'd just been through, Robinson couldn't help but be awed.

Inside the room, Isabel was still hooked up to monitors, but the drips were no longer connected, and the morphine had been replaced with more standard painkillers plus her own adrenaline and single focus. If she was suffering any trauma or residual shock, she wasn't letting anyone see it. She was plumped up in bed with pillows, her face stitched, plastered and bruised, her arm in a sling and every time she winced, Bert Robinson felt a sympathetic twinge himself. He couldn't see the bandages beneath the sheets, but Dr Cisco had explained in detail about the hypothermia, the ripped skin and leg muscle. She'd been a lucky woman to survive, let alone to be as on top of everything as she most clearly was.

Chief Franklin was whispering something to her while Attorney General Bentley was at the window surveying the security circus outside.

"Ah, Bert, you're back," she said acknowledging the Secretary. "Marcus, let's run through it again, okay?"

When the Attorney finished, Chief Franklin said, "Just to make it clear, if anything gets in the way of the President delivering his State of the Union Address, we will be 100-percent ready to swear in Madam Speaker instantly."

Plan B still rankled the two Cabinet members, and Robinson couldn't wait for his own call with Foster, not just so he could hear it all directly, but so he could have the comfort of hearing his friend's own voice.

"If people out there," Isabel looked at them each pointedly, "want to believe President Foster is dead, so be it. In any case, if I *am* going to be sworn in as President, it'll be when the two Houses of Congress are sitting together tomorrow night, not a moment sooner, not unless there's an emergency."

"Isn't this an emergency?" Marcus whispered to Bert as they left her room.

# 72

AFTER SECRETARY BERT Robinson's mobile phone battery died, the hour he spent drumming his fingers in Tom Cisco's office waiting for his call from Bobby Foster bled into a second and then into a third. His mounting stress that as the senior-most Cabinet member, he still hadn't made personal contact with the President almost made him puke. And this after he'd been on the head table at Foster's wedding and later godfather to one of his kids. Despite repeated calls to Chief Franklin, even to the First Lady, he couldn't access either.

But he persisted, both in the national interest and as a frantically worried friend, and eventually Franklin, who he viewed as a brick wall physically and who was certainly behaving like one, called him from one of the secure lines on the plane they'd flown down on after returning to the operations room he had temporarily set up there.

Robinson was praying that Franklin's call was to put the President through to him.

"I've checked with the President," said Franklin. "Yes, personally. And he apologises, but he can't speak to you till later today. Remember, he'll call *you*. Bye."

Secretary Robinson blinked. He didn't know what to say, even though Franklin was no longer on the line to hear it if he did. He simply stared into the phone still in his hand contemplating an explanation that, up to now, he had been reluctant to accept.

He slammed down the phone, and sprinted from Cisco's office back toward Isabel's room. The agent let him pass and he pushed her door open without knocking. Both she and the Attorney General looked up with stunned expressions. "Sorry, I…," said Robinson, recovering his own composure, "Marcus, I need you… Outside, please."

Once the two Cabinet members were in the corridor, Bert held his hand up and said, "Not here." He led the Attorney by the elbow back to Cisco's office.

Marcus Bentley listened carefully. Neither man had met Ed Loane before today, nor was either hoping for a repeat performance with him but, even so, both were now convincing themselves that Ed's suspicions simply had to be correct.

That the President, their friend, might truly be dead was shocking, a tragedy of vast proportions, personally and politically, but a conspiracy to conceal it would be even more alarming. What absolutely petrified them was the chill of not knowing who was exercising the President's authority… or why.

"As senior-most Secretary, if anyone should know what's going on, it's me, right?" Robinson asked Marcus.

The two colleagues tried several more avenues but they all led back to Franklin, a route as unhelpful as it was disturbing. The two men suddenly gaped at each other as though lightning had just struck them. Without a further word, they charged out of the office. They passed Ed as they ran through the corridor, but were going so fast they didn't see the smile of smug satisfaction crawl onto his face.

When they got to Isabel's room, Marcus was puffing. He was tall, but unlike Robinson, he was not a slight man. His career outside politics was as a trial attorney and though he'd made millions out of the tobacco companies for his clients, as well as himself, he'd never kicked the habit. "Ma'am. Bert and I… well, look… we don't buy what's happening."

Bert was nodding.

Marcus continued, "We can't get access to the President and…"

"He's fine," Isabel said.

"He's fine?" Bert almost exploded. "*I* don't know he's fine… *Marcus* doesn't know he's fine… *No one* knows he's fine except you and that damn Franklin. There's nothing *fine* about that in our book."

Marcus rested a hand on Bert's shoulder and looked at Isabel, "Your husband was right, wasn't he? Bobby *is* dead."

Isabel gingerly pushed herself back into her pillows, her flinch worrying the pair even more. Marcus moved to help her, but she frowned. "I'm fine."

"Now *you're* fine too?" spluttered Bert, his voice almost a screech. "Hey, Marcus! Everyone in this whole fucking world is fine. The Vice-President is dead, but that's fine. The President's suffered a life-threatening asthma attack, something he's never had before, ever, and that's fine, too. We can't even speak to the President, but he's fine, just trust me. The Speaker is in hospital, bandaged to the hilt and can hardly sit up in bed without wincing in pain, but she's fine too. It's all fucking fine. Well, Madam Speaker, it's not… fine."

"Bert's right," said Marcus, playing good cop to Bert's crazy cop. "In a situation where we can't even speak to the President to confirm he's alive… well, my advice to the Cabinet will be that we've got no choice but to assume he's unable to act in the Office, at a *minimum*, in which case it is our constitutional duty to invoke the succession…"

"And have me declared as Acting President until his inability is removed?"

"Yes. And if, Madam Speaker, you decline the role, as you might… you know, out of respect for the… ah… political situation… the next in line is Senate President pro tempore." The current Senate President was Eric Mallord, a Democrat.

"And after him, it goes to me," added Bert needlessly.

"Gentlemen," said Isabel, "please believe me. President Foster is certainly not dead nor is he unable to fulfil his duties as you and my hus… others are too willing to speculate."

"We believe you, of course, ma'am," said the Attorney. "But until we know that as a hard fact, and not hearsay, we have no choice other than to invoke the succession. Then, once we can be sure his disability has been removed, he'll be reinstated. But meanwhile, this country cannot be rudderless. We simply can't permit it."

"Actually, I'm afraid you must," she said, pushing herself further back into her pillows, this time without letting them see her pain. "You give me no choice…"

# 73

MANIFOLD'S AIRSTRIP COULDN'T take the highly modified Boeing-747 yesterday, so the presidential plane had instead landed thirty miles away by road, at the South Burlington Air National Guard airfield. And that was where it was now waiting to fly its passengers to Washington DC for the State of the Union Address that evening.

Back in the hospital carpark, Isabel and a small contingent of her entourage strapped themselves into the Sea King helicopter. As it lifted its precious cargo into the air for the short airtrip to South Burlington, the rest of the party of officials and security personnel were separately being ferried there in a fairly hotchpotch cortege of two bulletproof limos flown in earlier on one of the C-5 Galaxy heavy transport aircraft, several borrowed pickup trucks, some rented SUVs, and nine of Manifold's taxis.

Even with Secretary Robinson giving the orders, the symbolism of Isabel flying in the President's personal helicopter and then on one of the two presidential planes, as well as her being escorted by C-5s and protected by AWACS, F-15s and F-16s—while President Foster remained incommunicado for the second day running—was torturing an incredulous media and an increasingly jittery public.

Before boarding the chopper, Robinson and Bentley had fronted the media swarm outside the hospital. They repeated the lines they'd started parroting the prior afternoon: that because President Foster was physically weak after the debilitating asthma attack, even though he was fully competent and definitely in charge, the White House Physician had confined him to bed rest ahead of his State of the Union Address, due that evening. And yes, they had spoken to him personally.

That two such respected men, who were also known to be his personal friends, were standing side-by-side saying this so unflinchingly placated many people watching, but there were enough rumblings around the country to keep the nation on edge… that the President was dead… he was seriously incapacitated… there'd been a coup.

The hardcore conspiracy theorists were having a field day.

# 74

THE JOINT SESSION of the two Houses of Congress was scheduled for 8:30 PM, with the State of the Union Address being broadcast at nine. This time every network, not just C-Span and the news channels, was scrabbling to take the feed live. Tonight, virtually every eye in the nation would be glued to a TV screen.

In the corridor, just before she entered the Hall of the House of Representatives, Isabel sighed, "And now for the public hanging." Marcus Bentley hoped he knew what she meant, but after what was to follow they were words he would scarcely ever forget.

Ed went to take her wrist, her undamaged left one, to wish her luck but, so noticeably that even Secretary Robinson flinched, she shook him off. So far, she'd barely said anything to Ed, and certainly nothing about his affair or, for that matter, the President.

Ed's fingers had felt like sandpaper against her skin, and as his hand dropped away, she noticed flesh-coloured pads covering a couple of his fingertips.

"What're those?" she whispered, trying not to move her lips, aware that Davey wouldn't be the only one able to read them this time; there were no press or cameras permitted in the corridor, but it was abuzz with staffers, the Secret Service and the Capitol's own police.

"A couple of warts," Ed shrugged, leaning into her ear. "Got 'em burnt off."

Isabel didn't recall him having any warts recently, but didn't think about them further after a nod from the Sergeant at Arms signalled her to follow him in, leaving Ed and Davey with the two Cabinet Secretaries.

Bert pointed out the correct door for Ed and Davey to wait at, and he and Marcus turned, heading for the anteroom where the Cabinet was assembling.

CARRYING the traditional mace, the Sergeant at Arms walked slowly down the aisle to the rostrum. As Isabel limped behind him, the Hall kept an embarrassed silence, no one confident enough of the circumstances to lead any applause. Her cane was its own mace of sorts, reminding some of the now almost folkloric day she hobbled into George and Annette Hicks' diner. When her eyes located George up in the public gallery, the old guy, genetically contemptuous of convention, leapt to his feet and started to clap. His outburst seemed to trigger an electric shock through everyone's seats at the same moment and they all stood to follow him, though their applause was hesitant, unsure.

Isabel cracked a wrinkled smile, as genial as she was able given her stitches, and pushed on down the aisle until she stood unsteadily to the side of the podium.

The applause thickened, and with small, precise steps, Isabel cut a slow pivot to face the chamber simultaneously scanning over the faces while the hundreds of Representatives, those cramming the press and public galleries, and the millions more in the TV audience, all scanned her and stared back in shock.

She knew she wasn't the pretty sight they'd got comfortable with during the campaign but she'd scrubbed up well enough:

a gifted makeup artist had plastered over her facial bruises, though her stitches were there for all to see, and she was stuck with her right arm bent in its sling and her left having to lean on a gnarled oak cane. There was nothing she could do about any of that, but to her, even making it to stand here tonight was an extraordinary feat.

As the ovation clattered on, she turned and, with her back to the chamber and the cameras, she slowly climbed step-by-painful-step to the top tier of the rostrum where eventually she slumped into the Speaker's red leather chair.

THE air was thick with anticipation. Once Isabel had settled the House as best she could, she nodded to the Sergeant at Arms. He in turn signalled the Deputy Sergeant at Arms who announced that the Senators had arrived outside the Hall. As near to a single organism as 435 anxious people can be, the Representatives present rose, as was traditional to receive the members from the other legislative chamber. The public gallery followed suit, with George standing only when Isabel raised her eyebrow at him.

Spencer Prentice was down toward the front and three rows back. A student of protocol, he knew that the first senator to enter would be Eric Mallord, the Senate President pro tempore. For the joint sitting of both Houses, Eric would be taking the high-backed chair to Isabel's right.

With the flag draped behind her, Isabel waited to strike her gavel until Eric sat beside her and the bustle of senatorial silk and wool and the smattering of huffs and grunts had ceased.

"To escort the President of the United States into the Chamber, the Chair," she pronounced formally, "appoints as members of the committee on the part of the House: the gentleman from Missouri… the gentlewoman from Ohio…" and after appointing another eleven representatives, "the gentleman from Massachusetts, Mr Prentice." She winked at Spencer, but without a smile.

The glint when their eyes met spoke enough for him and, pumped up, the six-foot-six son of a Boston hospital nurse and pre-school teacher—hardly the black Boston Brahmin many people assumed from his bearing and diction—winked back at his old friend, also without a smile. Impassive, tough, she watched him as he stood and swivelled around to go to the doors.

As Spencer and the others headed up the centre aisle, Senator Mallord took his cue and appointed a similar number of senators as additional escorts.

Next, the Deputy Sergeant at Arms welcomed the Dean of the Diplomatic Corps and the Chief Justice and the Associate Justices of the Supreme Court.

Isabel caught the Chief Justice's smile, and searched for other friendly faces among the otherwise impressive gathering.

There were many faces, though few actual friends.

FOSTER'S Cabinet entered next, all except the Secretary for Health who, under the Continuity of Government plans that demanded one person in the succession be located elsewhere, had drawn the doomsday short straw.

The Cabinet members shuffled in with their heads appropriately grave and low. Their colleague and, for several of them, their good friend Vice-President Mitch Taylor had died; and only two of them were in the tiny loop of knowledge about what was really happening with the President.

Every Cabinet member, even Robinson and Bentley, was hoping or praying that President Foster would appear tonight safe and well. The repercussions would be enormous if he didn't: the unspeakable possibility of a double assassination; and with Isabel Diaz seated up ahead of them, the unthinkable toppling of a hard-fought, near-miss Democratic White House.

Paying evident respects to the tragic circumstances, they took their reserved seats at the front.

# 75

ISABEL CAUSED THE first real stir of the session when she asked Congress to grant the privileges of the floor of the House to Ed and Davey so they could take the two remaining seats up front. Normally the Speaker's relatives sat in the gallery, where George was. Even the President's family sat up there, though oddly neither the First Lady nor her children were there tonight.

"What the...?" was the most common reaction that flittered around the Chamber. Everyone present knew that they were in uncharted territory tonight and a hesitant acclamation granted her request. The doors opened and, preceded by the Deputy Sergeant at Arms, Ed and Davey brushed their way past the President's welcoming committee. Spencer Prentice, standing beside the doors, grit his teeth as the former General passed. If Ed had noticed the Congressman, he would have done likewise.

THE President's motorcade snaked towards the Capitol Building. The vehicles hadn't come from the White House—no one knew where they were from—so their mere approach was newsworthy.

"The motorcade is about three minutes away, Kevin," the newscaster told her ABC sidekick on air. "And as yet, no one has actually sighted of President Foster."

"Yes, Patsy, and with the First Lady not even in the Chamber, which is most unusual, there are many who could be forgiven for being in severe doubt that he's even behind those dark-smoked windows."

"There's been so much speculation about tonight's session that bloggers are calling it 'The *Fate* of the Union'..."

"A week ago, the events of the last few days would have been inconceivable... plunging the country into a turmoil that, hopefully, will be quelled tonight. Who could ever have contemplated that nothing—not a peep—could have been heard, or seen, of the President since his...?"

"Kevin, this attendance by the Speaker's husband and stepson on the floor of the House... it's most irregular, too. We're crossing now to Leighton Smith, a longstanding expert on House formalities... Leighton, what do you make of this?"

"As you know, Patsy, family members are always seated in the galleries. I've been covering Washington for fourteen years and I can't recall seeing anything like this before. For Madam Speaker's family to be admitted to the floor suggests something more than a State of the Union..."

"Like what...?" pressed Patsy.

"I know this will only fuel the rumour mill," Smith continued, "...an inauguration."

"But Leighton, the ceremonies swearing in a new president are held on the West Front of the Capitol."

"In modern times they are, but until 1850 they were usually held *inside* the Capitol, in fact mostly on the floor of the House..."

"Leighton, you're not suggesting...?"

ED strode down the aisle to the front with Davey nervously trying to keep up behind him. Davey was doing his utmost not to shake out of his skin or rather, his alien coat and tie. He stretched his shoulders back and held his posture as high as possible, trying hard to imitate his father's natural ramrod straightness, but his hands were useless and, without the comfort of holding Pip his fluffy penguin, they were dangling self-consciously by his side, and he knew he wasn't allowed to put his hands in his pockets. George had said so.

When Davey and Ed had settled into their seats in the front row, beside the Cabinet, Davey looked up at Isabel in awe, but caught her watching him with a sadness in her eyes, though he thought it was from her injuries.

Quickly, she collected herself and smiled, tipping her head to the side, so he would look over to the right of the Hall—his right, her left—where the signing interpreter she'd told him about earlier was poised so he could follow the proceedings.

Tonight, he would need to.

# 76

AT 9:01 PM, THE Sergeant at Arms re-entered through the main doors and closed them firmly behind him. He walked down the aisle and up to the rostrum. Spencer watched him lean over between Isabel and Senator Mallord, cover his mouth and speak. The three engaged in a fleeting conversation and when the Speaker and Senate President nodded, the Sergeant stepped down to the floor and back up the aisle. At the doors, he cleared his throat, and after a collective intake of air, a hush enveloped the Chamber.

Throughout the Hall, eyes closed in relief and hands clasped together as though in prayer. Then everyone twisted around to see Spencer and the other members of the welcoming committee tipping forward at the doors, set for them to swing open, or at least hoping they would.

Isabel struck her gavel twice, and the Sergeant at Arms announced, "Madam Speaker… the President of the United States."

A commotion erupted at the back of the Hall and ten plainclothes Capitol police ran up the centre aisle and around the sides. Several clusters of congressmen and women from the rear leapt from their seats and themselves charged to the doors, blocking the view from the front. Everyone rose, this time including George.

Three officers stepped up onto the rostrum to protect Isabel and Senator Mallord, though from what no one seemed to know. Four other officers hugged the front row just to the side, near where Ed and Davey were now standing, with Davey trying to peek toward the back between all the tall bodies.

Those who couldn't see were straining their bodies toward the cause of the hubbub, only adding to it by asking their neighbours either side if they could see anything.

The Chamber was descending into a rabble. Because of her injuries and the difficulties she'd have using her gavel while she was standing, Isabel had asked Senator Mallord to take temporary control of it and, with her cane, she carefully pressed herself to her feet.

Mallord slammed the gavel with no remit but the only soul who seemed to be paying attention was Isabel who judiciously kept her hands safely away from the bench. Mallord was forced to shout, "Order! Order!" Again and again, he smashed the gavel onto the bench and, stretching out his neck, even he couldn't detect what was going on in the ruckus down the back.

"Please!" shouted Mallord, "Members, Senators… Do you hear me? Order!"

The Sergeant at Arms was on the case. His single finger held aloft signalled to Mallord that he'd need a further moment as he pushed back through the swarm.

The authorised camera crew suffered similar obstructions though, briefly, a gap opened up among the crowd milling around the doors and, before it closed up again, they managed to zoom their camera through it.

One of the Capitol police officers stationed near the rostrum was pressing on his earpiece. He was refusing to trust what he thought he'd heard, but when it came through a second time he stepped between Mallord and Isabel to inform them.

"Truly?" Mallord exclaimed for everyone to hear, even over the hullabaloo, and pressed his fist to his mouth to suppress a nervous cough.

Never before had so many legislators with their mouths open been as silent.

# 77

UNUSUALLY FOR A President's entrance, if that's what was about to happen, no one was applauding. Instead everyone was listening and watching. Waiting.

Spencer Prentice stood near the doors in edgy silence, almost on his toes. He swivelled back to the front and saw Isabel was also standing, leaning on her cane, her blank eyes fixed on the back of the Hall not far from him. She wasn't unsteady, though there was something hard about her, pitiless. She was like a rock.

Spencer had never seen her like this. Sure, he'd seen her tough and resolute, but always tempered, with a softness to her edge. But he knew she'd been through a lot the last forty-eight hours, let alone the last eighteen months of her futile campaign. She was entitled to feel empty when the man she would easily have defeated, if she had been allowed to continue in the race, was about to deliver a speech that should have been hers. Just then, President Robert J. Foster swept through the doors into the Chamber.

To Spencer and everyone else Foster's face, too, was set like week-old concrete. His usual glinting Kennedy smile was gone. His eyes, thought Spencer—turning his head to and fro a few times to check—were aimed right at Isabel as though he were trying to fix her to the spot, and her own glare in return coldly matched his.

The aisle swarming before Foster cleaved open as though he were a prophet parting the sea. His eyes kept locked ahead, never deflecting from Isabel's, not acknowledging a single face to either side. Normally, a President would be smiling, chatting, shaking hands, hugging as he came down the aisle, but Foster did none of that, emitting a frigid shield that no one dared break into. The House didn't know how to respond. Ordinarily, they'd be giving his entrance a standing ovation, but all they could do was stand, and gape. The few weak attempts at applause quickly petered out.

Foster had a slight lean, preferring one side as he walked, but he had not a hint of a smile; not even a smirk. Just cold poison. As he strode to the rostrum, there was now only silence and this time not even George would interrupt it.

Everyone was wondering the same thing. Isabel Diaz? Had she…? Politics and disbelief were suspended. Guts were knotted and lungs constricted by the dread of what they were about to hear. If hands weren't glued to people's sides as if taped there, they were covering their mouths.

President Foster stepped up to the podium, a little less slowly than Isabel had, and went for the lectern at the Clerk's desk, just in front of the Speaker and the Senate President. He didn't shake their hands or catch their eyes, and he didn't follow the custom of handing them two manila envelopes containing his address.

To the majority of those present, familiar with House protocol, this made them even edgier. Faces around the Hall wrinkled, eyes blinked and eyebrows furrowed. Stomachs were clenched. Those watching in their homes were tipping on the edges of their sofas as the TV commentators explained the unexpected breaks with tradition. Bars were silenced as their customers stared at the TV screens hanging from the ceilings or on the walls.

Foster's jaw was grim, Spencer could see that, and there seemed to be nothing physically ailing him, despite the slight lean Spencer had noticed as he'd walked through.

Suddenly, it dawned on Spencer, and on many of those watching. Foster hadn't been recuperating… he had been in hiding.

But from Isabel? Surely not.

"Members of the Congress," said Isabel, interrupting these thoughts, "I have the high privilege and the distinct honour of presenting to you… the President of the United States."

Foster's head bowed as in prayer and the House clapped lightly. When he raised his head back up, all he could see were heavy, worried eyes, not unlike his own. He arced left and right as if blessing the grand hall. His right hand patted the air to signal those before him to sit.

"Members of Congress," he said, pausing until the tide of heads had subsided. "Distinguished guests and fellow citizens. Your eyes have not deceived you but your President has… and when you hear why, I pray you will forgive me."

He paused to pour himself a glass of water from the crystal pitcher, and took a sip, taking particular care to wet his lips. Eyes, still puzzled, met all around the Chamber.

"The Secretary of State," he said, pointing to the front row, "announced to the public that I was mentally alert, but because my physical state was weak, that my physician had temporarily confined me to bed. The truth is that I am not—nor was I—feeble nor so confined. You can see before you that I am fit, and you will be your own judges that I suffer no mental impairment. But there are people who were hoping otherwise… who had planned otherwise. And it was vital in the nation's interests that these people, these traitors, felt the possibility that they had… ah… that I had died."

As he twisted around for a long glare at Isabel, the House rumbled. He turned back to the microphone, "Why did

Secretary Robinson lie to you? Because I asked him to. A President does not deceive his people lightly, so why did I ask my friend and Cabinet colleague to do so for me? Several times in our more than two centuries of unbroken democracy, traitors or madmen have attempted to, and on four occasions have in fact assassinated our presidents. And this time… this week… such people—not madmen, but traitors surely—got close… perilously close… with a treasonous plan to assassinate both your President and your Vice-President. It was a plan to completely overthrow our elected administration, and our Constitution, and it nearly worked." As the murmuring rose, Foster said, "One of those traitors… is here among us… in this Chamber."

The House exploded in uproar and people leapt to their feet. The President looked back at Isabel, but signalled to her not to gavel. Instead, he raised his hand and waited until silence fell. The Chamber seemed to press in on itself.

As if to answer the obvious question—who?—the three security men who'd earlier marched onto the rostrum clamped themselves into a tight U-shape behind Isabel. The four who were on the side near Davey pressed forward, ready.

Until this minute, Isabel Diaz was a national treasure, yet now eyes all over the country were clouding with disbelief, many with tears. Isabel had been a shining light, an icon of hope. One Senator had even started humming to himself the Paul Simons' lyric, "Who'll be my role model now that my role model is gone?"

Isabel stared back at the Hall showing nothing but stony calm. She reached her good arm out toward Davey and Ed, and two of the police officers ushered them forward and escorted them up to stand beside her in support.

Spencer's blood seemed to drain from his head, a cold sweat had burst through his skin and his hands were gripping the back of the seat in front of him as though he was dangling from a crumbling ledge thirty floors above the ground. He bit his lip until he tasted blood. How could he have so badly misread her?

"Please sit," said Foster, but few obeyed him. "Initially," he continued regardless, "medical opinion was that Vice-President Taylor died of natural causes. That was wrong: his death was a cold-blooded, carefully plotted assassination. A plot to eliminate Vice-President Taylor first so that when my own death followed—yes, consecutive assassinations—America would have no vice-president to replace me and the presidential succession would automatically fall to the House Speaker, Ms Diaz here."

One congressman at the back shouted "Treason!" setting off a chain reaction. The President immediately raised his hand again, and when the clamour stopped, he went on, "To Julia, Mitchell Taylor's widow, and Oliver, James and Tyrone, his three children who, by regretful necessity, are hearing this for the first time… let me say this to you: be strong in your knowledge that Mitch, my great friend and a fine man… your dad and your husband… died serving his country… All of us owe Mitchell Taylor, and the four of you he has left behind, a debt this country will never forget." He bowed his head.

The Chamber flurried with whispers. Fingers accused Isabel from all directions.

The memory of a conversation flooded back to Spencer: when he'd pointed the finger at Ed, for manipulating her. "*What makes you think I'm not using him?*" she'd said. The comment had unsettled him at the time, but now… Spencer's legs turned to jelly and couldn't support him. He slumped back onto his chair and tears spilled down his cheeks, hidden from the cameras by the forest of legislators towering around him.

Isabel had been his trusted friend. No, it was more… the truth he could never admit before was that he had loved her. How could he have been so misguided… not to see the charade?

And suddenly what he had done hit him… his own unwitting role in this treachery with his fool idea to persuade Foster to get her appointed as Speaker… He, Spencer Prentice, had caused, or at least created the circumstances that killed Taylor and… worse.

Spencer wasn't the only one searching for answers. To the cameras doing likewise, George was an early target, but all he offered them was a grey head burying itself into an old man's trembling hands. Isabel had told him about Ed's affair, but this…? He couldn't believe it. But the evidence unfolding seemed to give him no choice.

Davey, too, was baffled. He was trying to follow the interpreter, but simply wasn't getting it. At the hospital, his dad had been yelling how the President was dead, but here was Mr Foster in front of them. And all this stuff about traitors? It was weird, like an episode of *X-Men*.

Isabel saw the confusion on the boy's face and spoke to him from behind her hand so only he could read her lips. He nodded, but it was slowly enough to make his continued bewilderment obvious.

President Foster raised his head, saying, "Our enemies plotted a double assassination," and he pasted a thin grin onto his ashen face. "Well," he said, turning back toward Isabel and lifting his voice, "I'm… still… here."

# 78

DAISY'S BAR & GRILL was packed tonight. It was the natural venue for folks in Manifold to congregate and party over the town's newfound—and to be short-lived—celebrity status. Andy Goodman was on his fifth beer and was more relieved than most to see President Foster alive on the TV monitor, and he took Bobby Foster's triumphant glare at Isabel Diaz as a mark that more was coming.

Suddenly, he jumped up, knocking the bar stool out from behind him. "She *was* the scheming bitch I said she was all along," he shouted. Paul Dawkins was standing nearby and picked up the stool for him. "Hey, Dawkins, we shoulda let her freeze to death. That woulda been patriotism."

The House camera zoomed in on Isabel and it seemed clear to Andy, his bar-room friends and millions of other viewers that guilt was oozing from her pores.

Unseen, a single bead of sweat slithered down the crevices in Ed's face. As he turned to face Isabel with disgust clouding his face, the drop fell from his chin, slipping down Davey's neck and prompting the boy to look up at his father, standing just behind him. The House TV producer had noticed the boy's move and directed one of his cameras to pull back from Isabel to capture the fractured family group in a single frame.

"Some of what I'm about to tell you," said President Foster, "is not what you would expect to hear from your President. For that, I apologise. All of what I tell you will distress you. But my solemn duty is to suppress none of it." He paused to look around the Chamber. His eyes were glassy. Those watching on television saw tears welling. He slid a handkerchief from his inside jacket pocket. It came out with an envelope but he slipped that back inside. He wiped his eyes and continued, "When the people of this Union voted me in, you expected a strong leader… yet I am ashamed to tell you my own weakness put this country in harm's way." His head dropped for a moment.

Already starting to ripple through the minds of his political detractors was a cynical question, *Is this emotion genuine or is he just working the jury like usual?* Foster's own supporters didn't know what to think either.

"Order. Order." It was Senator Mallord using the gavel.

Foster continued, "After we recently suffered the terrible threat of homegrown terrorism on our shores, and then a divisive and close-fought election, I asked the congressional leadership in a spirit of national unity to elect Ms Diaz to the post of House Speaker. Little did I suspect that this act of bipartisanship would place a death sentence on both my head and the Vice-President's."

The Hall exploded with more outbursts of "Shame!" and "Treason!" but again the President held up his hand for silence. He paused for more water, again glancing back at Isabel who was sitting yet still poker-faced, with Ed standing close by, his hands on Davey's shoulders.

"How did this happen? The conspirators—yes, there were a number of them—hatched their plot months before November's election, perhaps as early as July. Their scheming was intricate, exceptional. It also took considerable funds and was executed with a chilling precision and determination. Sadly, with Mitchell Taylor's death, they partly succeeded."

The Chamber erupted again.

"Order… Order!" Senator Mallord had to smash down the gavel five times before the legislators hushed. "Please continue, Mr President."

"Just a few months ago, Ms Diaz here," Foster's arm moved back to point to her, "was hot favourite to be elected president—a certainty, it seemed—until an unexpected and destabilising series of events unfolded…"

Foster then connected the dots in ways the public had previously had no inkling of. He explained that when Isabel was forced to withdraw, mistakenly as they now knew, a band of patriotic extremists decided they needed a way to stampede voters into the right arms—Republican arms—and that it was this group, not Karim Ahmed and his four friends, who were the ingenious perpetrators of the thwarted terrorist attack on New York City.

"These zealots framed and, in cold blood, murdered those five young men, innocents who were moulded so easily to fit into the radical Islamist stereotype.

"But it was homegrown *non*-Muslim pariahs who did this. Not only did they organise the subway attack, they orchestrated for it to be foiled, though only at the last possible moment… to maximise panic with minimum collateral damage. Their goal was not mass destruction, rather the upswell of relief that comes after a cataclysmic near-miss, expecting it to flood voters back into a safe, right-wing harbour. But their plan failed… despite their despicable deceit, the people still elected Mitch Taylor and me, though not by much, that is true. So, silently waiting until after my Inauguration, this despicable group triggered the final climax of their murderous plan."

He stooped to lift the pitcher to splash more water into his glass. "At this point, I have no choice but to reveal my own shameful part in this."

Silence temporarily descended on the Chamber but the speculation among the TV commentators was approaching fever pitch.

Foster continued, "During the campaign, a... er, photographer was travelling with our team, making a record for the archives. Her name was Niki Abbott and her award-winning work includes a photo-series for *Newsweek* on... on Ms Diaz's own campaign during the primaries."

Mallord shouted now, "If I have to call for order again..."

"Ms Abbott had become an associate of Ms Diaz, and we also now know that she was a, er, confidante of Ms Diaz's husband here." Foster gestured toward the pair on the rostrum as they exchanged a quick glance between themselves which, especially in close-up on TV, now seemed to be screaming with mutual guilt.

DAISY'S Bar was in uproar when Andy shouted, "Foster's not gonna admit he had sexual relations with that Niki woman, is he?" He slapped Paul Dawkins on the back. Paul's wife had sent him to sit with Andy at the bar to hose him down, to keep him quiet, but it clearly wasn't working.

★ ★ ★ ★ ★

TWO hours earlier on Butaka, under a canopy of stars and the glow of candlelight on her beach hut's veranda, Niki's soft pallor lingered alongside Mario's all-over bronze. Apart from his wavy black mane and the fine stroke of hair that tapered down from his navel, he was shaved smooth all over. She selected a few lonely strands to twirl and tweak just above his penis, enough to spring it back to life. She lay back on the day bed and looked up at the night sky, using her old Air Force survival skill training to estimate the time. Suddenly, she whispered in his ear, but it was hardly what he expected: "Get me new batteries for the radio."

She was an unusual customer, he reflected with just a little arrogance; their activities throughout the time she'd been here had so far proved that to his, and thus her, satisfaction. "You want music?" he asked. "Mario will sing for you?" He leant back on his elbows and broke into a lightly accented "Moon River" scraping even more rasp over it than Ol' Blue Eyes ever did.

"I want the news," she said, and the back of her hand flicked at his prick, setting it bobbing like a metronome.

"S-sure," he squealed, and jumped to his feet partly to mask the sting, and ran outside to his buggy.

Niki heard him start it up over the waves softly lapping the sand. She guessed he had to drive back to the main pavilion on the other side of the island to fetch the batteries. From the airstrip to her hut yesterday had taken them thirty minutes... but she had no idea how much further away the service pavilion was. She put her Ted Williams cap over her face and dozed off, smiling.

IF she'd heard the beat of the rotors, Niki's educated ear for aircraft would have identified it as a twin-engine Apache attack helicopter, but the chopper stayed far enough aloft not to wake her. A commando wearing night goggles tossed the end of a thick cable out the jump door, and once it hit the beach near her hut, he slid down it and thudded his boots into the sand.

"Mmm. Mario?" she murmured. She got no answer and rolled over to look, her only covering, her baseball cap, falling onto the mattress. The young man who was hovering over her—he'd been careful not to cast any shadows over her face—confirmed the telltale rose tattoo specifically mentioned in his order, then snatched at her wrists, in one slick motion handcuffing them behind her.

"Who the fuck are y...?" she started, thrashing her legs and twisting violently.

"No, it's who the fuck are you!" he replied as he clamped her ankles. "Niki Abbott... or Diana Hunter?"

Her eyes bore into him.

"Whoever... you're coming with me." With one hand at her feet and the other on her handcuffs, he rolled the naked woman, carefully, onto the canvas sling bag he'd just laid out on the floor next to the bed. Despite her writhing and squirming, he zipped the bag around her, leaving only her head exposed. He had tossed in her cap as well. Only a neanderthal would leave something as valuable as a Ted Williams Red Sox cap behind.

"Who the f...," she started to shriek until he pressed a strip of grey duct tape over her mouth with his thumbs. Her head twisted from side to side, spraying her red hair back and forward like musket fire. Suddenly, she stopped still. Her eyebrows furrowed, and she tried focusing her frigid blue eyes on the helicopter hovering in the dark above her. They pulled back so she could scan her captor's uniform, but it was also without any identifying insignia.

"To answer your question, ma'am... I'm not the fuck anybody." He grabbed at the zip and pulled it up further to encase her head. Next, he unclipped the stainless steel karabiner from his belt and snapped the straps from Niki's pod into it, stepped back to grab the loop at the end of the cable still dangling down from the chopper, and once he'd securely locked the karabiner onto it, he reclipped himself to the higher loop, ominously slipped a gas mask over his face and gave a circle-wave above his head with his finger. For good measure, he gave a tug on the cable and he shot up into the air, followed a split second later by Niki in her cocoon. From his fast-rising vantage point, he saw a car's headlights stopping just outside the hut and a guy, naked he thought, racing over and brandishing his fists to the sky.

Mario slid to a stop directly below the chopper, though not all of his body parts did at the same time. "Hey," he shouted, "what are you doing?" He was in a frenzy. No valet had ever lost a client in the entire history of Butaka although, unknown to him, all his colleagues were suffering similar fates simultaneously all over the secluded island. He ran around screaming up at the bird, feeling helpless as Niki was yanked on board. Stunned, he watched the chopper bank and fly away and, straining for an explanation, he just stood there oblivious to the fine mist of droplets that were drifting down from where the helicopter had been hovering, though he did wonder why, out of the blue, he was feeling so… drowsy.

★ ★ ★ ★ ★

NIKI Abbott! Spencer Prentice's blood was pounding. He pressed his thumb and forefinger into his temples as if forcing it out… SNAP! Outside Foster's campaign office. SNAP! On his plane. In his…

"Order! Order!" shouted Mallord. "Sergeant at Arms, please be at your ready should I have to order the ejection of any Member or Senator from the Chamber."

Foster again drew his handkerchief from his inside jacket pocket and patted his brow.

He wasn't prepared to disgrace himself any more than was essential. His wife already knew the details. Up in Air Force One, under the cutting knife, he had to tell her—how could he avoid it, given where the device had been secreted?—but he didn't have to completely humiliate himself, or Mitch, in front of the nation, let alone in front of the children watching. All he told Congress and the cameras was that Niki Abbott had through a complex ruse implanted tiny poison delivery devices under his skin and Mitch Taylor's, devices that a simple radio wave at a certain frequency would trigger whenever the conspirators chose. He held back her precise *modus operandi* but judging by the eyebrows he could see rising, at least some people in the Chamber were figuring it out.

"When Mitchell's device was activated—weeks after it was implanted, so as to distance his death from his, er, encounter with Niki Abbott—it caused a massive and fatal heart attack. I can tell you that Ms Abbott was captured two hours ago on a remote island in the Caribbean... Part of the deception I was forced to put you through the last two days was so we could accomplish that.

"I regret to say, however, that before we could interrogate her she took her own life using a similar device that she had already planted on herself."

Davey grimaced when Ed's fingers suddenly dug into his shoulders. He wriggled and looked up, but Ed's mind was elsewhere.

"With a similar device implanted on my... my own body, the reason I am standing before you... why I survived... is due solely to the patriotism, the bravery and, as you will hear, the astonishing self-sacrifice of someone who jeopardised their own life to save mine...

"Two nights ago, when we still thought Mitchell Taylor had died of natural causes, I was pulled aside from an official engagement for an urgent phone call. In that call, I learned of the murderous plot as well as its threat to me... and its imminence. Without delay, the President's protective division of the Secret Service rushed me on board Air Force One."

As the President took a moment to close his eyes and take a breath, Spencer wasn't alone in puzzling over the informant's identity or why there was such a rush to get Foster onto a plane.

Foster answered the second question first, "Air Force One is equipped with both an operating theatre as well as an elaborate defence shield which my quick-thinking Security Chief, when told of the threat, knew could be critical to saving both my life and this presidency. Once the shield was activated, no unauthorised transmission waves—whether infrared, radio, microwave or any other—could break through it to activate the killer implant. With the protection afforded by that shield, Rear Admiral Dr Raymond Jones, the White House Physician, had enough time, using the plane's emergency medical facilities, first to locate and then extract the tiny apparatus… before it could shoot out its drug dose to kill me."

As the President stood tall and silent, one of the cameras panned across to the empty seat where, traditionally, the First Lady would be seated.

# 79

"WAIT TILL THEY arrest that bitch," Goodman slurred.

"Andy, keep it down, okay?"

"Can't. Gotta go to the barfroom. Get it? *Barf* room?"

As the ranger staggered past, Paul Dawkins shook his head as though Andy had the shit hanging out of his pants already. "I don't know what's worse," he told the barman, "what the President's telling us, or drinking with Andy."

During the next few seconds of silent congressional anticipation, the TV commentators broadcasting into Daisy's struggled for banter that was any more intelligent than Andy's or Paul's. "An incredible story, Patsy. A lot of Democrats used to laugh about those elaborate defence shields, didn't they? No more, eh?"

"Kevin, the President's about to reveal the identity of the hero who made that call. My money's on Ed Loane. He's one of America's true patriots, a Medal of Honour..."

"Isabel Diaz's husband? You kidding me?"

THE President squared his shoulders. "Two people," he said, "there are two people on this podium who would have benefited directly... if this second stage of the plot had succeeded. I speak of Madam Speaker, Ms Isabel Diaz, and her husband who, as many of you know, was a four-star general and decorated war hero, General Edwin D. Loane. Ms Diaz, please stand. If you can." Foster kept his eyes forward. Ed was already on his feet.

The Attorney General, down in the front row, recalled Isabel's earlier comment: "*Now for the public hanging.*" What was she thinking?

Davey was trying hard to follow. Whatever was happening, it was bad and, terrified, he shook as he handed Isabel her cane and helped her up.

"Both of these people knew Niki Abbott. She was their friend, or at least an associate. General Loane's own pharmaceutical company manufactured the devices she secreted..."

Foster let this float for a few moments, until he heard it being sucked in by the intake of breaths around the chamber. Satisfied, he turned his head toward the couple up on the rostrum behind him. "My fellow citizens, I could never bring myself to admit this before but I must acknowledge it now... if Isabel Diaz could have continued her election campaign, I have no doubt she would have won.

"But that *didn't* happen, and *I* was elected. Democratically elected. The object of this treason was to usurp the presidency from me, for her, as though it were her divine right. But, with minutes to spare before I was...," he took another sip, "... assassinated, I was forewarned... knowing that it would keep me in my office... knowing that it would keep *her* out of it."

He turned back to the front and his eyes, tired, slowly scanned the room, "The person who phoned me, my fellow Americans, was Madam Speaker, Ms Diaz herself, only moments before she herself drifted into unconsciousness after the shocking wolf attack she suffered."

"NO-O-O-O!" howled Andy Goodman, doing his best to emulate one of his wolves. "Fuck no!"

CONGRESS erupted again, high fives being slapped all around the Hall, and not just among relieved Republicans. Spencer threw his head back and almost punched the air himself, but that would have been undignified. And George had leapt to his feet cheering.

"Order! Order!"

During the chaos, the Capitol police officers on the rostrum locked themselves closely around Ed. Subtly, the one directly behind him pulled the General's arms back and unobtrusively handcuffed him under a cotton cloth of a grey similar to Ed's suit.

Davey had felt Ed's hands leave his shoulders. He twisted around but didn't see the slick manoeuvre nor, of course, could he hear the click of the cuffs. He turned to the front ready to alternate as before between the signing interpreter and trying to read the President's lips on the TV monitor placed before the rostrum.

"And what I later learnt," said the President pointing back in Davey's direction, "was that Ms Diaz only found out about the plot herself because of this wonderful young man who I asked her to arrange to be here on the rostrum with me, and I thank this Chamber for permitting that earlier." Davey turned around expecting to see somebody behind him but there was only Isabel, Ed and the security people, and he looked back, puzzled.

"I mean you, Davey… Please come down and join me here."

A mask of fear fell over the boy's face. He looked toward Ed and Isabel for a hint of what he should do… was he in trouble? Ed was motionless but Isabel nodded, and nudged him to go to President Foster. The boy walked slowly, worried.

Smiling for the first time, Foster got down on one knee, "I can assure you I've never been more thrilled to meet a single person, Davey," he said and shook the boy's hand. "Do you remember this?" he asked, slipping a silver object out of his pocket. Davey nodded and Foster handed it to him before standing back up. "That was Davey's birthday camera. Davey turned nine only a couple of weeks ago, didn't you Davey?"

Davey shrugged, his mind was in a whirl.

"A few days ago, Madam Speaker flew up for a break at her retreat, located in the mountains above the historic Vermont township of Manifold."

"HE said 'Manifold,'" yelled Andy as though the rest of the bar hadn't heard it.

"Shh!" hushed everyone else.

"DAVEY," continued the President, "couldn't join her on the trip since he had school to go to, but he lent her his new camera so she could take snaps of the mountains and the snow and bring them back for him. But saved in the camera's memory were a couple of video clips that Davey had shot of General Loane with his back to the camera and talking on a speakerphone so Davey, who is deaf, couldn't tell what was being said. It was days later, up at her shack, that Ms Diaz played Davey's video clips—to her horror. What she heard was her husband, Niki Abbott, and others many of whom have also been rounded up, coldly handing down their death sentences on Mitchell Taylor… and me… all so Ms Diaz would become President… all so General Loane here would be in a position, as he thought, to pull the strings." He glanced over at Ed. "Well, General, your own wife has cut those strings."

The Attorney General shook his head in disbelief. Isabel Diaz was some woman.

"Imagine," the President continued, "Ms Diaz alone in her mountain-top shack, discovering all this, but with no communications with the outside world, hours from the closest town and with sunset almost upon her, the outside temperature sub-zero and dropping. Ms Diaz knows that if she waits till daybreak, Mitchell Taylor and I will both be dead... that she could walk casually, seemingly innocently, into the presidency herself.

"But Isabel Diaz doesn't wait, instead urgently setting off into the dark and the snow to get to a town and a phone. As we know, a wolf attacks her and, desperately, she fights back not merely to defend herself, but also this nation's Constitution. It's a struggle to the death," he said, and looked back at Isabel. Her eyes dropped to the floor in modesty, but he continued, "Both she and the wolf lie dying in the snow, losing pints of blood between them and her body temperature dropping fast to dangerous levels.

"Two unsuspecting heroes, park ranger Andy Goodman and his friend Paul Dawkins, are out searching for the female wolf in answer to a distress alarm from her radio-collar. She is part of an experimental regeneration program run by the Fish and Wildlife Service. They arrive at the blood-soaked scene and stumble on Ms Diaz, who is suffering acute hypothermia and from shocking, terrible wounds that you can only get a hint of today. They desperately race her to the county hospital for emergency treatment. On arrival at the ER, she is floating in and out of consciousness. Her ears pick up that Mitchell Taylor is already dead and her mind snaps back, just enough to demand a phone. And that... that was the call that saved this presidency and my life, though unfortunately it was too late to save Mitch's."

Davey ran back to Isabel and buried his head in her stomach as the once familiar chants of "Bel... Bel... Isa-bel" rang through the Hall to tumultuous applause.

INSIDE Daisy's, Andy and Paul had been hoisted up on their friends' shoulders and were being circled around the bar, their beers spilling over the floor as well as onto their friends who didn't seem to care. Brad declared an open tab and Paul, in between swigs, was chanting his own version of "Isa-bel" but Andy, for the first time this evening, was quiet, almost dazed. No matter which way his bearers turned or swayed him, his head and his eyes stayed locked on the TV screen as though he needed to check it was still there, as though this wasn't for real.

The shouts in the bar fell to a hush when President Foster started up again.

"DURING that same first phone call, Ms Diaz had enough lucidity, amazingly given what she'd gone through, to persuade me that we needed to throw her husband off guard, in case there was some back-up plan. She had thought long and hard about this during her trek down the mountain before she encountered the wolf. That is why we faked my asthma attack and created the uncertainty about my whereabouts. Ms Diaz," he said turning toward her again and placing his hand to his heart, "I thank you… America thanks you."

"HE'S bowing to her. He's fuckin' bowing!" It was Andy, still in a state of shock.

"Christ, Andy!" said Paul. "The woman saves the President by fingering her own husband. Doesn't that deserve a fuckin' bow?"

WHEN the congressional applause died down again, Foster explained that in the circumstances, he considered it was in America's national interest to install a new Vice-President immediately, that in view of the circumstances the nation could not afford even a moment's delay for the usual confirmation hearings. "And I can think of no better person than this fine woman. Right now, in this joint session of Congress, I formally nominate Isabel Rosa Diaz to the position of Vice-President of these United States of America. Ms Diaz, will you resign as Speaker and consent to my nomination?"

Everyone watching—in Congress, around the nation, even in Daisy's Bar—could see that Isabel was as stunned as they were. Clearly, this wasn't part of any script she'd agreed with Foster. A Democratic President nominating a Republican Vice-President was extraordinary.

Spencer's pulse went haywire. Foster doing something as gracious as this? Volunteering it, no less? Not having it shoved down his throat?

Isabel gripped Davey's shoulder and, leaning on him, stepped slowly to the President, everyone hanging for her words. When she was beside him, she gave a weak smile and said, "Mr President. I can think of no greater honour… no greater tribute to Mitchell Taylor… to this country… than serving under your Presidency. If the Congress wishes it, I will accept your nomination."

Davey's head was twisted up to watch for her decision, and once she'd given it, he squirmed out from under her arm to jump up and down. She edged down to give him a light hug. During the embrace, the boy cast a long look over her shoulder at his father, uncertain how to feel.

"Under Section Two of the Twenty-Fifth Amendment," said the President, whose lawyering skills had come in handy, "I ask that both Houses of Congress here jointly assembled confirm that nomination immediately."

Congress once again broke into applause and those who'd already sat down were rising back to their feet and cheering.

"Thank you, Mr President," said Senator Mallord, with the gavel in hand. "Unusual though this may be, unique I suppose, I will take it that the two Houses have just voted; that Ms Isabel Rosa Diaz's nomination has been confirmed by acclamation. Do

I have any dissent from my ruling?" He looked around, allowing for the dissent he knew would not dare show its face. "Chief Justice? Please step forward to administer the oath of office."

Once the formalities were over—they took only a few minutes—the President asked his new Vice-President to join him at the Clerk's desk. They smiled and stood side by side during the applause and, on impulse, Foster grabbed her unsplinted arm, thrusting it high above their heads in victory. "The Vice-President!" he roared.

Isabel winced with the excruciating pain.

"The Vice-President!" Congress responded.

★ ★ ★ ★ ★

THE First Lady, Marilyn Foster, was alone watching her husband on TV from the Residence in the White House, their young children already snug in bed. She lifted the fine porcelain cup and sipped her tea calmly as Bobby waved his own and Isabel's arm in the air. It was what she'd insisted on… what Bobby had no choice over, assuming he still wanted a wife and family to come home to. But it was only the first part of it.

"At the start of the campaign you promised me you wouldn't fool around any more," she'd reminded him while they were still on board Air Force One, but after the operation to remove the implanted *Clip'n'Drip*. "I warned you… Bobby, I told you… I'm not Hillary. And I *won't* be, either. This is one lady who won't hang around with the whole country snickering about who you've been fucking on the side. So, if you want me and the kids standing by you, the only way is if…"

★ ★ ★ ★ ★

AS President Foster lowered his arm and released Isabel's, the smile fell from his face, revealing once again the gravity that had dominated the session. The First Lady knew what was going through his mind that second: "Is Marilyn bluffing? Do I really have to go through with this?"

As Bobby tightened the knot of his tie, Marilyn leant forward expectantly, closer to her TV.

"I have one final duty," he said, "before I conclude my visit to this Chamber. Secretary of State Robinson," he called. "Would you please join me and the Vice-President up here?"

Foster imagined his wife's eyes boring into him, but in fact they were closed while she prayed.

As the Secretary rose from his front row seat, he quizzed his colleagues either side of him for an idea of what the President had in mind but no one had a clue. He stepped up onto the somewhat crowded podium to stand next to the President, on his side opposite Isabel and Davey.

Foster slid his hand into his inside jacket pocket and pulled out a buff-coloured envelope. He handed it to the Secretary and began speaking before Robinson could slit it open.

"Madam Vice-President, Mr Senate President pro tempore, Senators, Representatives, Chief Justice, other dignitaries and my fellow citizens. I have made some critical errors of judgment, errors that do not reflect well on this great office. What I am about to do…," he looked up at the ceiling, "what I'm about to do, however, is no error… no mistake. It is my solemn duty…" He threw back a mouthful of water.

Spencer Prentice's mouth was open, something his mother, a stickler for good manners had noticed on her own TV, but this time she forgave him.

★ ★ ★ ★ ★

MARILYN Foster opened her eyes. No, she decided, Bobby wouldn't do it. Even without her and the kids, the lust for power—his lust for fucking lust—would be too great for the philandering bastard. She stood, ready to pack her bags immediately if he faltered.

★ ★ ★ ★ ★

"TONIGHT," said Foster, "it is my solemn duty to… to resign as your President. Here and now. According to the Constitution, Vice-President Isabel Diaz will automatically succeed me. She is a woman whose courage and selflessness have demonstrated she is who this nation needs, and deserves, and as I said earlier, wanted in the first place. In the presence of Congress, I have just delivered my written resignation to the Secretary of State and thus, following Section Twenty of Title Three of the US Code, I stand here no longer as your President. Instead, I present to you… the President of the United States. May God bless her, and may God continue to bless America."

★ ★ ★ ★ ★

"HOLY fuckin' fuck!" Andy Goodman shrieked and he slid off his friends' shoulders onto the beer-swilled floor.

★ ★ ★ ★ ★

MARILYN Foster sat herself down again. He did it! The bastard actually did it… put his family ahead of his damn prick, and his career. She didn't believe it; that he was really going to keep his dick in his pants for the next three years… to prove himself worthy of another run at the presidency. To prove himself to her and, if he passed that test, she'd certainly stand there with him. Again. But next time it'd be for keeps.

# 80

FOR THE SECOND time tonight, the Chief Justice stepped forward to swear Isabel in. During the oath, Paul Dawkins' wife approached her husband, who was now perched on a stool at the bar. "Another idiot male blinded by sex," she said, slapping his back.

"Yeah?" said Andy, next to Paul and keeping his eyes on the beer the barman was pulling for him, "and another idiot female blinded by love. What's the fuckin' difference?"

"MY fellow citizens," President Diaz began, alert to the irony those words would have carried only months ago. There was much to say, but the row upon row of sapped faces before her, let alone her own flagging energy, told her she should save most of it for the next four years. What couldn't wait, what the moment decreed, was a tribute to Foster's astonishing altruism. But as she spoke, most of the Congress stayed flat, tolerating her words with barely glimmering smiles that might dupe a TV camera, but not her.

She was staggered… after what she'd been through, and *they* were exhausted?

But spurring her on, virtually alone on the floor of the

House—a beacon among flickering candles—was Spencer Prentice. The gleam in his eyes energised her, cheered her on.

"President Foster led us only briefly," she continued, "but lead us he has, and tonight, in a remarkable generosity of spirit and national renewal we saw him lead in the best way imaginable… by example. And in that same spirit, and by his example, I too will nominate my Vice-President…"

Hank Clemens, who'd kept his seat as Representative for North Carolina, was ready to step forward. He ran his fingers through his mop of brown hair, and still seated, pulled his jacket down as best he could to ensure the line at the back was smooth, perfect for when the TV cameras zoomed in on him as he got the call.

Isabel continued, "…a man who stood by me…"

Hank straightened his tie.

"… and has been my friend and counsel…"

Hank readied himself to stand.

"… the gentleman from Massachusetts, Spencer Prentice. Sir, will you accept my nomination?"

Hank's smile turned to stone but recorded history was saved the moment as the cameras zoomed in on Spencer, capturing the tall, elegant Afro-American moving to his feet amid the applause. Spencer's bowtie was still a little crooked, but he kept his large hands by his sides. His expression was severe.

"Mr Prentice, do you accept?" Isabel repeated.

"Madam President, I do, but on one condition," he replied soberly.

Isabel bit into her top lip, her stomach tightening. "And that condition is…?"

"That you won't ever resign on *me*," he said, and he split his face into the starburst grin his mother adored so much.

# 81

AFTER SPENCER WAS also sworn in on the floor of the House, Isabel took Davey's hand and, in turn, he took Spencer's. The three of them stood while the Chamber roared and stamped its final ovation. Davey's lip quivered and a tear slowly ran out of his eye. He snuck a peek back at his disgraced father surrounded by the tall men with the curly earpieces stretching down inside their collars.

His eyes met his dad's. Cold eyes. Hard eyes. Eyes that didn't even seem to see him… rather through him. Eyes that didn't show any sign of regret. The boy shook his little blond head as though to cast off the image and turned away, back to the front.

Spencer looked down and saw Davey wipe his eyes and screw his face up into a tight knot. It appeared the boy was thinking hard about something, or trying to make a tough choice. Poor kid, he reflected.

Davey tugged on Isabel's jacket. At first, she ignored it, but the little boy was insistent. Almost blanching, she bent down to him, leaning on her cane for support.

Davey opened his mouth and worked his jaw, breathing hard and, as his words came out, slowly, deliberately, Isabel took his hand again, squeezing it in encouragement.

"Please...," he said, his voice nasal and absent of tone or lilt, "can... I... still... go... to... the... shack...?"

Isabel's eyes burst with emotion and, though her back was still bent and sore, she couldn't restrain her joy and drew the boy toward her.

At that moment, they both knew that sometimes words aren't necessary.

# EPILOGUE

ED WAS BUSTLED off the podium. Still cuffed, he was shuffled out to a black van with heavily tinted windows. As the rear doors slammed shut on him, he leant forward to give his hands room behind his back. His thumb, with the flesh-coloured pad on its tip, where he'd said his wart had been removed, located his other padded finger.

Like Niki, he pressed the pads together for the crucial eight seconds, counting ten just the same. The forced contact of the specially coated pads caused a chemical reaction that itself, one second later, generated a shot of electric current, weak, but enough to trigger the release of the poison in the implant.

Ed's body spasmed and he flew forward from the seat, his head cracking on the cold steel floor. His pupils rolled back into their sockets revealing nothing.

★ ★ ★ ★ ★

"CARLOS who?" snapped Elia Cacoz, grouchy that she'd even picked up this call; what were assistants for, now she had one? For the last three hours she'd been chiselling her thoughts for the weekly news editors' conference about to commence—the first she'd chair since her promotion—and disruptions were not welcome. She stood, her foot tapping, and her shoulder crooking the phone against her ear while her eyes kept scrolling her notes as the others started to amble in.

"Carlos in La Paz," he said, and then to prompt her, "I do research for you?"

"Oh, yeah." Her mind wandered back to the interview with Isabel Diaz's mother, and her aborted attempt at shooting a follow-up once Isabel had become President. Maria Rosa had died.

But—she gathered her thoughts—what the hell did Carlos want now? She'd paid him for his work; paid him plenty, in fact.

Sensing Elia's irritation, Carlos filled the silence, "I do good for you, yes?"

"Yeah, good." She motioned to the other journalists to take seats. "Look, I'm busy, so what's…?"

"I find more for you, Miss Elia."

"More," she said.

"*Si*. I find him. *El jardinero*. How you say…? The gardener. The *papá* of your presidente."

Everyone in the room watched the sheaf of notes slip out of Elia's hand and flutter to the floor.

"Hallo… hallo?" pressed Carlos.

"You've got her natural father? The embassy gardener?"

"Not exactly, Miss Elia… *El jardinero* is dead many years. But I find his brother."

"And why should I care about his brother?" asked Elia, shrugging and then hunching down to pick up her papers.

"Is funny thing," said Carlos. "He tell to me his brother, the gardener, was *estéril*. How you say…? He could not have *bebés*. No *bebés*… never."

Elia left the papers on the floor.

★ ★ ★ ★ ★

# AUTHOR'S NOTE

MY MOTHER'S TEARS over John F. Kennedy's assassination led me, decades later, to create *Born to Run's* Isabel Diaz.

My late mother wasn't American, and her taste of US life was sweetened by episodes of *I Love Lucy* and Hollywood movies. We lived in far-away Australia yet JFK was idolised here and, for this kid in short pants, her grief fired a spark: that American presidents matter.

I have often scratched my head at why the charisma genie has blessed so few of the nine US Presidents since, and why they've mostly been Democrats. Only Clinton and Obama approached Kennedy's lustre, although Obama's is sputtering as I write. Many say Reagan had the gift, but it didn't seem like it at the time.

Before Kennedy's day, revered Republicans weren't as rare. Start with Abraham Lincoln, who abolished slavery, and the startling snippet of history that the Democrats were then the pro-slavery party.

Given recent history, it's high time for an inspirational Republican to pop up so, impatient for a real one, I created my own.

In *Born to Run,* the world yearns for Isabel Diaz to become US president. She's widely hailed as a saint yet, as the story's dark side unfolds, we begin to dread she is a demon. Isabel Diaz is a woman born to run, yet she faces two big questions… can she win… and should she?

I've been researching this story implicitly for years, visiting the US so many times that I've chalked up visits to towns and cities in around half the 50 states, including Half Moon Bay, California where Isabel Diaz, as a 15-year-old runaway, first hobbles into the greasy diner that will seed her fortune and, of course, Washington, DC from where she aims to lead the nation.

I've also been addicted to US presidential elections since Lyndon B. Johnson withdrew from the race after he visited Australia, and NSW Premier Bob Askin notoriously spat out "Run over the bastards" when anti-Vietnam War demonstrators lay in front of the motorcade.

One of the story twists in *Born to Run* springs from a glitch I teased out of the US Constitution and a dusty 1898 Supreme Court ruling over it. For confirming I correctly interpreted the law, I thank James C. Ho— then Chief Counsel of the US Senate Subcommittee on the Constitution, and now Solicitor General for Texas—and Todd Gaziano, Director of the Centre for Legal and Judicial Studies at Washington's Heritage Foundation. (For the nit-picky, see Jim Ho's article, "Unnatural Born Citizens and Acting Presidents," (2000) 17 Constitutional Commentary 575.)

To develop my character Jax Mason's cataclysmic subway shockwave model, I sat for many hours in both the New York Transit Museum and the London Transport Museum scouring books and historic resources for details of subway construction and history. But I owe my biggest debt for this to advanced analysis engineering guru Shane Donohoo. Shane works in a global engineering group devising "theoretical disasters" and testing their likely effects on complex structures such as oil rigs and dams. He shared not only his insights, but numerous technical papers that helped show me that while Jax's model is indeed technically feasible, it has enough barriers, thankfully, for it to be a snack in fiction, but virtually impossible in real life.

For colour and detail on what Washington's Capitol Police do during a president's State of the Union Address, I am grateful to Capitol Police Public Information Officers, Michael Lauer and Contricia Sellers. For advice on nine-year-old Davey Loane's likely strengths in lip-reading, I thank Professor Carol Padden, Professor of Communication at the University of California, San Diego whose work includes research on literacy in young deaf children. For details about the heart rates of grey wolves, thanks to Dr Terry J. Kreeger of the Wyoming Game and Fish Department and Professor Peter D. Constable, head of the Department of Veterinary Clinical Sciences, Purdue University, Indiana. For insight into Hispanic and Andean languages, I consulted Dr Luis Fernando Restrepo, Professor of Spanish, Comparative Literature, and Latin American and Latino Studies, University of Arkansas.

If you believe something is factually wrong in the book, it is more likely because I intentionally voted for pace or story over accuracy than because I garbled my research or advice but, if it was inaccuracy, don't blame the people above.

Thanks to Pam Holland for photos of New York trains and subways so I could get my imagery right after I misplaced my own. Raymond Teichman, Supervisory Archivist at *The Franklin D. Roosevelt Presidential Library and Museum* helped by digging up the full context of Eleanor Roosevelt's short quotation in the epigraph. Her article, "Women in Politics," ran over three issues of *Good Housekeeping* in 1940: Volume 110: January: pp.18-19, 150; March: pp.45, 68; April: pp.45, 201-203. The relevant part is:

> This country is no matriarchy, nor are we in any danger of being governed by women. I repeat here what I have so often said in answer to the question: 'Can a woman

> be President of the United States?' At present the answer is emphatically 'No.' It will be a long time before a woman will have any chance of nomination or election. As things stand today, even if an emotional wave swept a woman into this office, her election would be valueless, as she could never hold her following long enough to put over her program. It is hard enough for a man to do that, with all the traditional schooling men have had; for a woman, it would be impossible because of the age-old prejudice. In government, in business, and in the professions there may be a day when women will be looked upon as persons. We are, however, far from that day as yet.

With the right woman, such as an Isabel Diaz, I hope that this day is now not far at all.

For other help with *Born to Run*, thanks to: Bill Thompson, my editor in New York. Authors Stephen King and John Grisham said good things about him for a reason. Luke Causby for the jacket and internal book design. Graeme Jones for typesetting, Karen Young for production. Publicist, Trudy Johnston. The book's distributor in Australia and NZ, *Simon & Schuster*, especially Lou Johnson and Ed Petrie and their fabulous team and reps. And the bookseller who sold this book to you, or your friend who gave it to you.

I also shine a torch on *Pantera Press*. With our focus on discovering and nurturing previously unpublished writing talent, *Pantera Press* hopes to be "a great new home for Australia's *next* generation of best-loved authors." In its second year, it is already delivering on that dream, with a small but growing stable of authors, books with rave reviews and happy readers, including a best-seller, several books now in reprint, new editions, and one short-listed for the Commonwealth Writers' Prize.

Lastly, my family. My role-model wife, not least for the light bulb she flicked on for me when she tossed in her own business career to become a full-time professional sculptor. Visit her website: www.jennygreen.net

And our extraordinary two kids who have lived with this book and far, far more.

If you enjoyed *Born to Run*,
here is a taste of John M. Green's first novel...

# NOWHERE MAN

It's available from all good booksellers...

# 1

THIS CITY DOESN'T grow on you, it grows in you. It snatches your breath. It scratches its scarlet nails down your back so you squirm for more. Sydney is heaven without dying. But in eight minutes, for Sonya, it would become hell.

The bush track clung alongside the foreshore, a seductive stretch of dirt and rocks and water views. Professor Sonya Wheen pounded it daily so, even without checking her watch, she knew she'd been running fifty minutes. But after last night, who cared about time?

Dribbles of sweat kept filling her smile lines. It had been their first sex in three weeks, true, but what did she expect after nine, no, ten years. As Sonya was convincing herself once again that Michael wasn't a lousy lover, the lace frond of a fern camouflaged a sandstone outcrop and she almost tripped. Regathering her balance and her pace, she reminded herself that in the long spaces between the sex Michael was still, well, a gentleman; most at ease sniffing a vintage red or cradling a tumbler of good scotch—no ice, no water—and drawing back on one of his antique smoking pipes. And considerate. The word "companion" didn't endear itself to her, so she pushed it away.

She leapt, almost flew, over a tree root that caught her eye just in time but her shoulder swiped against a split branch of a eucalypt.

To her, Michael was a Mr Cool in a gallant, nineteenth-century kind of way, yet "cold fish" was the epithet more often whispered round their circle of friends; these days more a semi-circle, and mostly hers. To them, Michael soaked himself in solitude. "Reserve" was a word conceived for him, or so a friend had said once in Sonya's earshot. It was true he rarely sought friendships and when on odd occasions they were offered, he seldom accepted them.

For him, familiarity bred contentment, albeit one focused on few people and fewer things. Mostly, Michael was a self-contained, tight-lipped man who brushed off the prevailing fondness for approval or intimacy. Cool… yes. Detached at times… oh, yes. But for Sonya, also thoughtful… decent. Integrity and a quiet generosity gently shimmered from him, in soft beats.

He stuck to his guns in most things, even in his business affairs. His work since she'd known him was as a stocks and bonds trader operating from home, a perfect cocoon for his temperament. He'd chosen it well, she decided. Intellectual stimulation, the adrenaline of the markets, and no people. Plus, keeping yourself away from the daily hub-bub helped you filter out the noise and maintain perspective, a lesson he said he had gleaned from his earlier days freelancing as a journalist.

He claimed it was a useful tool in trading on the markets as well as in everyday life but Sonya was never as convinced about the virtues of isolation. It did have its moments, like when she powered her motor bike down after a day's lecturing and she'd find him at their grey sliver of fence that overlooked the beach, ready for their ritual chat over a freshly-poured wine or whisky. She never knew if it was his first drink since alcohol didn't affect him as much her. Sonya was tall and slim so her vulnerability was a metabolism and fitness thing, nothing to do with her being a blonde as a friend once joked. As she'd head through the house to join Michael at the back fence, she'd try to guess from the wafting aroma what he had cooking. As well as a journalist, he'd also worked as a chef. What jobs hadn't he done? She'd pass by the dining table, usually set for two, often with a spray of fresh tulips. Like last night.

For Sonya tulips went with everything, even her job lecturing in business studies. It wasn't just their cheeky cup shape or their splashes of vivid colour. It was also the history of the manic speculation they'd fired up four centuries ago. Every year, she got a kick out of telling her students how Rembrandt earned less for his 1640s masterpiece, The Nightwatch, than the hammer price a single Viceroy tulip bulb got knocked down for at auction.

There were other kindnesses: gifts, and especially conversations. But Michael kept that side of him to their private world; the modern fetish for public displays of affection, even warmth, repelled him.

Where would she have been without him? Living comfortably on a university salary, for sure, but not in their beach house… well, hers actually… but that was another story. One she had certainly rationalised but never quite worked out.

A barbed sapling brushed against her but she palmed it off, just as she'd done for years to the gibes and gossip. Like Michael she didn't care for the sneering but, truth be told, she yearned that he would occasionally display his emotions so others could see him as she did. Her late mother had always stereotyped him. That he was so reticent, so uptight, because he was British. It wasn't that, Sonya was sure, but there was something. An itch she couldn't scratch.

Sonya knew she should speak to him about it, and she would.

Today.

Six minutes…

Heck, did she really care if he was reserved? Live for the moment! And with him, there were great moments. She brushed back some loose strands of hair, for a change blasé that the whole world could see she had one ear with a lobe and one without. It was an oddity she normally covered up with longer hair, even though Michael claimed he found it endearing.

How often had she engaged in these same arguments with herself? She would definitely raise it all with him today. For sure. What better time, now that he'd agreed, finally, to a baby? Thirty-five on her last birthday, she had certainly been hearing her body. Tick… tick…

The early morning sun slanted through the treetops, leaping from branch to branch like flames. She stopped at the viewing platform, drawing in the crisp sea-spray of the sou'-easterly and watching the wind-shadow skip across the water. An augury perhaps.

Her thoughts lingered, imagining that the rhythmic swell of the water was Michael, his chest rising and falling just as it had been when she'd slipped out of their bed that morning.

Their relationship had always had its edges. Until last night, Michael's stand-off against children, though always gracious, had been as hard as flint. Despite that, compared to the ditch her first marriage had careened into, her decade with Michael was a yellow brick road. There were the unexpected things. Like last night: "Let's go barging on a French canal," he'd said, "before our baby." Before our baby, a phrase lightly tossed in like a vinaigrette, and without any fanfare despite her years of badgering.

Surprisingly, she'd almost not registered it; the mere mention of an overseas trip had thrown her completely off-guard. After they'd quit New York for Sydney nearly nine years ago and despite their, or rather, his money, they'd only ever flown together within Australia. Never internationally.

He, on the other hand. God! she thought, as she turned back onto the track, Michael was such a frequent flyer the airport security people probably knew his shoe size. He must have a trillion international frequent flyer miles but, she reminded herself, she had never enjoyed a single one.

His many, too many, business trips were fleeting, always rushed. Inevitably he returned dishevelled, as if he'd just been trekking for thirty days in Nepal rather than on a three-day flit to Los Angeles or some other business capital. In the beginning, she'd stressed herself about these trips—what wife wouldn't?—but time wore her down and tolerating them simplified her life, despite her mother's finger-wagging: one failed marriage was enough, she'd repeatedly warned.

Four minutes…

A child. Sonya hurtled off the end of the track and her shoes dug into the white sand, so fine and clean it squeaked as it stopped her short. She slipped off her sweatshirt and wrapped it round her waist for her cool-down. Her red leotard top was crimson with sweat and her heartbeat was even outpacing her mind.

She'd come round the headland and this end of the beach was tapped in behind, sheltered from the south. Here the palms and eucalypts stood motionless. The barnacled boats moored in close were rocking imperceptibly from the rising tide and there was scarcely a jangle from their glinting halyards. The sun continued to chin itself above the horizon and paint colour onto the eastern cliffs, giving the final crescent of moon a razzle of gold.

She watched the water nudge against the beach, up and back. It hissed up the sand leaving a froth of lace for the seagulls to trample. As her breath slowed she watched the grey scavengers fluffing up their wings and poking their beaks underneath, picking out lice for their breakfast appetisers. A fledgling with a pink-grey beak and legs and spotted wings scrabbled to the water's edge and dipped its head in and out several times, shaking it in between.

Apart from a drifting foam of cloud, it was a still winter's morning. Sonya strode over the sand for her final stretch, certain this would be a good day… a good year.

But in three minutes, she'd discover how wrong she was.

At the far end of the beach, the familiarity, the odd ordinariness of their grey slatted fence sandwiched between much grander walls caused her to question Michael's sudden new leaf and by the time she reached the boardwalk, she was stamping the sand out of her soles as well as her scepticism.

Once again she questioned how she'd lasted so long with a man so guarded, so private. Obscurity and vagueness about his past hovered around Michael like a cloud of summer sand flies but though it was irritating, years of practice had taught Sonya to swat it off as yet another tolerable eccentricity. No longer. Not from today. Today the itch would be scratched.

She recalled how weeks after she'd moved into his New York apartment on Central Park West, she'd knocked his passport from his desk and two strange dried flowers fluttered out of it to the floor. They were shrivelled, brittle and brown though she guessed they'd once been white. Daisies perhaps. As she slid a page of the passport underneath the wilted blooms, carefully so they wouldn't disintegrate, she'd wondered if they were a memento. But of what? Or whom? She'd never asked. Flipping through the tattered passport that day, she saw some pages were ripped. The corner with his birth-date was gone. Cut or torn, she couldn't tell. But for the first time she saw his full name: Michael Will Hunt. His name was a sentence.

One minute…

She unlatched her gate smack on what she assumed was 7 am. Courtesy of Ralph their pitch-black Labrador, the time seemed obvious. Ralph was not normally a barker but what usually got him yapping at this time was the racket from the builders a few doors up. Six days a week it was always the same. On the dot of seven the noise dam from the construction site legally sluiced open.

But wait. Apart from Ralph and the squawk of a seagull, and the hiss of the tide, there was no sound. No builders. Not yet. Sonya checked her watch: five before seven.

Something caught her eye and she jerked her head up at the house to see that the glass double-doors of their attic bedroom were ajar, swinging out onto their balcony.

Michael must be up but, at anything before 7:30, that was almost unheard of.

A lorikeet flashed past her, so close the green wingtip brushed her cheek. The bird perched on top of the left-hand balcony door and cocked its head, a scatter of sunlight fluorescing its blues and mauves.

As Sonya unconsciously wiped her cheek, the bird gave a raucous squawk and shot a repulsive stream of grey shit down the glass door panel. Sonya was not religious, yet the smear roused in her an ancient echo of parents daubing blood on their doors to ward away the angel of death.

# BOOKCLUBS

For bookclub questions,
opportunities to host the author at your bookclub
(via Skype) …

And more…

Please visit
**www.PanteraPress.com**

## ABOUT JOHN M. GREEN

*Born to Run* is John's second novel, and his first is *Nowhere Man.*

When it dawned on John that what got him up in the morning was writing not his day job, he quit the job. Until then he was an executive director in a leading investment bank. Much earlier he'd been a lawyer, a partner in two major law firms.

As well as a novelist, he is a well-known business writer and commentator and his non-fiction writing has appeared in a variety of publications in Australia and overseas including: *The Australian, The Australian Financial Review, Company Director, Business Spectator, The Age,* the UK's *Financial Times* and Canada's *Director Journal.*

As well as writing, John is a board member of two stock-exchange-listed corporations and some not-for-profits, as well as a co-founder of *Pantera Press.*

He lives in Sydney with his wife, the sculptor Jenny Green. They have two adult children who share their passions for the arts, books, business and philanthropy, as well as for the shimmering waters of an extraordinary city.

## Praise for *Born to Run*

"A spectacular political thriller that unfolds with more twists and surprises than real American politics, and you really care about Green's characters. *Born to Run* has intellectual weight, too. It takes genius to make fictional American politics more dramatic than factual American politics, and Green has done that. But, as an added fillip, Green makes American politics believable.

"I really enjoyed the book. It kept me up nights (and not much does)."

*P.J. O'Rourke, international best-selling author & US political commentator*

## Praise for *Nowhere Man*

"Michael Crichton is good but [John M Green is] no slacker either... I'm ripping through this book... chapter after chapter [until] the eyes are hurting...it's a really good read... A great mystery. A book has to get you from the opening paragraph... and [*Nowhere Man*] has..."

*— Nights with Walter Williams, 4BC Brisbane Radio*

"John M. Green is the new Michael Crichton... but better!"

*P.J. O'Rourke, international best-selling author*

"...a gripping thriller which will literally have you on the edge of your seat!"

*Saturday Breakfast, ABC 720 Perth (James Lush)*

"It's a futuristic, cyber-type thriller. I thought it was great fun. I enjoyed it."

*—Jennifer Byrne on ABC TV's First Tuesday Book Club*

"...an atmospheric thriller."

—The AGE

"I found myself very quickly caught up in the story and reading it far later into the night than I had anticipated."

*— The Book Show, ABC Radio National (Peter Mares)*

"I began reading last night and couldn't put it down until early this morning... I enjoyed it... I'm sure it will be successful... It's a good read."

*—Janine Perrett, The Perrett Report, Sky Business TV*

"... Every new discovery only compounds the enigmatic mood and teasing power of the plot... Green's strength lies in conjuring a bewildering landscape of betrayals." *— The Courier Mail (Gillian Bramley-Moore)*